DO OR DIE

The privateersmen would be desperate: they would realize that unless they escaped the *Calypso*, they would end up on the gallows, and to them the sword would be preferable to the noose...

Ramage heard a thud from forward and saw a puff of smoke beginning to drift from the *Calypso*'s side. Then another as the second gun fired in the frigate's raking broadside.

Having fired all her starboard guns into the *Lynx* while tacking northward across her stern, she was turning to pass southward across the *Lynx*'s stern again and fire all her larboard guns, into the unprotected stern, yet another raking broadside which every ship feared.

Again sails slatted; the yards creaked and rope rattled the sheaves of the blocks as the *Calypso* seemed to spin and sail back almost in her original wake. The first half dozen guns had fired when suddenly Ramage saw a huge blast of flame and felt, rather than heard, a roaring blast, and everything went black...

Other Avon Books by
Dudley Pope

RAMAGE AND THE GUILLOTINE
RAMAGE'S DIAMOND

RAMAGE
AND THE
RENEGADES

DUDLEY POPE

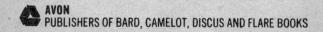

AVON
PUBLISHERS OF BARD, CAMELOT, DISCUS AND FLARE BOOKS

AVON BOOKS
A division of
The Hearst Corporation
959 Eighth Avenue
New York, New York 10019

Copyright © 1981 by Dudley Pope
Published by arrangement with the author
Library of Congress Catalog Card Number: 81-70574
ISBN: 0-380-60137-0

First Avon Printing, July, 1982

AVON TRADEMARK REG. U. S. PAT. OFF. AND IN
OTHER COUNTRIES, MARCA REGISTRADA, HECHO EN
U. S. A.

Printed in the U. S. A.

WFH 10 9 8 7 6 5 4 3 2 1

For KYLE and DOC

Author's Note

The tiny island where Ramage and his men fought out their battle actually exists as described, 673 miles from Bahia. Still uninhabited, it belongs to Brazil. It was first surveyed by Captain Philip D'Auvergne R.N., Prince of Bouillon in 1782 and his original chart, in the British Museum, shows he made an error of only about twenty-five miles in plotting its position.

D.P.
Yacht *Ramage*
Marigot
St Martin
French Antilles

RAMAGE
AND THE
RENEGADES

CHAPTER ONE

Ramage lowered the copy of the *Morning Post* and listened. A carriage was clattering to a stop outside the house and old Hanson, muttering "Coming, my Lord, coming!" as though someone was already hammering impatiently at the door, was shuffling across the hall. Pausing for a moment when he saw Ramage sitting in the drawing room he called: "The Admiral's back, Master Nicholas!"

Dear old Hanson; for as long as Ramage could remember the butler always muttered "Coming, coming" as he walked across the hall to answer the front door, and at every third step his right hand, with thumb and finger extended, lifted to his face to push his pince-nez back up over the bridge of his nose. It must be a most sensitive nose because Hanson's spectacles rarely slipped right off the tip to dangle from their black cord. Ramage remembered as a boy, fifteen or twenty years ago, watching fascinated as the butler lovingly polished the silver. Would they . . . would they . . . yes, there—but a quick movement of the right hand would, disappointingly, catch them just in time.

Hanson was always so relieved when any of the family returned home to the house in Palace Street, even after only an hour's absence, as though a social call or a shopping expedition was as dangerous as a foray into dense jungle. On this occasion Ramage's father had been over to Wimpole Street to call on Lord Hood (who, as a characteristically brief note explained, was beneaped in his house with gout). The two old admirals enjoyed gossiping and discussing foreign affairs, and certainly Bonaparte's latest move must have given them plenty to talk about. Had father been able to learn more than the rumour reported in the newspapers?

Gianna would be pleased the carriage was back: she was anxious to use it to call on her dressmaker. Instead of having the woman visit the house, Gianna wanted to go to her establishment to inspect rolls of materials, and Ramage was hoping his mother would go with her: as the first week of his first leave for nearly two years came to an end, he was at last managing to relax quite happily in an armchair. In a few more days he might agree to plunging into the London social activity, to be shown off by his mother and Gianna, but for the moment (as Gianna had grumbled last night) the bear was happy sleeping at the end of his chain, and would have been much happier to have come back to England and found Gianna and the family staying in Cornwall: Blazey Hall, sitting four-square among the crags and rolling hills, was always peaceful; the village of St Kew was "home", not London with its noise, smells and crowds.

Yet London this morning was still surprisingly quiet: the hucksters and piemen had not yet reached Palace Street, the air was still and the house seemed glad of the rest. The high ceiling made the room seem larger than it was, and his mother's choice of a very pale grey paint and a blue the shade of ducks' eggs set off the oak panelling. The glass of the diamond panes in the windows showed that Mrs Hanson had kept a close watch on the window cleaner, and the doorknobs shone with a brilliance that would bring an approving nod from most first lieutenants.

He heard the sharp clatter of the carriage steps unfolding. His father said something to the coachman, Albert, and a few moments later was in the hall, with Hanson taking his coat, hat and cane. Both Gianna and Lady Blazey had heard the arrival and were now coming down the stairs, greeting the Admiral. Ramage heard his mother ask if there was anything wrong, and the Earl must have answered with a gesture because she said: "We'll join Nicholas in the drawing room and you can tell us about it."

Ramage stood up as his mother came into the room, followed by Gianna. The Countess of Blazey, wearing the large amethyst brooch Ramage had given her last week on her fifty-first birthday (causing her to burst into tears, exclaiming that his unexpected return to Britain and a month's leave was the best present she could have), sat down and said: "Your father is just going to change into some comfortable clothes...Now, tell us what the newspapers have to say, so we are all prepared for his gossip."

Ramage knew Gianna was becoming excited by the rumours, but both he and his father had discounted them to her; there was no point in letting her build up hopes to have them smashed when it was discovered that the British government was the victim of a spiteful jest by Bonaparte.

"I haven't read *The Times* yet, but the *Morning Post* only reports what we've already heard."

"Read it, *caro*," Gianna said.

"There are a few lines on the front page and I am sure it's just speculation, not based on anything they've been told by the Secretary of State's office."

"Read it, anyway," Gianna said firmly. "This Lord Hawkesbury is still so pleased at finding himself His Majesty's new Secretary of State for Foreign Affairs that he talks only to the King and the Archbishop of Canterbury."

The Countess laughed. "Surely you hardly expected him to reveal matters of state at last night's ball, my dear? After all, the Duchess of Dorset was standing beside you, and she's a terrible gossip."

"I expect him to provide information for the ruler of a friendly state invaded by Bonaparte. After all, I *am* the Marchesa di Volterra!"

"Yes, dear," the Countess said, smiling at what she called Gianna's "imperious outbursts", "but if Hawkesbury had any news about Volterra or, indeed Tuscany or even Italy, he might tell you if you called at his office in Downing Street, or his home in Sackville Street, but hardly at a ball!"

"He did not suggest I call," Gianna said coldly. "Is he one of these new Irish barons? Wasn't he known as 'Jenks'?"

Her tone, Ramage knew, was haughty enough to freeze even the chilly Secretary of State. "He's the son of the Earl of Liverpool. He's also Member of Parliament for Rye and his nickname comes from his family name, Jenkinson."

"This Liverpool—a new creation?"

Ramage laughed and the Countess joined in. "Yes, 'a new creation'. His father received an earldom about five years ago and Jenks has one of his father's courtesy titles. Like me, in fact, except I don't use it."

"I wish you would," Gianna said, beginning to thaw. "You are not ashamed of being the son of the Earl of Blazey, and you inherited one of his titles, so why not use it?"

"Darling, I've told you enough times," Ramage protested. "Admirals with knighthoods don't like having young captains serving under them with titles like 'earl', or 'viscount'. It can often mean midshipmen and junior post captains have higher precedence at receptions than their commander-in-chief."

The Countess said: "If Nicholas had attended a dinner at which Hawkesbury was present, before he became a minister, Nicholas would have had much higher precedence—if he used his title."

"All the more reason for using it," Gianna said. "Jenks is a cold pudding."

"A cold fish," Ramage corrected.

"*Accidente!* I always know when I am winning an argument because you begin correcting my English!"

"Nicholas," the Countess reminded him, "you were going to tell us the news in the *Post*."

"Ah, yes. It says that—well, I'll read the item. 'We understand the M. Louis-Guillaume Otto, the French Commissioner for the Exchange of Prisoners, resident in London, has been a frequent visitor at the office of the Secretary of State for Foreign Affairs during recent days. It is believed that M. Otto, who has been living in London since the beginning of the present war, has been acting as an envoy of Bonaparte, discussing proposals from Bonaparte for a general peace.

"'We further understand that Lord Hawkesbury has put Bonaparte's proposals before the Cabinet and that Mr Addington has informed the King of the details. We believe Mr Pitt's supporters are violently against a peace. M. Otto can rely on the support of Mr Fox and his faction.

"'M. Otto has had little official work to do for the past two years: so few French ships put to sea that the Royal Navy cannot take many prisoners. On the other hand the bold British ships are constantly attacking the enemy's coasts and ports and naturally some are lost, so the French have many British prisoners in their jails. Unfortunately few can be exchanged because we do not have enough Frenchmen to make the numbers even.'"

Gianna sighed and rearranged the skirt of her pale dress. "Let us hope Bonaparte's terms are generous."

The Countess shook her head disapprovingly. "Gianna, I know you want to go back to Volterra, but don't let us fall into a trap just because we want peace."

"No, Bonaparte would not be offering terms unless it was to his advantage to end the war," Nicholas said.

At that moment the Earl came into the room: a tall, still slim man with silvery white hair and the same thin, almost beak-like nose and high cheekbones of his son. Gianna looked from Nicholas to his father. Yes, she thought, that is how Nicholas will be in thirty years' time. For the first time since she had met him, she felt she could think of him in old age: until now he had been at sea, being wounded regularly once a year, being in action at least once a month ... Peace would mean he could resign his commission and live in London and Cornwall.

And now, also for the first time, she could picture him growing old without her beside him. Until recently, she always thought of their lives after the war as being lived together, but now, after the years she had lived here in England, mostly at St Kew, she accepted that it was impossible. *Noblesse oblige.* It was a phrase, but for the two of them it was a code, a law— and for her a sentence of eventual banishment.

In the first couple of years, when she thought of little else than Nicholas and returning to rule her kingdom of Volterra the moment Bonaparte's troops were driven out, she had ignored religion. Yet she was Catholic and Nicholas was Protestant. Marriage would force Nicholas to agree that their children would be Catholic, and in turn that would mean one of the oldest earldoms in Britain would become Catholic the moment Nicholas died after inheriting from his father.

The twelfth Earl of Blazey a Catholic ... For the first year or two in England she could see no difficulty about such an old Protestant earldom changing its religion to Rome, but eventually she had come to understand that Britain was built on Protestant foundations, and to ask Nicholas (who would be the eleventh earl when he inherited from his father) to sacrifice the earldom—for that was how it would be regarded—was something that an enemy might do, but not the woman who loved him.

Her other plans—she saw now they were but dreams—were equally impractical, because of that same phrase. Her idea that Nicholas would resign his commission after the war and come to Volterra as her husband was hopeless, and Nicholas himself had made that clear. Volterra, still turbulent after years of French occupation and no doubt still affected by the talk of French revolutionaries, would be in no mood to accept a *straniero* as their ruler's husband; not even one who spoke Italian as well as any of them and who had rescued their ruler from Bonaparte's troops. A foreigner was someone from the next state; to some people a man from the next town. She thought that Nicholas might have in mind that she would hand over the kingdom to her heir, her nephew Paolo Orsini, at present serving as a midshipman in Nicholas's own ship but—as she had finally been forced to admit to herself—there were at least two things preventing that. First, Volterra, once liberated, would need a firm ruler for the early years of peace, someone who understood the complicated relations, friendships and enmities of the leading families. Paolo knew nothing of all this, and might well fall victim to an assassin. And secondly, his life was now the sea: it was unlikely he would exchange the Royal Navy for the falsehoods and sycophancy that made up life at Court.

Paolo was a new generation: he had never lived in an atmosphere of *noblesse oblige* so he would sacrifice nothing for it. For her and Nicholas it was as much a part of life as breathing and, she realized with something approaching bitterness, comparable with breathing: it was always there, unobtrusive, noticeable only when you thought of it, but an essential part of life itself.

Her other dream, after recognizing that the people of Volterra would not accept Nicholas as her husband, was to have Nicholas sent there as His Britannic Majesty's Envoy Extraordinary and Minister Plenipotentiary. The ruler could summon the British Ambassador as frequently as she wished. Yet she knew that neither she nor Nicholas could accept such a relationship.

This was all in the past and in the future . . . Miserably,

knowing she would eventually have to sacrifice her first and probably only real love, she wrenched herself back to the present. She watched Nicholas talking with his mother. The suntan was wearing off, and his brown eyes were just as deeply sunk beneath eyebrows that were like tiny overhanging cliffs, but the lines were going: years of squinting in tropical and Mediterranean sun, and commanding one of the King's ships in actions that usually resulted in a long dispatch in the *London Gazette*, had left pencil-thin lines on his brow, round his eyes and beside his nose, but they were disappearing as he relaxed here in Palace Street. Nor did he have the worry of the ship: the *Calypso* was having an extensive refit in drydock at Chatham, and from what he and his father could find out at the Admiralty, he would stay in command when she was commissioned again. Unless... unless a peace treaty was signed.

Then, she gathered, at least three quarters of the King's ships would be paid off; the Royal Navy would be reduced to a peacetime size. Admirals, captains, lieutenants—there would be dozens to spare. Nicholas might resign his commission because the routine of commanding a ship in peacetime would be too boring for him after the past years of continuous excitement and action.

Yet Nicholas's mother and father seemed almost hostile to the proposal of peace. No, Gianna corrected herself, not to peace itself but to dealing with Bonaparte. Well, no Tuscan trusted a Corsican, and if she was honest and dispassionate about it she did not trust Bonaparte either: he was the general who led the French army which invaded Volterra. Yet ironically but for Bonaparte she would never have met Nicholas, whose frigate had been sent to rescue her by Sir John Jervis (as he then was, but now Admiral the Earl St Vincent, First Lord of the Admiralty in the present government). So but for Bonaparte—and St Vincent—they would never have met and fallen in love.

Dreamily she returned to the Palace at Volterra: she pictured herself in the great state room, sitting in the chair reputed to be eight hundred years old. The big double doors would be flung open, His Britannic Majesty's envoy would be announced, and Nicholas in full diplomatic uniform would march in to present his credentials. Both of them would be hard put to keep straight faces...

She gave a start as the Earl clinked the heavy crystal stopper back into the sherry decanter, walked with his glass to a chair and sat down carefully.

"Hood sends his regards, m'dear," he said to his wife. "Terrible attack of gout; he can't bear anyone within ten feet of him—afraid they'll bump his leg. We were almost hailing each other across the room!"

"I think Gianna is anxious to know if you heard any news of Bonaparte's—er, offer."

"Yes, I did," the Admiral said grimly. "Too much. Hawkesbury called in while Hood and I were talking, and told us about it. The negotiations are nearly complete; Hawkesbury sees this fellow Otto for three or four hours a day and dispatches go off to Paris daily—apparently we have Revenue cutters waiting in Dover and they deliver Otto's diplomatic bag in Calais and bring back Bonaparte's instructions."

Ramage said: "Did you discover anything about the terms, father?"

The old man was silent for a moment, lost in thought. In memories, Ramage guessed. Thousands of British men had been killed, dozens of ships sunk, countless women widowed and children orphaned. Now the present politicians were likely to make all these sacrifices worthless in their scramble for peace: they would accept any terms Bonaparte cared to offer because they knew a peace treaty meant votes, just as the previous government had squandered thousands of soldiers and not a few sailors through sickness to capture worthless West Indian spice islands because "victories" were always worth a parliamentary cheer. Few members of Parliament realized that most such islands were only a quarter the size of a county like Kent. Few would remember that Bonaparte controlled everything that mattered, from the shores of the North Sea to the banks of the Mediterranean, including Spain, Italy and Egypt. Except for a naval base like Jamaica, the West Indian islands were irrelevant.

The Earl glanced up at Nicholas. Two scars on one side of his brow, another the size of a coin on his head—the hair there was growing back white—and a stiff left arm: wounds inflicted in the West Indies, Mediterranean and Atlantic. Nicholas and Lord Nelson had disobeyed Sir John Jervis's orders at the Battle of Cape St Vincent and in doing so had turned a miserable defeat into enough of a victory to earn Jervis an earldom, so that Earl St Vincent was now First Lord of the Admiralty. St Vincent was a fine administrator who had, by accident, won an undeserved reputation as a tactician. Had he ever forgiven that glorious act of disobedience by a young lieutenant called Ramage, which was spotted and backed by an almost unknown commodore in a seventy-four called Nelson? Now Jervis was Earl St Vincent; without those two he would still be Jervis, and few would have sympathized had he been put on the beach to draw halfpay for the rest of his life.

"Yes, and by the time the treaty is ratified I suspect we'll have surrendered every acre of land we've taken except Ceylon and Trinidad, and we may have forced Bonaparte to leave Egypt."

"And Italy?" Gianna said.

The Earl shook his head, as though trying to drive away his irritation. "Bonaparte has made offers on behalf of France, Sweden, Denmark and Holland. The negotiations concern only territory belonging to Britain or those countries. There has been no mention of Tuscany, Piedmont, the Papal States . . . Nor does Hawkesbury see how we can do anything about them— I asked him."

"He's a weak man," Gianna commented.

"He's a politician," the Earl said contemptuously. "No votes come from Italy for Addington and his cronies, but the House of Commons will give them three cheers for Ceylon and Trinidad . . ."

"When will the details be made public—officially, I mean?" Ramage asked.

The Earl shrugged his shoulders. "When Bonaparte, or this fellow Otto, say so. Officially Addington and Hawkesbury deny any negotiations are going on. That's where Otto is so useful: he's been the official French representative in London since the exchange of prisoners started, so no one takes any notice of his comings and goings."

"Gianna's dressmaker," the Countess said firmly. "We can do more good by visiting her than talking about the tidbits that Bonaparte tosses to us."

With that the two women left the room to put on outdoor clothes. Even though a watery sun made faint shadows, the chill of autumn was in the air.

The Earl sipped his sherry. "A sad business. Hood agrees with me that we are giving up just as the tide is turning in our favour."

Nicholas said: "Yes, the French are desperately short of wood, rope and canvas for their ships. Our blockade is really hurting them. I'd have thought that's why Bonaparte's offering terms: he wants a year or so of peace to restock his larder. Then he'll go to war again, knowing we'll have paid off most of our ships and disbanded our regiments. Once the men have disappeared the pressgangs will never find them again."

His father put down his glass. "Hood made the same points: he too reckons Bonaparte wants a rest, and lost his temper with Hawkesbury over the policy. But Jenks is only a politician, and for people like him no policy need cover more than the next division in the House of Commons. The frontiers of the world are bounded by the walls of the 'Ayes' and 'Noes' lobbies."

"Will the King agree, though?"

"They'll persuade him Britain is going bankrupt. It probably is, but better bankruptcy than Bonaparte!"

He held his sherry up to the light coming through the window. "When will the dockyard be finished with the *Calypso*?"

"Another three or four weeks. It'd be longer, but my fourth lieutenant's father is the Master Shipwright."

"At Chatham? Hmm, used to be a fellow called Martin. Very good. One of the very few honest men in all the King's dockyards."

"It must be the same man: his son is William Martin, known to his friends as 'Blower'."

"'Blower'? What an extraordinary nickname!"

"He plays a flute."

"Ah yes, you told me. Did very well in that Porto Ercole affair with the bomb ketches, and then with young Paolo in the convoy from Sardinia."

"That's the lad. If he goes on like this he deserves to get his flag."

"Won't stand a chance if there's peace. By the way, Nicholas, you ought to get Paolo up here from Chatham. Gianna is anxious to inspect her nephew, but she won't say anything to you for fear of it seeming like favouritism."

Ramage smiled and nodded. "Yes, I'd guessed that, and

20

talked it over with my first lieutenant and Southwick. There's an enormous amount Paolo can learn while a refit like this goes on, so we decided he'd get no leave for the first three weeks but they'd cram as much as they could into him and then make sure he has a week or two with Gianna."

"She's so proud of him."

"She's right to be. He's very much like her in some ways. Not so—well, explosive, but a very quick brain. Gets on very well with the men. Brave to the point of foolhardiness. If he survives and improves his mathematics, he'll pass for lieutenant at the first try."

Have you thought of taking Gianna down to Chatham so that she could see the ship as well?"

Ramage's face fell. "What a fool I am! She'd love it and all the old Kathleens—Jackson, Rossi, Southwick, Stafford—would go mad. Would you and mother come down as well?"

"Ah—well, I was hoping you'd propose it. Yes, we'd be delighted: we've already discussed it, so I know your mother's answer."

CHAPTER TWO

The black-hulled *Calypso* frigate had caused a stir of interest from the moment she sailed up the muddy Medway on the first of the flood, her ship's company racing round the deck working sheets, tacks and braces as she tacked and then tacked again the moment she had way on. The Medway narrows up as it nears the towns past the ruins of Upnor Castle (battered a century and a half earlier by the Dutchman, de Ruyter), and has some nasty bends, with mudflats a few inches below the water to trap the unwary.

Once she had moored off Chatham Dockyard, the ship and her men came under the authority of the Commissioner and was soon the target of all his minions. Ramage had managed to get a copy of a recent *Royal Kalendar* to see the names of the men who would be responsible for the *Calypso*'s refit and whom Aitken, the first lieutenant, would spend several weeks cajoling, persuading and threatening to get work done properly and reasonably promptly.

The first name in the Kalendar under "Chatham Yard" was the Commissioner Resident, listed as "F.J.Wedge, esq., 800 L., more for paper and firing 12L". Ramage conceded that the Commissioner probably earned his £800 a year pay, and probably quadrupled it from bribes and all the corrupt activities a man in his position could indulge in. The Navy Board were showing their usual parsimony in allowing only £12 a year to pay for stationery and fuel for the fires or stoves. Still, there must be plenty of old wood lying around.

The Master Shipwright, Martin's father, was paid £200 a year—the same as the Master Ropemaker, Master Boatbuilder, Master Mastmaker, Master Sailmaker, Master Smith, Master Carpenter, Master Joiner and Master Bricklayer. The Bosun of the Dockyard received only £80, but the storekeeper received £200 and was probably—because of the opportunity for fraud—the wealthiest of the Dockyard employees.

Most of them had come on board as the frigate was moored up, not because a 36-gun French frigate captured and brought into the King's service was an unusual sight but because the exploits of the *Calypso* and her captain had been mentioned in enough *Gazettes* to make them both famous. It would not mean any favourable treatment for the ship, because dockyard officials were by nature close-fisted men, issuing paint, rope, canvas and the like as though they paid for it themselves. There was the story of one eccentric and aristocratic captain, who receiving the Navy Board's issue of paint for his ship, wrote to their Lordships and asked which side of the ship he should paint. Their Lordships were not amused and the captain ended up doing what most captains did—paying out of his own pocket for the extra paint needed.

Ramage had stayed on board for a week as the *Calypso*

swung on the buoy with wind and tide until their Lordships answered his request for leave—no officer was allowed "to sleep out of his ship" without written permission, and that included admirals. Ramage had been given a month's leave and the ship was left in command of James Aitken. The Scotsman had no wish to go up to Perth on leave (Ramage discovered for the first time that Aitken's mother, the widow of a Navy master, had recently died) and he obviously trusted no one else to make sure the refit was done properly. Ramage knew that, however keen and eagle-eyed Aitken was, the man who really mattered was Southwick, the master, a man old enough to be the father and almost the grandfather of both his captain and first lieutenant.

Leave for the men, all of whom had been away from Britain for at least a couple of years, was always a problem for any captain. Usually half the men had in the first place been seized by pressgangs, and if the ship was an unhappy one because of the captain or her officers, giving the men leave would result in a number of them deserting: never returning to the ship and forfeiting a year or more of the pay due to them. Popular captains did not have to worry so much, but even if the men returned, a percentage of them would have spent their leave in and out of brothels and would come back riddled with venereal disease. This would put money in the surgeon's pocket, because he was allowed to make a charge for venereal treatment, but eventually it meant lost men: nothing cured syphilis.

Some captains gave leave only to selected men but Ramage disliked the system: it smacked of favouritism and the men not chosen were resentful. As he told Aitken, it was leave for all or for none, and he had decided on all: they would be allowed two weeks each.

One watch could go at once; the other when the first came back. He had mustered the ship's company aft on the quarterdeck and told them of his decision—and told them he trusted them to come back on time. In the meantime, he added, the watch left on board would have to work twice as hard.

Nor had that been an exaggeration. One of the most arduous tasks to be done was changing the *Calypso*'s guns: she still mounted the French cannons with which she had been armed when Ramage and his men captured her. Ramage had managed in Antigua to get rid of the unreliable French gunpowder and

23

stock the magazine with British, and there had been enough French roundshot on board to fit their size of guns, but the ship had been in action enough times to have the gunner reporting that the shot locker was now less than a third full.

The Ordnance Board had agreed to supply British 12-pounders to replace the French, and the shot to go with them, but not without a good deal of argument. Ramage never understood why the Ordnance Board, part of the Army, should have anything to do with naval gunnery, let alone control it completely. Anyway, hoisting out all the *Calypso*'s French guns and carriages and lowering them into hoys, and then getting all the shot up from the shot lockers—a deep, narrow structure in the ship like a huge wardrobe open at the top—was going to be hard work for the fewer than one hundred men comprising the one watch left on board. Then the hoys would bring out the new guns and carriages, and getting them on board would be more wearying than disposing of the French ones.

Once the new guns were at their ports, there would be new train tackles and breechings to be spliced up—the Master Ropemaker had agreed that the French rope had not been of a very good quality to start with, and two years' more service had brought it to the end of its life: when the rope was twisted to reveal the inner strands, they were grey; there was no sign of the rich golden brown of good rope.

Halyards, tacks, sheets, braces and lifts were all being renewed, along with many of the shrouds. The Master Shipwright and Master Mastmaker had inspected the masts and decided not to hoist them out for inspection. Only the foreyard, which had broken in the Mediterranean and been fished by the *Calypso's* carpenter and his mates, would be replaced. Then the *Calypso* would be towed by her boats into the drydock and, once all the water had been pumped out, leaving the ship sitting high and dry, shored up by large baulks of timber wedged horizontally between the ship's side and the walls of the dock, her copper sheathing would be inspected. All the sheets round the bow and stern would have to be replaced—this was a regular procedure for ships of war because, for a reason not yet understood (though there were dozens of theories), the sheathing there always became thinner and thinner and was eventually reduced to a mass of pinholes. Ramage hoped—

even though it would delay sailing—that all the sheathing would be renewed.

It was unusual to keep a ship's officers and men standing by her during a long refit; usually the captain was given another command, and the officers and men distributed among other ships, but as a gesture to Ramage's record, Lord St Vincent, the First Lord, had directed that the *Calypso*'s men should be kept together. Which was also more than a hint that he had a job for them all once the refit was over.

The *Calypso*, newly coppered, with new rigging and perhaps even new sails, would sail like a witch, he had told his father, who shared his enthusiasm for the skill of French naval architects: they had mastered that strange mixture of artistry and science which produced fast ships of war, particularly frigates.

"Jacko!" Stafford said as soon as he found the American on deck among the crowd of men who were preparing to hoist a gun out of a port.

"Jacko, you 'eard the scuttlebutt? About the captain?"

The tall, narrow-faced American whose sandy hair was thinning, seemed to freeze. He turned round slowly and stared at Stafford. "No. He's all right, isn't he?"

The Cockney seaman laughed, not realizing the effect his question had on the captain's coxswain. "Yus, he's all right—what harm would come to him in London? No, he's bringing the Marchesa down to see us. *And* his father and mother. Old 'Blaze-away' himself!"

"You gave me a scare," Jackson said, turning back to give orders to the men straining at the rope. "I thought something dreadful had happened."

"You don't trust him on his own!"

"I've picked him up unconscious enough times, bleeding like a stuck pig from a sword cut or a bullet, never to take anything for granted."

"An' he's saved you enough times," Stafford said, intending to tease.

"Five times up to now," Jackson said soberly. "If I stay with him I may reach old age and see South Carolina again."

"You don't seem very pleased at the idea o' seein' the Marchesa again."

"I am. It's just I'm still cold all over from your clumsiness.

25

And his father. What a sailor *he* was. The Countess must be a remarkable woman, judging from her husband and her son."

"There's Rossi—hey, Rosey, hear about the Marchesa?"

The Italian seaman looked up. He had no need to ask "What Marchesa?"; but because of the tone of Stafford's voice he suddenly grinned. "Are they getting married?"

"Nah, nothing like that. But they—she and the captain and his father and mother—are coming down to see the ship tomorrer. Probably coming down specially to see Signor Alberto Rossi, once the pride o' Genoa!"

"Watch out," Jackson muttered, "here comes the bosun."

The two seamen began heaving on the rope while Jackson went to the gun and made sure the cap squares holding the trunnions down on to the carriage had been pulled up and swung back out of the way. He checked that the sling was square, so that as soon as the men hauled down on the yard tackle the gun, weighing nearly a ton, would rise vertically and not damage anything. He went to the port and looked over the side. The hoy was secured alongside; the men in it were waiting patiently for the next gun to be lowered to them and join the five already lying in the bottom of the hoy, wedged with bags of sand so that they could not move.

Stafford gave a shiver as a gust of wind swept down the reach, pushing at the frigate so that she strained at the heavy ropes securing her by the bow to the mooring buoy. "This east wind—goes right through you. All that time in the West Indies and Mediterranington makes yer blood thin."

"Mediterranean," Jackson said, automatically correcting Stafford, who had a remarkable inability to pronounce place names correctly. "It's the damp in the cold that makes it worse. I'm surprised the captain is bringing visitors with the ship in such a mess. Anyway, how do you know about it?"

"That chap Hodges. He's the first lieutenant's servant while the other fellow's on leave, and 'e 'eard Mr Aitken and Mr Southwick talking about it. An' we're going to have to tiddly up the chair; the rats have been chewing the red baize."

"Anything to get away from these guns," Rossi said wearily. "*Accidente*, twenty men should make light work of hoisting one gun, but they seem to leave the hoist to me."

Stafford laughed and said: "You mean to say it's too heavy?

26

A *French* gun? You ought to be able to lift it up like a baby out of a cradle, without usin' a tackle."

He helped heave down on the fall and added: "'Ere, the Marchesa's goin' ter 'ave a surprise when she sees Mr Orsini. You'd never think he first came on board a shy boy trippin' over every rope in sight and slippin' on every step of a companionway."

Paolo Orsini had just left the first lieutenant and his head was in a whirl. He had expected to be given a couple of days' leave so that he could visit his aunt and the captain, and of course, the Earl and Countess, at the Palace Street house. He had never thought for a moment that all of them might visit the ship. His aunt knew what a frigate was like because one had brought her to England from the Mediterranean after the captain (and men like Jackson, Rossi and Stafford) had rescued her from a beach in Tuscany, but now she was to visit the *Calypso* she would see not only the ship in which he served but which he had helped capture. And since then the *Calypso* had been in action—well, how many times was it? He found he could not remember; his memory was blurred by the time he had been second-in-command to "Blower" Martin in a bomb ketch, and when he had (all too briefly) commanded a captured tartane.

He had grown a good couple of inches; the sleeves of all his jackets were too short, so that his wrists stuck out like sections of bamboo; the legs of his breeches ended just on his kneecaps, making them very uncomfortable—so much so that most of the time he felt like a hobbled horse, though on watch at night he pulled them down so that the waistband was tight against his hips.

There was no chance of getting on shore and buying new uniforms here in Chatham: he had hinted to Mr Aitken, who had pointed to the shiny elbows and mildewed lapels of his own uniform and said dourly: "This is ma best—you see what the Tropics did to it!"

The Tropics were a destroyer: leave a jacket hung in a locker for a week and it grew a fine crop of green mildew wherever a trace of food or drink had spilled on it. Leather, whether boots, shoes, belts or scabbards, grew rich yellow and green mildew as fields sprouted new grass and clover. Iron and steel rusted; a sword or dirk left in its scabbard for a few weeks

27

would rust even if coated with grease—the rust seemed to grow beneath the coating. Rope lost its springiness and became dead, apparently from the sunlight, although no one could explain exactly what happened. Sails suffered too; the humidity and constant tropical showers brought on the mildew, while the blazing sun took the life out of the threads so that it was easy to poke a finger through canvas which looked perfectly sound. Even worse, the material was so weak that the stitches securing a patch just ripped it away like a slashing knife. He had seen a patch blown clean out of a sail—and a few moments later the sail itself had split, starting from the hole left by the departed patch.

Yes, most interesting, but what the devil was it that the first lieutenant had ordered him to do? Quickly Paolo tried to remember the conversation. Mr. Aitken had said he had just received a letter from the captain saying he was bringing the Marchesa and his parents down to Chatham for a visit to the *Calypso*, and he wished Midshipman Orsini, able seaman Jackson, and ordinary seamen Rossi and Stafford to be available. Then he said they would be coming down by carriage and mentioning the name of the hotel they would use. And the Commissioner of the dockyard was making his yawl available and they would be leaving the jetty of the Commissioner's residence to board the ship at ten o'clock in the forenoon. Then what? The chair! That was it: the red baize needed replacing; and a whip had to be rove on the starboard main yardarm.

The English language was sometimes absurd. On land a whip was something you used on a horse or mule; in a ship it was a small block and a rope. Then there was a block—on land that was a large piece of something, like a block of wood. In a ship a block was what men on land called a pulley. And a sheet! That was the most hilarious of all—on land you found a sheet on a bed, although you could also have a sheet of paper. In a ship a sheet was a rope attached to the corner of a sail to control its shape. A seaman did not "put" a rope through a pulley, he rove it through a block, or he was ordered to reeve it. Paolo saw the first lieutenant coming up the companionway. Damn, where was the chair stowed? The bosun would know.

Aitken paused and looked round him. To an untrained eye there was chaos, with seamen running here and there like ants when their anthill was disturbed, but a seaman could distinguish order. Apart from young Orsini—clearly he had been standing daydreaming—the seventh 12-pounder was already hoisted out and slung over the side, the men under Jackson lowering it into the hoy.

But devil take it, how was he to have the ship ready for tomorrow's visitors? The captain would understand and, from what everyone said, the Marchesa would too. But Admiral the Earl of Blazey was the fifth most senior admiral in the Navy (he knew that because the moment he received the captain's letter, he had looked up the father in the latest edition of Steele's List of the Navy). Still, even a senior admiral would make allowances for the necessary activity. So that left the Admiral's wife. Well, all admirals' wives brought only misery and harassment to first lieutenants, whether of frigates or 100-gun flagships, and the Countess of Blazey was unlikely to be an exception.

Orsini had finally bestirred himself: no doubt asking the bosun where the chair was stowed. He was a remarkable young lad, and Aitken looked forward to meeting the aunt. It was curious how at first, when he joined the captain, he had assumed that Paolo's aunt, the Marchesa, was a wrinkled old Italian dragon, full of unpredictable whims and with enough influence to break a post captain with a pointing index finger and a mere lieutenant with a flick of a little finger. He had been quickly corrected by those who knew her—old Southwick, for instance, who doted on her—and told that she was five feet tall, about twenty-three years old, and the most beautiful woman they had ever seen. She had striking blue-black hair, large brown eyes—and, when she felt like it, was imperious.

Still, that was not surprising, because she had once ruled the kingdom of Volterra; her family had done so for centuries, until Bonaparte's invading army forced her to flee to the coast, to be rescued by the captain—then a junior lieutenant. And they had fallen in love. Hardened sinners like Jackson, Stafford and Rossi, who were in the ship's boat that rowed her to safety (even though one of Bonaparte's cavalrymen had put a bullet in her shoulder), fell in love with her too.

He admitted he had not at first been too pleased when the captain told him that the Marchesa's nephew would be joining the ship as a midshipman: he had visions of a spoiled Italian brat expecting privileges and constantly running to the captain.

Instead the Marchesa's nephew (who would inherit the kingdom of Volterra if she had no children) was quite as tough as a young Scot of the same age would have been. He had proved something of a contradiction. He was hopeless at mathematics (and he and Southwick had to be careful about that, because the captain's own mathematics were said to be sufficient and no more) and tended to daydream, and he was famous throughout the ship for his forgetfulness. But in action, with roundshot and musketballs whistling about his ears, cutlasses flashing and clanging, and the odds against him at about ten to one, then he had the quickness of a snake, the cunning and ingenuity of a highwayman, the clear thinking of a gambler, and the bravery of—well, someone like the captain, or Southwick.

Aitken knew little of Italian character, but from what he had heard and seen (people like the seaman Rossi) Paolo Orsini was a happy mixture of the best of the British and Italian characters. As important as his behavior in action was his attitude towards the day-to-day running of the ship: he was a leader. Aitken doubted if he was yet sixteen years old, but as a midshipman he had to give orders to seamen who had been at sea for twice as many years as he had lived. With many young midshipmen this led to trouble—and with old ones, too: failing their lieutenants' examination, or passing but not getting a ship, resulted in midshipmen of forty who were almost invariably bitter drunkards. Orsini had such a cheerful manner, and he had learned so fast and was so anxious to go on learning, that he was the ship's favourite. He had heard seamen exchanging stories of Orsini's exploits in action, and they were related with pride, as one man might boast about his village's prize fighting cock.

He spotted a white mop of hair up on the fo'c'sle, showing Southwick busy with some men. He had to discuss with the master the programme for tomorrow's visitors because the old men knew them all. Then, Aitken decided, he would inform the lieutenants and then, before the midday meal, muster the men and tell them: they would want to get their queues retied and start the day with clean shirts. It was a Thursday, so they had to shave, but they would have done so anyway.

"The Frenchies made it fancy enough," the bosun said as he held up the legless chair for Paolo's inspection. "The lady sits on the seat, then this bar drops across the front from arm to arm and locks to hold her in. She sits back and up and away she goes."

"Yes," Paolo said doubtfully. "As soon as someone's rove the whip I'll try it out. Then we'll change some of this red baize. It looks as though the rat did not like it."

"Not surprised, sir; it's the same baize that's used for covering the handle o' a cat-o'-nine tails and the bag to put it in. Not that we need it with this captain."

"No, I've never seen a flogging," Paolo said, with all the curiosity of the young. "Is it really bad?"

"You probably won't ever see one if you serve with Mr Ramage 'cos he don't believe in flogging; but yes, it's 'orrible. Most frigates like us'd have at least three or four a week. Not because the captains are cruel but a few bad men keep getting drunk or regularly make mischief. Mr Ramage managed long ago to get rid of the few bad apples and keep the good ones."

Paolo looked up at the starboard main yardarm. One man was passing a rope through a block while a second paid out more from a coil slung over his shoulder. Paolo picked up the chair and walked over to one of the guns, followed by a puzzled bosun. Holding it by the arm he lifted it and then banged the seat across the breech of the gun. Dust particles lifted in a cloud.

Just making sure there's no dry rot or woodworm at work under that baize," he said. "Seems strong enough." He looked up again and saw that one end of the rope had almost reached the deck. "Come on, hoist me up to the yardarm; I weigh a good deal more than my aunt or the Countess."

At ten o'clock next morning Ramage, once again wearing the heavy blue coat of a post captain, with its gold-braided lapels and the single heavy epaulet on his right shoulder indicating that he had less than three years' seniority, stood on the Commissioner's jetty and looked across the muddy Medway at the *Calypso*.

He had expected to find her heeled to starboard or larboard because the French guns had been hoisted out on one side or the other and lowered into the hoys. Instead she was floating on an even keel; all the yards were square.

"She looks very smart, Nicholas," his mother said.

"Very French, that sheer," the Admiral commented. "A handsome ship. Not surprised they bought her into the Service after you captured her. A nice pile of prize money for your men."

"With that and the money from the convoy we captured, most of them would be rated wealthy by their neighbours," Ramage said. "They deserved it!"

"The yawl, my Lord," Wedge said, gesturing to the white-painted boat at the end of the jetty. The dockyard commissioner looked to Ramage like a Gillray cartoon of a corrupt public official: rolls of fat began at his chin like canvas hose and circled to below his hips. His eyes were never still, jerking from face to face as if frightened of missing a proffered bribe or a warning glance.

"Yes, yes," the Earl said impatiently, "we're having a look at the ship from here."

"And very nice she seems, sir," Wedge said predictably, like an ingratiating parson entertaining the patron of his living to tea.

Ramage turned to Gianna. "Watch this," he said, having just realized that the two figures on the quarterdeck were Aitken and Southwick but there was not another man in sight on board the ship. Wedge had spotted this too, and was grumbling to himself just loudly enough for Ramage to hear. "Seem to be asleep on board there. So much work to be done. The rest of the guns to be hoisted out . . ."

Suddenly the shrouds of the fore, main and mizenmasts changed in appearance from thin cobwebs of rope to thick trunks of trees as scores of men raced up the ratlines. The first kept going and a couple of dozen walked out along the top-gallant yards while below more spaced themselves at arms length on the topsail yards and the fore and mainyards. In a matter of moments the men were equally spaced out on all the yards, facing forward with arms outstretched, the tips of each man's fingers touching those of his neighbours on each side.

Gianna gave a gasp of surprise and pleasure and the Countess, who had so often seen a ship's company man the yards years earlier, turned to her son. "You shouldn't have arranged that just for us, Nicholas!"

"I didn't," Ramage admitted. "You can thank Aitken and

Southwick when we get on board. Anyway, let's go out to her now."

The yawl came alongside the *Calypso* and hooked on. The Earl looked at Ramage, who nodded. By the custom of the Navy, the senior officer was the last into a boat when leaving a ship but the first out when coming alongside.

Two side-ropes hung down, one each side of the battens forming narrow steps, or ledges, secured to the ship's side from just above the waterline to the entryport at deck level. The ropes, knotted with diamond knots and covered with red baize, hung a couple of feet away from the hull, held out by sideboys at a comfortable distance for a climber to grip them, like the bannisters of a staircase, as he made his way up the side. The ship's side was manned—the normal routine for the visit of a flag officer or captain.

The Admiral went up with a briskness that surprised Ramage, and Gianna was just beginning to get up from the thwart and gather her skirt round her when Ramage gestured to her to remain seated. The Countess had not moved and smiled reassuringly at Gianna, guessing that although she had been in a frigate several times before she had never made an official visit.

Gianna's eye was caught by a red object high above her, and a rope dropped into the stern of the boat and then another dropped into the bow. A moment later a seaman slid down each one and nimbly scrambled to the middle of the boat in time to catch and hold the red object as it was lowered into the boat, and which she now recognized as a sort of chair suspended on a rope which went up to the mainyard.

Then suddenly she recognized one of the seamen. "Rossi! *Come sta!*" She held out her hand and the Italian lifted it to his lips, suddenly too shy to speak.

Then she saw who the other man was. "Stafford! What a wonderful surprise, the pair of you dropping out of the sky on me! Where is Jackson?"

Rossi pointed upwards at the deck and turned the chair, flipping back the arm but waiting for the Countess to sit in it first.

"I'll go first, dear," the Countess said tactfully, "then you'll see how it is done." The remark was spoken softly, and Gianna

33

was grateful, realizing that in the Navy's table of precedence the Countess of Blazey came first.

The Countess settled herself in the chair. Ramage quickly inspected it and swung over the bar to secure it. She smiled at the two seamen and spoke to them for a few moments while Ramage climbed up the ship's side.

Rossi, watching him disappear through the entryport, whispered something to the Countess, and then made a circular movement with his raised hand. Slowly but steadily the chair rose, taking the Countess with it. "I love this," she called down to Gianna, "it gives one such an unusual view of everything!"

The chair swung slowly inboard once it had been raised clear of the bulwarks and entryport and was then lowered until it was two or three feet above the deck.

"Jackson!" the Countess said delightedly as the seaman stepped forward with two other men to steady the chair, open the bar and help the Countess out. In a moment the chair had been pulled clear and men bustled about tactfully as she shook out her skirt, adjusted her hair and acknowledged her son's salute.

While the chair soared up and was then lowered over the side again for Gianna, Ramage said formally: "Madam, allow me to present my officers."

Ramage guessed he had about three minutes for the presentation before Gianna soared on board, and knew his mother was accustomed to all the ritual and timing of Court and naval etiquette.

"Ah, Mr. Aiken—my son's right hand! Will you have time to visit Perth? . . . Mr. Wagstaffe—you had a good voyage to Gibraltar with that prize frigate? . . . Mr. Kenton, I haven't had the pleasure of meeting you before, but I've read and heard all about your adventures . . . So you are Mr Martin. May I call you by your nickname and ask you to play for us—it is not often we can listen to a flute. My husband has known your father for years, of course . . . Mr Renwick, I've heard so much about you and your Marines that I feel I've known you for years! . . . Mr Orsini—Paolo!" She kissed him. "You left us a boy and you've come back a man! Your aunt will be with us in a moment! . . . Mr Southwick—not a day older. What is your secret? You have a recipe for eternal youth! . . . Mr Bowen, I

34

hope my son has not been giving you too many patients! Oh, so few? That's the way it should be in every action!"

She had just spoken to all the officers, with the Earl walking beside her, when seamen hoisting on the fall of the rope brought the red chair up above the bulwarks and Jackson hauled gently on the guy, fitted to an eyebolt beneath the seat, to make sure Gianna landed in exactly the right place. She was smiling with pleasure and recognized Jackson at once, laughing as he steadied the chair while Aitken appeared, apparently from nowhere, to swing back the bar and help her stand up.

"Blower" Martin, fourth in the line of officers waiting to be introduced to her, was suddenly finding it hard to breathe: he seemed to have an invisible band round his throat, like the Spanish garotte, and it happened the moment he first saw the Marchesa's face as the chair rose above the level of the hammock nettings on top of the bulwarks. He realized that without any qualification or argument she was the most beautiful woman he had ever seen. Her face was heart-shaped, her eyes widely spaced and—from this distance—seeming black. Her hair was as black as a raven's wing. As she stepped out of the chair, he saw she was tiny. Her dress was a very pale green, probably silk. Laughing over something Mr Aitken had said, she was pointing to Jackson. Now she was pointing at Southwick and hurrying—to Martin it seemed like dancing—over to embrace the old man. Embrace be damned, she had just given him a smacking kiss on the cheek. He was laughing and now they were dancing a jig—and from aloft the ship's company were cheering and singing!

Martin glanced round nervously: such behaviour with Admiral the Earl of Blazey on board, quite apart from the Countess of Blazey, could get Mr Ramage into trouble . . . Then he saw them both laughing, obviously delighted, and remembered that the Marchesa lived with them, was young Paolo's aunt, and that she and Mr Ramage were in love.

Now he understood why seamen like Jackson, Stafford and Rossi talked so much about her: she had more life and high spirits in her little finger than any woman William Martin had previously seen had in her whole body. Jackson and another seaman with Mr Ramage had saved her life. That was some years ago now, but Martin remembered he had seen the spot where it had happened: someone had pointed it out during the

35

attack on Port Ercole with the bomb ketches. He felt a sudden jealousy: to have helped rescue such a lady, and to know her so that when she kissed your cheek the whole ship's company spontaneously cheered.

Five minutes later, as she was formally introduced to the *Calypso*'s officers, "Blower" Martin was tongue-tied, able only to stare and then to bow, and it was Paolo who stepped forward and described how they had been in action together *"tante volte"*, which Martin guessed must mean several times, and how Lieutenant Martin had commanded the bomb ketch. The Marchesa knew all about it, and made him describe how they had aimed the mortars.

With all the introductions over, Ramage murmured to Aitken, and later repeated to Southwick, his thanks for the reception. When the men were piped down from aloft and descended like swarming starlings, excited at the presence of the Marchesa and the captain's parents, Ramage said to Aitken: "You aren't going to get much work out of them until we leave!"

"We're only doing the dockyard's work, sir," he said sourly. "Eighty dockyard men were allocated to get the guns and roundshot out. I haven't seen one of them. It took me three days of bullying at the Commissioner's office to get the hoys, and I began swaying the guns over the side with my own men just to get the job done. That damned Commissioner probably has those eighty men building a house for one of his friends—using Navy Board wood."

"Probably," Ramage said. He had seen long ago that corrupt transactions would be rated normal by the Navy Board; honest work was the exception. "Now, all the officers are invited to lunch with us—providing you can supply enough chairs from the gunroom. Kenton, Martin and Orsini could use a form. And was that hamper of food brought on board from the yawl? Ah, there it is; Jackson and Rossi are carrying it below. My mother has packed enough for a ship o' the line."

CHAPTER THREE

The family's visit to Chatham was still being talked about by Gianna, who had been excited at seeing again the men who had rescued her from the Tuscan shores and then sailed with her in Ramage's first command, the *Kathleen* cutter.

The Times and the *Morning Post* were delivered early that morning and Hanson brought them in on a silver salver, offering the Earl his choice. He took *The Times*, saying: "I know you prefer the *Post*, Nicholas."

The Countess pushed back her chair and stood up. "You men will want to read your papers. Gianna wishes to visit her dressmaker again, so unless you want it, John, we'll use the carriage."

"Good Heavens!" the Earl muttered. "Sit down a moment dear . . . Does the *Post* mention this?" he said to Nicholas without raising his head.

Ramage nodded but was engrossed in what he was reading. The Countess looked surprised and then slightly alarmed, but when she saw that Gianna was about to ask questions she held her finger to her lips.

Finally the Earl said, unable to keep the bitterness from his voice: "Bonaparte's done it, the scoundrel!"

The Countess sighed, needing no more explanation, but Gianna said excitedly: "What is it? Read it out!"

The Admiral looked across at his son. "You read it, Nicholas: I'd like to compare it with *The Times* report."

Nicholas flattened the page of the paper. "Well, peace has been signed. The *Post* says:

"'We are officially informed that yesterday, the 1st day of October, the preliminary articles for a peace between Great Britain and France were signed in London between Lord Hawkesbury, His Majesty's Secretary of State for Foreign Affairs, and M. Louis-Guillaume Otto, Commissioner for the Exchange of French Prisoners in England.

"'It is understood that ratifications will be exchanged within two weeks, and that they will be followed by a Royal proclamation in which His Majesty will order a cessation of arms by sea and land.

"'According to the preliminary articles, five months from the date of the exchange of ratifications will be the longest period during which hostilities can exist in the most distant parts of the globe.'"

As soon as he stopped reading, Gianna said: "It gives no actual details, then? Just that the preliminaries have been signed?"

"There is a second article, which may or may not be official. The writer simply says 'We understand . . .' That's often a way the government flies a kite to see how Parliament will react; sometimes it is simply gossip."

"Read it out, anyway," his mother said.

"I'll just tell you the main points. As far as I can see, we return to Bonaparte and his allies everything we've taken and he keeps everything except—Egypt. Anyway, starting with the West Indies: we return every island we've captured from the Dutch except Dutch Guiana but we don't return Trinidad to the Spanish."

The Earl sniffed: "That's Bonaparte punishing the Dons for making peace with Portugal without his permission!"

Nicholas nodded. His father understood the broader sweep of world affairs better than he. "Denmark gets back the islands of St Thomas, St Croix and St John . . ." For a moment his memory flicked back to the *Triton* brig, his second command, drifting dismasted in the Caribbean after a hurricane, with St Thomas and St Croix in the distance.

"The Swedes get back St Bartholomew."

A tiny island north of Antigua but one of the most beautiful in the Leeward Islands.

"France—well, Bonaparte gets back all the sugar islands except Guadeloupe. We lost thousands of soldiers and hundreds of seamen from sickness to capture them. Every capture raised a cheer in Parliament for the government. Now Bonaparte gets them back—by bluffing Hawkesbury, I suppose."

Every one of those islands was as familiar to Ramage as Whitehall: St Lucia, and his attack with the *Triton* brig; Martinique, where he had seized Diamond Rock and captured a convoy, and his present command, the *Calypso* frigate, raiding Fort Royal—or Fort de France, as the Republicans had renamed it; Antigua with its mosquitoes and corruption...

"Now," he continued, "the Atlantic. We return the Cape of Good Hope to the Dutch, and Portugal gets Madeira."

"So we lose provisioning ports on the way to India," his father said. "Hawkesbury is a bigger fool than anyone believed."

"You flatter him," Nicholas said dryly, "because, in the East Indies, Malacca, Amboyna, Banda and Ternate are returned to the Dutch, although we keep Ceylon. But in India Bonaparte gets back Pondicherry, Chandernagore and various settlements along the Ganges."

"It's unbelievable," the Admiral said, his voice revealing his despair. "We've lost so many lives and beggared ourselves and now we sign a peace treaty which would be harsh even if we'd *lost* the war."

"We won the war and Hawkesbury and Addington have lost the peace," Nicholas said bitterly.

Gianna said quietly: "There is no mention of Italy?"

"Not of Volterra, but I'm just coming to Europe," Nicholas said. "We return the island of St Marcouf, Egypt goes back to the Sublime Porte, and the Order of St John of Jerusalem have Malta, Gozo and Comino restored to them. France has to evacuate Naples and Roman territory—that is the only reference to Italy—while Britain evacuates Corsica, which means Portoferraio, and 'all other islands and fortresses she has occupied in the Adriatic and Mediterranean'. And, across the Atlantic, we restore St Pierre and Miquelon to Bonaparte so his fishermen have a base..."

"Can I return to Volterra?" Gianna asked flatly.

Ramage gestured at his father, who was obviously leaving him to answer. "Well, once the ratifications are signed, legally

39

we are at peace with France and British subjects will be free
to travel. Dozens will flock to Paris and Rome, I expect. But
Bonaparte is going to keep the Republic of Genoa, Piedmont,
Tuscany . . . all the Italian states, including Volterra. At least,
that's what the newspapers say, and I think they must have
been given special information."

"That doesn't answer my question, *caro* . . ."

He knew it did not; he was trying to evade it.

"You are the ruler of Volterra by right, custom, tradition
and the will of the people. But Bonaparte invaded it—along
with most of the rest of Italy—and this peace they are signing
still leaves the French in occupation. I can't see Bonaparte
allowing the rightful ruler back into any country he is occu-
pying."

"Why not? It is my Kingdom!"

"That would be sufficient reason for him to refuse . . ."

"This Bonaparte—he would be afraid that I would rally my
people and throw out the French?"

"Darling, you might—and would, I am sure—rally your
people, but you could never throw out the French." He loved
the way she always referred disdainfully to "this Bonaparte",
but the habit could be dangerous. "You must not underestimate
'this Bonaparte'. His armies probably total a million men.
You'd be lucky to raise an army of a thousand—"

"Nico!" she said angrily. "Many more than that!"

"*Cara*, you must be realistic," he said, choosing his words
very carefully: he wanted to convince her, but if she lost her
temper it was impossible to reason with her. "While you have
been in exile, the French will have set up a government, as
they did in Genoa, and new leaders will have emerged in
Volterra prepared to work with them. There—"

"You are not suggesting my people would cooperate—"

"I am not suggesting it, I am telling you. There are *always*
men who cooperate with an occupation army. If Bonaparte had
ever occupied Britain there would be men—perhaps even people you know—eager to cooperate to get some personal advantage. It is the same in Volterra. Some of those who did not
choose to escape with you when Bonaparte's Army of Italy
marched in—why did they stay?"

He waited for the question to sink in. After several long
moments she said: "They had land, family, responsibilities . . ."

40

The Countess said: "Gianna, you know that's not entirely true; you've complained to me about some that you suspected were staying to collaborate with the French."

Gianna nodded miserably. "Yes, but it is hard to believe people can be so wicked!"

Ramage said harshly: "They can be and they are. Bonaparte obviously set up a puppet government in Volterra formed by people you know. If they heard you were coming down the Via Aurelia in your carriage, you'd meet with a fatal accident before you were within a hundred miles of the city gates."

"But supposing I keep my arrival secret?"

"Assassins would find you in the palace corridors."

"Then why did not the British insist that Bonaparte withdraw his armies from Italy?"

"We are not strong enough. When a peace treaty is being negotiated, the country with the biggest army and navy has the most say."

"But you have just been saying that Hawkesbury—"

"Yes," Nicholas interrupted. "Bonaparte has the biggest *army,* but we have the biggest *navy,* and our blockade of France has left his dockyards empty of timber to build and repair ships, rope and canvas. France is short of food. That's why Bonaparte started the peace talks: he wants a year or two of peace."

"A year or two?" Gianna exclaimed. "Then what happens?"

"As soon as his warehouses are restocked Bonaparte will declare war again. There are still places for him to conquer. Britain, for example, quite apart from Egypt and India."

"Then why does Britain accept his terms? Why negotiate? Why not continue the war?"

"Because this present government is weak and doesn't believe we can finance the war any longer."

"Finance it! Which would Addington and Hawkesbury prefer—to be bankrupt or prisoners of Bonaparte?"

The Admiral coughed and everyone glanced at him. "The fact is," he said, "most of the present government don't have the imagination to see that ultimately that's the choice. The people in the country towns and villages can understand it, but not the Addingtons and Hawkesburys. Pitt has many faults, but when he's sober he is a brilliant treasurer."

By now Gianna was weeping and both had the embarrassed attitude of men facing tears. Nicholas deliberately avoided saying anything to comfort her because the "this Bonaparte" attitude had to be changed, for her own peace of mind and safety.

"So traitors rule Volterra," she sobbed. "Perhaps even my own cousins... Yes, they would do anything to hold on to their wealth and lands..."

"And get control of yours, too," the Admiral said quietly. "That is why people collaborate with an enemy—for power and material gain."

Two days later a letter arrived at Palace Street from the Secretary of the Admiralty, telling Ramage to report to the First Lord next morning at ten o'clock. Evan Nepean, the Secretary, gave no hint at what Earl St Vincent wanted to see Captain the Lord Ramage about, but it was typical of the irascible old admiral that he insisted on using Ramage's title.

Gianna was sure Ramage was to be sent to some distant part of the world with news of the peace, but both Ramage and the Admiral thought it more likely that the First Lord, as a gesture towards Admiral the Earl of Blazey, was seeing his son personally to tell him that once the ratifications had been exchanged—within two weeks at most, unless Bonaparte thought of more outrageous demands—half the Navy's ships were to be paid off and their officers put on halfpay.

"You have to admit that you have no experience of the Navy in peacetime, Nicholas," his father said. "I have, and looking at your service—where you've been able to pack more action into a very few years than any half dozen officers normally experience in a lifetime—I can't see you being able to put up with the boredom.

"Yes," he said, noting his son's raised eyebrows, "sheer boredom. The Navy in peacetime is concerned with filling in the right number of the correct forms punctually, doing every sail order in the signal book in the minimum time, and covering the maximum amount of ship with the minimum of paint. Your service in command of a frigate will probably comprise dancing attendance on an admiral who has enough political "interest" to keep himself employed.

"At sea you and the rest of the squadron or fleet will be in company with the flagship. When the admiral says tack, you tack; when the admiral says wear, you wear. Everything you do, as the ship's captain, will be governed by a signal from the flagship, from hoisting your colours by the flagship's drumbeat at daybreak to lowering them at her drumbeat at sunset.

"In port—which will be most of the time—you will dance attendance on the commander-in-chief, for several reasons. You are a very "eligible" bachelor, and the admiral's wife will have at least a dozen young officers or protégées she considers suitable matches for you. You have a certain fame as a fighting officer, so you will be required to attend all social functions arranged by the admiral and his lady to give *ton* which the proceedings would otherwise lack. And you should remember that one word spoken out of place could lose you your command: for every ship in commission in a peacetime Navy, there are twenty captains on halfpay only too anxious to take over, and a vindictive admiral can put you on the beach."

"I think you are deliberately painting a gloomy picture, father," Ramage protested, but his mother shook her head.

"If anything it would be worse for you, Nicholas," she said. "From your first day as a midshipman until now there has been a war, with action, opportunity and promotion. You have come to think of that as normal naval service. But it is not. You may spend the rest of your life without hearing another shot fired, with promotion depending upon the captains senior to you dying of old age, not being killed in action . . . Nicholas," she said with a seriousness he rarely heard, "I do not see you as a naval officer in peacetime."

Ramage laughed because he understood what his parents meant, but they were also forgetting a point which they had discussed only two days earlier, when he had read out the reported terms of the articles of peace.

"You forget that we shall be at war again in a year or two. Bonaparte is only resting. If I can hold on to my command for a while, it means I shall be ready with my present ship's company for whatever the French have in mind. It's taken a long time to sort out these men. Now I wouldn't change one of them."

Gianna, still upset at Volterra not being mentioned in the articles, and due to see Lord Hawkesbury next day, protested: "You talk as if war is going to last for the rest of our lives."

The Admiral said gently: "It may well do for the rest of *our* lives—" he gestured to include himself and the Countess "—and much of yours. Remember, Britain is now alone. Austria, Prussia, Portugal, the Russians—all have been our allies at one time or another. We've paid enormous subsidies to persuade 'em to fight—for their own safety, incidentally—but now we haven't the money and they've neither the ability nor courage. Britain alone can't defeat Bonaparte: just think how many men he has under arms and how many acres of land under cultivation. Ultimately they are the two things that matter. If he can grow enough wheat to feed his people and has a big enough army to defend his borders, our blockade can't hurt him. In the peace he's now arranging he'll restock his warehouses, as Nicholas says. Then he'll be beyond our reach. If he can last out five years he'll beat us because I'm sure we can't beat him: our people have been taxed enough, in order to try to save the Prussians and the rest of them."

"And I shall never again see Volterra..."

"Perhaps not: you must always have that in mind."

"So how can I argue with Lord Hawkesbury to have Volterra included in the peace, or the subject of a further treaty?"

The Admiral shook his head. "My dear," he said in his calm, gentle voice, "we have not encouraged you either to see Hawkesbury or to think Britain can help you. Just remember that Jenks is a politician, not a gentleman, and you should treat him as such."

Lord St Vincent's office was the next beyond the Board Room, high-ceilinged with a polished table on the far side, opposite the door and where the First Lord sat in an armless chair with his back to the window. His large head and a natural stoop made him appear smaller than he was.

The room smelled of guttering candles: St Vincent was usually the first to start work at the Admiralty, and the first officers he wanted to see would find their appointments timed for seven o'clock. Between seeing people—who ranged from captains receiving orders to politicians seeking favours for the nephews of friends—he attacked the papers neatly piled on his table, calling in the Board Secretary, Nepean, who often worked at the huge mahogany table in the Board Room itself.

The old Admiral wiped his pen with a piece of cloth and carefully placed the quill in a wooden rack before looking up at Ramage, who had been announced by a messenger, summoned into the room, and now waited while St Vincent went through the ritual of completing one task before starting another.

Unexpectedly he stood up and held out his hand. The two men shook in silence, and the Admiral gestured to the single straight-backed chair as he sat down himself.

"You've been busy since I last saw you. At the Duchess of Manson's ball before you went off spying in France, eh?"

"Yes sir," Ramage said.

"Since then you've been collecting a number of *Gazettes*."

"Thanks to you, sir."

A captain's dispatch after an action was addressed to Nepean, the Secretary to the Board, and began with the time-honoured phrase "Be pleased to lay before their Lordships..." A description followed, showing success or failure—and often revealing something of the character of the writer. Ramage's dispatches were concise rather than brief; he had long ago noticed that the officers cultivating brevity did so quite deliberately, knowing that a reputation for such a style would be useful when reporting near failure.

When their Lordships considered that an officer had done particularly well, his dispatch (after being edited in case it contained information of use to the enemy) was sent to the office of the Secretary of State for the Home Department, further along Whitehall, to be handed over to the *Gazette* printer, Andrew Strahan, who had his office there.

His father had been the first to draw Ramage's attention to the importance of writing careful dispatches. He pointed out that a good captain did not need his dispatch to be published in the *Gazette*, because the Board knew his worth, but for a deserving officer serving with him in the action, a mention in a dispatch was invaluable; it was often the only road to promotion. It was useful for a lieutenant seeking promotion to be able to show a *Gazette* or two in which he was mentioned. And, as his father had emphasized, if a man has a common surname, make sure you give the number by which he is known in the service.

The number of lieutenants John Smith in the Navy List was startling; it was not unusual to see "Lt John Smith the Fourth" or seventh or tenth in a *Gazette*. Yet, again proving that a dispatch often revealed a good deal about its writer, it was not unusual to read one in which not a single officer or man was

45

mentioned, so unwilling was the captain (or even the admiral—and St Vincent himself had been guilty of it after the battle which gave him his title) to share either credit or glory.

St Vincent tapped a copy of the *Gazette* lying on the table. "You read yesterday's issue?"

"Yes, sir," Ramage said, his voice neutral.

"What did you think of the main announcement signed by the Secretary of State and Otto?"

St Vincent was a friend of Addington; the Prime Minister was obviously proud of the treaty with Bonaparte, since his own Secretary of State had negotiated it. But Ramage, knowing that a wise man would tell a white lie but refusing to be a hypocrite, simply turned down the corners of his mouth.

"You don't like it, eh? Why?"

St Vincent never wasted words; he doled them out, spoken or written, as a miser might give a coin to an improvident nephew. Did a wise post captain with a good deal less than three years' seniority really reveal his views to the First Lord? Well, St Vincent was shrewd; probably he really wanted to know what Admiral the Earl of Blazey thought, and guessed his son's views were similar.

Ramage turned his hat in his lap, to give the impression he was taking time to consider his reply.

"With respect, sir: Bonaparte has made fools of us."

St Vincent's eyebrows shot up. "I don't think Lord Hawkesbury would like to hear you say that."

Ramage shrugged his shoulders. "My father has already told him that—and a good deal more—a couple of days ago."

"In what way is Bonaparte supposed to have made fools of us?" St Vincent asked sarcastically.

"Our blockade has emptied his warehouses; he has no rope, canvas or timber to repair his ships. Now he makes us lift the blockade. We captured many of his islands—you yourself took Martinique, sir—and now he gets them all back at no cost."

"Not all," St Vincent protested.

"All that matter, sir," Ramage said stubbornly. "We've lost thousands of men from sickness but very few from fighting, and spent millions of pounds on the war—to no purpose."

"I didn't know you were a strategist," St Vincent growled. "If you intend to go into politics, let me give you some advice—" the Earl broke off when he saw the expression on

46

Ramage's face. "Yes, well, you take after your father in that respect."

Ramage inspected the inside band of his hat.

"Now peace is signed," St Vincent said, "are you sending in your papers?"

Ramage looked up, startled. "No, sir. At least, not unless their Lordships ask me."

"You don't need the halfpay," St Vincent said.

"I had no intention of requesting it, sir," Ramage said tartly. "As far as I know, I am still on full pay in command of the *Calypso* and on a month's leave."

St Vincent had moved the *Gazette*, which had hidden a bulky letter bearing the Admiralty seal. The Earl picked up the packet, turned it over so that Ramage could read the super-scription, and slid it across the table to him.

"*Captain the Lord Ramage, H.M. frigate Calypso, Chatham.*"

As Ramage reached out for the packet, St Vincent held up his hand. "Don't open it yet: read the back."

Just below the seal, copperplate handwriting said: "*Secret orders—not to be opened until south of latitude 10 degrees North.*"

Ten North! That was south of the latitude of Barbados in the West Indies or the Cape Verde Islands off the coast of West Africa. So the orders concerned the South Atlantic. The coast of Africa or South America in peacetime? What on earth could be happening down there?

St Vincent stood up and walked to the window. There was not much to see; Ramage knew that this and the Board Room's three other windows overlooked a stable. The early morning sky with its scattering of cloud was now becoming overcast; there would be rain by teatime.

Abruptly, and with his back to Ramage, the First Lord asked: "How is the *Calypso*'s refit proceeding?"

Obviously the First Lord did not trust the daily reports he received from his dockyard commissioners. "Slowly, sir, as far as I could see when I was on board three days ago."

"Ah yes, you and your visitors took up a lot of time."

"Indeed, sir?" Ramage could almost see the Commissioner's report. "How so, sir?"

"The dockyard men could not get on with shifting the guns."

47

"Sir, there hasn't been a single dockyard man on board since the *Calypso* moored up in Chatham."

St Vincent swung round. "Rubbish! You've had eighty men!"

"Excuse me, sir," Ramage said carefully. "I was told by the Commissioner I would *get* eighty men, to shift the guns. In fact none arrived and my own men have been doing the work. My first lieutenant had a great deal of trouble getting even a few hoys to carry the French guns on shore."

St Vincent sat down at the table and quickly shuffled through a pile of papers. He found one page and ran his finger down it. His eyes flicked back and forth along the lines.

"The Commissioner has allocated 110 men to the *Calypso*. Eighty to get the guns out; twenty are riggers; and ten are to help strike that foreyard."

"When were those men supposed to start work, sir?"

The date the First Lord gave was the day after the *Calypso* arrived in Chatham. "We might have been allocated 110 men, sir, but none has come on board, unless they started today. I was there on Friday and I can't think they'd work half a day on Saturday. Yesterday, Sunday, was a holiday."

"The Commissioner himself signed this return, Ramage; are you calling him a liar?"

Ramage pictured the ingratiating figure at the jetty, rolls of fat quivering, servile to the Admiral—and using the Ramage family visit as an excuse for "delaying" men not even on board.

"A liar, sir, with respect, and a fraud too. Where *were* those 110 men working?"

"I intend finding out," St Vincent said grimly, "but don't you go down to Chatham until your leave expires; it's better that I stir things up at Somerset House."

The Navy Board occupied Somerset House, and there the Comptroller, Sir Andrew Snape Hamond, held sway. Probably the most dishonest man connected with the Royal Navy, he controlled the purchase of everything concerning the King's ships. Everything from rum to salt pork; timber to trousers for the men. All of it was bought from private contractors; all bought, Ramage thought bitterly, with "a token of our esteem" being sent by the contractors to people like Hamond. More than a hundred dockyard men should have been working on the *Calypso* for more than seven days. What *were* they doing?

Where had the Commissioner sent them? That many men in seven days could probably build a house, Aitken had said. Did one of the Commissioner's friends now have a new house on Gad's Hill?

The First Lord finished writing a note, rang a small silver bell and gave the sheet of paper to the clerk who hurried in. "Give that to Mr Nepean. I want it ready for signature before noon."

Once the clerk had left the room, St Vincent said: "I deliberately left you in command of the *Calypso*. Have you wondered why?"

"No, sir," Ramage said, trying to guess the reason for the question.

"You don't lack confidence, young man."

Something in St Vincent's tone angered Ramage and before he could stop himself he said: "Captains lacking confidence usually put their ships up on a reef, sir."

"Quite," St Vincent said amiably. "I was commenting, not criticizing. Your skin is too thin. However, your new orders. You rarely carry out my orders in accordance with their wording—"

"But always in the spirit of their meaning, sir!"

"—their wording," St Vincent repeated, ignoring the interruption. "Where do you stand on the post list?" he demanded.

"About tenth from the bottom, sir."

"An admiral tenth from the top of the flag list is more tactful when speaking to the First Lord."

"I apologize for my manner, sir."

"But not for your words, eh? Anyway, your new orders concern something where it is highly probable that your views and the Board of Admiralty's coincide." There was a hint of a smile round St Vincent's mouth. "They are also the first orders you have ever received in time of peace."

Ramage recalled previous encounters with St Vincent and his predecessor as First Lord, Earl Spencer. Always there was the heavy emphasis on his disobeying orders, but it seemed more a question of "give a dog a bad name" because the orders were always *carried out*. That was the important thing; no senior officer had ever told him to do something and then had to blame him for failure. The trouble was that senior officers soon regarded themselves as omnipotent. Instead of simply

49

writing orders telling the officers what was to be done, they went into details of *how* they were to be carried out, and that was the mistake. No one could anticipate every circumstance. It was the man on the spot, the captain of the ship, who had to make his plans according to the situation he found. Surely a general did not order a colonel to capture a particular fort and tell him by what highways, tracks and byways he was to approach it. Perhaps generals did . . .

"Do you know anything about surveying?"

"*Surveying*, sir?"

"Obviously you don't; the word has paralysed you. Well, you can go through the Marine Department and get some instruction from the Hydrographer, Dalrymple, or his assistant, Walker. You need to know how to survey an island and chart the waters round it."

"Aye, aye, sir. A large island?"

"No. Perhaps a couple of miles long by one wide."

"Do any charts or maps exist, sir?"

"A rough chart; nothing to rely on."

"Might I ask—?"

"Trinidade."

"Trinidad? Why, there's—"

"Not Trinidad," St Vincent said testily, "but Trinidad*e*." He was careful to emphasize the "e" by pronouncing it as a "y". "It's off the Brazilian coast, seven hundred and fifty miles east-north-east of Rio de Janeiro and seven hundred from Bahia."

"Does it belong to Spain or Portugal, sir?"

"What I am going to tell you remains secret until you open your orders. At present it—I'm referring to the service upon which you are being sent—is known to the Prime Minister, the Secretary of State, myself and Nepean, who wrote the orders. As far as your family and your ship's company are concerned, you are bound for the South Seas."

"But forgive me, sir, is it Spain or Portugal?"

"Have you read the full text of the new Treaty with Bonaparte?"

"Yes, sir. At least, what was published in the *Gazette*. There might have been secret clauses . . ."

"There were none," St Vincent said shortly. "Did you see any reference to Trinidade?"

"No sir, just Trinidad, which Spain loses and we keep."

"Yes, one of the few places Bonaparte allowed us," St Vincent said with the first indication of his own views about the terms of the treaty, although it was quite clear to Ramage that he welcomed the peace. "Now, have you Trinidade placed in your mind?"

"Yes, sir. A thousand miles or so south of St Paul's Rock and Fernando de Noronha, and about the same distance west of St Helena."

"Precisely. An isosceles triangle would have St Paul's Rock and Fernando de Noronha as its apex, Trinidade on the left of the base and St Helena on the right. Now, what strikes you about its position?"

"If it has water, then it is a perfect place for the King's and John Company ships to call on their way to or from the Cape of Good Hope. At present—or, rather, in the war—the Honourable East India Company were very nervous of having their ships call at St Helena for water because both French national ships and privateers usually lurked close to it. Trinidade would be a good alternative."

St Vincent nodded with his rare wintry smile. "And a good rendezvous for the trade bound to or from Rio de Janeiro, Montevideo and Buenos Aires, as well as the Cape. It has water, by the way."

"Who owns it, then, sir?" Ramage asked for the third time, guessing from the spelling it had been named by the Portuguese.

"No one," St Vincent said. "We used it occasionally in this late war and can claim to have captured it, but it belonged to Portugal before that. It is not mentioned in the Treaty."

"So whoever notices the omission and gets there first..."

"Exactly," St Vincent said. "Speed and secrecy, my dear Ramage. You have a fast ship and a good crew. Now go and claim it for His Britannic Majesty."

CHAPTER FOUR

The Hydrographic Office was simply a small room: Dalrymple sat on one side of a table and his assistant, Walker, on the other. One wall was taken up with what appeared to be tall chests of drawers, the drawers being wide but shallow, and each labelled. A small table at the far end of the room was piled high with volumes which Ramage recognized as masters' logs, and he recalled a paragraph from the *Regulations and Instructions* concerning masters: "He is duly to observe the appearances of coasts; and if he discovers any new shoals, or rocks under water, to note them down in his journal, with their bearing and depth of water."

A conscientious master usually did better than that. Many were skilled with a paintbox, enjoying making sketches of unfrequented coastlines and preparing good line and wash illustrations. Often a master would make two sketches, one to go into his own collection of charts and views, the other to be inserted in his log, which had in due course to be sent to the Navy Office. One of Dalrymple's most difficult tasks, Ramage guessed, was getting logs from the Navy Office: the Navy Board had a reputation for losing documents. The few hundred yards from the Navy Office in Somerset Place to the Admiralty in Whitehall might well have been a few thousand miles.

Dalrymple was courteous. Few captains visited his office; usually he saw only masters, who were, officially, responsible for the actual navigation of a ship.

Yes, he said, he had a map of Trinidad, but not a chart.

The map was in fact Spanish, and found on board a prize, which accounted for the Spanish spelling, with the final "a".

He went to his chests of drawers, pulled out the one labelled "T", sorted through some papers and then extracted a rectangular sheet of parchment measuring about two feet by one. He blew dust from it and brought it to the table, where he wiped it again with a cloth.

"You see, the cartographer—I'd hardly call him a surveyor—was more concerned with drawing the voluptuous cherubs in the corners than details of the island. There's enough giltwork to cover a ship of the line's transom!"

Ramage stared at the map. The island reminded him of a mole. It sat diagonally southeast-northwest, with the northern coast, the back, almost a straight line, with no bays. There were several small anchorages on the south side formed by pairs of peninsulas sticking out like teats hanging down from the belly. He picked up a magnifying glass and began reading the Spanish references to the "A", "B", "C" marks on the island itself.

The latitude and longitude were given, 20° 29′ South and 29° 20′ West. There were six hills, looking like sugar loaves in the centre of the island, and someone had pencilled in the heights in feet, the highest being nearly 1,500 feet and the lowest 850 feet. There was a small rivulet of fresh water on the north side and another almost opposite on the south. Three places were marked as possible positions for batteries while another could be a signal station. There was no date on the map; not one depth was shown in the waters round the island.

"What date was this drawn?"

Dalrymple shrugged his shoulders and glanced at Walker, who shook his head. "At a guess from the style and decorations, I'd say about 1700. I suspect a privateersman had thoughts about using it as a base against the Rio de Janeiro and Buenos Aires trade. Or perhaps the Spanish government wanted to keep privateers out. Whoever it was took care against the map falling into the wrong hands."

"The lack of soundings?"

"Yes, with that kind of detail of the land, normally I would have expected soundings. Someone did not want to encourage visitors."

"There must be some dangerous reefs, otherwise the soundings would be of little importance."

Dalrymple nodded and said: "I was just thinking that. It's a rocky island, so one would expect deep water close in, with rocks and foul ground. As you can see, it's an island the size of Hyde Park put down in the South Atlantic and rarely visited by the King's ships. The masters of those that have been there did not bother to do any survey work."

"Can you make a copy of this map?"

"Of course," Dalrymple said. "I'm sorry we don't have it ready, but we had no warning. Walker and I do the best we can to prepare charts we think might be needed, but you can see those logs..." he pointed to the other table. "Now the war has ended and scores of ships will be laid up, you can imagine how many more logs will be arriving for us to examine."

"Do you often find anything of consequence?"

Dalrymple shook his head. "No. The masters with the interest and ability to help us never seem to go anywhere interesting. They spot a fall of rock or a new battery along the French Channel coast, but apart from your Mr Southwick they don't benefit us much."

"Ah, you find Southwick's log of interest?"

"Yes—his are the best sketches of the coast of Tuscany. And the recent ones of the southwestern corner of Sardinia were invaluable."

"And the Catalan coast, sir," Walker added.

"Ah yes, and of course many places in the West Indies. The island of Culebra. Parts of Martinique—Diamond Rock, for example: his survey and line and wash sketches of the Diamond are among the best examples of a master's work that we have."

"May I tell him that?"

"Indeed you may, my Lord; we would welcome a good survey of Trinidade, of course..."

Ramage recalled St Vincent's warning about secrecy, even though the First Lord had suggested the visit to the Hydrographic Office. "If we ever visit it, I'll do my best. I was just curious about it."

"Of course," Dalrymple said politely. "Well, that's what we're here for. I wish more captains and masters would make use of us—and send us copies of charts! It's a slow business, building up a library of the charts of the whole world—which is what I intend to do. Who knows, one day we might be able to print and issue our own charts, instead of masters having to copy anything they don't have in their own private collections."

Ramage returned to Palace Street to find his father looking worried. The old Admiral glanced at him inquiringly. "Did St Vincent have good news for you?"

Ramage nodded and patted his pocket. "The *Calypso* stays in commission and we sail the moment her refit is completed."

The Admiral was quick to recognize the significance of Ramage's words and tone of voice. Knowing he would have been told more had it not been secret, he limited himself to one question. "A long voyage?"

"It could be, sir. Six months or more."

"I'm worried about Gianna," the old man confided, running a hand through his hair in a gesture Ramage knew also indicated exasperation.

"Where is she?"

"Visiting Hawkesbury. A messenger from the Secretary of State's office said she was free to call this morning. She left about an hour ago."

"Surely she couldn't be naïve enough to take advice from Hawkesbury?" But even as he spoke, Ramage knew that Hawkesbury's sole ability was delivering the most banal statement with all the authority and panache of the Primate of All England damning the devil in Canterbury Cathedral.

The Earl nodded his head sadly. "I've warned her and so have you, but she's drawn to Volterra: as its legitimate ruler she feels she should be there—"

"But Napoleon will arrest her the moment she sets foot in France!"

"I know, I know, and we've all told her that too. But will that fool Jenks? He's a poor specimen of a politician, and like any tradesman he'll tell her what she wants to hear."

"You think he'll tell her it's safe for her to return to Volterra?"

"Yes, because scores of people are packing for visits to Paris, Rome and Florence. It's the first time they've been able to visit France and Italy for eight years. Jenks hasn't the wit to distinguish between the case of an English person visiting

Italy and that of the ruler of an Italian state still occupied by Bonaparte's troops and deliberately omitted from the new Treaty."

Both men heard a carriage stop outside the door and Hanson shuffled across the hall with his cry of "Coming, my Lady, I'm coming."

Ramage said: "We could get her to see Grenville and ask his advice . . ."

Lord Grenville, who had resigned with Pitt and had been the previous Secretary of State for Foreign Affairs, was a shrewd man. "Grenville would certainly give it, and we know what he would say. The fact is," the old man said wearily, worried as if Gianna was his own daughter, "she'll listen to whoever tells her what she wants to hear."

"We may be wronging Hawkesbury," Ramage said, with no conviction in his voice, and he sat down to wait for Gianna.

"Interesting orders?" the Earl asked casually.

"Not very, sir. Almost routine for peacetime, I imagine. There's just one unusual aspect that makes 'em secret."

"Don't tell me any more; I was just interested to see how you regarded your first peacetime commission."

"My own ship and my own men—the First Lord is being generous."

"Yes, but you deserve it. How many *Gazettes* have you had?"

Ramage grinned and held out his hands, palms uppermost. "I've no idea; they're usually published while I'm at sea."

"Ask your mother or Gianna; they both collect 'em!"

They heard the front door open and Gianna's voice sounded gay as she greeted Hanson. Father and son glanced at each other; both guessed what Hawkesbury had said.

A moment later a bubbling Gianna came into the room, undoing the ribbon holding her hat.

"I can go!" she exclaimed. "Lord Hawkesbury says there is no danger! He is going to ask M. Otto for a passport for me, and he says Bonaparte is sure to approve it."

Ramage groaned as he helped her remove her cloak.

"Why are you so—so *pesante* about everything?" she exclaimed angrily. "You are not sad at the idea of me leaving, because you are at sea most of the time!"

56

"I am so 'heavy' as you put it, because I don't trust Bonaparte, and no one but a fool would listen to Hawkesbury—"

"Oh, so I'm a fool now!"

"—on such a matter. Yes, you *are* foolish if you believe Bonaparte is going to let you return to Volterra while his troops still occupy it and he's left it out of the Treaty. You might just as well expect him to allow a British army to land on the Tuscan coast and march to Volterra with bands playing and flags flying 'to pay their respects' to the Marchesa."

Gianna sat down with an angry thump. "You know about the sea, and Lord Hawkesbury knows about diplomacy—"

"Very little," Ramage interrupted bitterly. "He's had the job only a few months and the Treaty shows all he can do is lose a peace. He's given back to Napoleon just about everything we won in battle. Why, Volterra isn't even *mentioned*."

"Ah, *that* shows how little you know. Lord Hawkesbury explained it to me," she said, her voice dropping confidentially. "He has heard it direct from M'sieu Otto. Bonaparte is tired of bloodshed. He had to continue the war that the others started with the Revolution until he could arrange a fair peace that was honourable for France."

Ramage sighed and his father said gently: "Gianna, there isn't a labourer in England who would believe that. Bonaparte wants to rule the world. He'll start the war again as soon as his warehouses are full, and he'll fight until he rules India, Egypt, the Americas—the world, in fact."

"That's not what Lord Hawkesbury says."

"I don't doubt that," the Earl said soberly. "Would you listen to Lord Grenville? We can have him to dinner and you can talk privately to him."

"What does this Grenville know? He's out of office; he had nothing to do with the negotiations for the new Treaty."

It was the Earl's turn to sigh. "My dear, Grenville probably knows more about French diplomacy and Bonaparte's intentions than any other Englishman. But did you ask Hawkesbury the question I mentioned to you?"

"What question?"

"Why—if he approved your journey—he thought Bonaparte would let you remain free while his army continues to occupy Volterra."

"Well, no, I did not," she admitted. "It was—how do you

57

say?—*redundant*. Lord Hawkesbury, His Britannic Majesty's Secretary of State for Foreign Affairs, says it is quite all right for me to go back to Volterra and he is arranging my passports so—*allora!*"

The Earl took a deep breath. "My dear, we are only trying to protect you when we strongly advise you not to go to Volterra!"

"I know *caro zio*, but my mind is made up. There will be so much for me to do in Volterra!"

"You'll find it very different from when you left. You may well discover that people you trusted have—well, behaved differently from what you expected."

"Had a right to expect," Gianna said, an unexpectedly grim note in her voice. "This is another reason why I must go."

"What can you do alone?" Ramage asked harshly. "A dagger in your back would solve many problems for those with power."

"You could take Paolo," the Earl said, "although it'd be a pity to interrupt his training."

"No," Gianna said emphatically, "Paolo stays with Nicholas. *Come si chiama?*—not all my eggs in one basket!"

Ramage felt completely helpless. They had all argued the whole question since the first reports in the newspapers that a Treaty would be signed. From the first Gianna had said she would go; from the first the whole family had argued against it, refusing to trust the French. He had progressed through gentle reasoning to angry arguments; he had wanted to seize and shake her, refusing to believe she could be so stubborn. His mother was probably right: very early on she had told Nicholas: "She has a strong sense of duty. I am sure she understands the danger, but she feels she must risk it because she is the ruler of Volterra, and with the war ended she can at last return to her people. *Noblesse oblige*, my dear Nicholas. You men admire Lovelace for writing 'I could not love thee dear so much, lov'd I not honour more', but when a woman says the same thing you do not understand."

Clapping her hands, as if to signal a change in the topic of conversation, Gianna asked Ramage: "And you—how did you fare at the hands of milord St Vincent?"

"We sail again as soon as the dockyard finishes the refit."

"Back to the Mediterranean? That would be fortunate."

The Earl interrupted to save Ramage from the risk of provoking an angry outburst from Gianna. She was clearly on the verge of one of her "imperious" moods.

"His orders are marked 'Secret' so we can't ask him. All I've been able to worm out of him is that it will be a long commission—six months or more."

"There you are!" she said. "You were expecting to be half paid!"

"Put on half pay," Ramage gently corrected. "Yes, obviously the size of the Navy will be cut, and I expected . . ."

"Why would the government cut the size of the Navy if Bonaparte is not to be trusted?" she demanded.

"Because politicians are fools and optimists," the Earl said contemptuously. "They want to cut taxes to have everyone cheering and voting for them. *They* do not have to fight and die to correct their mistakes."

"You can take Paolo with you?" she asked Ramage.

"Yes, of course—but whether or not he will want to come when he hears of your plan . . ."

"He has no choice; I say he stays with you."

Ramage shrugged his shoulders: he found it impossible to be gracious, understanding or patient with a woman who deliberately handed herself over to Bonaparte as a hostage.

"I have to go down to Chatham tomorrow. Do you have any messages for him?"

"Will he have any leave before I go?"

"That depends when you go."

"Next week," she said. "I shall be leaving London next Wednesday morning. I am travelling to Paris with the Herveys: I met Lady Hervey at Lord Hawkesbury's office this morning and she invited me to join them—they have room in their carriages."

Later that afternoon Ramage was sitting in his own room on the first floor, glancing at the latest edition of Steele's *Naval Chronologist*. He looked out at the plane trees, and like calendars recording the passage of autumn, they were losing their leaves. The bark of the trunks reminded him of a beggar with some vile disease.

So she was returning to Volterra, but he was puzzled and troubled by his own thoughts and feelings or, rather, by the contradictions in them which had been emerging over the last year or two and he was now being forced to examine.

How should the love between a man and a woman develop? It was something about which he knew very little, because Gianna was his first real love. Since those early months (years, he corrected himself, the period between being a junior lieutenant and a junior post captain), the original blazing love had cooled slightly. Cooled? Well, changed, both in his actual feelings for her and in his eventual realization that they could never marry. Had that realization eaten into that love, silently like rust or old age?

Could love really continue and develop when both people knew it would never reach the final stage of marriage? Neither he nor Gianna had talked about it; rather each of them (he was guessing her thoughts) had felt the pressures mounting. First there had been religion, and it seemed obvious that a woman accustomed to her own way in everything, as only the ruler of a nation could insist on it, would not accept that one of the oldest Protestant earldoms in the kingdom could never become Catholic by marriage.

Nor did she ever consider that, even if marriage was possible, the people of Volterra would never accept their ruler back if she had married a Protestant foreigner while in exile. That the foreigner had rescued her from Bonaparte, that his family had given her shelter, that her heir served in the Royal Navy under him—no, the man was a *straniero* and a Protestant; and that would be enough. Gianna had mentioned that he could perhaps be appointed the British ambassador, but he wondered if she had considered whether either of them really wanted a lover-and-mistress relationship.

Did the "deep love" still exist? Love, yes; enough to make him want to bend iron bars with the frustration of failing to persuade her not to go to Volterra. In the old days he would kidnap her rather than let her go. Now he was apprehensive, but as though she was a favourite sister.

Guilt came into it, of course. The story of their romance was well known; the reception the Calypsos had given Gianna was proof of that. Ramage felt he had been urged on by what was expected of him—but with no opportunity of holding up a hand and explaining the difficulties: of religion and of the feelings of Gianna's own subjects.

He often felt that Paolo, young as he was, understood that he was in effect in a treadmill; as though instinctively Paolo had known there was no way round the twin barriers of religion and nationalism.

He sighed and watched a sudden gust of wind send more leaves tumbling down. Duty was forcing Gianna to return to Volterra and abandon the man she loved; duty had forced him to accept that he could never marry her because their son would have to be raised as a Catholic, which meant that when he inherited...Duty, *noblesse oblige*, was armoured against Cupid's darts.

CHAPTER FIVE

Although his head was buzzing and his nose painful because of the strong smell of paint, Ramage was glad to be back on board the *Calypso*, and through the sternlights he could see the houses of Chatham beginning to move round as the frigate swung at the turn of the tide. The misery of dry docking was over; the copper sheathing had been replaced; the only work remaining to be done by the dockyard was building some extra cabins forward of the gunroom. They would be insubstantial structures, merely large boxes with sides made of battens and canvas.

More cabins meant more men on board, and once again he looked gloomily at the latest letter from the Admiralty. "I am directed by my Lords Commissioners of the Admiralty", Nepean had written in the time-honoured opening phrase, "to direct you to prepare for the reception on board the vessel you command of the people listed in the margin . . . and who will accompany you on the voyage for which you have already received secret orders.

"Their Lordships further direct me to enjoin upon you the need for secrecy and none of the individuals named in the margin know the details of the service upon which you are engaged. The circumstances under which such details may be imparted are described in your sealed orders."

The list comprised seven men, each name followed by a description of his function. The first read, "The Rev. Percival Stokes, chaplain", and was the reason for Ramage's irritation. No ship smaller than a ship of the line was compelled to have a chaplain—unless one volunteered. There were captains whose religious beliefs bordered on fanaticism and who had the ship's company praying twice daily. Most captains were like Ramage, respecting the fact that a man's religious beliefs were his own affair and limiting the enforced observance to Divine service on Sundays.

Chaplains were not at this stage of the war—at the moment, he corrected himself—very popular among either captains or ships' companies. Some were splendid fellows who, in a ship of the line, kept the six or seven hundred men cheerful and were a help to the captain and officers responsible for their welfare. Others stayed remote from the men, regarding the wardroom and the quarterdeck as the limit of their perambulations. The third type were members of what Ramage always called "the pursed lips party": narrow-minded and self-righteous, regarding a ship of war solely as a floating house of God which they controlled, they were usually the centre of intrigue and complaint. Either they found a fanatical captain who listened to their every word, or else he ignored them and they whined at the most senior of the lieutenants who cared to listen.

The general dislike of chaplains, though, was based on something much simpler: there were so few of them that although ships of the line had in theory to carry them, only one in three had a chaplain: in wartime parsons, it seemed, preferred a rectory or vicarage where a fire blazed of a winter's night. The ship of the line with a chaplain was usually carrying a clerical friend of the captain. Frigates, with a ship's company a third of the size of a ship of the line, rarely saw one; Ramage could not remember a single case.

Now, however, with peace, were chaplains going to flock to sea? And what on earth made the Reverend Percival Stokes apply to join the *Calypso*? He was probably the penurious friend of a friend of one of their Lordships. Ramage saw an endless vista of members of the ship's company complaining: in one of the King's ships carrying a chaplain it was more restful, to say the least, being Church of England.

Well, Mr Stokes had better be a careful man: the *Calypso*'s first lieutenant was a Highland Scot and certainly Low Church; the master was, surprisingly a free thinker; the single midshipman an Italian Catholic. And the captain refused to discuss religion with anyone.

The next two names in the margin of Nepean's letter had "surveyor" after them, followed by two draughtsmen, an artist and a botanist. A previous letter from Nepean had told Ramage that six miners and six masons were being sent to join the ship's company, volunteers who should be entered in the *Calypso*'s books as supernumeraries for both victuals and wages. Several tons of bricks and materials for mortar were being brought by hoy from Maidstone, and shovels, plasterers' trowels and wooden buckets had already arrived on board. The *Calypso* was going to be sailing well down on her marks: he was under orders to provision for five months—only possible because the *Calypso* was to carry a peacetime quantity of powder and shot—and water for three. There would be difficulties if the map of Trinidade was wrong about the presence of fresh water . . .

Ramage pushed aside Nepean's letter and reached for the one which had arrived from London at the same time. He recognized his father's writing and broke the seal. The Earl had written:

I called on Hawkesbury, and must confess the only real information I received from him was extraordinary enough for me to note down. Up to yesterday, passports for visits to France had been requested by five dukes, three marquises, thirty-seven earls and countesses, eighty-five viscounts, seventeen barons and forty-one elder sons and heirs. This comprises a third of the House of Lords, so if Bonaparte wishes to play a trick he could tear up the Treaty and intern the peers.

Hawkesbury mentioned these figures to justify the advice he gave Gianna. When I pointed out that although one third of the House of Lords, and their women, were visiting France, all were British subjects and not one of them was the ruler of a nation which Bonaparte still occupied and obviously intended to keep.

He told me I worried unnecessarily, but when he said Lord St Vincent held the same views as himself and was already preparing proposals to place before the Cabinet for paying off two thirds of the Navy's strength, quite apart from a comprehensive plan for scrapping many older ships of the line and frigates, I must confess I lost my temper.

I pointed out that the newspapers carried reports that French transport ships were busy at places like Brest and Rochefort embarking troops, and ships of war were commissioning, and the same was true for Dutch and Spanish ports. He protested that Otto had already explained that French troops were intended to subdue a rising among the blacks in St Domingo.

I pointed out that such a powerful force could be used for recapturing Trinidad; that now we had just returned all his sugar islands except Guadeloupe, Bonaparte would be sending out large garrisons as soon as possible, and may plan attacks on our own islands. This wretched man Jenks—I can think of him only by that name—then produced the excuse used by all political scoundrels: it was Cabinet policy, he said. I took my leave; it was as much as I could do to stop myself rapping him across the shins with my cane. When I think of all our seamen and soldiers who died in the drunken projects of Dundas, and the risk at which sober idiots like Jenks put people like Gianna, I find myself ashamed of my country. Are we so impoverished of talented men that we are reduced to ministers like Addington and Jenks?

Ramage locked his father's letter away in a drawer and slid Nepean's among the pages of a book labelled "Captain's Orders—Received". With its companion volume, "Captain's

Orders—Issued", it was also kept under lock and key. All the years he had been at sea, such volumes were stored in a canvas bag secured by a drawstring and weighted with a bar of lead in the bottom. Now there was peace, a locked drawer in his desk was enough. That, and the use of lights when under way at night, would be the most obvious signs that Britain was at peace.

Quite deliberately Ramage had hurried over the last few paragraphs of his father's letter. They described the violent arguments Gianna had had with Paolo. Or, rather, the violent arguments Paolo had had with her. Ramage had said nothing to the boy when giving him leave to go to London. According to the Earl, Gianna had not mentioned her plans to her nephew for a couple of days. She had then chosen an afternoon when the Earl and Countess were out paying a social call. They had returned to find an outraged Paolo waiting for them, almost distraught and appealing to them to forbid his aunt to leave England. Paolo had immediately seen the dangers, though he thought they came mostly from certain members of his family who had remained in Volterra and, by fawning on Bonaparte, gained power they certainly would not give up to the Marchesa arriving back in Volterra on her own. And Paolo knew enough of the realities of Italian politics, where a dagger was more commonly used than a speech in the senate, to realize that nothing short of a few battalions would suffice to protect her. Traitors, he had told his aunt, especially related by blood, were not fish that willingly swam into the net.

The sentry outside the cabin door reported that Mr Southwick had arrived, and Ramage called for him to be sent in. The old master sat down as Ramage waved him to the only armchair, and skimmed his hat on to the settee.

"The dockyard chippies," he said crossly. "They work more slowly and make more mess than a band of monkeys. These extra cabins will never be finished. Their foreman as good as said five guineas would see them all completed by Friday, otherwise it would take a couple of weeks."

Ramage stared at Southwick. "'As good as said'? Was he openly asking for money?"

"Yes, I was being polite, sir. His actual words were, 'Tell your captain that five guineas will see it all finished by Friday: otherwise we'll still be here a week on Friday.'"

Ramage sighed and picked up the papers still on his desk. "The First Lord knows there's corruption in dockyards and throughout the Navy Board," he said as he locked the papers in a drawer. "The trouble is I can hardly bother him with the case of a corrupt foreman carpenter. Still, by next Monday I intend to be at sea. The extra people join the ship this Thursday—in three days' time."

"Perhaps if you saw the dockyard Commissioner, sir..." Southwick's tone showed he was simply being polite.

"I can tell you exactly what the Commissioner would say," Ramage said bitterly. He thought for a minute or two, saw and understood the glint in Southwick's eye, and nodded at the master.

"As you know, I have secret orders I can't yet open. The general orders I have, though, mean that we must sail as soon as possible. The ship's company are back from leave, we have the miners and bricklayers, and we are provisioned and watered. If the cabins were completed, we could even sail on Friday; we'd be clear of the Nore by Friday night..."

"But it'd cost us five guineas," Southwick said.

"You know, Southwick, I don't see why I should pay an Englishman five guineas to be allowed to go about the King's business...These fellows have grown rich by blackmailing captains anxious to get to sea again to fight the King's enemies. Now the king *has* no enemies, except these wretched crooks. Perhaps we should have a look at this particular scoundrel. Tell the sentry to send for him."

Southwick went to the door and passed the order, but he looked worried when he sat down again. "Corrupt they may be, sir, but if we make an enemy of Commissioner Wedge we'll never get anything done. It's not this refit nor even the next one I'm thinking about; it's the one after that. A commissioner can keep a ship and her captain locked up in a dry dock for months—he has only to keep finding defects which, he says, he's anxious to make good for the ship's safety."

"I know that," Ramage said shortly. "We are concerned now with a carpenter, not a commissioner. If you feel squeamish, you'd better take a walk in the fresh air."

"Squeamish?" Southwick grinned. "No, I think I shall enjoy this."

A knock on the door and the sentry's hail announced the

foreman's arrival. When he came in Ramage saw he was a big hulking man who had to crouch to walk into the cabin, with its headroom of five feet four inches.

The man was at least six feet tall and almost handsome, the narrow face and greasy black hair seeming not to belong to the broad shoulders and large hands.

"You are the foreman carpenter?" Ramage asked politely.

"Yes, sir." Now he had an ingratiating smile. Already he had noted Southwick's presence and (Ramage sensed) had probably guessed that the message about the five guineas had been passed.

"Your name?"

"Porter, sir. Albert Porter."

"You live nearby; I can tell from your accent." Ramage's voice was friendly, and from the way the man's eyes were sweeping the desk he was looking to see where the pile of coins were waiting.

"Ah yes, sir. Born in the Hundred of Hoo, I was, and served my apprenticeship at a shipyard that side of the river before starting in the dockyard. Twelve years ago, that was."

"Three or four years before the war began," Ramage commented.

"S'right, sir. Kept us busy, the war. Still, now peace is here and I got my little house and four children. Big expense, a wife, a house and children."

"So I believe," Ramage said dryly. "I've been at sea all the time, so they are three problems I don't have."

"Ah, you're a lucky man, sir, a lucky man."

"However, I've been wounded four times, and with Mr Southwick here I've lost a couple of ships. I've read the funeral service over more of my men than I care to remember..." Ramage let his voice die away, as though stifled by memories. He had the memories, but far from stifling him they were making him hot with anger, although this lout was too greedy to realize it.

"You must have saved hard to pay for a house—or do you rent it?"

"No, sir, all paid for it is; I don't owe any man a penny piece."

Ramage nodded understandingly. "Your children marry, you spoil your grandchildren, and enjoy a happy old age, eh?"

67

"S'right, sir," the man grinned. Here was an understanding captain who was in a hurry to sail. Five guineas had been pitching it much too low. Some said he was a lord, and ten guineas should have been the price. Perhaps he'd get the chance of saying that the master, Southwick or some such name, had misheard him.

"I wonder how many of the *Calypso*'s officers and men will live to become grandfathers..."

The foreman looked puzzled. The captain seemed to be talking to himself, and he was still almost mumbling. "...All the officers of the *Sibella* were killed except me...A lot of men killed when we lost the *Kathleen* cutter...Several died in the *Triton* brig...We lost Baker in Curaçao, when I had a bullet in the arm and this bang on the head..." He tapped a small patch of white hair. "No, they won't ever be grandfathers."

Albert Porter, his head and shoulders bent below the beams, suddenly found he was staring into a pair of deep-set brown eyes that seemed to be looking right through him and seeing, across the river, his house built with the bribes he had managed to extract from impatient captains—men impatient to get to sea, the poor fools, where they stood a good chance of having their heads knocked off by roundshot. Albert Porter just had time to realize he had made a mistake when a cold but quiet voice seemed to wrap itself round him and penetrate his clothes like a chill Medway fog.

"Porter, while you have been doing your job here in the dockyard, the officers and men in the King's ships have been at sea, fighting the weather and the French and the Dutch and the Spanish and the Danes. They've been collecting musket balls and roundshot and yellow fever and scurvy; you've been collecting tainted guineas to buy yourself a house, a wife and four children. Do you understand the two different kinds of life?"

The eyes and the tone made Porter agree at once.

"Good, Porter, so we understand each other. Now, I am going to tell you a story. The companionway down to the gunroom comprises ten steps. A man tripped at the top and fell down them once. He was picked up dead. The parish—he was a dockyard man—had to bury him. It's surprising how these sort of accidents happen. A chisel slips and cuts a vein and in

68

a trice a man bleeds to death; someone else slips on one of the sidebattens and falls into the boat and breaks his neck across a thwart. A third has his skull split as he walks along the deck and a double block falls on him from an upperyard. Indeed, Porter, as the chaplains tell us, 'In the midst of life, we are in death.' "

"Yes, sir," Porter managed to whisper.

"I called you here to give you some information, Porter. We have seven extra people joining the ship on Thursday; we sail on Friday. We need seven extra cabins ready by Thursday."

"Yes, sir."

"You are a conscientious man, I know. Do I have your assurance that the seven cabins will be ready in time, doors hung and glazed with stone-ground glass, and everything painted?"

"Yes, sir," Porter said, at last coming to life. "Oh, easily by Thursday, sir."

"Very well, thank you. You may go."

After the man shambled out, Southwick said: "You'd never have done it. Rossi, Stafford, Jackson—yes, any of them would have given him a push at a word from you. But I can't see you giving the word."

Ramage grinned, his eyes now warm, the hard line gone from his lips. He looked at the man who was old enough to be his father and who had served as master in every ship Ramage had commanded, from the earliest day when as a lieutenant he had commanded the little *Kathleen* cutter.

"It doesn't matter what *you* think, does it? Porter is convinced I can, so the cabins will be ready and we'll be off Black Stakes on Friday, taking on powder."

All ships, naval and mercantile, coming to London or the Medway had to unload their gunpowder into barges moored at Black Stakes, at the entrance to the Thames. The risk of fire and a ship exploding in the London docks or close to one of the Medway towns was too great to allow any exceptions. It delayed a ship, but many an officer late back from leave was glad to hire a cutter at London Bridge and be put on board at Black Stakes.

"Is it true we're getting a chaplain, sir?"

Ramage had mentioned it to the first lieutenant because Aitken, a Highlander, would not welcome what undoubtedly would be to him a High Church minister. The Low Church first lieutenant and the free-thinking master must have been discussing it.

"Yes. Someone has applied." It was a convenient way of telling the officers (which meant the ship's company would know soon enough) that he had not asked for a chaplain; everyone knew the regulations.

"I've never met one yet that was worth the room to sling a hammock."

"Perhaps not, but let's hope he plays chess."

Southwick chuckled and reached for his hat. A long time ago, he and Mr Ramage had joined the *Triton* brig at Portsmouth to find that the ship's surgeon was a drunkard; a very skilful doctor who had practised in Wimpole Street until his heavy drinking drove his patients away, and the Navy had offered him the only way of earning a living from medicine. Mr Ramage had other ideas: no drunkard would be allowed to treat his men, but he had neither the time nor the influence to have the man changed. Being Mr Ramage, Southwick reflected, he found no difficulty in solving the problem: the drunkard must be cured. It had been a terrible time for Bowen, the surgeon, for Southwick, and for Mr Ramage, but they had cured Bowen. And once the drink no longer clouded his brain, left his eyes bloodshot slits and his face a sweat-stained mat of unshaven whiskers, they found the surgeon was a highly intelligent and amusing man. But part of the convalescence had involved preventing Bowen returning to the drink, and once Ramage found that he was a skilful chess player, Southwick had been made to play seemingly endless games of chess.

Actually Southwick himself, now considerably more skilful, enjoyed an occasional couple of games with Bowen, but four or five games a week were enough for him, whereas Bowen was good for four or five games a day. A parson *had* to be able to play, he told himself as he left the cabin. If he could not, then he could dam' well learn.

Although the seven newcomers had come by different coaches, starting off from London Bridge or the Bricklayers Arms, all had of course followed the Dover Road, stopping for fresh horses at Blackheath, the Golden Lion on Bexley Heath, again at Dartford, at the Chalk Street Turnpike beyond Gravesend, and finally at Rochester before getting out at the Star Inn to spend the night ready to join the *Calypso* early on Thursday.

Aitken had left written orders at the Star for them to come on board at ten in the forenoon. At nine o'clock he reported to Ramage.

"The foreman carpenter and his men have just left the ship, sir. I inspected the new cabins. The smell of paint is a bit strong, but they've swept up all the shavings and scraps of canvas. They even polished the glass windows in the doors. The hinges are greased and all the bulkheads swing up nicely and the doors have drop-on hinges. The doors aren't marked, sir: I can have one of the men who's a passing good signwriter paint on 'chaplain' and so on, if you like."

"We won't bother yet. Let them decide. They're going to be spending a lot of time together, and letting them choose their own cabins should sort them out!"

Aitken paused, as if he had bad news he was reluctant to report. "It's about the last lot of men returning from leave, sir."

Ramage felt a sudden depression. He had trusted the first half of the ship's company and all but one had returned on time, and the man had come back a day late with a story, probably true, of being waylaid and robbed. Why was there trouble with the second half of the ship's company?

"How many?"

"Three, sir."

Ramage sighed with relief. "I thought you were going to say thirty-three. The dockyard Commissioner wrote to the Navy Board, telling them that I was giving everyone leave and forecasting that I'd be lucky to get fifty men back."

"He must have been basing the estimate on his own men."

"Or himself. Now, everything is ready for the chaplain and his party? If we can drop down to Sheerness on this afternoon's ebb we can be alongside a powder barge at Black Stakes soon after daylight tomorrow and be off through the Four Fathom Channel by early afternoon."

"Everything is ready for them and we're ready to sail. I've hoisted in all our boats—they can hire a local sloop, or use a dockyard boat. Young Martin has said goodbye to his father and the letter bag has gone on shore. The tradesmen have been on board to get their bills settled, and I've ordered all the women to be off the ship by noon."

"Wouldn't ten o'clock have been better—before the chaplain, ah . . ."

"No sir," Aitken said emphatically. "Unless you give orders to the contrary, I'd like to watch the parson's face as the women go down into the boat. We'll learn more about him in two minutes than we would otherwise in two months."

Aitken was quite right, of course. The whole thing was a coldblooded business because it meant a captain had to allow whores on board, but like most other Navy captains Ramage insisted only that a man had to vouch for each woman and be responsible for her behaviour (obeying the Admiralty instructions which said only that a man "claimed" the woman as his "wife", with no limit on the number of ports in which the man could have a "wife"). If she misbehaved (quarrelling with others of the sisterhood or smuggling her man liquor were the most usual offences) she was turned off the ship and the man could not replace her.

The Admiralty were, he admitted, very sensible in their attitude. Their Lordships knew that in wartime few seamen could be given shore leave without "running", but fear of the men deserting did not stop their Lordships understanding that men at sea for months (sometimes a year or more) without seeing women, let alone sharing a hammock with one, had to be given some freedom in port. If they could not be trusted to leave their ships to find the women on shore, the women had to be allowed on board. The price everyone had to pay was to accept the man's declaration that the woman was his wife, and that he took responsibility for her while she was on board. A ship coming from abroad and staying a week or so at Plymouth before going to Chatham meant that a man could claim three wives, the only proviso being that he could afford them. The price tended to drop the further east the port. The highest price was at Plymouth with the Channel Fleet in: a large number of ships meant plenty of demand.

Curious how these women would quarrel with each other: frantic screeching from below was the signal for the master-at-arms and the ship's corporals to hurry down to stop a hair-pulling, nail-clawing fight. Indeed, the reason why the cockpit was originally given that name was that the raucous noise of quarrelling women was reminiscent of fighting cocks in a cock-pit.

Aitken said, with elaborate casualness: "Orsini still seems very unhappy after returning from leave, sir." The Scotsman thought the lad might have fallen in love or received some news of his family in Italy. But whatever it was, his sadness was affecting the men. Orsini was their favourite; he had a way of getting twice as much work out of them just because of his cheerful manner. At least, that had been the case until he came back from leave. Now he was as dour as John Knox on a rainy sabbath in December.

Ramage thought for a minute or two. The Marchesa was very well known to a few of the ship's company—men like Jackson, Rossi and Stafford, who had helped rescue her—and known to most of the others. All were interested in any news of her, and undoubtedly Paolo as her nephew benefited from the relationship. Seeing the lad so downhearted must have led to a good deal of speculation. Perhaps now was the time to pass the word that Gianna was already travelling to Paris with the Herveys, on her way home to Tuscany.

"His aunt, the Marchesa, is on her way back to Italy." Ramage had kept his voice neutral, but Aitken stared at him, obviously shocked by the news.

"But Bonaparte . . . He still occupies Volterra, which isn't included in the Treaty . . . He'll seize her, sir!"

"She insisted on going, to be with her people. She would not be persuaded—by anyone."

At once Aitken saw the reason for the gloom that hung like a thunderstorm over the captain, and for Orsini's dour bad temper. They both loved her in their different ways but they shared the same fear and the same distrust of Bonaparte. If he seized her—*when* he seized her, rather—there would be nothing they could do. The British government would be powerless. Today Bonaparte did what he wanted, unchallenged; the Treaty was proof of that.

"Shall I tell . . . ?"

"Yes. And have a quiet word with Orsini. It's difficult for me to say anything at the moment."

Aitken straightened his hat and spoke slowly, his Perth accent more pronounced than usual, something which Ramage noticed happened whenever the first lieutenant expressed deep feelings. "With us sailing tomorrow, sir, and being provisioned for five months and watered for three: we're likely to be away for half a year. That'll be half a year when ye'll have no news of the Marchesa, sir?"

Ramage nodded. "I'm assuming we'll be away six to ten months, but as you know, I have secret orders which I've not yet read."

Aitken excused himself, both embarrassed and yet relieved to know the reason for the captain's and the midshipman's sadness. He could imagine the arguments that had gone on in London at the home of the captain's father: the men—the Earl of Blazey, Mr Ramage and Orsini—would have been arguing for reasons of affection; the Marchesa for reasons of state. It must have been a dreadful decision for a woman to make on her own: no husband, no relatives, no ministers could help her; she was—had been, rather—alone in a foreign land. Aitken was suddenly glad to be simply the son of a long-dead officer in the Royal Navy. It seemed inhuman to make a woman choose between some vague loyalty to a country and the man she loved.

CHAPTER SIX

Ramage had purposely not watched the seven men come on board (Aitken had proudly reported that there were in fact nine: two of the three seamen thought to have "run" had come on board from the same cutter), preferring a more individual approach after they had time to settle in. All except the chaplain were likely to be complete strangers to life afloat.

Had he watched them come on board through the entryport he would have saved himself the shock of the chaplain's appearance. Ramage had told Aitken to bring him to his cabin and introduce him at noon. For a moment he thought there had been some mistake until he saw Aitken behind the man.

Small, with narrow shoulders and stance that looked as though he was half crouching, a ferret face with stained protruding front teeth that reminded Ramage of splayed fingers, shifty and bloodshot eyes: the Reverend Percival Stokes looked more like a trapped pickpocket as he stopped inside the door and then lurched forward a few more paces, obviously pushed by Aitken.

"My Lord Ramage? I am—"

Aitken stepped in front of him. "Captain Ramage, sir: may I introduce the Reverend Percival Stokes? Mr Stokes—Captain Ramage."

Aitken had managed the introduction very well, but Ramage doubted if Stokes had noticed that the captain did not use his title or, if he did, whether he could let his proximity to a member of the aristocracy go unremarked. The Reverend Percival Stokes, Ramage decided within seconds, would create havoc in the gunroom with his ingratiating brand of snobbery, fawning where he thought necessary and bullying where possible. Obviously someone with influence was indebted to the man—or, perhaps more likely, wanted him out of the way.

"Oh, my Lord, I am honoured and grateful to be the chaplain to such a distinguished officer—"

Ramage held up a hand. "You have been appointed chaplain to the *Calypso* frigate, not to me, and at your own request, Mr Stokes. I did not apply for a chaplain."

At first Ramage regretted speaking in such chilly tones (which clearly delighted Aitken), but a moment later he saw that neither the words, the double correction nor the snub had registered. Stokes, his hands clasped as though leading a congregation in prayer, was eyeing the sherry decanter and glasses on Ramage's desk.

In that moment Ramage thought he saw Stokes's life as though glancing along a narrow, shadowy corridor, and three words came to mind—debt, drink, hypocrisy. The wretched man was probably heavily in debt and, because of drink, had been neglecting his parish more than usual when the shopkee-

75

pers decided it was time their parson paid some attention to Mammon as well as God. With the debtors' prison suddenly presented to him as an alternative, it was likely that Stokes decided his vocation—for a year or two, anyway—was the Navy in peacetime. There he was paid, food was cheap and drink, duty-free, even cheaper. The Treaty ensured that no roundshot would spin past his ears.

Why did the man choose a frigate? Since his pay depended mainly on the number of men in the ship, a ship of the line offered eight hundred or so souls to be saved. A frigate like the *Calypso* had only two hundred souls. In both ships a chaplain received nineteen shillings a month, but he also had his "groats", four pence a month for every man in his ship. In a ship of the line this meant an extra thirteen pounds a month, which was £156 a year. In a frigate like the *Calypso* it was about £3 6s a month, or about £40 a year.

Why a frigate? Perhaps, despite the perpetual shortage of chaplains, even the Chaplain General had baulked at Mr Stokes; given that the Admiralty was prepared to grant him a warrant, perhaps the Chaplain General decided that he could do (or come to) less harm in a frigate.

Aitken stood to attention and said: "If you'll excuse me, sir, I have—"

"No, no, Mr Aitken," Ramage said genially, having no intention of letting his first lieutenant desert him at such a moment, "you have the ship so well organized it can run for fifteen minutes without you."

Aitken noted the fifteen minutes and sat down on the setee as Ramage gestured towards the armchair for Stokes. It was a seat from which a man of his stature would have to look up at both officers.

"Your first ship, Mr Stokes?" Ramage asked amiably.

"Oh yes, indeed, my Lord, oh yes, my goodness—"

"My title is not used in the Navy, Mr Stokes; you address me as 'sir' and refer to me as 'the Captain'."

"Oh yes, indeed, Captain sir," Stokes said hurriedly, and Ramage noticed the man sprayed saliva as he talked, his protruding teeth tending to act like fingers over a hose.

"Where were you—" Ramage just avoided saying "practising". "Where were you—I mean, where was your benefice before you decided to come to sea?"

"Oh, in Essex, captain," Stokes said vaguely.

"Then you decided you would like to see more of the world?"

"I had a row with my bishop," the man said crossly and then, realizing his indiscretion, added with an ingratiating smile: "I considered I could best serve the Lord by saving souls among our brave seamen, exposed as they are to greater temptations than my flock in Essex."

"Ah," Aitken said, glancing at Ramage, "that's an interesting point of view which I know the captain has considered before. At this place in Essex where you had your kirk—did ye not have whores and thieves and vagabonds, like anywhere else?"

Stokes raised his hands, palms outwards, and assumed what he must have considered a man-of-the-world expression. "Ah, a few of each, I must admit; the flesh is weak and a chaplain can only advise and pray and point the way . . ."

"I'm thinking ye've abandoned your flock," Aitken said, his voice sorrowful, "because while ye could perhaps have converted the whores and thieves and vagabonds in Essex, we dinna have one of any of those on board this ship for ye to practise on, Mr Stokes."

"Ah, lieutenant, there you are mistaken," Stokes said patronizingly, assuming that the fact that Aitken deferred to the captain meant that the chaplain's position was between the two. "No man is without sin, is he Captain?"

"He is in *this* ship," Aitken said crisply, "otherwise he gets a flogging!"

Ramage was hard put to keep a straight face: Aitken had set the trap. Stokes had walked in and Aitken had sprung it. Stokes was not to know that Ramage had ordered only two men to be flogged since he first commanded a ship, and anyway, he was technically correct.

"Flogging?" Stokes's eyes jerked from Aitken to Ramage, as though—as though what? Ramage was not yet sure. Did the thought of flogging horrify him, as it did Ramage and many other captains? No, it was more fear than horror in the man's eyes.

"Yes, flogging. As you mentioned, no man is without sin; likewise no man is beyond the reach of the cat-o'-nine-tails."

"Except the officers, of course!" Stokes tried to smile at his

77

own joke, but Ramage decided to stretch the truth to see what effect it had.

"Officers, too," he said. "The captain of a ship has more power than the King—you realize that, Mr Stokes?"

"Er, well, I did not realize that. In what way, sir?"

"The King cannot order a man to be flogged; I can."

"So let us pray," Stokes said unctuously, "that everyone behaves himself."

"They won't." Aitken commented gloomily, "they never do. Well now," he said, looking at his watch, "your fellow warrant officers will be busy taking all the food, so perhaps . . ."

The first lieutenant picked up his hat and Ramage was thankful to see that Stokes was obviously going to follow him. However, there was just one thing to make clear right at the beginning of the chaplain's ecclesiastical reign. "Mr Stokes—neither I nor the ship's company like long sermons. Apart from anything else, the weather is seldom suitable: too cold in northern waters for them to sit around for long, and too hot in the Tropics. So remember, ten minutes!"

"Oh captain," Stokes said reproachfully, "what can I tell the men in ten minutes?"

"I can read the Articles of War in less," Ramage said. "They are the rules governing the behaviour of every man in the Navy, from an admiral to a boy, in peace or war, at sea or in harbour."

"But all my sermons—"

Ramage pictured a packet of a couple of dozen sermons, written by some hack cleric and sold at fourpence each.

"The men don't like shop sermons," Aitken said. "Funny how they spot them, isn't it sir? They can tell at once whether a chaplain is talking from his heart or just reciting."

"I'm not sure about all the men, but this captain can, and he's certainly not about to sit through a fourpenny tract."

It was unfair to harp on fourpence, but Ramage was sure that one of the first questions asked by Stokes when he boarded the frigate was aimed at the purser—how many men did the *Calypso* muster? That number, multiplied by fourpence, told him how much his monthly "groats" would total.

Aitken opened the door and Stokes scuttled out, obviously distraught at the loss of his sermons for twenty-four Sundays.

The first lieutenant returned two or three minutes later. "I think you've squared his yards, sir."

Stokes had been brought to heel, like a wayward gun dog. "But," Ramage said sourly, "that doesn't alter the fact we've got to put up with him lurking round the ship for the next few months."

"'Lurking'—aye, ye've got him there, sir; the man's a lurker, that's for sure. But he's the worst of the bunch; the rest o' them seem pleasant enough."

"I'll see them two at a time this afternoon, beginning with the surveyors."

Aitken brought in two young men whom Ramage assumed were brothers until the first lieutenant mentioned their names. David Williams, the elder, was a Welshman, black-haired and blue-eyed and with what Ramage thought of as a laughing face; Williams obviously saw the humorous side of life, while his fellow surveyor, Walter White, also black-haired and blue-eyed, came from Kettering and obviously took a far more serious view of his work and his immediate future. One could imagine his notebook showing the distance between two distant points as being correct to half an inch, while Williams would prefer rounded figures.

"Can you give us any idea what we'll be surveying, sir?"

"No, I'm afraid not. I'm not being unnecessarily secretive: we are sailing with sealed orders. But I can assure you there'll be plenty of work for both of you once we arrive."

Williams grinned happily. "It's our first voyage, sir, so we're excited. We're lucky it's with you, sir!"

Ramage smiled and said: "You've heard of me?"

"I've got a copy of every *Gazette* mentioning you, sir."

White said it in such a lugubrious voice that it took Ramage a few moments to realize that the young man was making a proud boast.

"I didn't realize the *Gazette* was so popular in Kettering!"

"Ah, no, but we both worked in the Navy Office, sir."

"The Navy Office?"

"Yes, sir. The Hydrographer came over to Somerset Place one day and talked to the head surveyor, and we were offered this job. Neither of us is married, sir."

"Well, I wish I could tell you more about the work. It'll be typical of the naval service, though; weeks of tedium getting

79

there, then a frantic rush where eighteen hours' work a day won't be enough, and then weeks more tedium."

He nodded to Aitken, and the surveyors were replaced with the draughtsmen. They had been recruited in the same way and were equally anxious to know their destination. Their task, they explained, was to take all the measurements supplied by the surveyors, mostly angles and distances, and turn them into maps for people to look at.

The last pair, the botanist and the artist, seemed at first to be an ill-assorted couple. The botanist, Edward Garret, a grey-haired man with the weathered face of a fisherman or farmer, promptly denied that he was a botanist. "I'm a farmer who likes to experiment," he told Ramage. "The Admiralty asked the Board of Agriculture for someone likely to make plants grow on a barren island, and they recommended me. I'm still not sure if the Board want to get me out of the way for a few months—I'm always chasing them, you know!"

"The Board of Agriculture?" Ramage inquired. "What does it do?"

"Not enough!" Garret said crossly. "The office is in Sackville Street and its membership looks like the House of Lords at a Coronation—the Archbishops of Canterbury and York, the Dukes of Portland, Bedford and Buccleuch, and dozens of earls, among them Chatham and Spencer—you'll recall he was the last First Lord of the Admiralty. And plain politicans—Mr Pitt, the last prime minister and Mr Addington, the present one. You'd think that with such a membership the Board would be very powerful."

"Yes," Ramage agreed. "Archbishops and prime ministers—they should be able to move Heaven and earth!"

"You'd be quite wrong, sir; quite wrong. Apart from Arthur Young, the secretary, they're all nincompoops. Just look at the price of flour and bread. Yet farmers feed grain to their livestock. Your father's not a member!"

Ramage raised his eyebrows. Father was notoriously a non-joiner. He would send a subscription each year but he refused to be a patron. The "Sea Bathing Infirmary in Margate, Instituted for the Benefit of the Poor" ended up asking the Prince of Wales; the "Society for the Relief of the Ruptured Poor" managed to persuade Henry Dundas to be their president (and thus nearly lost the Earl of Blazey's annual subscription). There was another philanthropic institution that his mother favoured, and was cross with the Earl for refusing to be the patron (but the Duke of York finally agreed). He recalled that it was "The Benevolent Institution for the Sole Purpose of delivering poor Married Women at their own Habitations". His mother occasionally went to their meetings at the Hungerford Coffee House in the Strand to make sure the forty midwives it employed were competent and clean.

Garrett laughed at Ramage's obvious interest in the Board. "I mention your father, sir, because he is one of about a dozen landowners I hold up as examples to the Board. And not one of the others is a member either."

"Well, the Board must have some use, or you wouldn't be here."

"Ah yes, sir: I owe that to Lord Spencer. He was talking to your Mr Nepean, who mentioned something about settling a desert island and needing a botanist. Obviously your Mr Nepean is not very clear about botany, but Lord Spencer understood and suggested me."

Ramage reflected that more secrets were revealed in London's drawing rooms than anywhere else: Nepean should know better than confide in a former minister. They were the worst gossips of all, trying to make up for the loss of power by retailing tales passed on by people like Nepean, who were adept at keeping in with anyone ever likely to get back into office.

"Don't discuss your forthcoming work with anyone, Garret; it's a secret."

"Ah, yes sir," Garret said, in what Ramage realized was the preliminary to anything he said, just as other men might take a deep breath, "but planting potatoes and maize can't be very secret."

"No," Ramage agreed, and then added sharply: "But *where* you plant them not only could be but is, so guard your tongue." He turned to the artist, finding he did not like Garret's marketplace oratory, which seemed to be combined with a horse-coper's sharpness. "Now, Mr Wilkins, how came you to be included in this expedition?"

The artist was young—Ramage guessed he was about the same age as himself. Curly blond hair, skin very white, eyes blue, a thin face but eager. A man who would have to watch the sun in the Tropics.

"Nepotism, really," he said frankly. "An uncle of mine is professor in painting at the Royal Academy. I studied under him and through him know several of our leading painters—people like Sir William Beechey, Hoppner, Opie, Zoffany and the sculptor Joseph Nollekens... with such friends one does not need much merit!"

"You're very modest!"

"You look alarmed, sir, but I've specialized in painting flora and fauna—and can turn my hand to landscapes, if they're needed."

Ramage nodded, relieved at Alexander Wilkins's natural assurance. "If you get bored, you have some unusual fauna in the gunroom!"

Wilkins grinned and glanced at Aitken, as though he had asked the first lieutenant about something and had been told to ask the captain. "Since you mention it, sir, I would like to attempt a portrait of Mr Southwick. Would you have any objection?"

"Of course not. You are free to do anything that does not affect the running of the ship, and I've known Mr Southwick long enough to be sure he won't want to sit for you when he should be on watch!"

Ramage realized that Wilkins had been quick to spot what must, to an artist, be the most interesting and challenging face in the ship: Southwick, now well past sixty, had unruly white hair that he usually described as being like a new mop spun in a high wind. His face verged on plump, but it was the plumpness of contentment rather than soft living. His eyes were grey, revealing a sense of humour. At first sight he appeared more like the bishop of a rural diocese than the master of one of the King's ships, but the more observant might detect a delight in wielding a huge fighting sword with all the facility that a bishop would handle a crozier.

Aitken took out his watch and looked at it significantly. "It'll be high water in an hour, sir; if we want to catch the first of the ebb..."

CHAPTER SEVEN

The first few miles on a voyage which would take them a quarter of the way round the world were bound to be the most tiresome, Ramage thought. The wind was light from the south-west when they dropped the moorings off the dockyard, and with topsails drawing there was enough strength in it to carry them over the last of the flood: the *Calypso's* smooth bottom, newly coppered, more than made up for the fact that with extra provisions and three months' water she was floating lower on her marks than at any time since she was first captured.

Ramage disliked sailing down a river on a tide which would be falling before he was a quarter of the way to the entrance: going aground meant the ship would stick for a whole tide. Sailing with the flood, on the other hand, meant waiting a few minutes and the ship would float off...

The Medway was the worst of the rivers the King's ships normally navigated: it twisted and turned every few hundred yards between banks of mud and acres of saltings, across which snipe jinked and startled duck quacked, watched by seamen who pictured them plucked and roasted.

Southwick had a chart spread over the top of the binnacle box and held down by weights. The men at the wheel and the quartermaster were not concerned with the compass as Southwick tried to pick out where the channel lay in stretches of water that were greenish-brown and gave no indication of the depths.

Aitken, speaking trumpet in hand, kept the men busy trimming the sails to every change of course; yards were braced, sheets hauled or slacked. A seaman standing in the chains heaved the lead and sang out the depths in a lugubrious monotone, but everyone knew the ship would be hard aground before anyone could react to shoaling.

"Not far to Sheerness now, sir," Southwick said. He had long since taken off his hat, and the wind ruffling his white hair once again reminded Ramage of a mop. "That's Hoo Fort on our larboard beam, and Darnett Ness on our starboard bow." He gestured to a tiny island marooned in a depressing stretch of sea and which, at low water, would be reduced to a knob amid a vast stretch of smelly mud.

"Once we round the Ness, we pass Bishop Ooze to starboard, and Half Acre Creek joins us. Beats me where they get the names from. Past the Ness we're in Kethole Reach. I wonder if it was once 'Kettle'? Then we come into Saltpan Reach. Oh, just look at that . . ."

Southwick delivered one of his prodigious, disapproving sniffs, and Ramage, who was thinking of a woman with black hair in a carriage on the Paris road, gave a start and looked ahead. At least four Thames barges were coming up Kethole Reach. For the moment he could see only the big rectangular sails, a deep red ochre from the red lead and linseed oil with which they were painted.

"Don't give 'em an inch, sir," Southwick said. "I know they're beating and we're running, but they only draw about four feet laden. If there's dew on the grass a barge can float! They can sail in to the bank until they see the leeboard lifting as it touches bottom, and then tack with plenty to spare. Don't forget we're drawing sixteen and a half feet aft, sir."

Aitken had walked over to stand beside Southwick, as though to lend his weight to the master's comments.

"The trouble with you," Ramage said, keeping an eye on the sails, "you're afraid they'll scratch your paintwork!"

"Scratch the paint!" Southwick snorted. "If they're laden with stone, they'd stove in planks, and I'm sick of that dockyard!"

Ramage noticed that the barges had tacked one after the other so that they were now sailing diagonally across the river, their hulls hidden beyond the bend. They were on the starboard

84

tack, steering south, each great sprit holding out the sail like a matador's sword extending his red cape.

"Sir, the channel's but forty yards wide here; you remember coming up to Chatham we had to club haul and even then touched."

Ramage glanced at the chart and said mildly to the master: "You really mustn't be a bully, Mr Southwick. Just because we're so big, we can't just force barges aground. They've got a living to make. A man and a boy and a dog handling a vessel eighty feet long—more, some of them."

The barges were in line ahead now. At first glance this was not obvious, because the gap between each of them varied, but Ramage decided to continue for a few more minutes. Aitken was looking worried now but turned away to shout orders for sail trimming as Southwick gave a new direction to the quartermaster and the wheel turned a few spokes.

"It's soft mud, anyway," Ramage said dreamily. "We'd sit snug as a duck until the tide made again."

"But sir!" Southwick was certain that worrying about the Marchesa had temporarily deranged the captain. "The sides of the channel slope; if we ground we'll side and probably roll over as the tide leaves us!"

"The Good Lord will provide," Ramage said, "you forget we have a chaplain now."

"Sir—those barges can sit on the mud: they're flat bottomed and built to dry out . . ."

By now the first barge was bearing away a point, having been allowing for the ebb, and shooting up Half Acre Creek. Southwick, alarmed by his captain and keeping a sharp eye on the river bank each side, with its unappetizing expanse of mud, had not looked ahead again.

The second barge shot into the Creek. Aitken spotted it and turned quickly, about to tell Ramage. He caught sight of Ramage's face and grinned, turning away to face forward again.

"I really can't be responsible, sir," Southwick protested. "We ought to have an anchor ready. Those four barges are so close to each other we don't have a snowball in hell's chance of getting through without hitting one of them."

The third barge went into Half Acre Creek and Ramage said: "The war is over, Mr Southwick. We can't bully these poor bargemen. I'd be court-martialled if we sank one!"

"Sir, sir," Southwick said desperately, "you'll be court-martialled if you damage this ship and delay the expedition—God bless my soul!"

Southwick had glanced up and found Kethole Reach clear of sails as the last barge went into the creek. He turned to Ramage, a sheepish grin on his face. "Sorry, sir, you fooled me! Did you know they were going into Half Acre Creek?"

"No, but I thought they might," Ramage admitted. "They can make a couple of tacks, then come out again after we've passed."

Once past the entrance to Half Acre Creek the Medway widened as Sheerness came in sight to starboard and the flat expanse of the Isle of Grain stretched away to larboard, a rough green and brown carpet of marshes and saltings and mudflats that reached across to the banks of the Thames.

"Looks as though we could anchor for the night off Warden Point, after getting in the powder," Southwick said. "We'll be close by the entrance of the Four Fathom Channel, ready for an early start tomorrow, and there'll be enough moon later on for the watchkeepers to see the cliffs between East End and the Point."

Ramage nodded. "We must be one of the few ships ever to sail on the proper day after a refit."

By dawn the *Calypso* was steering along the north Kent coast under all plain sail with a brisk westerly breeze and an almost calm sea. The Great Nore and the Thames narrowing on its way through Sea Reach and up to London were astern. Southwick ticked off the bays and the towns, and Ramage was reminded of his days as a young midshipman.

St Mildred's Bay and then Margate; Palm Bay and then Long Nose Spit, with Foreness Point making the northern end of Botany Bay and White Ness the southern. Ramage called Paolo to his side and pointed out the North Foreland, the northeastern tip of Kent, unimpressive under a watery sun to a youth who could compare it with Tuscany or some of the West Indian islands.

The *Calypso* then turned south to steer through the Gull Stream, leaving the Goodwin Sands to larboard. The yards were braced up, tacks and sheets hauled, and the frigate began to pitch slightly with the two men at the wheel watching the luffs of the sails as carefully as the quartermaster and Martin, who was officer of the deck.

Ramage occasionally pointed out places of interest as the frigate sailed the fourteen miles between the North and the South Foreland, which was the official name of the famous "White cliffs of Dover". Seas breaking well beyond the larboard beam showed the main banks of the Goodwin Sands while on the other side of the shore was Deal, nestling amid the shingle behind the Downs, which was the favourite anchorage for ships waiting for bad weather to ease before beginning the long beat down Channel.

A cast of the log showed the *Calypso* making eight knots, and soon they were hardening in sheets as the frigate passed Dover and bore up for Dungeness, the wedge of flat land, a mixture of beach and marsh, forming the southeastern corner of the country.

With Folkestone abeam to starboard, Ramage pointed to the long, low, grey shape on the horizon to larboard. "You can see the French coast," he told Paolo. "There's Calais."

Jackson was the quartermaster and standing only a few feet away. Ramage's mind went back to the time when he had received orders from the Admiralty to see how near the French were to launching an invasion, and the only way of finding out was to go to France. He had enlisted the help of smugglers and gone to France with Jackson, Stafford and Rossi. The smuggler who risked his life for them had, ironically, been a deserter who had once served with Ramage.

"I wonder if 'Slushy' Dyson still smuggles out of Folkestone," he said to Jackson.

"I was just thinking the same thing, sir; we must be crossing the wake of that boat of his. Probably a rich man by now, with a big estate!"

"Not 'Slushy'—if you remember, he was born under an unlucky star."

Jackson peered down at the compass on the weather side and then at the luffs of the topsails. "Not so unlucky really, sir. He should have been hanged for mutiny, but I seem to remember you gave him a couple of dozen lashes and transferred him to another ship!"

Ramage laughed at the memory. "Just as well I did; if he

87

hadn't become a smuggler we might never have got back from France!"

By now Paolo, all ears, was begging to be told the story, but Ramage shook his head. "Too many ships for us to watch. Every fishing boat must be out, and you saw how many merchant ships were pouring out of the Thames. No more convoys now; the first ship at the market place gets the highest prices!"

Paolo, telescope tucked under his arm, tanned and far from the nervous youngster Ramage had first taken to sea (as a grudging gesture to Gianna, he had to admit), said: "I've never seen so many ships scattered across the sea, sir. But this is the first occasion I've ever been to sea in peacetime!"

"You get just as cold and wet and tired," Ramage said, "with many more chances of collisions."

"And no chance of action," Paolo said sadly. "No more actions, no more prizes..."

Ramage spoke quietly as he said: "For a while, anyway. Remember, we were trying to persuade your aunt to stay in England."

With that Paolo cheered up. "Yes, sir; I suppose we should consider this a holiday. Is that one of the packet boats?" he asked, pointing to a schooner crossing ahead.

Ramage looked at it with his telescope. "Yes, the Dover-Calais packet. Started again after being stopped for eight years."

The wind remained steady in strength and direction and Ramage tacked the *Calypso* as they approached within six miles of Fécamp, easily recognizable because it sat in a gap in the cliffs. The frigate could comfortably steer north by west, and by nightfall they tacked to south by west as the Owers, off Selsey Bill, came abeam. Ramage's only concession to peace was that the *Calypso* had four lookouts on deck at night, one on each bow and each quarter, instead of the six of wartime. With so many ships sailing up and down Channel, the risk of collision was considerable, and the *Calypso*, with a newly coppered bottom, new sails and well trained ship's company, was probably one of the fastest. This meant she faced the added risk of overtaking some merchant ship lumbering along without lights and running into her stern. Which, Ramage thought gloomily, would mean carrying away the *Calypso*'s jibboom and bowsprit, and that in turn would send the foremast by the board . . .

Southwick, after filling in the new course and the time, put the slate back in the binnacle drawer and, as if guessing Ramage's mood, walked over and said: "It's like hopping across Whitehall with your eyes shut, isn't it sir? I'd forgotten what peacetime was like. Still, war can be worse: I remember once in a ship of the line finding myself in the middle of a West India convoy one night. More than one hundred ships, we found out afterwards."

To Ramage it had all the qualities of a nightmare: far more dangerous than battle. A ship of the line could cut a merchant ship in half; with the bowsprits of a couple of merchant ships caught in her shrouds she could lose her masts. "What did you do?"

"Ah, Sir Richard Strachan was the captain." Southwick laughed at the memory. "I was only a passenger but I happened to be on deck, and so was Sir Richard. A pitch-black night; we hadn't seen a ship for a week. Suddenly we hear shouts nearby and sails flapping. Then our lookouts start shouting; a ship on each bow and one on our larboard beam—all crossing from the starboard side. You know what a cusser Sir Richard is: well, he cusses, but in a trice he has the foretopsail back and we heave-to on the larboard tack and start burning blue flares. That was quick thinking, I must say: we hadn't a hope of seeing and dodging all those merchant ships; but we were so big that once they saw us—we must have looked a splendid sight, all lit up with those flares—they could do the dodging. It must have taken an hour for them to pass us, and there was Sir Richard with the speaking trumpet swearing at every one that came within hail."

"He *can* swear," Ramage commented.

"We could hardly stand for laughing, sir. 'Here's another one sir,' the first lieutenant would say, and if she was going to pass ahead Sir Richard would run up on the fo'csle, jam the speaking trumpet to his mouth and bellow at the master something like 'Call yourself a man of God, do you? You look more like Satan to me!'"

The wind veered slowly northwest during Saturday night and by dawn on Sunday the *Calypso* was making nine knots, steering southwest, and Ramage intended to make his departure from Ushant. It was more usual to keep to the north, so that the Lizard was likely to be the last sight of land for a ship's company. The danger of being far enough south to use Ushant was that a sudden gale usually made it a lee shore, but the weather was set fair.

Hammocks were lashed and stowed; the ship's company had eaten breakfast; Ramage had carried out the usual Sunday morning inspection of ship and men. The smell of paint was at last disappearing. Ordering the wind sails to be rigged had helped—the tall cylinders of canvas, the tops open and winged and used in the Tropics to funnel a breeze down the hatches, had forced a strong draught through the ship which had made men shiver, but it had cleared the air.

Finally the order was given "Rig Church". Long wooden forms, used by the men to sit at the tables on the lowerdeck, were brought up to the quarterdeck, a chair was carried up from Ramage's cabin and put in front. A large Union flag was draped over the binnacle box, which was to serve as the altar. The quartermaster would not be able to look at the compass until the service was over.

Down in his cabin Ramage changed his shoes—his steward always had his newest pair, fitted with the heavy silver buckles, ready for the Sunday service. Ramage wondered where they spent the rest of the week. He stood still while the steward fitted the sword belt, and then slipped the sword into the frog. Just as he was looking round for his hymn book and prayer book, the Marine sentry reported the first lieutenant's approach.

Aitken came into the cabin. "All ready for you, sir. The chaplain is holding a bundle of papers as thick as a pound loaf. I hope they aren't the notes for his sermon."

"You haven't forgotten what I said?"

"No, sir," Aitken said with a grin. "And the wind is freshening."

Ramage walked across the deck and sat down in his chair, facing aft. The chaplain stood immediately behind the binnacle, just in front of the two men at the wheel. The Marines under Renwick were drawn up across the after end of the quarterdeck; most of the ship's company were sitting on the forms. As usual Catholics sat among the Church of England men; Methodists sat near the front and John Smith the Second stood to one side with his fiddle. The ship's officers sat on a form to one side.

Ramage thought that at a time when a prime minister had resigned because he disagreed with the King over religion, it would do them all good to see practical religion functioning in a ship of war. Most captains knew that sailors liked a good sing; two hundred voices seizing on to a rousing hymn, with John Smith's fiddle to help them along, did the men good. More important, as far as the Navy was concerned, the way men sang hymns told an intelligent captain if he had a happy or a discontented ship's company.

Stokes, watching Ramage sit down, clasped his hands as if in prayer, but there was something odd about the man. His surplice was not only creased but filthy: not the smears of some recent encounter with a dirty object but the greyness of grime: it had not been washed for months. And the man was standing strangely. The *Calypso,* on the starboard tack, was rolling with a slightly larger dip to larboard. Men standing on deck were tensing and flexing their knees to remain upright, but Stokes had the wrong rhythm: he was like a single stalk of corn that moved against the wind while all the others bowed away from it.

Ramage glanced across at Southwick, who was watching the chaplain closely, but none of the lieutenants had noticed anything. The man's voice was blurred but punctuated by the hiss of passing swell waves, the creak of yards overhead, and the thud and flap of a sail momentarily losing the wind and then filling again with a thump that jerked sheet and brace.

Stokes announced a hymn, John Smith tucked his fiddle under his chin and poised the bow. Stokes lifted a hand, John Smith scratched the opening bars and the ship's company, standing and swaying with the roll like the field of corn Ramage had pictured, bellowed away happily. Most of them knew the entire hymn by heart, and Stokes was beating time with his left hand. Not the time for the hymn and its music, Ramage noted; rather as though he was a tallyman counting as sheep ran through a gate.

There was still a little warmth in the sun but measurable only because of the chill when the increasing number of clouds hid it. The sea was a darker blue now as the *Calypso* approached the Chops of the Channel and deeper sea. The ship's company was going to be lucky this year; there would be no winter for them. With more than a hint of autumn in England, they would within hours be turning south, towards the Tropic of Cancer and the Equator, before stopping just short of the Tropic of Capricorn. Ramage doubted if many of the men had ever crossed the Equator. As far as he was concerned, the ship could not get back to the Tropics fast enough. Admittedly he had returned to England after several months in the Mediterranean, but after the Tropics, the Mediterranean seemed a wretched climate: scorching hot and windless in summer, without the constant cooling breeze of the trade winds, and bitterly cold in winter, though never a Spaniard, Frenchman or Italian would admit it, building his house as though there was always sun, and the bitter wind of winter did not blow through, chilling marble floors so that, even as far south as Rome, men and women hobbled about like lame ducks, almost crippled by chilbains. The trade winds made the West Indies as near Paradise as Ramage could imagine; and providing one avoided yellow fever which killed, and rum, which wounded first . . .

He stopped daydreaming as Stokes announced his text for the day. It was, he said from Romans, chapter fourteen, verse eight: "If the trumpet give an uncertain sound, who shall prepare himself to the battle?"

A curious text. In fact twenty or thirty seamen were openly laughing: whatever else they might consider the captain lacked, Ramage guessed it was not an uncertain sound when the time came to prepare for battle. That was assuming that Stokes had the sense to preach a sermon remembering he was talking to seamen, to whom "battle" meant "battle" and not some philosophical state of readiness.

Stokes began talking rapidly, like a nervous child reciting something in front of grownups, something little understood so that all the pauses for breath came at the wrong time and punctuation was ignored.

Southwick glanced across at Ramage: a look that said, without equivocation: "I told you so."

Well, the man was half drunk; Ramage was prepared to admit that, but he was also prepared to overlook it on this occasion, because a new chaplain could be forgiven for being nervous when conducting his first service.

Out of habit, Ramage glanced at his watch and slipped it back into his fob pocket. The wind was holding from the north-west; almost a soldier's wind to round Ushant and stand across the Bay of Biscay, heading for the Spanish Finisterre. It was going to take months to get used to the idea that every ship sighted was a friend. For so many years the lookout's hail of a sail in sight was the beginning of a sequence which involved identification and then, if French, chase and battle and, if British, the challenge and exchange of the private signals for the day and hoisting of the three-figure pendant numbers by which each ship in the King's service could be identified by name.

Stokes was not only gabbling but he was doing it in a monotone. Ramage concentrated on listening to the words. After what seemed an hour, he looked again at his watch. Stokes had been talking for five minutes, and he kept referring to "whom the Lord loveth he chasteneth", as though that was his text. Ramage again concentrated. Certainly there was no reference to trumpets giving uncertain sounds or anyone preparing for battle, but there was a great deal about punishing only those one loved; that one demanded higher standards from loved ones, and chastened them if they fell below them.

As Ramage reached for his watch again, he realized what had happened: Stokes was quoting from one of the two dozen sermons he had bought. Because the captain had forbidden him to use them, he had learned one by rote, or near enough, so he would seem to be speaking without notes and apparently directly from the heart. The only trouble was that he was preaching the sermon he had learned, but he had announced the text from another—presumably the text on the pile.

The watch showed the man had been talking for ten minutes. Ramage saw Aitken was also holding his watch and looking across at him.

Ramage stood up. "Mr. Aitken, I'll trouble you to take a reef in the foretopsail!"

The first lieutenant leapt up, shouting: "Topmen, look alive you topmen! Afterguard lay aft—come on, fo'c'slemen, I don't see you moving!"

Southwick leapt up and jammed his hat on his head. "Clear the binnacle," he roared, "get that flag off so we can get a sight of the compass!"

"Watch your heading!" Jackson shouted at the men at the wheel, unceremoniously pushing the chaplain to one side and helping to increase the confusion. He had more than a suspicion of what was going on, having seen the exchange of glances between the captain and first lieutenant. "Damnation, you're a full point off course!" He winked at the men before they had time to heave on the spokes of the wheel.

Renwick had been too far aft to see what was going on and had never listened to a sermon in his life, having in childhood perfected the art of sleeping while looking awake, but he realized that pandemonium was required, and instead of marching his men forward and dismissing them on the gangway, he shouted: "Marines—at the double, fall out!" Three dozen Marines in heavy boots suddenly began running forward in a cloud of white pipeclay which their movement crumbled off their crossbelts.

The bosun's mates were soon busy, repeating orders after the piercing trill of their calls. Topmen leapt over forms, knocking several over as they ran to the shrouds.

The Reverend Percival Stokes, unsure what was happening, wisely crouched down behind the binnacle, reminding Southwick of a frightened whippet cowering behind its kennel. Beside him a seaman was calmly folding the big Union flag, careful to line up the previous creases.

By now Ramage, still standing beside his chair, looked over the starboard quarter and then up at the sky. "What do you think, Mr Southwick? That squall will pass us to windward, eh?"

"You're probably right, sir. By a mile, I think."

"At least a mile. Mr Aitken! Belay that last pipe! Get these forms stowed below, and then you can pipe 'Hands to dinner'." With that Ramage strode to the companionway and went down to his cabin, and Stokes finally bobbed up in the sudden silence, lifted his surplice and scurried below.

Ten minutes later, after Ramage had passed the word for them, Aitken and Southwick reported to his cabin. In answer to Ramage's wave, Southwick subsided into the single armchair with the contented groan of a man whose back ached and Aitken sat on the settee, very upright at first until he realized this was to be an informal visit, when he leaned back.

"Drunk and a filthy surplice," Ramage said.

"And smelling like an overworked dray horse, sir," Aitken added. "The gunroom reeks like a stable."

"Did either of you notice anything about the sermon?"

"He's learned it by rote," Aitken said quickly. "If he'd had to stop, I'll bet he couldn't have got started again."

"Aye, and the sermon had precious little to do with the text he announced," Southwick added. "He said it was about the trumpet giving an uncertain sound, but even tho' I'm a free thinker I'd have sworn it should have been that line about 'whom the Lord he chasteneth'. I know it well; my father always quoted it, nigh on sixty years ago, when he laid on half a dozen across my buttocks with his belt. I always waited for his trousers to fall down. They never did."

Both Southwick and Aitken watched Ramage. Southwick had served under him for many years, starting the day the young lieutenant was given his first command the *Kathleen* cutter, by Commodore Nelson. What always struck him was that as an inexperienced young lieutenant or one of the best frigate captains in the Navy today, even though in terms of seniority his name was almost at the bottom of the post list, Mr Ramage was never indecisive. He collected all the facts, seemed to shake them up in a dice cup, and throw the answer across the green baize table. So far it had always been the right answer, with the result that his officers and ship's company had suffered few casualties in battle and collected a good deal of prize money.

Southwick had been surprised, when news reached Chatham Dockyard that the Treaty had been signed and Britain was at peace with France, that at least a quarter of the ship's company had not asked for their discharge. Ships would be paying off by the dozen, and the seamen who had served with Mr Ramage could go home to a tidy pile of money; enough to set up a small business, open a shop in their village, pay for a small house.

While the captain was in London on leave some had even come to Southwick to discuss it, and as soon as he was back on board many of them had asked to see Mr Ramage, and Southwick knew they were just making sure the master's advice was sound. Both master and captain, however, had said the same thing: that they thought the peace would be brief and the men risked being hauled back by the pressgang in a year's time . . . Neither he nor the captain had said, in as many words, that there would be no chance of them serving together again. For all that, each man had apparently weighed it up for himself: on one side a year's leave with money to spend, but ending up fighting another war in another ship, and on the other the wish to serve under Captain Ramage and his officers and with the same shipmates, but at the cost of a year's liberty.

Southwick disliked tale-bearing and he hated sycophants, but he was in some respects a jealous man: he was jealous of anything concerning his ship and anything concerning his captain. Jealous or, some might say, protective. He had been thinking about Percy Stokes for some time and this morning's service had decided him.

"There are one or two things about Stokes, sir. He's been selling liquor to his servant. Brandy and gin. The servant has been buying it for a crowd of drinkers on the lowerdeck. He's tried to borrow money from Orsini and Kenton, against IOUs. Fortunately neither of them have any left."

Aitken nodded in agreement. "I'd heard about Kenton, but not Orsini. The liquor is a bad business: we'll be finding seamen drunk on duty in a day or so. Even the best men don't seem able to control themselves while there's another tot left in a bottle."

Ramage listened to the two men and considered what they had reported. He guessed that both men had deliberated for several hours before saying anything and, but for the ludicrous service half an hour ago, might well have tried to deal with the chaplain in their own manner. "Pass the word for the wretched fellow—and stay here: I'll need witnesses for what I may have to do."

Stokes arrived still wearing his surplice but almost glassy-eyed: he had obviously been drinking again, but he was nervous, his tongue wetting his protruding teeth like a scullery maid washing a draining board.

Ramage remained sitting beside his desk, the chair sideways so that his right arm rested on the polished top. He inspected Stokes once again, the eyes, the face, the grubby surplice—and the hands, clasped in front of him like an unctuous prelate or a nervous beggar. He thought for a moment of the Chaplain General interviewing Stokes. It must have been a rare event; clerics had never pounded on his door. The Horse Guards was a more popular port of call; for a cleric the mess of a fashionable regiment seemed to Ramage infinitely preferable to the gun-room or wardroom of a ship of war. The only advantage of serving in one of the King's ships was that it took a man out of the country. Ramage suddenly stared at Stokes. If he was wrong, the Chaplain General's protest to the First Lord would be vociferous, querulous and acidulous. The First Lord would be his usual cryptic self: he would simply order a court martial to be held on Captain the Lord Ramage.

"Ah, Mr Stokes, when you were last here, you said you had never before been in one of the King's ships."

"That is correct, sir."

"But the sea is not unfamiliar to you?"

"Oh yes, indeed, sir; I'm a complete stranger to the sea."

"To the North Sea?" Ramage asked casually. "To the Irish Sea? *To the Marshalsea?*"

The knuckles of Stokes's clasped hands turned white; the man shut his eyes and began to sway, but he was forgetting the height of the beams, and when he raised his head he immediately cracked his brow. His body jerked as though someone had hit him with a cudgel and slowly, like a sack of grain emptying, he subsided to the deck in a faint.

None of the three men moved, but Southwick gave one of his disapproving sniffs. "The Marshalsea—aye, he looks the sort of fellow that's cruised in that jail more than once!"

"Did he escape or was he released?" Aitken mused. "Or has he been there before and knew his creditors were about to send him back?"

"He's bolting from his creditors," Ramage said. "He's been there before and wasn't risking another visit. Probably so much in debt he knew that once inside he'd never get out again."

The Marshalsea Prison was unlike the Bridewell. Thieves, rogues, murderers and vagabonds sentenced by the courts were sent to the Bridewell. But the Marshalsea was reserved for debtors. A creditor could apply for a court order which, if granted, locked a debtor in the Marshalsea and kept him there until the debt was paid.

"It's the drink," Aitken said, his voice sombre. "I'm sure his thirst overtook his pocket. But how did he persuade the Admiralty? Is his warrant forged?"

"No, I'm sure it's genuine enough, though I haven't inspected it," Ramage said. "I'm equally sure he's not a clerk in holy orders—he seemed to be conducting the service as if by rote, and we know about his sermons—ah, he's recovering: now he can tell us himself!"

Slowly Stokes sat up, a puzzled expression on his face. His head was obviously spinning from the fall; Ramage had the impression it was spinning the other way from the drink.

"I must have fainted," he mumbled. "It's the rolling."

"I should stay there," Ramage said. "Not so far to fall. Now, you were going to tell us about your cruise in the Marshalsea."

"I don't know what you mean, sir. This is an insult to a man of the cloth—I shall protest to the Chaplain General!"

"We shall not be seeing England again for half a year or more, so your complaint will have to wait. In the meantime, tell me how you obtained a warrant."

Stokes swallowed and his tongue slid from side to side over the front of his teeth, but his lips were too dry and they stuck on them, giving him a curious, rabbit-like appearance which contrasted with the ferret-like shape of the face.

Ramage said softly: "Stokes, at the moment you are trying to decide whether to attempt to brazen it out, or admit to what amounts to fraud. There are no courts and judges where we are going. I am the judge and jury. I can tell you now that I do not think you are a clerk in holy orders, despite your warrant, and I shall not let you minister to the ship's company."

"You could get yourself into a lot of trouble, Mr high and mighty Lord Ramage," Stokes said viciously.

"Oh yes," Ramage said, hoping to draw out the man even more, "I could face a court martial; I could be dismissed from the service."

"That's right; the famous Lord Ramage court-martialled for ill-treating his chaplain. What a scandal *that* would cause. Be the death of your father, the shame of it."

"How much did you owe?" Southwick suddenly asked.

"Owe who?" Stokes said sharply.

Ramage said: "Stokes, you are not a clerk in holy orders; you do not even have the education necessary for a sexton, so let us agree on that. I am not really interested in your debts or why you bolted. I'm concerned only with that warrant. You are not entitled to it, but somehow you got it."

"Ah, frightens you, doesn't it? You daren't touch me while I have the warrant. That proves the Admiralty believe me."

"It's issued by the Navy Office, not the Admiralty, and it

certainly does not prove the Navy Board believe you. Describe the Chaplain General," Ramage said suddenly.

The question took Stokes completely unawares. "Well, he's—he's rather like me. No, perhaps taller. A very nice man; sympathetic, and concerned that the Navy has only the best men as chaplains . . ."

"What does he look like," Ramage persisted. "Bald, white hair, grey, black, fifty years old or eighty? Does he walk with a limp? Deep voice or shrill?" He has seen him once at Lord Spencer's, and like many such clerics who owed their position to patronage, the Chaplain General was portly and pink, but his nose was an object few would forget: it was purple, bulbous and almost incredibly long, like an elephant's trunk. Also the voice emerging from the bulky cleric was little more than a squeak; not a voice to fill a modest drawing room, let alone a vast cathedral.

Stokes shrugged his shoulders. As the fainting fit receded in his memory and the word "warrant" obviously took on the role of a talisman, his cunning was returning and with it a shoddy bravado. "Can't remember; I only saw him for a moment or two."

"If you saw the Chaplain General only once and at a distance there are things about him you would remember."

"Well, I don't, and that's that."

"Get up," Ramage said, the quietness of his voice making both Southwick and Aitken prepare to move swiftly. Stokes, too, realized that there was a change of mood in the cabin. "Take off that surplice."

"Whoa, my Lord!" Stokes protested, "you can't give orders like that to a man of the cloth!"

"I know, but you are a vagabond, not a man of the cloth, and I'm not having vagabonds walking about this ship disguised as men of God. Take it off or the Marine sentry will strip you bare."

Stokes suddenly realized that the quiet voice was a danger signal. Swaying and frightened, he pulled off the surplice and cassock and stood in his underwear, holding them out to Ramage like a peace offering.

"What happened?" Ramage asked.

"When, sir?" Stokes was admitting defeat, but now fright was changing to panic.

"How did you get that warrant?"

"It's all legal, sir," the man whined. "I wrote to the Chaplain General applying for a position in one of the King's ships, and saying I looked forward to visiting foreign countries. I enclosed a recommendation from the Bishop of London and the Dean of Westminster."

"How did you get them?"

"Oh, that was easy. I knew their names and styles, you see."

"How did that get you recommendations?" Ramage asked, puzzled by Stokes's patient explanation of what seemed so obvious to him.

"Well, it means I got all the details right in the letters of recommendation. I write a fair hand and a change of pen is a change of style."

"Oh, you forged them!"

"Of course, sir," Stokes said contemptuously. "I got my new name out of a university register, so if anyone looked up Percival Stokes they'd see he had a good degree and was a clerk in holy orders. The Chaplain General was ill and his secretary accepted my letters, and the next thing was an Admiralty messenger delivered my warrant and orders to report to 'His Majesty's ship *Calypso*, frigate'. And I did."

"So you are not 'Percival Stokes'?"

"Not likely!" the man said scornfully. "Percival—what a name. No, the Reverend Percival Stokes lives in Bristol, according to the University register."

"What's your name, then. Your *real* name?"

"Robert Smith."

"Very well, Robert Smith. What debts are you bolting from?"

"Well, there are several," he admitted.

"Were all your creditors taking you to court?"

"Well, no, only one, but the others would have the minute they heard about it."

"How large is that one debt?"

"Sixteen pounds."

Southwick sniffed and Aitken grinned: they could see the way their captain's mind was working.

"Listen carefully, Smith. I can stop a ship returning to England and have you landed under an arrest, charged with impersonation, defrauding the Admiralty, and various other things that will put you in the Bridewell—the Bridewell, not the Marshalsea—for several years, and when you're released your creditors will still be there waiting to pop you in the Marshalsea. Or..."

Smith was now pale and shaking; the perspiration was pouring down his face and he was too panic-stricken to lift a hand to wipe it away. He was watching Ramage, waiting for the next words.

"Or what, sir?" he exclaimed.

"Well, the Navy won't surrender a seaman for a civil debt of £20 or less. Although we're now at peace, the wartime laws concerning our seamen still apply. If you want to volunteer for the Navy, you're free to do so. Sleep on it and tell Mr Southwick tomorrow morning. In the meantime Mr Aitken will tell the purser to issue you with a hammock. Now, clear your gear out of the cabin you've been using and get forward!"

Smith almost ran through the door, remembering to keep his head down.

Aitken said: "Not one of the King's best bargains, sir!"

"No, but it's got him out of the gunroom."

"Aye, and for that many thanks, sir."

"And as soon as we meet another of the King's ships, we can transfer him."

Southwick said, "I have to admit I admire the rogue, sir. Fancy forging references from the Bishop of London and the Dean of Westminster! He was lucky the Chaplain General was ill: if there'd been an interview...he doesn't look much like a chaplain."

"I've seen worse," Ramage said, "even if they smell fresher, but I admire him, too."

CHAPTER EIGHT

Because Ramage hated all the paperwork attached to commanding one of the King's ships, he set aside one complete afternoon a week. On that day his clerk brought him the pile of forms, reports and letters that he had to read or sign—rarely both—and Aitken and Southwick trod carefully, knowing the captain would be ill-tempered and, so the master claimed, equipped with a magic shovel that in a couple of seconds could make a mountain out of a molehill.

He opened the muster book, curious to read the latest entry. Robert Smith was now entered and rated a landman. He was noted down as being thirty-eight years old and born in Peckham, London. The purser had dated the entry the day before the *Calypso* sailed from Chatham. In that way, Smith would be paid from the day he joined the ship—but at the rate of a landman, not a chaplain. Ironically the pay was about the same; it was the "groats" that lined a chaplain's pocket.

Closing the muster book, he looked at the muster table, and then at a single sheet of paper which showed all that was known and needed to be known about the ship's company of the *Calypso* on her first voyage in peacetime. Ironically the form was still drawn in the usual wartime wording.

There were four "classes" of men—ship's company, Marines, supernumeraries "victuals and wages" and supernumeraries "victuals only". Each of these four had then to be placed in one of five categories, "Borne" (which meant carried on the *Calypso*'s books), "Mustered" (paraded and answering their names as read from ther muster book), "Checqued" (not on parade but their presence on board confirmed), "Sick on shore", and "In prizes".

So today the *Calypso*'s ship's company totalled ("borne") 211, with 199 mustered and 12 checqued, with none sick on shore or away in prizes. The figure sixteen appeared in the "supernumeraries victuals and wages" column because in addition to the dozen masons and bricklayers, the surveyors and draughtsmen were being paid and fed as part of the ship's company, while the figure two in the "supernumeraries victuals only" showed that the botanist and the artist were being fed but not paid—the Admiralty or Navy Board had made some private arrangement.

He pushed aside the muster documents and pulled over the *Calypso*'s log. There were in fact two, one kept by Southwick and referred to as the "Master's Log", and his own, known as "the Captain's Journal". He had not filled it in since leaving Chatham, and he used Southwick's times and positions. He filled in the words "*Calypso*", "Ramage", "fourth" and "September" in the blank spaces at the top of the page where it said: "Log of the Proceedings of His Majesty's ship_____, Captain _____, commander, between the ___ day of _____, and the ___ day of _____." The last two spaces were left blank. There were certain superstitions few officers cared to ignore. One was never to write the final date in a log book or journal (they were supposed to be sent to the Admiralty every two months) until it was actually completed, and even though a page equalled a day, and another was not to write in the final entry of a voyage which said "From _____ to _____" until one actually arrived. Life was uncertain enough without teasing fate.

He began to fill in his journal. The first column headed "H" was a series of numbers from one to twelve—the time. The next two columns were headed "K" and "F", the knots and fathoms run, entries that land people rarely understood because in the log a knot could mean speed, one nautical mile an hour, or a distance (one nautical mile) with any extra distance measured in fathoms, or units of six feet. "Courses" and "Winds" headed the next two columns, while "Remarks" occupied the right-hand half of the page, and recorded such mundane matters as the opening of a cask of salt beef, and the number of pieces it contained, compared with the number stencilled on the side by the contractor, which was the Navy Board's figure.

Now for the course, distance, longitude and latitude, recorded at the bottom of—surely that was a lookout hailing? He wiped his pen and listened. Yes, young Martin was answering.

"Deck here!"

Then, from high above: "Sail ho, dead ahead, approaching fast!"

"What do you make of her?" demanded Martin.

"Need a bring-'em-near, sir, but reckon she's got everything set to her royals."

"Very well, I'll send someone up with a telescope."

Ramage thankfully jammed the lid back on the inkwell, slid the books and papers into the top right-hand drawer of his desk and, out of habit locked it. Royals set almost certainly meant a ship of war—except, he corrected himself, the world is at peace now. But no merchant ship, not even one of the Honourable East India Company, would be bowling along with royals set in this breeze. Only a ship of war had enough men to handle a cloud of sail in an emergency. The approaching ship could be British, French, Dutch, perhaps even Danish. Unlikely to be Swedish and definitely not Russian—both because few were still at sea and because they were handled in an unbelievably lubberly way.

By now Ramage had collected his telescope from its rack on the bulkhead beside the door and his hat from the hook just below it. He arrived on deck in the weak sunlight to find the western edge of the Bay of Biscay still reasonably calm despite the freshening wind.

Most likely a French ship of the line making for Brest or Rochefort, although, come to think of it, very few French ships of the line had been at sea in the last few days of the war.

"I was just going to send down Mr Orsini, sir," Martin said. He knew the captain could hear hails through his skylight, but overhearing had no official existence, and Martin added: "Foremast lookout reports a sail dead ahead steering towards us, and he thinks he can see the royals over the horizon." Martin pointed at Jackson going hand over hand up the shrouds. The American was reckoned to have the best eye for identifying ships—not just the rig but often the name as well.

104

Martin was excited, and so was Orsini, but both youngsters, the frigate's fourth lieutenant and the midshipman, had forgotten one thing: there was no war on. Three months ago, such a sighting would have meant sending the men to quarters, opening the magazine, wetting the decks and scattering sand over them, loading the guns, the surgeon setting out his instruments and the galley fire being doused. Now, it was peacetime. But Ramage saw Aitken and Southwick coming up to the quarterdeck, both aware there would be no action but both unable to break a habit—of a lifetime for Aitken, of many years for Southwick.

Ramage pulled out the brass eyepiece tube of his telescope, slid it back a fraction of an inch so that the focusing mark was against the end of the larger tube, and looked ahead, where by now he could see an occasional fleck of a sail as the *Calypso* rose on a swell wave. The other ship was not quite on an opposite course because the masts were not in line: she was steering to pass along the *Calypso*'s starboard side and, at a guess, pass perhaps a mile off.

No new private signals or challenges had been issued as a result of the Treaty; the only flags now to be routinely hoisted, apart from the colours, were the three from the numerary code giving the *Calypso*'s number in the List of the Navy. And they would be hoisted only to another British ship of war. Ramage saw that Orsini had the flags ready.

Ramage felt curiously naked and unprepared: never before had he sailed towards a ship of the line—he was fairly sure that was what she was—with no more preparation needed than making sure three flags were bent on to a halyard. He knew from the aimless way they were walking round the quarterdeck that Southwick and Aitken were having similar feelings.

"Deck there—Jackson here, sir."

Martin glanced at Ramage, who nodded to emphasize that the youngster was officer of the deck.

"Deck here—what d'you see?"

"Ship of the line, sir; British, may be the *Invincible*, and probably a private ship."

A private ship: Jackson could not make out an admiral's flag. With luck, the ship being so near home, she would pass with just a cheery signal, instead of heaving to and her captain ordering Ramage to report on board with his orders, and generally making the most of many years of seniority but knowing that, with Ramage sailing under Admiralty orders, he could not interfere in any way.

"Fetch Jackson down," Ramage murmured to Martin. The reason was mundane enough—the binnacle drawer had opened and slid out a couple of days ago and both telescopes in it had landed on the deck and cracked their object glasses. There were now only three working telescopes left on board—Ramage's own, the second that Martin had been using but had sent aloft with Jackson, and the third being used by Aitken.

When the American was down on deck again he said to Ramage: "She's been at sea a long time, sir; I had one last look as I came down and she and us lifted to waves together so I could see her hull as she rolled. Plenty of copper sheathing missing and her bottom green with weed. Topsides need work on them and her sails have more patches than original cloth."

"Probably coming home from India, and only had time to call at the Cape for water."

That remark, directed at Southwick, brought a knowing nod. "She won't want to delay us, then!"

There was nothing more irritating than having to heave to and launch a boat at the whim of a captain whose name was higher on the post list—particularly when the boats had been well secured for a long voyage.

The two ships were approaching quickly: Ramage guessed that the *Invincible*—if that was who she was—must be making ten knots, with a soldier's wind, and the *Calypso* a good seven. He looked again with his glass. Yes, he could make out the patched sails now and, as both ships rose on swell waves, saw what Jackson meant about the weed. She must be three or four miles away. Her masts were coming in line now—she was altering course to close with the *Calypso*. Perhaps she intended just asking for news. Ramage suddenly realized that if he had to board her he could take Robert Smith, landman, with him. The report to the Admiralty about the "chaplain" was already written; the letter needed only dating and sealing.

There was something very impressive about a ship of the line running dead before the wind: ahead of her the waves swept on in regular formation while she, her sails straining in elegant curves, seemed to curtsey as her stern lifted to a swell wave, her stem sliced up a sparkling bow wave and the whole ship seemed to rise with a massive eagerness until, the swell wave passing under her, she slowed and the whole process began again with the next wave.

And she was hoisting a lot of flags!

"Hoist our pendant numbers," Ramage snapped, "and stand by to answer some signals!"

Orsini now had Martin's telescope because he was responsible for signals.

"Well?" Ramage asked impatiently.

"I—I'm not sure, sir. Do we have the old signal book, sir?"

"Of course not. Why?"

"I think she's making an old challenge!"

"Rubbish! You'll say she's hoisted the private signal in a moment!"

"I think she has, sir," Orsini turned to Ramage. "My memory is not good, sir, but I'm sure that's one of the challenges for last July, and one of the sequence of private signals also for July. If she—"

Aitken interrupted, a note of urgency in his voice: "Sir, if you don't have the latest challenges and private signals, you use—in wartime—the ones for the same day but two months earlier!"

"We don't have the replies," Ramage said, thinking aloud. "All the books were returned to the Admiralty when the Treaty was signed."

Suddenly he felt chilled and swung his telescope to his eye again.

The *Invincible* was furling her royals and courses; in a few moments she would be sailing under topsails alone, the canvas for fighting. At that moment the *Invincible*'s starboard side, which he could see most clearly, had changed: the curving black tumblehome with its single white strake, greyed with dried salt, now had two gashes running parallel above and below the white strake: two dull red gashes where her gunports had suddenly been opened. And now, like ragged black fingers, her guns were being run out.

"She doesn't know the war is over!" Ramage exclaimed.

"And as far as she's concerned, we're a French frigate flying false colours and not answering the challenge," Aitken said.

"*Senta,*" Orsini murmured, "*siamo amici;* listen, we are friends."

For a moment Ramage stared at the approaching ship. Impressive, terrifying, majestic, irresistible...she was all of these things; he had the same view of her that a frog in a pond would have of an approaching swan. The *Calypso*'s magazine was still locked, the portlids still down, Bowen's surgical instruments stored in their chest—there was no war on, and the *Invincible* was British. In the *Invincible*, though, all her guns—32-pounders on the lowerdeck, 24-pounders on the maindeck, and 12-pounders and carronades on the upperdeck—were loaded and run out; the locks were fitted, the gun captains would be holding the trigger lanyards, crouched beyond the reach of the recoil, and the second captains would be waiting the word to cock the locks; the *Invincible*'s decks would be wet and covered with sand to prevent men slipping and soak up any spilled powder. The captain at this very moment must be preparing to luff up or bear away to bring one or other broadside to bear. And he must be surprised that the captain of the apparent French frigate had a strong enough nerve to trust his bluff with the false colours. One broadside from the *Invincible*, well aimed (as it must be, in such a comparatively calm sea, and the first broadside was usually the decisive one), would destroy the *Calypso*.

How, then, to prevent the *Invincible* from firing it?

Surprise...surprise...surprise...The word, which he had so often dinned into his officers, echoed like a flat note repeated on a pianoforte. How on earth did one surprise a 74-gun ship which was bearing down from to windward of an unprepared frigate, guns loaded and run out?

She was now barely half a mile away: as she rolled he could see black rectangles below the waterline where twenty or thirty sheets of copper sheathing were missing; the boats stowed on the booms were newly painted. The stitching of a seam was just beginning to go in the foretopsail; in ten minutes they would have to furl the sail for repairs—but ten minutes would be too late for the *Calypso* as she stretched along on the starboard tack. In a few minutes there would be roundshot as well as wind coming over the starboard side.

A glance forward showed the *Calypso* and the Calypsos utterly unprepared: forty or fifty men were standing by the bulwark, watching the ship of the line bearing down on them, but in the last moment or two they had realized the significance of the opened gunports. Aitken, Wagstaffe, Kenton, South-wick, Orsini, the Marine Renwick and even the surgeon Bowen, on the quarterdeck to watch the *Invincible* pass, and Martin on watch, stood as though paralysed: in a few minutes not one would be left alive; they would all be cut down by a hail of round and grapeshot.

Surprise: the unexpected: what could stop the *Invincible*'s broadsides? A sudden threat—but to what? Her masts and rigging...her bowsprit and jibboom?

"Ready ho, Mr Martin," Ramage suddenly bellowed, his voice carrying across the ship and turning every seaman's face up to the quarterdeck eagerly awaiting the order that might save their lives. "Orsini, a white sheet!" There would be no time to do anything with it, but...He continued the sail orders. "Put the helm down!... Quartermaster, the helm's a'lee, eh? Right, now men, raise tacks and sheets!"

To a stranger, the *Calypso*'s decks were chaos, with men running, hauling on ropes, glancing up at the trim of a sail, easing a sheet, hauling on a tack, hardening in a brace.

Ramage saw the *Invincible* appear to slide across from the *Calypso*'s starboard bow to her larboard; overhead canvas flogged as sails lost the wind. The frigate steadied as the quartermaster repeated a helm order from Martin.

The after sails had lifted, then he could see the wind was out of them. "Maintop bowline—haul it well taut..." Now the bow had passed through the eye of the wind. "Mainsail haul! Step lively men!" Ramage's throat was already sore and Southwick handed him the speaking trumpet.

Already, crashing and bumping as the wind filled the sails with a bang on the new tack, jerking yards and making ropes whiplash, the *Calypso* was beginning to pay off.

"Foretacks and head bowlines...haul taut!"

The *Calypso* was coming alive in the water again; he could hear the spilling water sound of her bow wave. The *Invincible* was—damnation, she was just abaft the *Calypso*'s beam and although still racing along she was simply turning a few degrees to bring her larboard broadside to bear, instead of her starboard. The *Calypso* had tacked too quickly. Very well!

"Ready ho!" Ramage bawled into the speaking trumpet. "Put the helm down!"

He saw the men spinning the wheel the other way again,

ready to turn the *Calypso* back in the direction from which she had just come.

"The helm's a'lee! Keep the foretopsail backed, men!"

The frigate swung back through the wind's eye so that the *Invincible* was almost ahead again.

"Put the helm up!" Ramage roared. "That's it, hold her there hove-to!"

Hurriedly he trimmed the main and mizen sails. The foretopsail had the wind blowing on its forward side, pressing sail and yard against the mast and trying to push the *Calypso*'s bow round to larboard, but the after sails, trimmed normally, were trying to push the bow to starboard.

Ramage gave a few more orders—bracing the foretopsail yard until it was sharp up, easing the helm slightly, letting fly one of the jibs—until the thrust trying to force the *Calypso*'s bow to larboard exactly equalled the thrust of the after sails trying to push it to starboard. Then the frigate was stopped, balanced on the water like a gull, all her sails set but none of them moving her.

Then he prepared to look round at the *Invincible*. Southwick, Aitken, and all the others in the ship not busy with heaving-to the frigate were already staring at her, and Ramage knew he had probably failed: first he had tacked the *Calypso* too quickly, giving the ship of the line plenty of time to bring her other broadside to bear; then he had taken too long to heave-to the frigate on the other tack: instead of stopping the *Calypso* a few ship's lengths in front of the *Invincible*, forcing the great ship into some violent manoeuvre to avoid ramming the frigate and probably sending at least her foremast by the board, it seemed he had left her just room to dodge and fire a raking broadside as she passed.

The distant rolling like thunder finally spurred Ramage to look: he was sure it was the rumble of broadsides but he could not believe that the *Invincible* could be so far away.

Not guns, he realized, but flogging canvas: faced with the *Calypso* suddenly heaving-to, the only way the *Invincible* could avoid a collision was to put her helm hard over and now, as she swung round, not fifty yards from the *Calypso*'s bow, every sail in the ship was flogging, the foretopsail ripping from head to foot.

And the muzzle of every gun in the *Invincible*'s starboard

broadside was pointing right at the *Calypso*. The *Invincible* was swinging fast and Ramage saw a group of officers on her quarterdeck staring across at the frigate. Then he saw they were in fact staring at Orsini, who was standing on the hammock nettings slowly waving a white sheet.

Suddenly and quite unaccountably angry at the group of men, Ramage ran to the bulwark and climbed up on to the nettings to windward of Orsini. He put the speaking trumpet to his mouth and screamed: "British ship! The war's over, you numskulls!"

He swung the speaking trumpet forward. "Come on, men, *sing!* 'Black-eyed Susan!'"

A moment later he was leading two hundred men as they bellowed the words which echoed across the sea to the *Invincible*, gradually bearing away now as she cleared the *Calypso* and slowly trimmed her sails.

"You can stow that sheet now," he said to Paolo. "Where on earth did you manage to find it so quickly?"

Paolo grinned as he folded it. "Your cabin was nearest, sir; it's from your cot! I'm afraid I tore it as I climbed up on the nettings."

"Did you, by Jove," Ramage said, for the moment finding his knees weak. Knowing that the strain was easing he wanted to giggle, and Paolo's apology, coming moments after the boy's signals had probably done more than anything to save the ship, could be enough to start him off.

CHAPTER NINE

"Look here, Ramage, I distinctly heard you call me a 'num-skull'," Captain William Hamilton protested querulously in a broad Scots voice. "'Numskull', you shouted, and every one of my officers heard you, too."

"Yes, sir, and I apologize: I was in a hurry when I spoke."

"I should think you were," Hamilton said, slightly mollified, and subsided into a chair, his lips drawn back to expose his teeth, reminding Ramage of a hissing snake. His complexion was purplish, his face narrow and the flesh sunken.

"I am twenty-eighth on the post list but you, Ramage, who aren't even named in *my* copy of the List, regard me as a 'numskull'."

"I've already apologized, sir: it was said in the heat of the moment. Now, sir, I must inform you that the war is over; we have signed a Treaty with Bonaparte and—"

"Silence!" roared Hamilton, half rising from his chair. "I won't listen to such nonsense! Here I have a man claiming to be a post captain, but whose name is not in my Navy List, coming on board from a French-built frigate and telling me that Mr Pitt has signed a Treaty with the enemy! Why—"

"I've been posted a year, sir; you have been in Indian waters a long time."

"And we all know captains serving in Indian waters for any length of time go off their heads, don't we, eh Ramage?"

The man's voice took on a slightly hysterical note, rising at the end of each sentence and emphasizing his Scots accent.

Lowland Scots, Aitken would pronounce with all the contempt of a Highlander.

"I didn't say that, sir: I'm trying to describe to you the terms of the new Treaty. If you wish to reassure yourself about me, you'll find me among the lieutenants in the Navy List you have."

"Ah, but how do I know you really *are* Ramage?" Hamilton's thin face now had the cunning look of a horsecoper, and then suddenly he grinned. "Very well, I believe you. Do you speak French?"

Ramage saw the trap. "Very little, sir; a few words."

"When was the Treaty signed?"

"The early part of October, sir."

"You tore my foretopsail," Hamilton said solemnly. "You must go and inspect it. They'll have sent it down by now."

"But sir—"

"Don't argue. Seeing a torn foretopsail is part of your training." He called to the sentry to pass the word for the first lieutenant, motioning Ramage to remain where he stood.

When the first lieutenant came into the cabin, Hamilton smiled amiably. "Ah, Todd, Mr Ramage was expressing interest in our torn foretopsail. Is it sent down yet? Ah, good: please take Mr Ramage to inspect it."

Ramage followed the obviously bewildered lieutenant out of the cabin and along the maindeck. The lieutenant was perhaps thirty years old, obviously once a burly man but now thin, the skin of his face seeming grey beneath the inevitable tan. He walked slightly bent, as though he had a painful stomach ulcer, and so far had not spoken a word.

As they reached the foremast, where one group of seamen were preparing to send-up a new topsail while others began stretching out the torn one on the deck, ready to repair it, Ramage realized that the lieutenant had not been present during the first conversation with Captain Hamilton.

"What is your name?" Ramage inquired.

"Todd, sir."

"Ah yes, I remember Captain Hamilton mentioning it. You'll be glad to get to Plymouth, I imagine."

"Yes, sir," Todd said tonelessly.

"You know the war is over, I suppose?"

"War? Finished, sir?"

The man looked at him like a starving man promised a meal.

"Yes, it's all finished: the one we've been fighting against the French—and the Spanish and the Dutch!"

"My God! So that was why—" Todd stopped abruptly and looked round, as though frightened someone could overhear.

"Bend down and inspect the tear with me," Ramage murmured. "Now listen carefully. You've another two or three days at sea before you reach Plymouth, perhaps more. Ships are coming out of the Chops of the Channel like sheep through a hole in the hedge. Ships of all nations . . ."

"I understand, sir," Todd murmured.

"You don't," Ramage said. "Captain Hamilton won't believe me when I tell him peace has been signed." "I *do* understand, sir," Todd said quietly. "I began to suspect peace had been signed because we saw two British merchant vessels sailing alone. The captain would not question them, but that was why you didn't get a broadside. I was certain you were British, so when we had to bear up to avoid hitting you, I pretended to mishear him when he gave the order to fire. I'm still under open arrest . . ."

Ramage bent down and hauled at a piece of canvas, inspecting the heavy cringle. "Is he mad?"

"Most of the time. Yet he'll go a couple of days with no trouble: laughing and joking, teasing his steward, an Irishman who stutters."

"Do you think you'll get to Plymouth without attacking another ship?"

"Not much chance," Todd said gloomily. "I'll warn the lookouts not to see too much: that might save us. Do you think he believed you about the Treaty?"

"No, but he's watching from the quarterdeck. Come here and inspect this cringle with me. You daren't confine him, eh?"

"Articles of war," Todd muttered. "He's not obviously mad—we officers would be brought to trial and on his good days any court would think he was sane."

"But supposing you sink a French merchant ship on the way home?"

"That'll be too bad, sir," Todd said. "If I confine the captain, they'll charge me under Articles Nineteen, Twenty and Twenty-two and Thirty-five; it'll be mutiny, and the penalty is death.

114

So let him kill a few Frenchmen instead. All I want is to get a berth in another ship."

Together they hauled a torn section of sail to one side and bent over again, inspecting the tear.

"I'll give you a letter addressed to the Board Secretary describing how he nearly sank my ship, and another letter outlining your dilemma. Listen carefully, because we must rejoin him in a couple of minutes. The second letter will cover you should you have to confine him: I shall say flatly that in my view he was insane when I saw him and that I'm prepared to give evidence in court to that effect. Obviously I can't supersede him because I lack the seniority. But I'll get both letters to you before we part company."

Todd nodded. "That should do it, sir. Your name'll carry weight. We've read about you in the *Gazette*."

"My officers will give evidence, too, if needed. I'll list them in my letter. And you'll have copies, too: they'll be marked. Don't mix them up."

"Sit down, sit down," Hamilton said. "Can I offer you refreshment? I have a good Madeira—shipped some when we called in. Damned customs fellows will be after me for duty, but it's worth it. Not many wines travel like a good Madeira."

Hamilton forgot his offer and Ramage was startled to see that the man, who had changed into another and newer uniform while he and Todd inspected the sail, had his feet encased in carpet slippers. When he saw Ramage looking at them he nodded and tapped the side of his nose with an index finger. "Gunpowder," he whispered. "These slippers don't make it explode if I tread on it. Leather-soled shoes would ignite it— and the whole ship could go up in one dreadful explosion."

"Indeed?" Ramage said politely. "I must get myself a similar pair."

"Yes, do, my dear fellow. I bought these in Calcutta. Anyone'll tell you where to go. 'Captain Hamilton's slippers wallah'—just ask, they all know. Now, tell me what's going on in London."

Ramage thought of his brief conversation with Todd. At the moment Hamilton was changing quickly from sanity to insanity, but it was almost uncanny how he could say something which was quite crazy yet make it sound perfectly normal. The

115

carpet slippers, for instance. There was no reason why a captain on board his own ship should not wear carpet slippers with his best uniform. His explanation would sound quite sane to a landman, and with his perfectly normal behaviour in every other respect, what court martial would believe a witness relating the gunpowder story? Hamilton would only have to mention corns or bunions and the slippers would seem perfectly normal.

"London—I was asking you about London, Ramage."

"Oh yes, indeed. Very quiet now—everyone that matters has gone off to France and Italy. A third of the peerage, I'm told."

"Indeed? Still, they haven't been able to visit Paris and Florence for years. The ladies want to see the new fashions, I suppose. Still, what's the news from the Admiralty?"

"Changes, of course. Lord St Vincent is the new First Lord, and there is a new Board."

"St Vincent? That was Sir John Jervis? What's he doing at the Admiralty? Pitt must be mad!"

"Mr Pitt is no longer the prime minister," Ramage said patiently. "Mr Addington has formed the new administration—"

"Addington? I don't believe a word of it!"

Hamilton stood up and jammed his hat on his head. He stared at Ramage and took a deep breath. "A court martial, Ramage, I shall ask for a court martial on you as soon as I reach England. Plenty of charges; oh, yes, plenty of charges."

"Indeed, sir?"

"Oh yes. Apart from the 'numskull', there will be—now, let me see. Negligently hazarding a King's ship. That will cover the way you risked the *Invincible*. The same charge concerning the *Calypso*. Cowardice, of course—"

"Cowardice?" Ramage exclaimed, hardly believing his ears. "When?"

"You were waving a white flag—surrendering your command to the enemy, and never a shot fired! Articles Twelve and Thirteen, 'In time of action keeping back', and—well, you know the wording well enough."

"Ah, indeed," Ramage said, determined to get back to the *Calypso* before this poor, crazy man did something absurd, like ordering his master-at-arms to arrest him.

116

"Now, Ramage, let me see your orders."

"They are sealed orders, sir. I have only general orders to take me south, and then I open sealed orders when south of ten degrees North."

"Give them to me: I can open them. All things are open to those with faith."

"They are locked up on board my ship, sir."

"Then go and unlock them, my boy," Hamilton said in a perfectly normal voice. "I must inspect them. One doesn't know *what* they might say."

He spoke as though the Admiralty's orders might contain obscene phrases that Ramage was too young to read.

Ramage nodded agreeably. "Yes, indeed sir, who knows. You may remember that when I first came on board I said the war with France was over—"

"Ah yes, so you did," Hamilton interrupted. "And if you don't refer to it again, I shan't mention it at your trial. But it is a clear breach of one of the Articles of War, number Three to be exact, 'If any officer shall give, hold or entertain intelligence with an Enemy...'"

Ramage would have agreed, in order not to provoke the man further, but the *Invincible* still had a couple of hundred miles to sail before she reached Spithead, during which time she could meet and sink a dozen French, Dutch or Spanish ships.

"Sir, I have something to say that I insist is heard by your first lieutenant and at least one other officer, either the second lieutenant or your master."

"My dear Ramage, by all means. Tell the sentry to pass the word for them. Now, may I once again offer you refreshment? As I told you, the Madeira is good, but I have spirits, a poor brandy or some of those Dutch East Indies drinks, all spices and perfume: what shall it be?"

Now Hamilton's voice was that of a good host: a rational man pleased at meeting another of the King's ships after a long period at sea.

Ramage examined the bottles as Hamilton displayed them, playing for time and trying not to refuse anything until the two officers arrived. A knock on the door and a call from the sentry showed both men had been waiting close by.

As soon as they came into the cabin, Hamilton nodded to

117

Todd and introduced the second lieutenant, smiling as though they were all about to sit down to a specially-prepared *rijstafel*.

"Gentlemen, Mr Ramage couldn't make up his mind what he wanted to drink, and asked me to send for you."

Todd glanced at Ramage, knowing that his captain could not see his face. It was obvious to Ramage that quite apart from Todd, the other lieutenant too was almost at the end of his rope: they had been serving many months under this mad captain. He looked at them both and said slowly and carefully: "I have made a statement to Captain Hamilton, and I intend repeating it before the two of you. I want you to remember word for word what I say."

Before he had time to speak again, Hamilton said in a conversational tone: "Yes, remember what he says, word for word, and remember the Articles of War, numbers Three, Twelve and Thirteen. I shall be bringing him to trial, of course, and we shall need all the evidence we can get."

"Aye aye, sir," Todd said.

"Now," Ramage continued, "a treaty of peace has been concluded between Britain and France. All hostilities have ceased—"

"Note well what he says," Hamilton commented. "A clear case of 'intelligence with the enemy'."

"—between Britain on the one hand and France, Spain and the Netherlands on the other. Now, repeat that."

Todd repeated it word for word, with Captain Hamilton beating time with his right hand.

As soon as the lieutenant finished, Ramage continued: "Ratifications have been exchanged and all fighting anywhere in the world shall cease within five months of that date, which was—"

"It's absolute rubbish," Hamilton interrupted, "but humour him: I've known these cases turn violent."

Ramage then took a folded newspaper from his pocket and gave it to the first lieutenant. "Your captain has refused to read this. It's a copy of the *Morning Post* and reports the exchange of ratifications."

It had been lucky that there was a copy on board the *Calypso*: Orsini had used several to pack some crockery he had brought back from London.

Todd nodded as he read and then passed it on to the other

lieutenant. When he was holding it again he said respectfully to Captain Hamilton: "There are various interesting items here, sir. The parliamentary news, for instance. You were worrying about your constituency . . ."

So Hamilton was a Member of Parliament. He must be one of those Members who occasionally visited Westminster with a sprig of heather in their hair and salt staining the leather of their boots.

"I may not still be a Member," he said irritably. "The government could have fallen and new elections been called. No letters for nearly a year . . . who knows *what* has happened. Still, Lord Spencer will put everything right."

Before he could stop himself, Ramage said: "I've just told you, the present First Lord is St Vincent: Addington became prime minister when Pitt resigned."

Hamilton looked at him as a hostess might stare unbelievingly at a guest wiping dirty boots on her best Persian carpet. "Addington? St Vincent? You'll soon be telling me that Jenks is Secretary of State!"

Ramage sighed and took back the newspaper, which referred to Lord Hawkesbury and Otto conducting negotiations. "Captain Hamilton, you will not accept anything I say and refuse to look at this copy of the *Morning Post*, which refers to negotiations with the French conducted by Jenks. However, I must delay you no longer, sir: I shall make an entry in my log concerning our encounter, note that I informed you in front of your two most senior lieutenants that the war is over and attempted to show you a newspaper, which I am giving to your first lieutenant. I must ask you to wait while I write a letter for the Board. I will send it over as soon as it is written."

"Stop him!" Hamilton said excitedly, "he's under an arrest!"

Todd did not move and the second lieutenant stopped after taking two steps.

Ramage heard Todd ask conversationally: "Should I pipe hands to dinner, sir, or would you prefer that we should get under way first?"

At once Hamilton stopped, his brow wrinkled. "Why are we hove-to?" he inquired.

"We are receiving an extra man from a frigate, sir, a seaman Smith," Todd said, "and we are waiting for letters."

CHAPTER TEN

As the *Calypso* stretched southwards towards the invisible lines round the globe marking the Tropics and the Equator, Ramage was surprised to see how many ships were at sea. While tacking across the mouth of the Bay of Biscay, from Ushant to the Spanish Cabo Finisterre, still marked on the British charts by the French spelling, it had been easy to guess the ports for which merchant ships had been bound.

Few made for Brest because it was primarily a naval port, but several were probably heading for the mouth of the Seine with a following wind, hoping to catch the first of the flood to take them up to Honfleur and Rouen. Three outward bound had obviously left Bordeaux and were working their way out of the Bay with a steady westerly wind in several long tacks.

As the *Calypso* sailed down the Spanish and Portuguese coast, just in sight of the high land, they could tick off the ports simply by watching the sails of ships arriving and departing: Vigo and Oporto had been followed by an increase in numbers as they approached Lisbon and the wide but treacherous entrance to the Tagus. Many ships passed inshore as the land trended away to the eastward, curving round from Cape St Vincent to Lagos, the Rio Tinto, Cadiz, Cape Trafalgar and sharply to the Strait of Gibraltar.

"Amazing," Southwick commented as he replaced his old but carefully preserved quadrant in its brass-cornered mahogany box. "Half a dozen ships always in sight. In the war—surprising how long ago that seems now: all of three months,

I suppose—one passed a convoy of a hundred ships, and then saw nothing for a couple of weeks. Now, the same number of ships sailing independently means you're likely to see seven a day in the Atlantic. Many more along the coasts, of course."

For young officers like Kenton, Martin and Orsini, Ramage's deliberate tack in towards Lisbon and the Tagus had given them not only their first sight of the Portuguese capital—a view which might come in very useful in future because, as Southwick commented, one look is worth two charts—but their first look at local coasting craft.

Martin had at once compared the graceful fregatas with Thames barges, and was soon in an argument about them with Kenton and Paolo. Both types of vessel were built for the same function—to carry bulky cargoes up rivers and for short distances along the coasts. The fregatas had apple-cheeked bows and were gaily painted, often with an ancient eye painted on each side. The mast was stepped well forward but raked aft at a considerable angle like a hurricane-swept tree so that the masthead was over the cargo hatch. Nor was this a coincidence—a heavy tackle at the masthead made it easy to use the mast to hoist up the cargo, and another tackle hauled it over the side and on to the quay. The sails were loose footed and limited in size. The Thames barge, Kenton was quick to point out, was just a large box: it had none of the graceful curves of the fregata.

The practical Martin asked the obvious question: given a vessel of, say, eighty feet in length, what did you want: beauty or cargo space? It was almost impossible, he declared, to have both. With her flat bottom, straight sides, bluff bow and almost vertical stern, a Thames barge could use every possible inch for cargo. She hoisted the head of her great mainsail up the mast, and then extended the other corner with a long sprit, so that for a given length of vessel, a Thames barge could set half as much again more canvas than a fregata. And with her flat bottom, the keel in effect on the inside of the hull, she could carry a cargo up the River Crouch, the Medway, the Colne, Orwell, Yare—not to mention the Thames and the Rother and dozens of places in the Solent—and dry out to sit on the bottom when the tide left. *That* often meant, said Martin triumphantly, that the cargo could be unloaded directly into carts because the horses could come over the sand.

121

"Or get stuck in the mud," Kenton said, waving aside Orsini's claims for the polacca of the Mediterranean. The argument was stopped when Southwick pointed out that not one of their noon sights agreed with another. "According to Mr Kenton we must have made one great sternboard since noon yesterday, because he puts us so far north; Mr Martin would have us believe we've been making seventeen knots for the past twenty-four hours; and Mr Orsini must be teasing us."

Gradually the latitude and longitude columns in Ramage's journal began to change radically. The longitude started off from a few minutes of arc east of Greenwich, because the *Calypso* had sailed from the Medway, crossing the meridian while passing westward just south of Newhaven and Rottingdean. Since then the longitude had increased as they slanted southwest while the latitude grew less. Thirty-six degrees North showed they were level with the Strait of Gibraltar; thirty-five meant they were almost as far south as Rabat and bearing away to the southwest for Madeira, having completely failed to find the northeast trades which should have hurried the *Calypso* down the Portuguese coast.

And at last it was getting warmer. For the time being the sun was brighter rather than hotter, but the sea was certainly not so cold and Ramage slept with the skylights propped open.

Ramage enjoyed and re-lived his own first voyage into the Tropics by seeing it through the eyes of Wilkins. The present voyage must be the fifth or sixth that would take him across that magic latitude, twenty-three degrees thirty-three minutes, which marked the Tropic of Cancer, the northern limit of the band circling the earth like a cummerbund and called the "Tropics".

Wilkins, his blond hair blowing in the trade winds, his blue eyes rarely still for a moment, was looking at the flowing waves, the sky dappled by trade wind clouds, the *Calypso*'s sail, her deck, the movement of the men.

His first attempt to paint on deck had been disastrous: he was just settling down with brushes and palette, having drawn in with a few swift charcoal strokes the curve of the mainsail, when the combination of a lurch to leeward and a sudden puff of wind caught his canvas. The wooden frame of the stretcher hooked in his easel as it blew away and in a moment both had gone over the side, leaving a startled Wilkins still sitting on his folding stool, brush in one hand and the palette and more brushes in the other.

Ramage had run to the ship's side and seen that the easel, heavy with metal fittings, had sunk. To his surprise the seamen who had seen the accident were even more upset than Wilkins. Instead of laughing at the sight of the artist sitting on his stool apparently working on an invisible canvas, they had offered to get some more canvas from the sailmaker. Then, catching Ramage's eye and correctly interpreting the nod, the *Calypso*'s carpenter had gone up to Wilkins and asked for a sketch of an easel with dimensions, promising a replacement by the evening in bare wood, but tomorrow evening with two coats of varnish.

While he waited for the carpetner and his mates to produce a new easel, Wilkins talked to Ramage of his plans.

"The amazing thing is," he said, "that in the last few days my entire world has changed. For the whole of my life the sea has been various shades of green, even though poets insist on calling it blue. The sky has been a pale blue, as weak in colour as the shell of a duck's egg.

"Now, as we've come south and into this good weather, just look: the sea *is* a deep blue, the sky an exciting blue, the trade wind clouds *are* just the funny shapes you predicted."

Ramage had earlier tried to describe the day's routine at sea in the Tropics but Wilkins, looking at the Channel off Ushant, had not really believed him. The day, Ramage had predicted, would begin with dawn revealing a band of cloud on the eastern horizon which, as the sun was behind it, would be menacing. Then, as the sun climbed higher the band would disappear and the sky clear.

By nine or ten o'clock, there would be an occasional tiny cloud, like white blanket fluff; within half an hour more would be gradually forming into narrow columns, like marching men, and all borne westward by the trade wind, which would be increasing as the sun rose. Although it was an optical illusion the clouds would seem to be converging on a single point on the western horizon, and each would be changing shape until the underside was flat but the upper part would turn into a strange shape. To Ramage and to Wilkins when he first saw them they looked like the white alabaster effigies he had seen on tombs: a recumbent knight in armour, feet sticking up at one end, head complete with visor, at the other. There might

123

be one which clearly represented a woman. Then Wilkins was spotting faces: just the profile staring up into the sky as though its owner was lying flat on an invisible bed.

The first real day of trade wind clouds had Wilkins, the botanist Garret and Ramage vying with each other to spot and then identify the faces of well-known figures. Wilkins swore he could see the head of Sir William Beechey, the artist, but both Ramage and Garret protested they did not know what he looked like. They all agreed on the Prince Regent, followed ten minutes later by the bloated face of Dundas. Neither Ramage nor Wilkins could give a verdict on Garret's recognition of Arthur Young, the Secretary of the Board of Agriculture, but all three soon spotted Evan Nepean, the Secretary to the Board of Admiralty.

A delighted Wilkins then spotted Southwick's profile and the master, made to hurry on deck, claimed the cloud flattered him.

Wilkins, continuing his survey of the voyage so far through an artist's eyes, had one complaint. "You say the sea and sky will get much more blue before we reach our destination, but who in England will believe me if I paint what I see *now?* I hadn't realized how few of my fellow artists ever travelled south of Rome—and many, like me, haven't been able to set foot on the Continent yet because of the war. I have seen many paintings of subjects like a 'Frigate action off Martinique', or 'The Battle of the Saints'—they are islands nearby, are they not? The sea and the sky look like the Channel or North Sea: look like the sea should look—or so I thought. Now I realize that those artists had never seen tropical seas and skies; they were painting actions as described by individual captains, who would make sure the naval details were correct—the position of ships, the rigging, and so on. But they never told the artists—or the artists would not believe—the colours. Why, just look at that row of fire buckets—have you ever seen polished leather look so rich in England? The canvas of the sails—white be damned; just look at how much raw umber and burnt sienna there is. I'll show you when I mix some colours.

"Gaudy, my dear sir, what's what the Tropics are, and I love them: colours are beginning to *live!*"

"For real colour you should see the West Indies," Ramage said. "The colour of the sea over a coral reef—light blue that

124

seems alive, or a pale green like silk. The colours of the black women's dresses: they take three pieces of cloth of unbelievable gaudiness, put them on their bodies and on their heads, and seem more fashionable than milady riding in Rotten Row."

Ramage was sitting at his desk looking through the journals kept by Kenton, Martin and Orsini. They were supposed to be diaries of happenings on board the ship, with navigational facts, descriptions of "any unusual events" and sketches of any coasts the *Calypso* passed. Kenton and Martin were, for practical purposes, almost illiterate, and Orsini was lazy. Kenton and Martin had gone to sea at an early age; they could knot and splice, box the compass, load a cannon and fire a musket at an age when most boys on land were still scared of the dark, but they could not parse a sentence and even now would not know what to do with an adverb. Paolo's ruthless tutors at home in Volterra made sure he had a remarkable knowledge of grammar, so he spoke English, French and Spanish fluently, as well as Italian. This was normal for most intelligent aristo-crats. Paolo's trouble was sheer laziness and almost a *nostalgie de la boue* for the rougher side of seamanship. He preferred rope-work to navigation; he would sooner paint Stockholm tar on to rigging than study elementary ballistics. He picked up a pen with the same reluctance other men might grasp a smoking grenade.

It was curious how three clever, perceptive young men could fail to see—or, rather, to note—interesting events. A few days ago several whales were sighted, some young ones among them; last Sunday a school of dolphins played under the bow for hours like huge joyful children; on Monday seamen towing a huge hook caught a large shark and the task of killing it after it had been hoisted on board had made the decks run with blood—more blood than had ever flowed in battle. And the next day there had been a tropic bird.

For Ramage there were five things that he would always remember about the West Indies—the Tropics, in fact—even if he never visited them again: tropic birds, flying fish, blue sea, pelicans and palm trees. This tropic bird, the first of the voyage, had come up from the east, alone, passed high over the ship with a casual elegance, and flown on to the west— where the nearest land was nearly three thousand miles away.

It was not a big bird but a striking one—all white with a very long forked tail. In fact the tail was three or four times longer than the bird—V-shaped like a swallow's, and very thin, as though each part comprised a single feather.

But there was no mention of whales, shark, dolphins or tropic bird in any of the journals. They were accepted like sunshine and squalls as part of a daily routine. How did one make people aware of their surroundings?

Ramage was just closing the last journal when the sentry at the door called: "Mr Southwick, sir."

The master came in, a cheerful grin on his sunburned face, his white hair now greasy because of the water shortage, and put a slip of paper on Ramage's desk. Usually he brought down the slate on which he had written the noon position, and the use of a piece of paper made Ramage look carefully at the figure.

The longitude was of course west of Greenwich and in the thirties, but the latitude stood out as though Southwick had written it in large figures: 9° 58′ 12″. The *Calypso* was now south of ten degrees North!

Ramage looked up at the old master and smiled. "So we've crossed our own personal Equator! Pass the word for Mr Aitken while I find my keys. Time to break the seals!"

By the time the first lieutenant arrived in the cabin, Ramage had unlocked the drawer and taken out the packet with its four seals, each bearing the three anchors symbol of the Admiralty. It was addressed to him and bore the instructions: "Not to be opened until south of the 10th parallel of latitude."

It was far more exciting for Aitken and Southwick because Lord St Vincent had already told Ramage the *Calypso*'s final destination although he had been unable to mention it to anyone else.

Ramage slid a paperknife under the seals, levered them up and opened the letter, which comprised two sheets of paper folded into three, the two ends then being folded inwards and a seal applied to each corner of the flaps. In the top right-hand corner was the usual "By the Lords Commissioners of the Admiralty..." Then the elegant copperplate opened in the time-honoured way: "I am directed by my Lords Commissioners of the Admiralty to acquaint you..." He continued reading to himself.

Having resumed command of the *Calypso* frigate after her refit, and received on board the extra provisions, stores and equipment listed in the margin of the second page, and having received on board the supernumeraries also listed on the second page and . . . Ramage stopped: the habit of making a letter one long sentence, a series of statements linked by "and" and "whereas" was both confusing and tiring to read. Very well, now the *Calypso* is south of ten degrees North and the orders are opened.

You will make the best of your way to the Ilha da Trinidade situate to the best of our knowledge in 20° 29' South latitude and 29° 20' West longitude, or thereabouts, and upon arriving there you will take possession of the island in the King's name and erect plaques permanently recording the fact and recording your name and that of the ship and the date.

You will then cause the island to be surveyed and mapped, with particular concern for the watering places, and any sheltered bays suitable for use as anchorages should be sounded and proper charts drawn.

If wells are necessary they should be bored and lined with brick by the masons you carry; the botanist should choose and mark suitable land for the planting of maize, Irish potatoes and sweet potatoes. This land should be cleared, dug, prepared and sown under his instructions.

The surveyors, with the Marine officer, should pay particular attention to siting batteries to cover the main anchorages and the watering places, and those batteries should be built as expeditiously as possible. Appropriate magazines and kitchens should also be built.

He glanced up at Aitken and Southwick, both of whom were controlling their impatience. He resumed reading to himself.

If the island proves suitable, a signal station should be established which will also serve as a lookout tower, permitting an all-round view.

Having surveyed the island and its anchorages, provided it with batteries and a signal station, ensured a ready supply of water and planted the crops you are carrying, and having taken possession of the island in the King's name and leaving a Union flag flying at the signal station or lookout tower, you will return with your ship to the United Kingdom and report to their Lordships in detail and without delay upon your proceedings.

No surprises then, simply more details. Ramage turned to Southwick and, with a straight face said: "Well, you take us to twenty degrees, twenty-nine minutes South, and twenty-nine degrees, twenty minutes West, and anchor as convenient."

"Do I, by Jove," Southwick said, his brow wrinkled as he worked out the position. "Fernando de Noronha? No, too far south. It's about a thousand miles east of Rio de Janeiro, isn't it sir? It'll be rather deep for anchoring..."

Aitken's eyes were shut as he searched his memory and looked at an imaginary chart. St Paul's Rocks... no, they were north of Fernando de Noronha. Twenty north—that must be about the same as Rio de Janeiro—ah! "Abrolhos Rocks!" he said triumphantly; they were a hundred miles or so off the Brazilian coast.

Ramage shook his head.

"Martin Vaz island!" Southwick exclaimed. "Although how we'll find it I don't know; enough people have looked."

Again Ramage shook his head and told a crestfallen Southwick: "You are close. Ilha da Trinidade, which is nearby."

Southwick sniffed and Ramage recognized the sound as expressing the master's contempt. "How big is it?"

Ramage shrugged his shoulders. "Big enough to show on a chart; small enough, I suspect, to miss on a hazy day. I trust our chronometer is behaving itself."

"It didn't like those couple of months in England any more than I did," Southwick grumbled. "My rheumatism was playing up, and so was the chronometer."

"Might one ask why we...?" Aitken ventured, tactfully tapering off the sentence.

"No one can leave the ship before we arrive, so there's no reason why the pair of you don't read my orders," Ramage said, sliding them across the desk at the first lieutenant.

Aitken was halfway down the first page when he said: "We *claim* it? Who owns it now?"

128

"Let Southwick read it, then we can go over the questions together."

Aitken finished the first page and then ticked off the items listed on the second page. He knew all about them, and his curiosity why one of the King's ships should be carrying bricks, plasterers' tools, spades, rakes and hoes, sacks of seed potatoes and grain as well as surveying equipment was now satisfied.

Southwick read, folded the orders and gave them back to Ramage. "Whatever it is," he said slowly, "don't let's forget that the Ilha da Trinidade lies beyond the Doldrums . . . At this time of the year we could take weeks to cross them."

"The Spanish aren't very original about names are they?" Aitken complained. "There's the big island of Trinidad at the entrance to the Caribbean, a city in Cuba and I seem to remember seeing a reference to another island with that name off Bahia Blanca, three hundred miles or so south of Buenos Aires."

"There'll be more," Southwick commented. "It's like Santa Cruz. When in doubt the Dons call a place either Santa Cruz or Trinidad."

"This one was named by the Portuguese," Ramage said.

Southwick sniffed again. "Not much difference, except the language. Maybe the Portuguese are better sailors." He thought for a few moments and then amended his remark. "They were, a couple of centuries ago, but not now. But if they named the island I presume they own it."

"I've no idea what the legal position is except that Trinidade is not mentioned in Bonaparte's treaty. Nor are many other islands, I suppose, but Trinidade is the one that interests their Lordships. Anyway, we are to take possession and plant. The potatoes and grain will run wild, but they'll seed so that in an emergency a visiting ship will find something. If it looks a promising place it might even become a minor Ascension."

"But anyone could seize it after we've gone, sir!" Southwick protested.

"Orders," Ramage said. "We obey them. I could think of worse. It's a cruise, really. But I imagine that if I return and report that Trinidade will make a good base, their Lordships— the government anyway—will send a garrison. If the batteries are built by us, a passing John Company ship on her way to

India could land the guns and gunners and a battalion of infantry."

Aitken asked, "Do the government think of this island as a place for the Honourable East India Company ships to call for water in an emergency?"

"I don't really know," Ramage admitted. "It's rather far to the west for ships bound to and from the Cape of Good Hope and India. More likely their Lordships have in mind a wooding-and-watering island which a British squadron covering the South American coast could use. Somewhere they can refit, get fresh vegetables, land any sick . . . Seven hundred and fifty miles southwest to Rio, six hundred and fifty miles northeast to Bahia, and just over fifteen hundred to the mouth of the Plate."

"And two thousand across to the West African coast," Southwick said. "This place begins to sound interesting. But why has no one garrisoned it before? After all, it sits astride the South Atlantic like a jockey on a nag."

"Well, the Spanish and Portuguese don't need it because they share all the ports from one end of South America to the other," Ramage pointed out. "The French are really only concerned with the West Indies and India, and anyway the Dons are their allies so they can always use places like Rio—even though it is Portuguese—and the Plate for provisioning and watering. Only Britain needs bases to attack South America and cover the route to the Cape and India."

"How big is it? How high, rather?" Southwick asked.

"No one was very sure at the Admiralty, but as far as I could discover it's roughly a couple of miles long in a northwest, southeast direction, a mile wide and with hills in the middle a thousand feet high."

"A thousand feet, sir? We can rely on that?"

"We can't rely on anything. Mr Dalrymple at the Hydrographic Office admitted he knew nothing much about it—he just warned me not to hit Martin Vaz, which is either a tiny island or a reef of rock's a day's sailing from it."

"Once we're through the Doldrums, we'll get a lift to the westward from the current," Southwick commented. "But just think of it, once we make a landfall we go on shore to plant potatoes . . . I hate gardening," he admitted, "but it'll make a change to carry a spade and not a sword!"

* * *

The Doldrums had been empty days when the *Calypso* sat dead on the water, the heat haze merging sea, horizon and sky into what seemed to Wilkins a pool of molten copper. It was a time when he wanted to paint, wanted to capture on canvas the sense of the empty vastness of the ocean when there was no wind, where the sails were furled on the yards because there was no point in leaving them chafing against masts and rigging with every movement of the ship. Some days there was a slight swell, and Captain Ramage said it was caused by some distant storm, probably several thousands of miles away. He wanted to put it on canvas, but the sun was too hot. Even under the awning stretched across the quarterdeck it was an oven which sapped everyone's energy. Tempers were fraying and the sentry on the scuttlebutt watched closely as a man dropped in the dipper and took a drink.

The sheer stark simplicity of the life fascinated Wilkins. The intense heat, the lack of wind, and the fact that the *Calypso* was taking twice as long as expected to get through the Doldrums meant the men were twice as thirsty but had only half the water. It was interesting that the men had a basic ration, but in addition some extra was put into a butt each day and this was left by the mainmast with a Marine sentry guarding it.

And there was a dipper, a cylindrical, open-topped container, the diameter of a broom handle and about four inches long. There was a hole on each side of the top through which the line threaded, and a man was allowed to drop the dipper down through the bunghole and draw out as much water as it would hold. But because when there was a water shortage the butt was stowed on its side with chocks, the dipper usually tilted before it could fill completely. And the Marine sentry made sure that it was "one man, one dip".

Still, Wilkins had made up his mind about the colours, sketched in the outlines on the canvas with charcoal, and was ready when the first teasing but cooling puffs of wind had come. First of all there had been an excited hail from a lookout at the masthead—a man perched in what looked like an open-sided tent with strips of canvas to protect him from the rays of the sun. "Wind shadow on the larboard quarter!" he had shouted. A couple of minutes later he reported it was approaching, but, just as suddenly, it vanished. Five minutes later another, also on the larboard quarter, reached the ship, a wind shadow that danced across the surface of the sea like a swarm of gnats on the edge of a pond. Suddenly they all had a teasing breath of cool air, but then it was gone.

Yet Mr Ramage was quite confident the wind would set in: topmen swarmed aloft to drop the sails—"let fall", rather. And by then more wind shadows were being reported, the men becoming excited, and he was hurriedly mixing paints on his palette, the sudden breeze blowing away the lethargy. Now they were at last in the southeast trade winds which Southwick said started off down towards the Cape of Good Hope.

Crossing the Equator a few days later was best forgotten as far as Wilkins was concerned: Neptune had dozens of victims because the *Calypso* had spent most of her time in the Caribbean or Mediterranean, and few men had crossed the Line. So the unlucky ones were given stiff "tonics" of soap and water, shaved, ducked and five men, who had objected violently, were ordered by King Neptune to be tarred and feathered. Three others had their faces and backsides given a liberal coating of black gun lacquer.

Wilkins found it hard to get used to the sun's position. It was sufficiently late in the year and they were far enough south for the sun to be almost vertically overhead, so his shadow at noon was tiny, extending only a few inches from his feet, as though he was standing in a small puddle. Flying fish skimming just above the waves like great dragonflies had been common-place for a long time and although the *Calypso* was now almost midway between West Africa and South America, he was surprised by how many sea birds they saw. He had painted some of them, putting the date and position on the back of the canvas. He enjoyed painting birds in flight because it gave him good practice at painting the sea—surely the most challenging of all subjects. It was never the same, varying with the wind, cloud, sun, or rain, and, according to the captain, with the depth of the ocean and the latitude. At Trinidade, their destination, the captain promised that if there were reefs, he would see three or four different colours in as many hundreds of yards. For the moment, though, everyone was relieved that they were now in the southeast trades.

Now Southwick, legs astride and balancing himself against

the gentle roll, flipped down one more shade of his quadrant because he found the sun bright, once again "brought the sun down to the horizon", rocked the quadrant slightly to make sure that the lower edge of the sun was precisely on the horizon, made a slight adjustment and a moment later saw the sun had moved. He read the figures on the ivory scale of the quadrant. The ritual of the noon sight was, as far as the sun was concerned, now over: he had measured the highest angle that it made with the horizon, and that was that: only the angle mattered, not the time: if he had measured its highest angle, then that was the angle at noon local time, and he did not have to bother to turn a half-minute glass, bellow at Orsini to note the chronometer... Now he had to apply some corrections, add or subtract figures from the almanac, and the answer would be the *Calypso*'s latitude. It was the simplest thing to do in celestial navigation; it was how the navigators from the oldest times crossed oceans—they knew the latitude of their destination and sailed along it until they arrived. The only danger was running into the land at night. Longitude was a different problem; without an accurate chronometer there was no way of being sure of one's exact distance east or west of the Greenwich meridian.

Young Orsini was working out his answer using the top of the binnacle box. Kenton and Martin were sitting on the breeches of guns. Southwick could see Mr Ramage walking up and down on the windward side of the quarterdeck, having his spell of exercise before his meal. And waiting to hear the latitude... Normally Mr Ramage left the navigation to him, but for the last three days he had been taking a close interest. The reason was not hard to guess—the *Calypso*'s latitude and longitude were almost the same as the figures they had been given for Trinidade.

In fact, according to Southwick's reckoning, they were within a hundred miles of it. Allowing for the chronometer being a bit out, he was sure that putting the point of a pair of compasses down on Trinidade and drawing a circle with a radius of fifty miles would enclose the *Calypso*, but there was a high haze, so it was impossible to guess whether they could see ten miles or sixty.

This was always the difficult time when making a landfall: did one set more canvas to increase speed in the hope of sighting land before nightfall, or go slowly and cautiously and hope to sight it at dawn? Martin Vaz should be on the larboard bow and Trinidade dead ahead. If one left Martin Vaz too far to larboard—thus making absolutely certain of not hitting it— there was a risk of passing Trinidade out of sight to larboard. The life of a master in the Royal Navy, Southwick thought to himself, could be summed up by that situation: trying to find one rock in the middle of an ocean without hitting another . . .

He wrote the final row of figures, $20° 01' 50''$. And that, he knew without looking it up, was within thirty miles of the latitude of Trinidade.

A cast of the log half an hour ago had given just over six knots and they were able to lay the course. By five o'clock they might be there; it should be in sight at the latest in an hour or two—if it was as high as reported and the chronometer was anywhere near passing for correct.

Southwick walked across the quarterdeck and reported to Ramage, who grimaced and nodded ahead. "A thousand or fifteen hundred feet high? We should be seeing it by now."

"It's hazier than it looks, sir," Southwick said confidently. "Had you given any thought about who might . . ."

"All right, all right, pass the word through the bosun. Though why I should always pay up a guinea to the first man to sight such a place, I don't know!"

"It's the trickiest landfall we've ever made, sir. The Atlantic is 2,500 miles wide here, from Trinidade to the nearest tip of West Africa, and we're looking for somewhere two or three miles long."

"That's a fine argument to impress old ladies," Ramage said unsympathetically, "and it'd impress me if I thought Trinidade could lie anywhere along that gap of 2,500 miles. But you have a quadrant, almanac, tables and a chronometer that allow you to be rather more precise."

"Well, yes sir," Southwick agreed and added with a grin, "but I can't make it seem too easy!"

He walked back to the binnacle to inspect the calculations made by the two young lieutenants and midshipman.

He looked first at Orsini's slate and his brow furrowed. "I can assure you, Mr Orsini, that the *Calypso* is about seven hundred and fifty miles from Rio de Janeiro; in other words, about four fifths of the way across the South Atlantic between the Cape of Good Hope and South America, not far from the tropic of Capricorn. But you, Mr Orsini, seem to be not only north of the Equator, almost on the far side of the Torrid Zone, but close to the Cape Verde Islands, which the rest of us left thousands of miles away some weeks ago..."

Orsini, his face crimson, hurriedly rubbed out some writing on his slate and corrected it. "The latitude is north, not south. I'm sorry, I mean, I should have named it south, not north."

Southwick grumbled and picked up Martin's slate. He put it down again. "Lieutenant Martin has made a mathematical discovery of note: three and two make four. Well, the rest of us will continue to struggle along with five. And Mr Kenton? Ah, the method of calculation is correct, but the original altitude is wrong. Check your sextant, Mr Kenton; I suspect you have knocked it and it now has an error."

Ramage had listened to this daily routine for weeks and it varied little: Orsini made some enormous mistake that was due to lack of interest in mathematics; Martin made some silly mistake; and Kenton worked out the sight correctly but had been careless with his sextant. It was almost new, and one of the few sextants on board: Southwick and Aitken used quadrants.

Yet Southwick was right to keep nagging these young officers. One of them might be in command of a prize one day when war broke out again and responsible for navigating her thousands of miles to port, or even to a rendezvous at a place like Trinidade...

The lookout's hail came at exactly at three o'clock in the afternoon; his shout was partly drowned as six bells was being struck.

There was, he called, what might be only a cloud on the horizon but it was a different shape from the trade wind clouds and seemed to be lying athwart their course.

An excited Orsini asked "May I, sir?" and, when Ramage nodded, grabbed a telescope and raced up the shrouds, climbing the ratlines as fast as any topman.

He braced himself beside the lookout and glanced ahead as he pulled open the telescope. Low on the horizon there was something the colour of a fading bruise.

He held up the telescope, balancing against the *Calypso*'s roll and focused his eye in the circle of glass. It was land. As the lookout had said, it was athwart the *Calypso*'s course, probably lying northwest and southeast. Low at each end and rising towards the middle. There were some peaks in the centre of the island—he counted four which seemed the same height and a fifth quite a bit lower. It sounded like Trinidade, but where was Martin Vaz Rocks?

"Deck there!" he hailed. "It's land lying across our course and I can distinguish five peaks in the centre part of the island."

"How far?" Aitken shouted.

"Difficult to say, sir; there's nothing to use as a scale. Fifteen miles, I reckon; I think haze must have been hiding it, then the wind cleared it away."

Paolo felt like saying that even at this distance it looked like an island off Tuscany; cliffs with rounded hills just inland. Mr Ramage would understand—but so many islands in the West Indies looked like Tuscany, too, and neither of them wanted to be reminded that it would be months before they were back in England and receiving news of Aunt Gianna.

Down on deck Aitken and Ramage, using the only two other telescopes, sighted the island at the same moment.

"I don't know what happened to Martin Vaz," Ramage said, "but that must be Trinidade. We'll pass round the southern end to the lee side, so that we can run down the west coast."

"Supposing we don't find an anchorage, sir?"

"Then we'll be wasting our time, because the whole reason for taking the island will be gone."

What Ramage did not say was that he had been thinking a great deal about that very point, which was not covered by his orders. He knew that the Admiralty's only interest in Trinidade was as a base, and a base meant a safe bay in which ships could anchor, and with fresh water available on shore, from a river or wells. It had not occurred to their Lordships that there might be neither, although, to be fair, many ships had visited the island in the last hundred years. Presumably if they had found neither anchorage nor water they would have reported the fact: no one looked for either at Martin Vaz.

But supposing . . . Well, he could do one of two things: first he could say: "This island is no use to anyone" (after having put landing parties on shore to be certain about water) and return to the United Kingdom, calling in at one of the South American ports for water before crossing the Doldrums again. That would mean the *Calypso* would stay less than a week.

The alternative was to do a survey of the island anyway, plant the vegetables on the basis that although there was no river there was sufficient rain, and make soundings so that their Lordships at least had a record of the island, even if it was no good to them. That would take a couple of months, perhaps longer, and he might return to England to find that their Lordships considered he had wasted their time and his own.

Although Aitken had just raised the point, Ramage had made up his mind three or four weeks ago, when he first thought of the possibilities: he would survey, sound and plant, even if the *Calypso* could not anchor and had to back and fill in the lee of the island for as long as it took. Two months backing and filling . . . if he was more sure of the situation in Rio it would have been worth landing a survey and planting party on the island, leaving them with a couple of boats, and taking the *Calypso* on a visit to Rio—or even up to Bahia, which was nearer—where he could also provision and water.

As he looked over the quarterdeck rail Ramage saw the surveyors and draughtsmen standing on top of the hammock nettings, eager for a sight of the island that would comprise their world for several weeks. Indeed, the *Calypso* at the moment looked far removed from a ship of war.

There were ten or eleven of Wilkins's canvases lodged in various places on deck, to help the oil paints to dry, and his new easel was by the mainmast with a canvas clipped to it, so several square yards of deck looked like an artist's studio.

Round the foremast several sacks of Irish potatoes and yams had been emptied out and spread over the deck, and a dozen seamen were patiently sorting them out and throwing away those that had gone rotten or showed signs of mildew. The smell drifted aft, and Ramage was reminded of a country barn. For a moment, as his memory went back to Cornwall, he thought of swallows jinking through shafts of sunlight and shadow.

Already Southwick had assembled a party of foretop and fo'c'slemen to prepare anchors and cables. As soon as the *Calypso* was clear of the English Channel, her anchor cables had been taken off the anchors and hauled below, to be stowed in the cabletier. The hawsehole, one each side, out of which the cable led when the ship was at anchor, had been blocked first with a hawse plug the size of the hawsehole, and that had been reinforced by a blind buckler, yet another circular wooden disc backed up by iron bars, and ensuring that waves could not force water into the ship.

Now men were driving out the iron bars and then levering out the blind bucklers. The plugs were harder—men had to drive them out with heavy mauls while others, scrambling over the bow, caught them and made sure they did not fall over the side.

Meanwhile men were busy down in the cabletier, a hot and dank part of the ship, where several cables were coiled down but which was always damp because the cables, impregnated with salt (as well as sand and shell scraped off the sea bed and ingrained in the lay of the ropes) never properly dried out. Now they were hauling first one end up to the hawse and then the other. Each end was led round, one to be secured to an anchor on the larboard side, the other to starboard.

Soon Southwick was back on the quarterdeck reporting that the ship was ready for anchoring, and Ramage offered him a telescope to inspect the island. The master was not impressed by what he saw. "If the other side's like this, then there are no anchorages," he grumbled. "All I can see are steep cliffs. Those mountains must be a good fifteen hundred feet—one looks like that big sugarloaf at Rio de Janeiro. I grant they should put the other side in a lee, but a lee's no good without a bay. Nothing for that fellow Wilkins to paint . . ."

At that moment Ramage saw that "that fellow Wilkins" was collecting his canvases together and taking them below. He was one of the *Calypso*'s more welcome guests: he had quickly picked up the routine of daily life in a frigate, and quietly went about his painting without asking for special favours. The result was, of course, that he had become popular. He had painted several striking portraits. The first, of Southwick, was one of the best likenesses that Ramage had seen of anyone: looking at the canvas, one half expected Southwick's face to break into a grin. The second one, of young Paolo, had revealed his Italian lineage but in some subtle way merged it into his midshipman's uniform. The next venture had been a large canvas with three seamen sitting on the deck with a sail across their legs, busy stitching. Wilkins had contrived to let the viewer feel he was sitting among the men, Jackson, Stafford and Rossi, with the canvas round him. The portrait of Bowen sitting with his head

138

bowed over a chess board made Ramage think that Wilkins had somehow diagnosed something of the surgeon's tragic past, when drink had nearly ruined him, but the painting showed Bowen's victory, not a defeat. And, knowing Southwick's frequent defeats at Bowen's hands while playing chess, Wilkins had painted in the chessmen so that Bowen was trying to find a way out of checkmate.

Within another hour the *Calypso* was reaching fast and only two or three miles from the southern tip of the island. Aitken came up to Ramage and saluted formally.

"Do you want the men sent to quarters, sir?"

Ramage shook his head and smiled. "It's a hard habit to break, isn't it! But we're at peace and this is a deserted island, so we'll keep your decks free of sand."

Ramage thought for a moment and then said: "Send Jackson to the foremasthead, and Orsini to the main: tell them to watch out for any dark patches in the water that'll warn of rocks. And light patches for reefs, too!"

Aitken passed the order and then Ramage said: "Have the deep sea lead ready. I hope we don't have to use it, but if we can't anchor on the other side we might as well have some idea of the depth."

The deep sea lead was a very long line with a heavy lead weight on the end. The lead was taken out to the end of the jibboom and the line led back aft, clear of everything, and then forward again to the forechains, where it was brought back on board. As soon as the word was given the lead was dropped, taking with it line nearly twice the length of the ship. The leadsman and his mates could let more run, but initially more than 300 feet went in a matter of seconds. The usual hand lead was used only for depths of twenty fathoms and less.

Ramage, now holding the only telescope on the quarterdeck, because the other two had been entrusted to Jackson and Orsini, went through all the evolutions the *Calypso* might need to perform and could think of nothing they had forgotten. He could rely on Aitken and Southwick remembering the various drills, while Kenton and Martin had enough ingenuity to think of anything unusual.

"Quarterdeck there, foremast here!"

Aitken lifted the speaking trumpet and answered Jackson.

"Thought I saw a puff of smoke at the southern end, sir, like a bonfire being put out."

"Can you see smoke now?"

"No, sir, it only lasted a few moments."

"Keep a sharp lookout," Aitken said, in the standard response. He turned to Ramage, an eyebrow raised. Jackson was one of the best lookouts and probably the most reliable seaman in the ship.

"Could have been a flock of small birds flying off," Ramage said. "I've known the movement being mistaken in the distance for a puff of smoke."

"Aye, sir. It's hardly the place one would expect to find a gillie roasting a deer!"

CHAPTER ELEVEN

Colours could now be distinguished, although the sun dipping to the west was already beginning to throw shadows across the near side of the mountains, giving shape and design to apparently smooth peaks. There was some grass on the lower slopes, not many trees and those were evergreens stunted by constant exposure to the trade winds. Although he had only seen paintings of it, Ramage could understand Southwick's reference to the sugarloaf hill being like the famous one overlooking Rio de Janeiro.

"A tiny Antigua," Aitken said. "It has that same dried up and wasted look in places, like a deserted Highland hill farm."

"I'm glad I'm not going to command the garrison," Ramage

said, "although it seems a good spot for young subalterns dodging gambling debts and the furious fathers of jilted brides!"

He caught sight of small waves breaking on the nearest shore and noted that they showed the *Calypso* was now less than two miles away. Curious how one had these little mental pictures to help estimate distance when anything was close. At two miles one could see a small building on the beach; at a mile the colour of its roof was distinguishable. A man standing on the beach could be picked out at 700 yards and if he was walking one could spot him at half a mile.

"Pass this southernmost headland about a mile off," Ramage instructed Southwick. "That should keep us clear of any reefs. As soon as we round it we'll then stretch along the leeward side of the island under topsails and hope to find an anchorage for the night."

Aitken came up holding a slate. "If the highest peak is fifteen hundred feet, sir, I calculate the island is almost exactly two and a half miles long."

Ramage nodded: the figure coincided with his rough and ready measurement some minutes ago, when he divided the height of the peak into the length of the island and got an answer of nine.

Now the men were at sheets and braces and the quartermaster kept an eye on Southwick, waiting for the order that would begin the *Calypso*'s turn round the narrow southeastern corner of the island. It was, Ramage had to admit, an island with little to recommend it. Rocky—every inch of coast he had seen so far was backed by jagged cliffs—it had patches of green, indicating grass, but the trees were little more than overgrown shrubs. Something of the coast of southern Tuscany, something of the Leeward and Virgin Islands, but nothing of the lushness of Grenada or Martinique. This was not suprising, because it was only just inside the Tropics, receiving the full force of the Atlantic winds and very little rain.

It was a long, narrow island: as the *Calypso* sailed diagonally across the end he could see it was less than a mile wide. Ah, now the western side was beginning to open up and almost at once Southwick began bellowing a stream of orders to wear ship: for several hours the *Calypso* had been on the larboard tack, the wind coming steadily over the larboard quarter. Now she was coming round to starboard almost eight points, nearly ninety degrees, to steer—Ramage walked over to the binnacle and looked down at the weatherside compass—northwest.

The creak of yards being braced up, the thump and slam of sails filling again, the grunts of dozens of men hauling on sheets and braces, the cries of bosun's mates, the curses of the quartermaster as the two men at the wheel swung it over too far, making the *Calypso* bear up a point or two and bringing a glower from the master.

Ramage was relieved to see that although the weather coast was sheer and inhospitable, the lee coast had half a dozen prominent headlands poking seaward into the distance.

Aitken gestured towards them. "There should be some good bays between them, sir," he said. Ramage nodded, for a moment puzzled, but as the *Calypso* surged ahead on the new tack he shook his head as if to clear his thoughts: he had been at sea too long and was imagining things.

"Deck there—foremast here!"

"Foremast—deck!" Southwick answered.

"I saw a small boat beyond the headland, sir! Red it was," Jackson shouted. "Then it went behind the cliff."

Ramage said quickly: "Just acknowledge: I saw it, too!"

"Very well, keep a sharp lookout!" Southwick said in the usual response to a routine hail.

"What's an open boat doing here, sir?" the master exclaimed.

"From a Brazilian fishing boat, perhaps. Or maybe there is a settlement here after all."

Even as he said it, Ramage realized the problems mustered behind that one brief glimpse of a boat. A settlement meant people lived here; presumably they, or the country to which they belonged, claimed possession of Trinidade. Most probably it was Portugal, but it could be Spain.

It was a point not covered in his orders; the Admiralty had assumed the island was uninhabited. Yet...Lord St Vincent had, verbally, given what would undoubtedly be the Admiralty's view: ownership of the Ilha da Trinidade was not covered in the Treaty, so Britain could claim it. Any settlers would have to leave; he would take them back whence they came—Brazil, probably.

Aitken said matter-of-factly: "Probably just fishermen: their

142

vessel anchored in a bay while they get water, and their jolly boat is rowing round looking for lobster to make a nice supper!"

That would be it. Ramage felt sheepish and was thankful he had kept his mouth shut: once again his imagination had outdistanced his reasoning. A fishing boat from Bahia—it was so obvious! At that moment Jackson yelled excitedly.

"Deck there—there's a ship anchored in that first bay!"

Ramage grabbed the only telescope and before he could lift it Jackson was shouting again: "Merchant ship . . . British colours . . . a John Company ship."

Southwick said: "Her water's gone bad and she's come here to fill casks!"

"Deck there! I can just make out the stern of another merchant ship, French colours . . ."

By now Ramage could see the first ship. Yes, John Company, flying faded but distinctive red and white "gridiron" colours of the Honourable East India Company, the Union flag in one canton, with horizontal stripes. And now he could make out the stern of the French ship as the headland appeared to slide to starboard with the *Calypso*'s approach, beginning to give a glimpse of the rest of the bay. She was almost as big as the John Company ship and her sails neatly furled, too. A quarterboat was hoisted in the davits and there was another boat streaming astern on its painter.

Ramage found himself listening to the monotonous chant of the depths coming from the leadsman busy in the chains, and picturing the shape of the sea bed. It was shallowing only gradually and the old adage of high cliffs and deep water seemed true. But there could be no rocks or reefs at this end, since these ships had sailed in.

"We'll probably anchor to seaward of those ships," Ramage snapped, and Southwick hurriedly grabbed the speaking trumpet and quickly gave orders to clew up the main and forecourses. Almost immediately and as if by magic, because the appropriate ropes were hauled from the deck, the *Calypso*'s two largest sails lost their curves and were hauled up to the yards like window curtains lifted by an impatient busybody.

At once the frigate began to slow down. Earlier, the bow wave curling back from the stem had sounded like water pouring through a sluice gate; now it chuckled happily and at the same time, as the ship reached the sheltered water in the lee of the island, she stopped the gentle pitch and roll. Instead, sailing upright under topsails only and with a soldier's wind, the *Calypso* was like a cheerful fishwife losing her boisterous gait.

"Foremast here, sir—there's a third ship—"

"Mainmast here—and a fourth!" Orsini yelled, not troubling to hide his excitement.

As they came into view round the headland Ramage examined them carefully through the telescope. "The third one's British, I can make out her colours. She's in good order; sails neatly furled—too neatly, it seems to me! And the fourth is . . . yes, Dutch. I thought for a moment she was French; the wind plays tricks with her colours."

"Four ships at anchor in a place like this? What the devil's gone wrong?" a puzzled Southwick asked, preparing to give orders to clew up the foretopsail.

"Could be water," Ramage said. "If they all called at the Cape and took water from the same place and it later went bad . . ." Then he shook his head. "No, it couldn't be that; French and Dutch ships wouldn't call at the Cape—coming from India or Batavia they wouldn't know about the Treaty."

Aitken said: "Should I send the men to general quarters, sir?"

Ramage smiled at the Scot's reluctance to abandon wartime routines. "There are a couple of British ships anchored peacefully in the bay, Mr Aitken!"

"Aye, sir, but it's like walking into a glen twenty miles from the nearest village and finding a dozen men camped there—it gives you a shock and makes you suspicious."

"Yes, because they're unshaven and you don't know who they are, but these ships have their colours flying." Ramage looked at the four ships again. "New colours, too, most of them!"

Southwick sniffed—clearly he disapproved of the whole thing—and inquired patiently: "Where do you want us to anchor, sir?"

Now the *Calypso* was almost past the headland and Ramage saw a deep bay was opening up surrounded by cliffs, the northern end formed by a less prominent bluff. The four ships—

144

"Foremast lookout here, sir—there's a fifth ship, almost hidden by the third and fourth, French flag."

"Very well. Any—"

"Sixth, sir!" Jackson interrupted from aloft. "She's close in to the cliffs. Smaller, looks fast, twelve guns. Might be a privateer, from her appearance. Ah, I can just see her colours. British, sir."

Five merchant ships and a possible privateer, all peacefully anchored. A *former* privateer, Ramage corrected himself. Well, obviously Trinidade had plenty of fresh water, and equally obviously the Admiralty might know nothing of the island, but it was well known to merchant ships regularly sailing to the Cape, India and Batavia . . . Probably, Ramage thought, if the Admiralty had written to the Honourable East India Company and asked them for details, a delighted John Company would have sent a chart with the watering places marked.

"Mainmast, sir," Orsini called down. "The small boat we first sighted—she's going alongside the one we think is a privateer."

Suddenly Ramage found himself feeling cheerful: with five merchant ships in the anchorage, there would be some entertaining. The John Company ship would have passengers, and John Company masters, well paid, lived well and were often interesting men. The second British ship looked interesting. The Dutch ship was big enough to be one of the Dutch East India Company's fleet. And the Frenchmen, he thought, might not yet know of the peace treaty . . . no, they must, he realized, otherwise they would not be in here peacefully at anchor with British ships. They must all know—but how? The only way the British would know would be for a frigate to have reached the Cape with dispatches. That could have happened. But Dutch and French? Well, they could have met other Dutch and French ships, outward bound. That was obvious, he realized, irritated with himself.

"Anchoring, sir," Southwick reminded him.

"Ah yes. From the way all the ships are on the south side of the bay, we must conclude there's foul ground on the north side. Two cables astern of the seaward British ship; have her bearing northeast."

Southwick gave a quick helm order to the quartermaster and bellowed to the men to brace the topsail yards up. Sheets were

145

hauled home and the *Calypso* turned to starboard, hard on the wind for the last few hundred yards.

"Foretop—quarterdeck: that boat's leaving the privateer, sir."

"She'll be calling on us: keep an eye on the others—especially the John Company ship."

"Quite a social life, it'll be, sir," Aitken said, and Ramage was not sure whether the first lieutenant was pleased or depressed.

"Yes, the first time any of us except Southwick has met a merchant ship in peacetime. We must mind our manners: very proud gentlemen, these John Company masters. Always anxious to put the Navy in its place."

"Aye, and wealthy, too, sir, so I'm told. Silver cutlery, expensive china, only the best wines, fresh meat nearly every day because they carry so much livestock . . . Even fresh milk."

"Unless the cow goes dry. But the luxury is for the passengers: they are paying a great deal of money for a first class passage to or from India."

"These nabobs can afford it!"

"How I envy them," Ramage said. "If he had to go to India even your John Knox would have chosen an Indiaman and fresh milk in preference to a frigate and salt tack!"

"Make no mistake, sir, it's envy in my voice, not criticism," Aitken said with a grin. "Now, I'd better give Mr Southwick a hand."

The master gave him a speaking trumpet and went down to the maindeck, walking forward to the fo'c'sle where a group of men stood near the cable and bitts while others waited at the anchor, now hanging over the side ready for the order to let go.

Aitken glanced aloft and saw that the topsails were just drawing. Without bothering to look over the side he knew the *Calypso* was making less than three knots.

As he stood at the quarterdeck rail, deliberately leaving the handling of the ship to his officers, so that they increased their experience, Ramage watched the frigate's supernumeraries. Wilkins, sitting on the hammock nettings, was sketching: he would draw a few brief lines, write some words and tear off the page, stuff it in his pocket and then start work on a fresh sheet. A study for the *Calypso*'s arrival at Trinidade? The five other ships against the harsh grey curve of the cliffs and the five peaks rising high behind them would be a challenge some-one like Wilkins could not resist. The surveyors and draughts-men seemed more interested in the land than the ships: they were probably discussing how they were going to find their way across the ridges, some of which looked very sharp, and up to the peaks. The botanist stood alone but he too was looking from one end of the island to the other—or, rather, what he could see of it as the *Calypso* glided into the bay, the southern headland and the northern bluff seemed to enclose her like welcoming arms.

Aitken was just shouting the order to back the foretopsail, to bring the *Calypso* to a stop within a hundred yards or so of the Indiaman, so that when the frigate settled back on the full scope of her cable she would be exactly where Ramage wanted, when Jackson hailed again.

"Foretop—four men in that boat, sir, apart from the oars-men, and one of 'em is holding up something like a boarding pike."

"How do you mean—threatening us?" Ramage lifted his telescope but could not for a moment sight the boat.

"No sir—he's sitting on a thwart with it vertically between his knees. May be just a long stick."

"Very well. Keep an eye on it—and watch for other boats: they'll be flocking over soon."

"No one's moved yet, sir. Just a few people on the deck of each ship."

Kenton, who had been standing to one side, waiting for orders, laughed to himself and then said: "We surprised every-one and the ladies have rushed below to change into their best dresses and attend to their hair."

"And you're hoping that some of the nabobs have eligible daughters, eh?"

"They'd have been snapped up by now, sir: Trinidade isn't famous as a place where impoverished lieutenants find rich young ladies to marry!"

"Not famous *yet*," Ramage said. "You might start a fash-ion."

There was a creak from the foretopsail yard, and then a dull thump as the wind caught the sail on its forward side, pressing the canvas back against the mast, slowing and then stopping the ship.

Southwick was standing on the fo'c'sle, watching Aitken. The first lieutenant's left arm shot up vertically and at once Southwick turned and barked out an order. The heavy anchor dropped into the water with a splash and the cable ran out the hawse with a noise like a hundred galloping cattle. A few moments later the familiar smell of scorched rope and wood drifted aft.

By now the bosun was standing beside the larboard quarterboat, waiting for it to be lowered so that he could be rowed round the ship to give the appropriate signals for squaring the yards, while aloft seamen were furling the courses. The moment the foretopsail had finished its present task of giving the *Calypso* sternway, putting a strain on the cable and ensuring that the anchor dug itself in, it and the maintopsail would be furled and the jibs neatly stowed at the foot of their stays.

Ramage was pleased that there were ships here for another reason. Aitken had kept the ship's company busy, except during the hottest part of the doldrums, smartening up the *Calypso*. Long days without rain and with the sails furled meant that masts and yards could be painted, leather fire buckets polished, capstan painted in blue and white with some of the patterns and the crown on top picked out in gold. He was thankful now that he had bought a few books of gold leaf: they were expensive, but gilt work was always an economy because gold paint did not last and always turned into the colour of grey mud under the twin assault of sea and sun. The *Calypso*'s boats looked new: the hulls were a little darker than sky blue, the top strake white, and the metalwork black. The rowlocks had been picked out with gilt, and the oars were white. It seemed a pity to put the boats in the water: within a few weeks green weed and limpets would be growing thick and fast on their bottoms.

With guests coming on board, and the *Calypso*'s captain and officers paying social calls on other ships, Aitken's work would be seen and admired, and Ramage knew that an ounce of praise from the master of a John Company ship was worth the same from the captain of a 74-gun two-decker.

The lookout on the fo'c'sle shouted: "Quarterdeck there— boat approaching, sir: a hundred yards on the starboard bow."

148

Aitken acknowledged the hail and looked round for Renwick. A glance over the quarterdeck rail showed a Marine sergeant already marching a couple of Marines to take up their posts at the entryports on the starboard and larboard sides once the *Calypso* was at anchor. The sentry's task was to hail any approaching boat and, from the reply, find out who was in it.

The Marine sergeant, Ferris, had heard the fo'c'sle lookout's hail and marched the two Marines to the starboard side first: officers boarded on the starboard side, and the visitors were almost certainly officers. He halted the two men, detached one amid a volley of orders and a cloud of pipeclay, and then marched the second Marine over to the larboard side.

Aitken looked at the boat with the telescope in the few remaining moments before it was hidden by the frigate's bow. After his inspection he looked grim, shut the telescope and put it away in the binnacle box drawer. He walked over to Ramage. "I'll meet our visitors, sir; I don't think you'll need to see them."

Ramage nodded, because no one in the Navy had much time for privateers; in fact he assumed these privateersmen had been cruising well down in the South Atlantic and had only just learned of the new Treaty that put them out of business. Their licence, or letter of marque, to give it the proper name, gave them permission to wage war on the King's enemies (the Republic's enemies if French, of course) providing there was a war on. A hostile act against any ship in peacetime was piracy, and the penalty for piracy was hanging.

As he walked down the ladder from the quarterdeck towards the entryport, Aitken heard the sentry's challenge, and, from beyond the ship, a reply that sounded like a single word, the name of a ship. So the captain of the privateer—the former privateer, he corrected himself—was paying a visit. Probably, he realized, to get news of the Treaty: they would have heard only gossip and hearsay from the merchant ships, and were now seizing the opportunity of having it—officially, as far as they were concerned—from one of the King's ships. After all, hearing that a profitable way of life was now illegal—well, even privateersmen could not be blamed for wanting to have the news confirmed by a reliable source.

"Sir," the sentry said, obviously puzzled, "the boat's alongside and they've got a white flag flying—lashed to a boarding

149

pike. They've only just lashed it this moment because I saw a fellow sitting there with a pole, and there weren't no flag . . ."

Aitken went to the port and looked down at the boat. The bowman had hooked on; a man at the stern was waiting for one of the *Calypso*'s seamen to throw down a sternfast while the bowman waited for a painter.

In the meantime the four men sat in the sternsheets, one of them, a big negro, holding between his knees the boarding pike with a square of grubby white cloth secured to it.

Aitken noticed that the four men had pistols in their belts, and there were cutlasses in the bottom of the boat, but that was reasonable enough: the *Calypso* herself had flown false colours in the late war to get herself into a position to attack the enemy—after hoisting her true colours. And privateersmen, he had to admit, would be among the most cautious and distrustful men afloat.

Nevertheless, Aitken wanted an explanation of the flag of truce before anyone stepped on board.

"Why are you waving that truce flag?" he demanded.

"Not waving it," one of the men answered. "Holdin' it still."

"Answer my question."

"S'bluddy obvious. We want to come on board under a flag of truce."

"A truce for what? The war's over."

"Oh—it's true what they tell us, then?"

"I don't know who's been telling you what," Aitken said, his tone more friendly, "but Bonaparte signed a treaty of peace with Britain on the first day of last October."

"That's good news. Can we come on board, then?"

"Of course. What's your ship?"

"The *Lynx* of Bristol, letter of marque."

"*Former* letter of marque," Aitken said.

"Well, yes, give us time to get used to the idea of peace!"

Aitken laughed and watched as the speaker stood up and reached for the battens.

"I don't rate sideropes, eh?" the man looked up but started climbing.

"You could have been a bumboat selling bananas," Aitken said sarcastically. "But we'd have fired salutes and piped you on board, if you'd given us due notice."

The man looked up as he climbed. "You didn't give *us* any notice."

Aitken stood back several paces, with the Marine sentry to his left, musket at the slope, and Orsini and Martin to his right. He knew that Kenton was on the quarterdeck ready to pass any messages down to the captain, and Southwick would be within earshot. It was quite surprising, he noted ironically, how many seamen now had tasks that kept them amidships where they could watch the *Calypso*'s first visitors since she left the Medway.

The man coming on board was tall and thin; so thin that Aitken had the impression the skin had been shrunk on to his head. The face and head had sharp angles, like a five-sided lantern, and the man was completely bald. Not just bald, Aitken realized, but hairless: the result, presumably, of some illness like malaria. As if in compensation, he had a full set of perfect teeth, which were only slightly stained from chewing tobacco.

"Jebediah Hart," he announced, "master and part owner of the *Lynx*, schooner."

"James Aitken, first lieutenant, His Majesty's ship *Calypso*, frigate."

By now a second man had come on board: as fat as Hart was thin, shorter than Aitken, he had a large and black drooping moustache and thick, bushy eyebrows. His eyes seemed black and flickered round the *Calypso*'s deck, as though expecting a trap.

Hart said: "I must introduce the mate, Jean-Louis Belmont. Unfortunately he speaks no English."

Aitken nodded and bowed. The first lieutenant noted that despite the fatness, the man had climbed up the side without getting out of breath. And he was French. Presumably a royalist and a refugee from Bonaparte's regime. He took a risk if ever the privateer had been captured while the war was on: the French would have hanged him at once as a traitor.

The next man on board was small, muscular, with blond hair beginning to turn grey. Unlike the others he wore breeches instead of trousers and had a severely-cut coat of dark green. Aitken was unsure whether meeting him on shore he would mistake the man for a farmer or a rural dean. Unexpectedly he stood to attention, bowed his head, and moved to one side. Hart was busy looking round the ship and did not introduce

151

the man, who did not give his name. Aitken was sure, from his appearance and manner, that he was Scandinavian.

The fourth man to come through the entryport was the big Negro, still carrying the boarding pike, although he had spun it a few times to wind the white flag round it.

Hart turned and said: "Tomás—he's Spanish; speaks no English."

"You have a language problem in the *Lynx!*" Aitken said, but Hart shook his head.

"I've picked up a few words here and there."

Aitken waited for him to continue, but the four privateersmen stood in a half circle, as if waiting for him to make the next move. The first lieutenant glanced over towards the *Lynx* as if intending to admire their ship but in fact to see if boats were coming from the merchantmen. No boats had moved; those with their boats made up astern with painters still had them sitting like ducklings behind the mother and the rest of the boats hoisted up in quarter davits or still amidships, stowed on the cargo hatches.

Aitken looked across at Hart, puzzled by what he now recognized as a strange sight. Hart stared back at him and said in a flat voice: "We want to see your captain."

"Explain your business," Aitken said brusquely, "then I'll see if he has time: he is very busy."

"What's his name?"

"Ramage, Captain Ramage."

"Christ," Hart said in a low voice, "of all the ones the Admiralty pick it has to be him!"

"You know him?"

"Know *of* him," Hart said, "who doesn't? Well—" he shrugged his shoulders and said something in rapid Spanish to Tomás, who swore "—fetch him."

"I don't *fetch* the captain," Aitken said stiffly.

"Now you do," Hart sneered. "You see those ships?" he gestured at the anchored merchantmen.

When Aitken nodded, Hart said: "They're all our prizes. Now fetch your precious Mr Lord Ramage."

CHAPTER TWELVE

Ramage sat in his chair behind his desk, not because he needed the desk in front of him but because his cabin was crowded with the four privateersmen, Aitken and Southwick. Aitken had hurried in to give a quick explanation of why he was bringing the privateersmen down, and a couple of minutes later had led them in, Southwick following presumably because he realized something strange was happening.

"Strange" was the appropriate word. For the moment the privateersmen were settling themselves down with the leader, the Englishman calling himself Hart, sitting in what was usually regarded as Southwick's armchair and his three companions taking up the settee. Southwick stood one side of the door and Aitken the other, both stooped because there was not enough room to stand upright under the deck beams.

This is the first time I have taken my ship to a foreign island in peacetime, Ramage reflected, and I meet a situation more perplexing than any I met in the war. Perplexing because more than a hundred and fifty innocent lives are at stake: people I have never seen; men and women passengers, officers, petty officers and seamen from five merchant ships: Dutch, French and British. What did this fellow Hart want or intend? Well, the privateersmen seemed to be waiting for him to start the proceedings.

"Well, Mr Hart, my first lieutenant tells me you command the *Lynx* privateer, and you claim that the merchant ships anchored here are your prizes."

"Correct, except for the 'claim'. I'm not 'claiming'; they are."

Ramage nodded, as if accepting the point, but he said quietly, as though mentioning it apologetically: "Britain and France have signed a treaty: Britain is now at peace with France, Spain and the Netherlands. Can you take prizes in time of peace?"

"We can," Hart said bluntly. "We have."

Again Ramage nodded. "The two British, two French and one Dutch ships I see at anchor here?"

"Those very ones. And probably another two or three within a week: our sister ship is still at sea."

"Yes, it must be quite easy taking prizes now," Ramage said. "No one expecting trouble: guns not loaded—in fact I expect many merchant ships will have landed their guns."

"They will, they will," Hart said confidently.

"What do you propose doing with your prizes?"

At that moment the black spoke to Hart in rapid Spanish, demanding to know what was being discussed. Ramage was surprised at the words the man chose. He was careful to keep the tone of voice suitable for a seaman who was probably a bodyguard, but the actual words in Spanish were those an officer would use to a seaman. Clearly neither Hart nor the black had the slightest idea that Ramage spoke Spanish. The only trouble was that Ramage's Spanish and accent were Castilian, while the black spoke the crude and heavily-accented Spanish of the New World; almost as hard to understand as the Creole spoken by blacks in the French islands.

"What are you telling this man?" the black was asking.

"Just that the ships are our prizes, Tomás."

"You be sure he makes no argument."

"He is not. He is accepting everything."

"Why?" The black was shrewd and probably the real captain of the *Lynx:* Ramage was becoming quite sure of that.

"I do not know," Hart said vaguely. "What else *can* he do?"

"Find out," Tomás said.

Hart turned to Ramage with a friendly smile. "Tomás speaks no English; I was explaining what we had been discussing."

"Perhaps you'd like to translate for the benefit of your French mate as well?"

Hart nodded and quickly related to Belmont the gist of the

154

conversation so far, and Ramage's suspicion was confirmed: Belmont was of no consequence. Once again the tone was right but the words used were those a master would use to a petty officer, not his second-in-command.

The hierarchy of the *Lynx*, Ramage guessed, was that the big Spanish Negro, Tomás, was the leader, with Hart the second-in-command, while Belmont and the silent blond would be mates.

"Well, Captain," Hart said smoothly, "you do not seem very surprised to find five prizes anchored here at Trinidade!"

"Oh, I wouldn't say that," Ramage said vaguely. Tomás would not understand the words, but he would be quick to notice if a foreigner was an ineffectual man. Clearly Hart knew of Captain Ramage—he had made that clear at the beginning—but Tomás would not believe him if he saw that this Captain Ramage had a vague and indecisive manner. Even Hart might begin to wonder. "Well, yes, I suppose I was surprised to find ships here. After all, it isn't a very big island. It takes a lot of finding."

"You had trouble?" Hart asked casually.

"Oh yes. Our chronometer is not very accurate." He was careful not to look at Southwick as he added: "Fortunately one can run the westing down."

Hart said quickly in Spanish to Tomás: "They had to run their westing down to find this place."

Tomás said nothing and Ramage said innocently to Hart: "You did not say what you were going to do with your prizes."

"No, I didn't. It now depends on you, to some extent."

Ramage thought quickly, and then yawned, delicately picking fluff from his coat. "Oh, does it? It's not really *my* responsibility, you know. After all, you're the privateer. Well, the war's over now, so I suppose your letter of marque has expired, or whatever it does when a war ends. But your prizes are your affair—after all, even if the war was still on, they'd still be no concern of mine."

"I'm glad to hear you say it," Hart said.

"Oh indeed," Ramage said, as though politely delighted that Hart agreed. "I have my orders from the Admiralty and I really can't get involved in anything else—not without orders from their Lordships."

155

"Might one ask if your orders will keep you here for long?" Hart asked cautiously.

Ramage shook his head and resumed the search for fluff on his coat. "There's no secret about my orders: I've come here to survey the island and map it, and make a chart of the anchorages."

"Why? Are the Admiralty going to start using it?"

"Use it?" Ramage said scornfully. "I doubt it! Who the devil could find it! Anyway, it's a long way to anywhere else. No, Ascension is good enough for the Cape and John Company ships."

"Why the sudden interest in Trinidade, then?"

"It's not a sudden interest in Trinidade," Ramage said, with another yawn. "The war is over, but the Admiralty have to keep a certain number of ships in commission, especially frigates. So they are sending several of them off to survey various unusual places. I expect one has gone to St Paul Rocks and another to Fernando de Noronha, for example. And probably Ascension; the charts for them are terrible, I know."

"So how—" Hart was interrupted by Tomás asking what was being discussed. Hart told him that Ramage was not concerned about the privateer; that he wanted to avoid any responsibility, and that he was only concerned with carrying out his orders, to survey Trinidade.

"How long does he plan to be here?"

"I'll ask him."

"You had better tell him why he cannot interfere with the prizes."

"But he does not intend to anyway."

"If he is going to be here long," Tomás said, obviously controlling his impatience with Hart, "it is only a matter of time before someone from one of the prizes raises the alarm. Anyway, this Ramage will expect to be invited to dinner by the other masters. When no invitations come, even he will get suspicious—if he can stay awake long enough."

Ramage managed to keep his face blank at this unwitting praise for his acting. But what on earth was Tomás talking about?

"How long do you reckon on staying here, then?" Hart asked.

Ramage held out his hands, palms uppermost, in a gesture

156

well understood by all Latins. "Who knows? How big is the island, how long will my surveyors and draughtsmen take with their maps? How long will my lieutenants take with their soundings? Two months, four, six? Blessed if I know. I should think you'll be long gone before we've finished."

Hart nodded, but was obviously puzzled how to carry out the important part of Tomás's instructions.

"Captain Ramage," he said, a more formal note in his voice. "About these prizes of ours..."

Ramage raised an eyebrow. "Your affair, my dear chap. If you take prizes that's your responsibilty. The courts decide, as you know. You might have trouble over those two British ships, of course—unless they'd been captured by the French, and you recaptured them. But I'm not the judge and I'm sure you know all about the Prize Act."

"Oh yes, don't worry your head about that, sir," Hart said, a confidential note in his voice. "No, what I was going to explain is that of course we have prize crews on board each of the ships."

"Oh yes, I assumed that."

"Yes, and our men have orders," Hart said casually but there was no mistaking the warning, "to kill all the passengers the minute they see there's any danger of losing a ship."

"What if the prize crew run a ship on a reef, they murder the *passengers?* Hardly seems just, I *must* say."

Hart clucked like a disappointed schoolteacher. "No, no, no sir, not that sort of danger. I mean if they saw there was any chance of their ships being recaptured..."

"Can't see who'd try to do that," Ramage said, obviously puzzled. "After all, the war is over. Why, that'd be an act of piracy, surely?"

A contented smile spread over Hart's face. "Why, of course, sir, that's exactly what it would be, and that is why our prize crews have those orders; we have to be on our guard against piracy."

Again Ramage looked puzzled, scratching his head with one hand and tugging at the knee of his breeches with the other. "Yes, but I can't see how killing the passengers keeps pirates away."

"Oh, I see what you mean, captain, but if you just think of it as insurance, you'll understand."

"Ah yes, just insurance. Very wise too: never sail under-insured, somebody once told me. 'Beware of barratry by master and crew and pay the premiums promptly'—that was what he said, and it's wise advice, don't you think?"

"Indeed it is," Hart patiently agreed, "and we have the officers and men staying in a camp on shore." He turned to Tomás, saying in Spanish: "I have told him about the hostages and he sees nothing wrong about us having prizes. He might be a brave man—he must be, to have his reputation—but he's a fool. He's swallowed our story like a pike taking a minnow. So we can wait for our friends with more prizes, and then we can all sail in one convoy, leaving this pudding to finish his survey."

"Good, so now be helpful: tell him where to get fresh water. Then he will not be suspicious."

Hart waved away the idea. "It is not necessary, Tomás. He is not short of water, or he would have asked us about rivers and springs. No, believe me, I understand these people. We say goodbye now and go."

"Lead the way and say the right things then," Tomás said, and anyone listening but unable to speak Spanish would not have realized that the big black had been giving orders.

Fifteen minutes later Southwick was sitting in the armchair, Aitken leaned back on the settee with his hat beside him, and Ramage sat at the desk, looking far removed from the vague, hesitant and languid individual who had talked to the privateersmen.

"What was the flag of truce all about?" Southwick asked.

Ramage looked at Aitken, who shook his head. "I think they thought we might have known what they were doing," Ramage said. "The sight of one of the King's ships sailing into the bay must have startled them. But as we didn't have our portlids up and guns run out, they were puzzled too. By coming out under flag of truce, perhaps they thought they were safe-guarding their own necks."

"I couldn't understand the Spanish parts, sir," Aitken said, "but why did Hart take so much trouble to translate for that black while ignoring the other two?"

"The black is the leader," Ramage said. "He's the deep one; ten times the brains of Hart."

Southwick gave a deep sniff and Ramage guessed that he was impressed by the black's shrewdness. "What was his name? Thomas?"

"The Spanish version. Hart speaks reasonably good Spanish and good French."

"Comes from the West Country," Southwick commented. "Bristol, I reckon."

"Probably, because he said the *Lynx* hailed from there," Aitken said. "Mind you, it's a fake name, I'll be bound."

Ramage let the two men gossip for a few more minutes because, having just had a shock when they did not expect it, they needed some idle talk to let their thoughts settle. Then the questions would come poking up, like fish in a stream looking for flies. Finally Aitken coughed and both Southwick and Ramage looked at him.

"When that fellow Hart said that their prize crews had orders to kill the passengers if the ships were in danger, sir, what did he mean?"

Ramage's face hardened and his brown eyes seemed more sunken than ever, his high cheekbones becoming more pronounced and his narrow nose more beaklike.

"We were being warned. Hart was telling us that they have armed men in each merchant ship, guarding the passengers, who are in fact hostages. He said the officers and men are on shore 'in a camp'. That means there are a dozen or more hostages in each vessel, and if we make any attempt to recapture any of the ships or attack the *Lynx,* they'll simply massacre the hostages."

"Stalemate," Southwick said crossly.

"I wish it was," Ramage said. "At the moment the privateers hold the pistol at our heads. We can do nothing. That devil Tomás has probably given orders that if we so much as wave a musket, all the hostages get their throats cut. Remember, a privateer carries a large number of men solely to provide crews for the prizes. I doubt if the *Lynx* needs even one man from an original crew to sail a ship, so the officers and men could be thrown over the side. I've no idea if they'll bother to ransom the hostages—they might think it too much effort and risk for too little profit.

"They'll sell each ship and cargo for cash to unscrupulous owners anxious to increase their fleets. Paint out the old name,

159

line in a new, hoist fresh colours and no one will ever guess that's a ship which apparently vanished while the war was on."

Southwick nodded admiringly. "Privateers in wartime and pirates in peace. More profitable in peacetime—they're not at the mercy of the Admiralty court judge's valuation of a prize: they get the full market value with no deductions for agents, court fees and bribes. And, being pirates, they can disregard a ship's colours—look at the ones they've got out there: French, Dutch and British. No Spanish, though; perhaps this fellow Tomás draws the line at that!"

Ramage shook his head. "That man has no loyalty to anything. There are no Spanish simply because there are so few Spanish ships at sea. Wait until the *Lynx*'s sister ship comes in—she may have picked up a Don."

"Well, what are we going to do?" Southwick asked angrily. "We can't just look at these devils knowing that the ships are prisons for the passengers."

"We can send the men to quarters and weigh and sink the *Lynx*. Mind you, you wouldn't have the bars in the capstan or the portlids raised before every hostage would be dead," Ramage said quietly.

Aitken said: "What do you propose, sir?"

"Let's wait a few days and just watch. We'll put the surveyors on shore each day, and you can send off Martin and Orsini in boats to take soundings and start that chart. Get the privateersmen accustomed to seeing our boats bustling about—but keep away from the prizes. Not obviously; just don't let any boat pass within hail."

Southwick sniffed doubtfully, because he was not a man to play a waiting game, and the privateer had provoked him. "How long do we wait, sir?"

"'Wait' is not the correct word. We 'observe'—like one of Aitken's poachers hiding in a clump of trees for a day or two before shooting one of the laird's deer. I want a detailed watch kept on the ships day and night: one man for each ship. Note what boats come and go, men leaving and arriving, stores, what work is done, the guards and where they are and how often they're changed, what the passengers do and how many . . . I want some good men who can write given this job. Jackson and people like that."

"Bowen gets bored, sir," Southwick commented. "Just the sort of thing he'd like doing."

"Very well, but they must keep out of sight: I don't want the privateersmen to realize we are keeping a special watch on them. But of course they might try to board *us!*"

"Do you think they'll try?" Aitken sounded hopeful.

"It probably depends on whether or not brother Tomás believed my play-acting. He'll have about a hundred men in the *Lynx,* and he can guard the hostages with twenty-five. Would he risk trying to capture a frigate with seventy-five men..."

"You would," Southwick said.

"Only if I had no choice! But I don't think Tomás feels trapped: I'm sure he believes having the hostages is enough insurance."

"Plus having a sleepy and vague captain commanding the frigate," Southwick said. "Your performance would have convinced me—and I speak English! The way you tried to avoid any responsibility: Hart was delighted with that! Little does he know how many times First Lords and admirals have lost their tempers and accused you of taking *too much* responsibility!"

"Being sleepy and vague gave me a little time to think," Ramage admitted. "I was sitting here expecting the pompous master of one of the John Company ships to invite me to dinner to make conversation with his tedious passengers. Instead Aitken brings in a quartet of the most improbable scoundrels with a story that almost beggars the imagination!"

Aitken grinned and stood up. "If you'll excuse me, sir. I think I'll go and arrange the first watch of lookouts: I'd like to take each man and 'introduce' him to his ship. We had better start a log for each ship, so that in a day or so we will know how many are on board, who are prisoners and who guards."

Ramage opened a drawer of his desk and took out a polished mahogany case. As he opened it, Southwick grinned. "The Marchesa would like to see you getting those pistols out and loading them, sir: it's a long time since she bought them for you."

"The day I was made post," Ramage recalled, "we went to Bond Street with my father. In fact I remember the Admiral and I waiting in the gunsmith while the Marchesa was in another shop buying lace. Then she came in and bought pistols!"

* * *

"Impasse." Ramage crossed out the words and wrote "checkmate". Then he ran a line through "mate": it was certainly "check" as far as Tomás and Jebediah Hart were concerned, but not checkmate: Ramage guessed he still had a move—if only he could see what it was.

The privateersmen—curious how he avoided thinking of them as pirates: perhaps because it seemed absurd in these modern times to realize that pirates still existed—had five ships and nearly fifty passengers as hostages. Neither Hart nor Tomás had threatened the safety of the ships' companies, who would number about two hundred and fifty.

Very well, he had written down a single word describing the situation, but what did he know, or guess? First, there were two privateers, the *Lynx* and another which was still out looking for more victims and which was due back in "a few days".

Where would the prizes be taken? Unless cargoes and hulls could be sold, there was no point in capturing the merchant ships. Well, obviously not to British, Dutch or French ports, judging from the nationality of the present victims. Tomás was Spanish-speaking; the nearest ports—conveniently to leeward, as well—were Portuguese in Brazil or Spanish to the southwest.

Ramage wrote "Prizes sold in River Plate ports?" That gave him a choice of Montevideo or Buenos Aires. The River Plate, nearly a hundred miles wide, was a busy area; the Spanish merchants there would always need ships. Particularly now, he realized. The war had meant that many, if not most, of the merchant ships trading in that area, and occasionally making a bolt for Spain to sell hides and bring back manufactured goods (what the Jonathan traders called "notions"), had been captured by the Royal Navy. They were not restored to their owners by the absurd treaty, so Spanish shipowners would be looking round for suitable replacement vessels to buy. And they must be in a hurry, because every merchant along the banks of the River Plate would be anxious to ship something to somewhere else: goods made a profit only when they moved to the market place; stored in warehouses they cost money. Nor was that an original thought: it had been pointed out to him several years ago by Sidney Yorke, the young man who owned a small fleet of merchant ships.

Anyway, that answered the question of what happened to

the ships. What about the hostages? The ship's officers would not be worth anything; they would probably be killed or, with the crews of the ships, put on shore at one of the remoter Brazilian ports. But how was a ransom demand for the hostages going to be sent on to those able (and willing) to pay? A message for the hostages' respective governments could be put on board homeward-bound ships, naming the prices and where the money should be paid over—somewhere like Madrid, or Cadiz, he presumed.

Yet compared with the value of the ships, the problems of collecting ransom entailed a great deal of work for very little profit, quite apart from the delays involved. Governments or relatives would want assurances that the hostages would be handed over safely. Neither Hart nor Tomás seemed the kind of man for that sort of work.

Ramage wrote "Fate of hostages?", and then added: "Murdered or released without ransom?" He guessed that Tomás would vote for murder and Hart for release. Which of the two men really was the leader?

Then he wrote down the question whose answer he hardly dared to think about: "What is the consequence of the *Calypso*'s arrival?"

The privateers had been quick to act. Obviously they had a lookout on the island who had spotted the *Calypso* on the eastern horizon, but the speed with which they arranged the hostages and made their plans showed that the *Lynx* was commanded by a decisive captain, not an argumentative committee of privateersmen. Tomás or Hart? He needed to know because one of them would murder without hesitation.

The final question was: "Can they blackmail me into leaving with the *Calypso*?"

Of course they could! But would they? From the *Lynx*'s point of view, having the *Calypso* at anchor here ensured she was helpless: any action by her could provoke the murder of the hostages. On the other hand the *Calypso* at sea and out of sight could be fetching reinforcements (not much of a threat, considering the distances involved) or by chance meeting another of the King's ships (quite likely farther to the east, on the Cape route). Or could be intercepting the second privateer, surprising her with her prizes and sinking her.

Ramage cursed to himself: he was far from sure that having

163

reached a stalemate here with the *Lynx,* he should not sail and try to catch her consort. But would Tomás and Hart *let* him sail? On the whole it seemed unlikely, and the decision certainly rested with them. Suddenly to sail with the *Calypso* would panic the privateersmen, causing them to murder everyone, abandon their prizes and flee.

Abruptly he realized that the sentry was now rapping on the door of his cabin, a sure sign that previous calls had gone unheard. A shout from Ramage brought Orsini into the cabin to report that the survey and sounding parties were now ready and Mr Aitken had them paraded along the gangway.

Ramage wiped his pen, put the cap on the ink well, stood up and reached for his hat. The difference between a young midshipman and a post captain, he thought sourly, is that the midshipman goes off on an expedition while the captain stays behind and scribbles...

He found three groups of men waiting for him. The largest, under the second lieutenant, Wagstaffe, comprised the surveyor Williams, both draughtsmen, the gray-haired botanist, Garret, and five Marines with Renwick.

His instructions were brief. The party was to land at the most suitable place, choosing somewhere they would use for the next few days. The boat would then anchor off, leaving a couple of seamen in it as boatkeepers. The survey would then start, continuing until there was not enough light, and without being too obvious Renwick would choose the sites for batteries. The posts with the plaques would be erected, claiming the island as British.

"It is most important," he emphasized, "that you all go about your business as though the privateer was not here. For the time being we have to pretend this is simply an anchorage for six ships. Don't do anything to spoil the impression I've given the privateersmen—that I will do nothing without orders from the Admiralty. So go ahead and measure your angles and distances. What will be your base?"

"I thought we'd erect a flagpole on the highest peak—or on a suitable platform which can be seen from all parts of the island," David Williams said.

"Yes, but don't forget a signal platform will have to be manned eventually, and that means soldiers or seamen climbing up to it, perhaps in the dark."

Williams nodded and admitted: "Yes sir, I'd forgotten that aspect. I was looking at it from a surveyor's point of view."

Ramage turned to Renwick. "You may find the camp on shore where the privateersmen are guarding the crews of their prizes. If so, give it a wide berth, but note its position and, without being too obvious about it, see how many men are on guard."

"Details we'd need if we planned to rescue the prisoners," Renwick said confidently.

"Exactly—but don't arouse the privateersmen's suspicions."

With that he went on to the second survey party, led by Walter White and commanded by the *Calypso*'s third lieutenant, Kenton. They had five Marines under Sergeant Ferris, but like Renwick's group they were dressed as seamen. Ramage was anxious not to alarm the privateersmen. Men dressed as seamen would arouse no curiosity but Marine jackets and cross-belts would. For the same reason the men were armed with cutlasses and pistols, not muskets. The pistols would not be very obvious; everyone knew that cutlasses were needed to cut a path through the waist-high brushwood covering much of the island.

With the second survey party following the first to shore, Ramage turned to the soundings team, commanded by Martin. They had, as instructed, all their equipment on the deck in front of them: two leads, the lines neatly coiled, an old butter firkin full of tallow, a boat compass, three notebooks, a quadrant and a telescope.

Ramage picked up one lead and inspected it, then the other. Each was a solid cylinder of lead, with an eye at one end to which the line was attached, and a depression cast in the other, to be filled with tallow.

Pointing at the firkin of tallow, Ramage said: "Don't forget it's as important to know the type of bottom as the depth, so make sure you keep on inspecting what sticks to the tallow, and wiping it off before the next cast. Sand, small shell, broken coral, volcanic mud, silt . . . note it all down, and make sure you get your abbreviations right: don't rely on "s"—it could mean sand, silt or shell.

"Have you decided your base lines for triangulations?" He addressed the question to Martin, but was just as interested to see what Orsini had learned about chartmaking from Southwick in the last few hours.

"Yes, sir," Martin said. "Those two rocks that stand up like chimneys." He pointed to one near the privateer, and a second one halfway along the peninsula forming the northern side of the bay.

Orsini said: "That first rock means we can keep on looking at the privateer, too."

Ramage nodded. "Yes, the number of men and the times they leave or board the *Lynx*. By the way, Martin, if you suspect there are isolated rocks, get a second boat so that you can sink a line between the two of you and sweep the bottom. Or anyway drag to a definite depth."

"How deep, sir?"

"Five fathoms," Ramage said. Few ships drawing thirty feet would ever anchor here; the phrase "Swept to thirty feet" written on a chart was a warning that below five fathoms there might be isolated rocks to foul an anchor cable. It was all too common for a ship's cable to wind itself round rock or coral as she headed first one way and then another with each change of wind or tide, and often the first hint of trouble came only when trying to weigh—or the rock chafed through the rope and the ship found herself drifting, her cable cut and an anchor lost.

Turning to Rossi and Stafford, each of whom was now wearing a canvas apron to keep some of the water off them as they hauled up the lead, he said: "You'll find Mr Martin will take you close to one or two of the prizes as you row a line of soundings. Tell him anything you notice—number of guns, how many guards, if any passengers are on deck, if sheets, braces or tacks have been unrove . . . you know the sort of thing."

A few minutes later the boat was heading for the first rock, and through the telescope Ramage could see that she was being watched by the privateersmen. Once she was past the *Lynx* and the men started heaving the lead as the boat was rowed slowly across the bay, the privateersmen lost interest: the *Calypso*'s boat was doing what their captain had said he had orders to do . . .

Ramage snapped the telescope shut and said to Aitken: "You have your shipwatchers at work?"

166

Aitken grinned and said: "The privateersmen won't spot them if you can't see them, sir."

Together they walked over to Bowen: the surgeon was wedged into the shadowy corner of a gunport, a slate on his knees.

"Not much to report, sir. There are at least eight guards. They had eight women walking the deck for half an hour, and then eight men—I presume the husbands; they were not dressed as seamen—for another half an hour. They used the after companionway."

That was an important point: it meant that in the *Earl of Dodsworth*, one of the Honourable East India Company's newest ships, the sixteen passengers were almost certainly being kept prisoner in their own cabins. Eight married couples, eight cabins. Or were some of the women daughters with separate cabins? Or one or two of the men bachelors? It was a hopeless problem to work out. East Indiamen varied in the number of passengers they carried: there were different classes, the people ranging from important members of the Company and its military service to clerks and writers, as they were called. Those big ships normally carried a couple of dozen passengers, the dozen most important paying a hundred pounds each (with food and linen extra) for the passage and the honour of dining at the captain's table.

Bowen grunted and wrote on his slate. "Another four women, and the same eight guards—I recognize their shirts." He picked up the telescope again. "The guards have cutlasses. I presume pistols, too, but I can't distinguish them."

"Looks as though they put a limit of eight prisoners on deck at any one time," Aitken commented. "Probably means eight guards. These four women will have four husbands..."

"Why not exercise the four men with the women, then?" Bowen asked.

"I've no idea," Aitken answered. "Modest privateers, no doubt."

Ramage said: "Keeping the wives separate from the husbands creates uncertainty. The men worry about their women; the women are lost without their husbands." And I should know, he thought; the Herveys will have long since arrived in Paris and Gianna will have gone on to Volterra—providing Bonaparte has not already arrested her or the Herveys persuaded

167

her to abandon the journey. At that moment he realized for the first time that the Corsican was cunning enough to keep his secret police away from her: his spies might well have told him that there were desperate men in Volterra who, the minute the Marchesa returned to rule again, would do Bonaparte's work for him . . .

"Have you any idea if she's homeward or outward bound?" Aitken asked Bowen.

"Homeward, I should think," the surgeon said promptly. "Every piece of standing and running rigging is grey; the sun has bleached the John Company's colours—" he indicated the flag flapping in the breeze, the red bars now a faded pink. "Before the first of January this year John Company ships flew that ensign, seven white and six red horizontal stripes, now with an old Union in the upper canton of the fly. If she's come from India she won't yet know of the change in the Union."

Aitken nodded and grinned. "For a surgeon, you're well informed on flag etiquette."

"I always remember Southwick saying it looked like alternate slices of lean and fat bacon, but the only change now is adding the red saltire of the Irish after the Act of Union."

Ramage watched Martin turn his boat as it reached the first rock and stop while a seaman hove the lead for the first sounding. Not above four fathoms, from the look of it, and close to the *Lynx*. Would the privateer draw more than a couple of fathoms, twelve feet, on that length? Perhaps, to give a bite when she was driving to windward after a prize. If they had any sense, they'd anchor closer in, where it was too shallow for the *Calypso*, to guard against a surprise attack. Still, it was proof enough of their confidence that they had not done so: they must be sure that Captain Ramage would never risk the hostages who at the sound of the first shot would have their throats cut . . .

He walked with Aitken to where Southwick, with the second telescope, was watching the second British ship and the Dutch one. "Nothing very exciting sir," the master reported. "The British ship, the *Amethyst*, seems to have ten passengers and four guards. They had three women on deck for half an hour, then seven men. Same four guards, and I haven't seen anyone else. The Dutchman's the *Friesland*. I reckon both ships are

168

homeward bound: new rigging here and there, but simply replacing worn."

"*Amethyst* ... do you remember the *Topaz?*" Ramage asked.

"Why, surely she must be one of Mr Yorke's ships—weren't all of them named after precious stones, sir?"

"Yes, but I don't know how many he has. A dozen or so, I think."

"Well," Southwick said, as though announcing his verdict after judging a case, "I've seldom seen a ship in such good shape: I was going to comment that her owners didn't stint the master when it came to paint and ropework. So she could be one of his fleet. He'll be grateful to us."

"So far all we've done is look at her," Ramage said sourly. "Are you sure about the number of guards in the ships?"

"Yes, four in each. What's Bowen report on the *Earl of Dodsworth?*"

"Eight guards for sixteen passengers."

"Ah, Army officers going on leave! The privateersmen are wary of those in John Company's military service. A few wild subalterns will not take kindly to being prisoners."

"Good thinking," Ramage said, irritated that he had not worked it out for himself. "But why not keep them on shore with the seamen?"

Southwick sniffed, a slightly patronizing sniff that Ramage, who could have answered his own question a moment after he had spoken it, knew only too well: it said, without uttering a word, that "old Southwick" knew most of the answers. He often did, too, which was why the sniff infuriated every officer in the *Calypso.*

Very well, the Company's military officers were being kept on board the *Earl of Dodsworth* because it was easier to guard prisoners locked in a cabin than kept in a tent among a few score seamen. The passenger cabins of a John Company ship were substantial, probably mahogany; the cabins of a man of war were canvas stretched over light wooden frames ...

The bosun, lying comfortable along the barrel of the fourth gun on the starboard side, proffered his slate but Ramage, glimpsing the sprawling writing, said: "Tell me in your own words."

"Well, this *Heliotrope*—" he pronounced the name correctly, having listened to his orders from Aitken, but spoke it with the distaste of a bishop's wife referring at breakfast to an errant curate, "—has four privateersmen on board as guards, an' six passengers—two men and two women and two children, a boy an' a girl. Guards armed with cutlasses. No muskets. Perhaps pistols but I couldn't see any. Passengers kept aft—probably in their own cabins. They pump the ship once an hour for about ten minutes. All French ships leak, so it's nothing to worry about. Sails furled, sheets, tacks and braces rove . . . s'about all, sir."

It was very good, considering the bosun had no telescope.

"Did they pump while the prisoners were on deck?"

"No, sir: they brought up the women and children first and exercised 'em: then pumped; then brought the men up. They're due to pump again any minute."

The gunner, the only man in the ship Ramage disliked and regarded as incompetent, but did nothing about changing, had kept a sharp lookout on the remaining ship, The French *Commerce*. "No prisoners brought up while I've been watching, sir. Four privateersmen just walking about and leaning on the taffrail, spitting. Not all at once; I've distinguished four different men. Seem to have no duties; one comes on deck and looks round, then I don't see anyone for half an hour."

As they walked back to the quarterdeck, Aitken said to Ramage: "The *Earl of Dodsworth* seems their prize of prizes, then the *Amethyst, Heliotrope* and *Friesland* rank equal."

Roughly one guard to two hostages, Ramage noted. Tomás and Hart were not making idle threats about murdering them if necessary: each guard would have a pistol and a cutlass . . .

He left Aitken on the quarterdeck watching Martin's progress sounding towards the second rock. He saw the other two boats lying to grapnels off the beach, so the two surveying parties should be at work. Ramage sat down at his desk with a sigh and pulled his notes towards him. He wrote a second page, naming the five ships, and listing the number of passengers and guards. Then he added up the totals—forty passengers (seventeen women, twenty-one men and two children) and twenty-four guards.

Assuming the five ships had the usual number of officers and men, there would be sixty-five or seventy officers and men being guarded on shore, and given that there was no suitable building, this would be the biggest task for the privateersmen—unless... Ramage's stomach shrivelled at the idea: unless all those officers, petty officers and seamen had been warned that any attempt at escape would mean the massacre of the passengers. *That* would explain why the passengers were under guard in the ships and the crews on shore when the *Calypso* arrived. The passengers were already the hostages; it had taken no stroke of genius to tell the *Calypso* what they had already told the crews of their prizes.

Ramage was just realizing the hopelessness of his position when he thought of the second privateer, due in any day with more prizes. More ships, more passengers, more guards, and her own crew to reinforce the *Lynx*'s men watching the prisoners on shore. There was no reason to suppose she would be less successful than the *Lynx*, so any day now there could be another five prizes here, with forty-eight guards watching eighty hostages... Enough privateersmen with enough hostages, Ramage realized—and wished he had gone on halfpay, as Gianna had wanted—to force the *Calypso* to surrender. And he knew, without giving it a moment's more thought, that the instant Tomás or Hart demanded the surrender of the *Calypso* as the price for not massacring eighty hostages, he would agree. He had no choice, although no court martial could ever agree because none of the captains forming the court would ever believe that Tomás and Hart would carry out their threat. One had to see both men's eyes to understand that: they were both outcasts from the human race by their own choice. In wartime, privateers with genuine letters of marque were permitted, but privateersmen who, when the peace came, made the cold-blooded decision to become pirates and prey on ships of all nationalities, were turning their backs on civilization; they were quite deliberately striding into the jungle, and no naval captain sitting at a table in the great cabin of one of the King's ships listening to the evidence against Captain Ramage on several charges—he heard an echo of the crazy voice of the *Invincible*'s captain—would understand, or even think of, the law of the jungle.

"But what made you think, Captain Ramage, that, ah, the privateersmen, would carry out their threat to murder the hostages?"

"The look in their eyes."

"So you thereupon surrendered His Majesty's frigate the *Calypso*, and her ship's company?"

"Yes, sir."

"Because of the look in a privateersman's eye?"

It sounded ludicrous and it sounded unbelievable, and he could hear the knowing laughs of the other members of the court. There would be pressure, too, from the Honourable East India Company, who would probably be smarting from the loss of the *Earl of Dodsworth*—the underwriters might well not pay out for a ship lost to pirates in peacetime: Indiamen were armed to beat off pirates in the Eastern seas, but the *Earl of Dodsworth* did not expect to find an enemy this side of the Equator. Along the Malabar coast, yes, every John Company ship expected to find pirates there, but not in the middle of the South Atlantic.

There is only one way out of it, he thought miserably. Boarding parties will have to swim over on a dark night and deal with the guards.

Suddenly he sat up. There were enough swimmers in the ship's company. It might work—it depended on how often the guards were inspected by people from the *Lynx*. It would take a day or two of observation to find out.

CHAPTER THIRTEEN

The first survey boat to come back, commanded by Wagstaffe and with Williams's party, carried two excited men: Garret and Wilkins both came up to Ramage, who was walking up and down the quarterdeck hoping a practical plan would suddenly emerge from the tiderace of ideas coursing through his mind.

Garret's grey hair looked as though it was going to compete with Southwick's white mop, and his boots were dusty and his breeches torn. "Splendid, splendid!" he exclaimed. "There's water, and anyway I estimate there's enough rainfall for the crops we want to plant."

"What about clearing land?"

"Several flat areas—we'll need a few men to cut down some bushes, but I recommend burning. Burn and then dig. A few heavy showers and then we can plant. Then we can go home!"

Ramage turned to Wilkins. "I trust your notebooks are full!"

"Full enough," Wilkins said. "The sight of the ships anchored in the bay. Why, we could see a big reef lying along here—" he pointed over the larboard side. "If we'd gone outside the prizes, we'd have run into it. A wonderful effect it gives, seen from the hills. It'll be a challenge to get it on to canvas."

"The Irish potatoes will do well," Garret said, as though he had been spending the time Wilkins was talking coming to a decision about it. "Not sure about the sweet potatoes, though."

"The sailors will shed no tears if you can't make the yams grow," Ramage said. "They were brought up on Irish potatoes and most of them hate yams. Same goes for soldiers, I imagine. I mean, they'll hate yams," he added for the sake of the literal-minded botanist.

"What about the wild life?" he asked both men.

Wilkins grimaced and Garret said: "Very little that we saw. Some turtles. The land birds you'd expect (and very tame), the usual sea birds of course, but no sign of coneys. I'd have expected some wild dogs—a couple landed from a ship would breed and quickly turn wild—but saw none. Signs of goats, but they're a mixed blessing because they rip out everything."

Wagstaffe said: "I saw half a dozen tortoises walking about, and a turtle swimming near the beach, so we might catch one to give us a tasty dinner, sir. There is a fantastic amount of fish."

Wilkins interrupted excitedly: "The water is so clear you could see them from the boat, especially round rocks. I've never seen fish like them before—bright colours, gaudy designs, odd shapes."

Garret shook his head mournfully. "All colour and no taste, typical tropical fish. Same in the Mediterranean; the French disguise the lack of taste with spicy sauces. Hot water fish has to end up as a foreign kickshaw, I say. You can't beat cold water fish for taste. And I know the captain agrees with me."

It would be a brave man who disagreed with Garret, Ramage thought, but the botanist was right and he nodded, remembering too late that Garret was in fact repeating a comment of his.

He beckoned to Williams, who hurried up the quarterdeck ladder, dusty yet happy, like a man who had had a successful day's rough shooting.

"Did you see enough today to set your draughtsmen to work?"

The Welshman waved a handful of papers he was carrying. "There's a week's work for them here, sir, and I expect White has as much or more."

"What have you done today, then?"

"We've established where the signal station will be. Mr Renwick and Mr Wagstaffe agree on it, and we are using that as the base for all our calculations. We agreed on the site for two batteries, covering this bay, and one at the signal station. All subject to your approval, sir," he added hurriedly.

"If Mr Renwick approves, I'm sure I shall," Ramage said, reminding himself that the gunner, the one man whose opinion should have been of most value, was in fact keeping watch on the French *Commerce*—precisely because everyone knew that his opinion, if he could ever be persuaded or trapped into expressing it, would be worthless.

He caught sight of Rossi and Stafford walking forward and called to the maindeck: "Pass the word for Mr Martin and Mr Orsini."

The fourth lieutenant arrived first, the skin of his face red from the day's sun, his hat having protected his brow so that his hair seemed to be sprouting from a white skull cap. Ramage guessed the sunburn was painful; the skin of Martin's face seemed stiff and his eyes were bloodshot.

"A successful day's soundings, Martin?"

"I was just coming to report, sir. Yes, four fathoms over most of the inner half of the bay, we've sounded round that reef on our larboard beam. I have the depths where the privateer's anchored, and depths close to the nearest prize to her, the *Commerce*."

"Was the privateer at all suspicious?"

"No sir. Some of the men gave us a wave as we passed them soon after we began; otherwise they took no notice. I let the men make plenty of noise and sing out the soundings, so there was no doubt what we were doing."

"Where's Orsini?" Ramage asked impatiently, for no reason other than to relieve an impatience which was born of frustration. The Calypsos are going to have to pay for what should be charged to the *Lynx,* he thought sourly.

"He took his quadrant below to wipe off the salt spray and clean the shades and mirrors, sir. There was plenty of spray about. Er, there seems to be about thirty men on board the privateer."

"'About'?"

Martin, suddenly remembering how the captain hated vagueness, said hurriedly: "We counted thirty-six during the morning. I recognized the men who came on board yesterday. The tall man and the Negro were walking together for five minutes, watching our survey parties landing. They did not seem very interested and didn't bother to look with a glass."

Twenty-four guards in the prizes, thirty-six men in the *Lynx.* He still reckoned she would carry a round hundred. So forty men must be on shore guarding the officers and seamen taken from the prizes. Forty to guard a hundred? Anyway, how and where were the *Lynx* men keeping their prisoners?

Wagstaffe was walking towards him. He saluted and said: "I waited because I saw one of the surveyors was describing his work."

"Yes, I've heard about the potato patch. Tell me about the prisoners."

"Well, you can't see from here, sir, but just southeast from where we landed that line of hills goes round in a tight circle to make a sort of amphitheatre. All the prisoners are camped in the bottom with the guards round the top looking down on them. Both guards and prisoners have rigged up scraps of canvas to make awnings. The prisoners cook over a fireplace made up of rocks."

"What are the chances of escaping?"

"None, sir: the only way out is over the rim, which means climbing up the side of the hills. There are only a few bushes and rocks. We counted about forty guards."

Ramage nodded, thankful that the details he had so far did

not rule out the sketchy plan beginning to take shape in his mind. "By the way," he told Wagstaffe, "you'll have to make do tomorrow without Stafford and Rossi, and any other good swimmers."

Soon after dawn next morning the sentry called that Aitken was at the door of Ramage's cabin and a moment later the first lieutenant arrived holding a sheet of paper.

"The list of swimmers you asked for, sir. I started with the twenty men you gave prizes to in Gibraltar. I didn't expect the five-times-round-the-*Calypso* race to have results a year later! If you remember, sir, Renwick won, Martin was second, Rossi third, Orsini and Jackson tied for fourth position and the gunner nearly drowned!"

"And five guineas cost me six," Ramage said.

Aitken grinned at the memory. "Ah yes, the judge's interpretation of 'the first five positions', and nothing being laid down about ties."

"Yes. Judge Aitken and his interpretation of Scottish law! Well, what sort of list do we have?"

"The totals are quite good, sir. Twenty-three are powerful swimmers, fourteen more are good for a steady mile, another eight are fine for a fast half-mile but no good over a long distance, while sixty-eight are weak but can swim. In fact all but fifteen of the ship's company can swim. Of the supernumeraries, one draughtsman, Garret, and the four masons can't swim at all. Wilkins is a powerful swimmer—I've seen him, and when I spoke to him this morning he asked if you'd consider him for—well, whatever you have in mind."

"Oh, just another swimming competition," Ramage said innocently. "I thought we could practise on the larboard side."

"Yes, we'll be out of sight of the privateersmen and the prizes, so the women hostages won't be offended at the sight of dozens of naked seamen splashing about."

"Exactly," Ramage said. "I want a boarding net slung over the side, so the men can hold on to it when they want a rest. And three or four Marines with muskets, in case of sharks."

"Aye aye, sir," Aitken said, thankful that the first moves were being taken against the privateersmen.

"And Aitken," Ramage said quietly, "don't look so cheerful. I'd just as soon have everyone looking miserable. It shows with

176

a good telescope, you know, and we'd better assume those scoundrels Tomás and Hart are keeping an eye on us. A cheerful man has a jaunty walk. Those scoundrels think that none of the Calypsos have anything to be jaunty about—the officers, anyway."

"I understand, sir," Aitken said. "I can get very miserable at the mere thought of our problems, let alone solving them."

"That's the spirit," Ramage said, "looking sad may keep us alive—and those passengers too."

He folded Aitken's list of swimmers and put it in his pocket, after taking out another folded sheet of paper which he smoothed out on top of his desk and gestured to Aitken to come across and look at.

The first lieutenant was puzzled by what he saw. "A raft, sir or one of those South Sea things? A proa, isn't that the word?"

"A cross between the two. Two stout pieces of wood form the floats, and light planks join them and make a sort of deck. And an eyebolt at each end—one for towing, the other for steering."

"Ah, yes sir," Aitken said, obviously puzzled not by the raft but by its purpose. "About—" he looked at the dimensions which Ramage had scribbled in "—five feet long and two and a half feet wide."

"I want two, each with eyebolts," Ramage said.

"Indeed, with eyebolts," the Scotsman echoed and then looked up. He smiled and said; "Maybe I could better explain to the carpenter what's needed if I understood its purpose, sir."

"I'm sure you would," Ramage said and explained it.

As the rising sun neared the horizon in the east, Ramage went up to the quarterdeck and watched the island turn from a vague grey blur into a heavily-shadowed shape that Wilkins would no doubt call an exercise in the use of black. A sudden movement by the taffrail made Ramage swing round, to be startled by the sight of Wilkins himself perched on the breech of a carronade, legs astride the barrel, a pad in one hand and a stick of charcoal in the other.

"Good morning to you, Captain," the artist said breezily. "Sorry I made you jump. I hope you don't mind me making free with your quarterdeck, but these fat carronades are more comfortable than the 12-pounders."

"Go wherever you wish. What are you doing now?"

"A study for a dawn painting of the island, with the prizes in the foreground. Curious how you can really only see the shape of hilly or mountainous land when the sun is low, rising or setting."

"Yes, a high sun washes out the shapes," Ramage said.

"Ah 'washes out'—the exact phrase. You've noticed it, then?"

Ramage gave a short laugh. "Not living in a house means I've seen nearly every dawn and sunset for the past few years, most of them in the Mediterranean, or the West Indies, so I've watched shadows spreading across flat islands and mountainous islands, across the Pyrenees and the Atlas mountains, the Sierras of Spain and the Spanish Main. And at the end of it, Wilkins, I've a confession to make."

"A confession?" The startled artist swung round, lifting a leg so that both feet were on the top of the carriage.

"Yes, they total more than a thousand wasted dawns, because I am no artist and I haven't been able to record even the dullest of them."

"Except in your memory," Wilkins said. "Don't envy me," he added, almost a bitter note in his voice.

"But I do. Not just landscapes, but your portraits as well."

"Well, perhaps a dozen portraits, but no landscapes. With portraits rarely does the sitter, and never his relatives or friends (but particularly his wife) see him through the artist's eyes, or brush. The more worthwhile the landscape, the less popular it is. How many 'patrons of the arts' have ever seen dawn breaking from seaward of a West Indian island, or a Tuscan hill town as the first sun of the day washes it with pink? Or the sun setting through the Strait, with your Atlas mountains on the African side and Gibraltar or the High Sierras on the other? Wonderful sights, beautiful enough to make an artist weep for sheer joy—and weep, too, because no visitor to an exhibition of his work, no patron with the money to buy it, is going to believe what he sees on the canvas. 'Very imaginative,' the patron will say, keeping a firm hand on the strings of his purse. And he will move along the line and buy some miserable daub showing a wet sun setting over the damp Nor-

178

folk Broads—a sun looking as though it had been drowned a few times before setting through all that cloud."

Fascinated at this glimpse of the world of objects, subjects and patrons seen through the eyes of a painter, Ramage said: "If you can capture Trinidade on canvas just after dawn, noon and sunset, I'll be the first to buy them!"

"That's good of you," Wilkins said politely, "but it's not the point I'm making. You've seen it: you know what it's like. I'm grumbling about the people who don't know and refuse to let the painter show them. You probably know the early Florentine painters were laughed at because no one in the north could believe that the light they painted actually existed in Tuscany. Finally, enough people visited Tuscany and saw for themselves, and the Florentines were accepted. But that was a long time ago, and I assure you that Tuscany is still the southern limit of people's credulity!"

"When we get back to London we'll hold an exhibition, showing all your paintings of this expedition—like the paintings of Captain Cook's voyages."

Wilkins slid off the gun and stood in front of Ramage, the sun's rays giving him a ruddy complexion which did not disguise the serious look in his face.

"Do you really think we shall ever see London again, Captain?"

The sudden question startled Ramage. "Yes, why ever not?"

Wilkins gestured towards the *Lynx* and the anchored prizes. "Those fellows seem to hold all the aces."

Ramage's harsh laugh was not one intended to reassure Wilkins; it came quite naturally as his memory flickered back over the past few years, when a variety of men had seemed to hold enough aces, yet...

"I'm not a gambler, Wilkins; none of the *Calypso*'s officers is. But we've all learned one thing—three aces can be taken by the two of trumps!"

"So we have a two of trumps?"

"I didn't say that; just that we need to find only the two or three if we want to see London again, not necessarily an ace."

Wilkins laughed, a cheerful laugh which also revealed the relief he felt. "Tell me, Captain, all those actions of yours described in I don't know how many *London Gazettes*: how

179

many of those were games won with a two of trumps and how many with an ace?"

"You'd better ask Southwick, he watches the games more closely than I. But I don't remember any aces—or court cards—at all. We always seem to get dealt fives or under!"

Ramage saw the soundings and survey teams assembling on the maindeck and went down to give instructions to Martin.

"Don't be obvious about it, but each day I want you to take three or four soundings and get a rough idea of the depths between us and the *Lynx*. You'll soon have that reef on the western side of the bay charted, but make sure you cover the eastern side, too."

Martin grinned and said: "Aye aye, sir; it'd be easier to tack than wear to get out of the bay!"

"Indeed?" Ramage said, his face expressionless.

He found Wagstaffe with Kenton cursing the tardiness of Williams, one of the surveyors.

"Once you can look down on the *Lynx*, I want you to give someone the glass—perhaps you had better do it yourself; it'll be a welcome change from tramping up and down the hills—and watch the *Lynx* for a few hours. See what you can tell me about the state of discipline, condition of her sails and rigging, check her armament and see if she can mount swivels, and try to see exactly how many men she has on board. Tomorrow I want to know exactly how many men are guarding the prisoners. And, of course, note the boats leaving or arriving at the *Lynx*."

Wagstaffe saluted. "Surveying is a very boring job; I seem to end up holding these striped poles and measuring angles. By the way, sir, once the draughtsmen really get to work, we're going to have to give names to the bays, headlands and peaks. I mention it, sir, in case you want to state your preferences."

Ramage was still absorbing Wagstaffe's tact when Southwick came bustling up, holding a slate. "You want the same watch on the prizes, sir?"

"Yes. Not a boat visited any one of them yesterday."

"No reason why one should, come to think of it, sir; each ship must have plenty of water and provisions. Any trouble with hostages, and the privateersmen would be going over to the *Lynx*."

"Ah, what eyes and brains lost to the Revenue Service," Ramage teased.

Southwick sniffed contemptuously. "My big mistake, sir, was not joining the *smugglers* when I was a boy. I'd be retired now with a big mansion, a stable of horses, two carriages . . ."

Aitken came up and saluted. "The swimmers, sir. They're ready for inspection, and the carpenter and his mates have nearly finished the first raft. Would you care to look at it before they put the last nails on the decking and start on the second?"

The raft looked in fact like a large toboggan with wide and deep runners. On the front of what would be the section on which a person would sit to slide on snow was an eyebolt, with another at the back.

"I want a couple of fathoms of line on each eyebolt, and secure line along the sides, so that men can hold on."

"How many men, sir?"

Ramage shrugged his shoulders. He looked at the raft and said: "She won't take more than six holding on each side, plus one forward and one astern. That'll make fourteen, and should be enough. Put a batten each side on the decking, carpenter, here and there, so that something put on top won't roll off."

He left the raft and walked along the line of men drawn up on the larboard gangway. They represented the *Calypso*'s best swimmers, and he jumped on to the breech of a gun. "Gather round," he said. "This is what you'll be training to do in the next few days."

Four days later, as he listened to the splashing of a couple of dozen men swimming beside the ship, out of sight of the privateersmen, Ramage sat at his desk staring at several sheets of paper held down by a large polished pebble.

His life at the moment seemed divided into halves. One was Gianna, the other was the problem of the *Lynx* and her prizes.

Since leaving the house in Palace Street and joining the *Calypso* at Chatham, he had tried to avoid thinking of her. He realized now that he had in fact tried deliberately to destroy every memory of her, particularly of their first meeting, in the darkness and mystery of the Torre di Buranaccio, and the desperation he felt holding her in an open boat knowing she had a musket ball in her shoulder and fearing she would die before he could find a surgeon . . . So many memories, some of danger,

181

some of peace. When she came out to Lisbon to see him and the way she had the ambassador, Hookham Frere, dancing a jig in an effort to please her, and quiet days at St Kew when they had walked together over the Cornish moors or rode as far as Roughtor and Brown Willie, the distant peaks which looked as though they had been dropped by a giant . . . When her eyes glinted and she became imperious, the Marchesa breaking through, revealing a childhood spent in the palace at Volterra with dozens of servants and an early adulthood surrounded by ministers, the ruler of her own state, Volterra. He remembered the walled city of Volterra with its dozens of towers, tall, very narrow rectangles rising high like treetrunks.

Was she safely there, consulting with her ministers, restoring order and without French troops? Had the French removed their guillotines and rusty iron trees of Liberty? Was she ruling wisely and patiently, realizing that forgiving and forgetting might be a wiser policy than judging and revenging? Or was she dead, an assassin's victim?

Because he had previously refused to think about it, chasing away the random thoughts that leapt at him from dark corners of his mind before he went to sleep, or when he woke at night, his head a turmoil and his muscles knotted, he found that new fears for Gianna had spawned and demanded his consideration.

He tried to fight them off by imagining what had happened to her from the time she had boarded the Dover packet with the Herveys. They would have arrived in Calais and presented their passports, duly signed by Hawkesbury and probably, because Jenks was a fool, countersigned by Otto. The Herveys' carriages would have been loaded with their baggage, and knowing both the Herveys and Gianna, he could imagine just how many trunks would be involved. Then they would have set off along the Paris road, probably intending to spend the first night of the journey at Amiens.

They would be little prepared for what they saw: Bonaparte's secret police, the near-starvation, the nearness of the guillotine, the sheer lack of an occasional coat of paint on houses—all had combined to give French towns the appearance of places that have been stripped by locusts, or at least occupied by an enemy army. In fact France's own army had taken so heavy a toll of able-bodied men that the inhabitants of towns and cities were mainly women—many in the eternal black of mourning—and old men. There would be many cripples, too; men who had lost a leg or an arm in battle or even in the ice and snow of the Alps or Apennines.

They would see—particularly in Amiens, where he had once been imprisoned and threatened with it—the Widow set up in most squares. The guillotine had become part of every French square; *La Veuve dans la place,* usually set up high on a platform so the crowds could watch the spectacle, a wicker basket to catch the head . . .

This the Herveys and Gianna would see—well, not the basket and not the darkened bloodstains, which the rains would have washed away, nor the heavy blade of the guillotine, which was removed by the executioner when not required, so the edge could be sharpened again and greased well to protect it against rust. They would see the gaunt, wooden framework and probably sigh that it had ever been used. It was all over now, they would say, the Treaty had been signed, the war was over. Would Hervey himself, or Gianna, realize that *La Veuve* had nothing to do with the war and with the Treaty; that it was used by the French government of the day against the French people?

Anyway, eventually they would arrive in Paris, and there they, along with all foreigners, would have to register their presence and their address at the Prefecture. So if they were waiting for her, Bonaparte's secret police did not have to look for the Marchesa di Volterra; she would come to them . . . Leaving the safety of England, she would have walked like the fly into the parlour of the spider Bonaparte. And all he thought bitterly, in the completely mistaken idea that she was doing it for the good of Volterra.

What good was she to Volterra if she was lodged in a French jail? What influence could she have on Bonaparte when he had her behind a locked door? She argued, of course, that while in England she had no influence on Bonaparte, and both Ramage and his father had immediately pointed out that while she was free she *had* an influence on Bonaparte: he always knew that the rightful ruler of Volterra was waiting patiently to return; that his French regime there were simply puppets.

There was only one way that Bonaparte could destroy the Kingdom of Volterra, and that would be by destroying its rightful ruler, and Ramage found he had crushed the quill pen with which he had been tapping the pile of papers representing the other half of his problem.

Destroy... another word for murder. And murder was another word for what? Not the guillotine, that would be too public. The garotte—did Bonaparte's police favour the Spanish garotte for simple killings of women? Or perhaps just a pistol shot in the head. God help him, he was considering the fate of the woman he had loved. Yes, he had to admit now it was in the past tense. Had loved but still respected, like a favourite sister. Yet now was hardly the time to think about it any further. He had to keep the door shut in his mind, otherwise dreadful thoughts sneaked out. Gianna dead, murdered on Bonaparte's orders; Gianna locked in a cell, wasting away in darkness and subsisting only on sparse prison fare, and no one knowing what had become of her, outside the upper circle of Bonaparte's police...

Deliberately he picked up the top pages. They were the reports of four days' watch on the prizes, four pages for each of the five ships. He selected another quill, found it had been cut to give too broad a tip, and took a knife from a drawer in the desk and cut it again. He then found the ink, removed the cap, found a blank sheet of paper, and on the left side wrote down the names of the five ships. To the right of the names he drew four more columns, and at the top of them he wrote, in sequence, "Passengers", "Guards", "Crew", "Flag".

Starting with the *Earl of Dodsworth,* he saw that each day Bowen had reported seeing sixteen passengers (eight women and eight men) and he filled in the first column. Eight guards— he saw the same eight men each day, so it was reasonable to suppose they were the only eight on board, and that filled in the next column.

Southwick's four daily reports on the *Amethyst* and the *Friesland* showed the same consistency. Yorke's ship—Ramage found himself picturing the young shipowner as he read the name—had three women and seven men on board as hostages, and four guards. Southwick noted that on the second day he had seen only three guards, but the fourth man, easily recognizable by his red hair, reappeared next day and was there on the fourth day. Ramage filled in the appropriate columns, and then worked through the *Heliotrope* and *Commerce*, slowly filling in the columns.

Then he drew a line across the bottom and filled in the totals: exactly forty passengers (seventeen women, twenty-one men and two children), and twenty-four guards.

But most important: in four days, no boats had visited the prizes. No one had come round from the *Lynx;* no men from one prize had visited another. It would be such a normal and commonplace thing for them to do so that obviously Tomás or Hart had forbidden it.

Southwick's estimates of the sizes of the ships' companies of the five prizes before they were taken agreed with his own and showed there should be ninety-five or a hundred British, Dutch and French ships' officers and men held prisoner in what Wagstaffe had called an amphitheatre on shore.

The John Company ship, apart from being the most valuable, was physically the nearest: the *Earl of Dodsworth* was anchored about two hundred yards away. Close enough, he noted ruefully, for him to see that at least four of the women were young, two were elderly, and two had been impossible to guess at because they wore large, flopping hats, presumably to keep the sun off their faces.

The problem, he thought to himself, was going to be keeping the hostages out of the way when the fighting started.

He unrolled the first rough draft chart of the bay. There was an outline of the shore, from the headland forming the southern side to the other peninsula forming the northern. From each of the two rocks being used as starting points, a series of straight lines radiated out to seaward; they represented the compass courses steered by the soundings boat, and along the lines, at ten yard intervals, were written numbers, some with a small figure followed by a large one. The larger figure represented fathoms, the smaller feet. Also marked in were the positions of the five prizes, the *Lynx* and the *Calypso*. The nearest sounding to the *Lynx* was four fathoms and three feet, or twenty-seven feet. The inner bay itself, Ramage noted, was quite shallow; none of the soundings showed more than forty feet, although many more runs were needed before the boat had got out as far as a line joining the two headlands.

The big reef to larboard was a long and slightly crescent-shaped sausage, lying east–west and almost cutting the bay in two, with all the ships anchored in the southern half. The reef, made up of rock and staghorn coral—so named because it grew up from the bottom like the horns of a stag, flattening out near the surface—varied from a couple of feet over the coral to two fathoms over the rock. Martin had marked each end with a dan buoy, and once the sun was up it was easy to see the brown patches formed by the staghorn.

Ramage then unrolled the rough map showing the small section of the island surveyed so far. Williams and White had, at his suggestion, begun by concentrating on a broad band between the landing beach and signal hill. This included the approaches to the amphitheatre, where the crews of the prizes were kept prisoner, and the two sources of fresh water.

Finally there was Wagstaffe's report on the "forum" and on the *Lynx*. Jebediah Hart and the small grey-haired Frenchman had been on shore once in the only boat to leave the *Lynx* in four days. Their boat had been pulled up on the beach and the two men had climbed up to the "forum," stayed half an hour and then gone back to the ship. A routine visit, it seemed to Wagstaffe; they did not take provisions or water, so presumably the camp was adequately supplied.

He tidied the papers and rolled up the chart and the map. There, reduced to words and lines on paper, were all the facts he needed to carry out his next task, yet nothing there provided an answer to the most important question of all, one that was screaming in his brain like a descant sung by a mad chorus in an empty cathedral: how to keep the hostages out of harm's way when the fighting started.

He had worked out the general plan, and he was certain that he had reduced chance to the minimum. He could only attack two ships a night: it would be too exhausting for the swimmers to try more. Tired men made mistakes, and he had to be sure that the risk he took was reasonably small. By seizing the *Earl of Dodsworth* and the *Amethyst* on the first night and the *Heliotrope* and *Friesland* on the second, he was releasing the majority of prisoners first. The risk was simply that privateersmen from the *Lynx* might come to the *Earl of Dodsworth* or the *Amethyst* on the second day, before the other two ships could be secured. The *Commerce* could be left: she had no passengers, and the four privateersmen on board her were obviously little more than shipkeepers.

How to warn the hostages . . . Confound it, as far as the *Earl of Dodsworth* and *Amethyst* were concerned it was already too

186

late: he had set the time for the attacks at 3 a.m., a time when he reckoned the privateersmen on guard would most likely be all asleep, and there was no way of getting a warning to the two ships.

Well, the two boarding parties were now well trained: every one of them could swim a mile and at the end of it silently board a ship by shinning up the anchor cable if a rope ladder had not been left hanging over the side. At the moment all four ships had ladders down their sides: obviously the privateersmen were confident they had nothing to fear. However, a plan to board could not be based on the chance of a rope ladder, or the hope that no sentry would be waiting at the top.

He would be leading the *Earl of Dodsworth* party with Martin and Orsini; Aitken would be tackling the *Amethyst* with Kenton. That left Wagstaffe and Southwick in the *Calypso,* and both men had protested violently at being left out of the rescue. Finally Ramage had pointed out that if anything went wrong, it would be up to the two men to get the *Calypso* out of the bay and back to England . . .

There was in fact one way of warning the hostages, he realized, and shivered with a fear which was not only for his own life but, in the case of the *Earl of Dodsworth,* for the lives of eight women and eight men hostages. And how would Aitken react?

CHAPTER FOURTEEN

Silkin gave a sniff which, registering disapproval, would have outdone anything Southwick could have produced. Ramage was standing naked in the middle of his cabin, trying to arrange an old stock as a loincloth. "It's no good, the damned thing keeps slipping!" he grumbled.

"Breeches, sir, or even these trousers I bought from the purser: they will answer the purpose admirably."

"Silkin, I have a good half a mile to swim, and I'm not going to be weighed down by heavy clothes."

"These trousers, sir, they're not really heavy. Just nankeen, they are. Just enough for the purposes of modesty."

"The devil take modesty," Ramage snapped. "I'm not anticipating parading in front of the women passengers. I'd go naked but for the fact that it would remind an enemy that the quickest way of disabling a man is to kick him in the groin."

"What are the seamen wearing, sir?"

"I don't know, but they don't have such vivid imaginations as I do. Here, this stock is fine now. Give me a big pin. Ah, that's it. Now, that belt. Slide the frog round, so that it's in the small of my back."

The sailmaker had been busy adapting cutlass belts which were normally worn slung over one shoulder; the swimmers had demanded a way of keeping the cutlass from getting between their legs as they swam, and the best he could do was devise a waistbelt stitched to the shoulderbelt which kept the cutlass to one side. Ramage had not liked it; instead he was just using a waistbelt but fitting it much higher, under his armpits, so that as he swam horizontally the cutlass blade lay along his back, the point on his buttocks. He preferred this method to the other because, with the blade to a man's left, it could cause trouble if he swam to the left or the right.

"What's the time?"

Silkin picked up Ramage's breeches and took the watch from the fob pocket. "Just ten minutes past two o'clock, sir."

"Good, time I was off. Quickly, that knife and sheath. Now, strap it round my right shin." Ramage put his foot up on a chair. "Tighter . . . that's fine. Now take the line at the bottom of the sheath—yes, it goes round my ankle."

With the sheath knife secured on the side of his right shin, the cutlass slapping against his back, and dressed only in the stock round his hips, Ramage felt more than faintly ridiculous, but no one was going to see him for some time . . .

He met Aitken and Southwick at the top of the companion-way. Aitken was naked to the waist and wearing seaman's trousers, a cutlass belt across his shoulder.

"You look like an Indian, sir," Southwick said cheerfully. "I half expected you to try to sell us mangoes."

"I'm off to demonstrate the Indian rope trick," Ramage said. "Well, Aitken, do you still feel as confident?"

"No sir," the Scotsman said bluntly. "I didn't feel confident when you first mentioned it, but as I don't feel any less so now, we needn't worry."

Ramage took his hand in the darkness and shook it. "I'll give you a wave when we take our exercise in the morning!" With that he went to the entryport, acknowledged the murmured good wishes of the small groups of men waiting there, and reached out for one of the two manropes hanging down into the water.

As soon as he grasped them, two seamen held them away from the hull, and two more scrambled down the side battens to hold them out farther down, where they would otherwise touch because the hull curved outwards in the almost exag-gerated tumblehome.

Slowly Ramage let himself go hand over hand down the rope, acknowledging the good wishes of the sidemen as he passed them. Then the lapping of water against the hull became louder, and the curious mixture of seaweed and fishmarket smell peculiar to the waterline of a ship in the Tropics warned him he was almost in the water.

He felt chilled. A slow descent into the water or a sudden plunge? He let go and a moment later gave an agonized gasp: for a moment the water seemed icy cold, and he held his breath until he surfaced again.

Then, kicking away from the side of the ship, he checked first the cutlass and the knife and then, as an afterthought, the stock. Then, swimming on his back, he identified the particular stars he needed. A cloudless night: the one thing that would have postponed tonight's attempt would have been cloud, because it was impossible to see the *Earl of Dodsworth* or the *Amethyst* from the sea on a dark night.

The water was not as cold as he had expected and as he began swimming away on his back the *Calypso* seemed huge, her rigging and spars making a complex pattern against the stars, a vast net made by a crazy fisherman.

The cutlass was hanging down vertically, now he was swimming on his back, and the hilt was digging painfully into his shoulder blades. Aitken would be in the water by now and beginning his swim to the *Amethyst*. Because she was lying more to the south the first lieutenant had no further to swim: the *Calypso* was the centre of a radius whose circumference went through the *Earl of Dodsworth* and the *Amethyst*.

Ramage turned over and began swimming on his stomach. All the men had practised keeping their feet well below the surface, to avoid making any noise, and he was sure he was silent. He hitched the cutlass into the middle of his back and suddenly thought about sharks. No one had seen any sign of one all the time the *Calypso* had been anchored at Trinidade, but now, with only the stock round his hips, he suddenly felt vulnerable. It must be the darkness, he told himself, because he had never given it a thought while swimming naked with the men in daylight. Not only shark but barracuda, of which they had seen many. He found himself swimming faster, then realized that his strokes were making a noise.

He turned over on his back and saw from the stars that he had been swimming round in a half circle. He looked back and was surprised to see that the *Calypso* was now some distance away. He checked the position of Orion's Belt, which was acting as his compass, and after a few strokes decided to tread water and look for some sign of the *Earl of Dodsworth*. When he could see her masts clearly against the stars he began swimming again in a powerful overarm stroke. There was little or no phosphorescence, and at this distance if the guards heard a splash they would assume it was a fish leaping to escape a predator. A predator like a shark or a barracuda . . .

The sea now seemed warm and the air cooler on his face while he was treading water. In the Tropics at night the sea usually stayed at more or less its daytime temperature while the air temperature dropped below that of the water.

Where was Gianna now? Thinking of her took his mind off the thought of sharks and barracuda possibly circling below him, but as he congratulated himself on not feeling tired so far, he thought of the two dozen men who would be swimming in his wake from the *Calypso* in half an hour or so, and the twenty who would follow Aitken to the *Amethyst*. Was it possible that all of them would escape cramp, shark or barracuda? Was it possible that the whole operation would be achieved without someone screaming with pain as a shark's teeth took off a leg or the backward-pointing teeth of a barracuda ripped out a great piece of flesh? He shivered and wanted to clutch himself protectively, but to do so would miss a stroke and armour him about as effectively as a shrivelled fig leaf.

He began counting the strokes and stopped at a hundred for a rest, not because he was tired but to avoid arriving at the *Earl of Dodsworth* out of breath. There was no hurry; once on board and his first task accomplished, he would have to wait for the boarding party to arrive. Wet feet. Suddenly he realized that once he was on board he would have to be careful that his wet footmarks did not give him away. Even in the moonlight they would show up on the dry decks like blobs of black paint. He should have brought a towel, or a length of dry cloth, in a sealed glass jar. A thin roll of nankeen slid into a bottle which was then tightly corked would have done the job. Well, he had not thought of it and now it was about a quarter of a mile too late.

What else had he forgotten? He coughed as a wavelet slopped at the moment that he opened his mouth to take a breath. The salt water seared his throat and he immediately trod water and turned his face away from the ship. The sound of a racking cough like this would carry for miles; it seemed that he was coughing up his lungs as well as his throat. Finally the spasm ended and he thought of the two dozen swimmers who would soon be following him. If only one man in four accidentally swallowed water, as he had just done, that would mean six of them rasping away in the darkness . . . .

He resumed swimming once his breathing returned to normal. This swim was taking longer than he anticipated, although he had cured himself of the tendency to swim in a half circle. It was hard on the neck trying to keep an eye on a star constellation which was almost overhead: he should have thought of that and chosen one nearer the horizon—except none in the right direction were as obvious as Orion's Belt, which could be identified at a glance.

All of a sudden—or so it seemed—the *Earl of Dodsworth* was in front of him, like a huge castle wall in the moonlight. For the last few minutes he had been swimming and distracting himself by having a furious argument with Gianna in his imagination as he tried to persuade her to get into a carriage he had waiting outside the Herveys' Paris residence.

The bow was to his left and he swam cautiously towards it, propelling himself by slow strokes with his feet as he checked the cutlass, the stock and the sheath knife strapped to his shin. There was little or no wind and the *Earl of Dodsworth* had her bow to the northeast, riding to the current which, weak at the moment, ran continually to the southwest and meant that her anchor cable would probably be hanging down almost vertically.

The mainyard seemed to show up strangely, as though it was emitting a faint orange glow. Then he caught sight of a glow in several gunports and realized that a lantern on deck amidships was lighting up part of the deck, rigging and mainmast. How would he get aft from the fo'c'sle without being seen if the guards were amidships with a lantern?

He turned towards the stern. Unless an odd rope or an extra rope ladder was hanging over, there was scant chance that he would be able to board there, but it was a chance he could not afford to neglect.

Now he was swimming as carefully as if he was walking across a frozen pond in hobnailed boots: the *Earl of Dodsworth*'s sides rose almost sheer out of the water and he could make out the gunports—East Indiamen were always heavily

192

armed; from a distance an unskilled eye often took them for warships. Now the outward curve of the stern and the stern-lights, the big windows which lit the main cabin. Again there was the glow of a lantern, but no rope or ladder hung down.

He had arrived—just the length of the ship to cover, to reach the anchor cable—and he was feeling cold, but he was not puffing. All that would change soon: he would be hot and puffing by the time he reached the hawsehole after climbing the cable.

He stopped from time to time, keeping himself afloat by holding the tips of his fingers against the edges of copper sheathing, and listened for voices, but he heard nothing. The eight guards in the *Earl of Dodsworth*—did they stand a two-on-and-six-off watch at night?

Here was the cable: eight inches in diameter, perhaps ten, as thick as a man's leg at the knee. He checked the cutlass and knife again, paused for a few minutes while he breathed deeply, and then clasped his legs round the rope and pushed up while grasping it and hauling with his arms. The cordage was new and the thick strands of the cable-laid rope made it much easier to hold. Quickly he found the rhythm: clasp tight with the ankles, straighten up the body and then hold with the thighs; reach up with the hands, haul higher by making the body jacknife while sliding the legs higher... Ten feet above water, fifteen, twenty... Supposing a guard's bowels were troubling him and he came to the head, to so-called "seat of ease" built in the stem, one each side of the bowsprit in an Indiaman like this and merely a wooden form with a circule hole. A seaman sitting there would hear someone climbing the anchor cable.

He had slowed down, his breathing shallow, until he realized that the chances of anyone being there were negligible and anyway it was too late to do anything about it. He resumed the scissor-cutting movement and worked his way up to the hawse hole, where he paused and listened. As soon as he was satisfied that no one had heard him he reached up, carefully holding the blade of the cutlass so that it did not hit a piece of metal and make a clang, and climbed on board.

Looking down at the sea he was almost hypnotized by the reflection of all the stars. He began to shiver as the water dripped off him, and he tried to squeeze as much as he could from his hair. His teeth were going to be chattering in a moment unless he did something about it. He walked aft until the belfry hid him from anyone abaft the fo'c'sle and reached over his shoulder to draw the cutlass, which he put flat on the deck and then removed the belt, now stiff and cold from the salt water. Then he pulled the pin from the stock and unwound it so that he was standing naked, except for the sheath knife on his shin.

Using the edges of his hand he wiped the drops of water from his body like a cook rolling dried pease into a jar; then he rubbed his body briskly. He twisted the stock between his hands, like a washerwoman squeezing the water from a towel, put it on the deck and smoothed it flat with his hands, and then wound it round his hips again, finally securing it with the pin. It was cold and clammy, but even as he put the wet and unyielding cutlass belt round his ribs again and tightened the buckle, he could feel the cloth warming slightly to his body.

Well, he was on board the *Earl of Dodsworth* and he could have been feeling a lot worse. His shin muscles were telling him he had swum a long distance; his thigh, shoulder and arm muscles were protesting at the climb up the rope, but he felt he could (in case of dire need) swim back to the *Calypso* and climb up *her* anchor cable.

As he warmed up and the salt water dried in his nostrils he realized that the ship smelled and sounded almost like a farmyard. There were several hen coops on the fo'c'sle, presumably supplying fresh eggs and white meat for the passengers. And turkeys, too. He could smell sheep's wool and guessed that several animals were tethered below with a couple of cows— no doubt, to provide fresh milk. Passengers were charged so much that they expected fresh food. Some of these passengers probably controlled areas of India as big as a dozen English counties, and were certainly not going to eat salt beef and sauerkraut!

The lantern just abaft the mainmast was dim; in fact the candle inside was obviously guttering, the wick probably fallen over so that it was only partly burning, the rest lying below the melted wax.

Ramage picked up the cutlass. The lives of sixteen passengers and the fate of an East Indiaman depended upon him not making any mistakes in the next few minutes. From infrequent visits to East Indiamen years ago, when he was a hungry mid-

194

shipman and glad of an invitation to dinner on board—the richness of John Company food was famous among naval officers no matter what their rank—he remembered that the captain's cabin was right aft, with cabins for the most important passengers further forward on the same deck, and the cheaper cabins (for passengers who dined at the tables of the second and third mates) one deck lower.

Well, he needed to find the nearest passenger cabin that he could enter without a privateersman seeing him. He decided that going up and down companionways was the riskiest thing he could do; if a guard saw him, or he accidentally met one on the steps, there could be no doubt that a man rigged out with only a loincloth was an intruder and the alarm would be raised in moments.

Obviously he had to find the forwardmost passenger cabin on the upperdeck. Whether it was starboard or larboard depended on the route he had to take to dodge the guards. How long since he had left the *Calpyso?* It seemed hours ago. Weeks ago, in fact. It was probably only about twenty minutes at the moment, and very soon his boarding party would be slipping down into the water and beginning their long swim.

He came out from behind the belfry and saw the chimney of the galley. He continued moving to his right, his bare feet occasionally stubbing against an eyebolt or a coil of rope. After kicking one metal fitting—he could not see what it was—with a violence that seemed for a moment to have broken his left big toe, Ramage slowed down: he would have to look ahead at eye level, and then look down at the deck, before he moved. Looking ahead and trusting his feet to luck was an invitation to go sprawling.

Here was the companionway from the fo'c'sle down to the maindeck. He stood at the top and stared aft. Just the flicking lantern: no voices, no movement. Somewhere there a guard or two must be standing or sitting. A guard or a lookout—or a privateersman doing both jobs. Eight guards—surely there must be at least two on watch?

The bottom rung creaked, but there was enough swell to make the *Earl of Dodsworth* pitch slightly, so that she gave a slight bow every minute or two, just enough movement for the masts to creak as they strained the shrouds and to make the yards grumble as they tried to swing round against the pull of the braces. But for the creaks, he thought, he could be moving through a graveyard: lockers, hatches, hen coops and scuttles looked in the darkness like tombs and gravestones, the rising moon, in its last quarter, beginning to give enough light to make the white paint look like marble.

Keeping close against the bulwark, just far enough away to clear the breeches of the guns, Ramage crept aft. Past the foremast and all its dozens of ropes forming the shrouds, halyards, topping lifts... Past the third gun, and the round-shot in racks round the hatch coamings, man-of-war fashion, each shot like a black orange resting in a cup-shaped depression cut into the wood.

Halfway to the mainmast he crouched down behind the breech of a gun and concentrated on the lantern. It lit a cone about ten feet in diameter on the deck, and it was set on a low table. Several things glinted to one side, like winking glass eyes. A cut-glass decanter and glasses? Ramage could think of nothing else that would flash in that fashion as he moved his head slightly.

Then, each side of the table, he picked out two easy chairs. The shape of them was indistinct—then he could just make out the figure of a man sprawled in each one. Not just lying back asleep but sprawled in the shapeless lump of a drunken man who had passed out.

The two guards on watch? It seemed likely. That left six others who would presumably be sleeping peacefully until the next pair was roused by these two. Well, the half-dozen were going to get a good long sleep, from the look of it.

He kept still for a few more moments. The hens in the coops forward clucked and then went back to sleep. Finally he was certain these were the only two men on deck, so six privateersmen should be sleeping somewhere below, and so were sixteen passengers, who would be locked in their cabins or bundled all together in a large cabin that could be guarded easily.

Would there be more guards on duty somewhere below? Was it likely? Why put the passengers in a separate cabin when they could be locked in their own cabins? In turn, that meant the other six guards would be sleeping near the passengers' accommodation, ready in an instant should anyone try to escape.

What were these two doing on deck, then? Presumably they were really lookouts; men whose task it was to watch for a boarding party from the *Calypso*. Could these men be the key to capturing the *Earl of Dodsworth?* It seemed so; they were (as far as the *Lynx* and the six guards off watch were concerned) the ones who would raise the alarm, whether the *Calypso* or the passengers made a move.

They were also, he realized, two of the men who would massacre the hostages in cold blood if they saw any rescue attempt being made from the frigate. At that moment Ramage found that he could cut their throats without a moment's hesitation.

He stood up and walked softly along the deck towards them, keeping well over against the guns so that if the lantern threw any shadow of him in the last few paces it would be seen only from over the side.

In the few moments he was standing beside the nearest man, breathing an unpleasant stench of rum and sweat. Beside him on the deck were an empty decanter and a glass, both on their side, both sparkling as the lantern flame danced and flickered. The man was lean with a narrow face, and he was breathing heavily with his mouth wide open to reveal at most three blackened teeth. The top of his head was bald but the hair growing on each side and the back was long, so that it resembled a mangy black cat curled up asleep. The second man was plumper, his hair tied in a queue, and there were several gold rings on the fingers of his hands, which were clasped across his stomach. There was an empty decanter and glass on the deck beside him, too.

On the table, opposite each man, gleaming dully in the lanternlight, was a pistol. Each was cocked. Each could be reached without the man standing up.

Cut their throats as they sagged back in a cloud of rum fumes? When he thought about the hostages, Ramage guessed he could do it—but was it necessary? He reached out for the nearest pistol, opened the pan and shook out the priming powder, blowing gently to remove the last trace. He repeated it with the second pistol. They still looked ready for use, but anyone squeezing the triggers would be disappointed; there would not even be a flash in the pan.

There was some rope a few feet away, neatly coiled, and

197

in half an hour at the most the Calypsos would be on board. He picked up a pistol by the barrel and hit the nearest man on the side of the head with the butt. He took three steps to the other and hit him, careful not to bang anything with his cutlass, which he had transferred to his left hand.

The startling thing was that the men hardly moved. Perhaps they had slid further down in their chairs, but they still looked as though they had susided in a drunken stupor, which of course they had, having exchanged in the last few moments one kind of stupor for another.

Ramage quickly pullled a length of rope from the coil, slashed it with his cutlass and then pulled off a second length. It took longer than he anticipated to roll the first man out of his chair and tie his arms and ankles. The second was equally difficult. Each was completely relaxed, as though every bone in his body had turned into calves-foot jelly.

Ramage dragged the two men to the guns, pushing each one into the deeply shadowed area under a barrel. Then, pausing as he decided to leave the lantern there, swinging its doors open for a moment to straighten out the wick, he crept over to the main companionway and made his way down the steps.

There was another lantern hanging from the deckhand and it lit a row of doors, eight of them, four on each side. The first was open, the entrance to a black cavern; the rest had keys sticking out of them like tiny branches. The noise of several people snoring was coming from the first cabin. He tried to count the different tones. At least four people.

He crept closer to the door and listened again. Five. Yes, and there was another faint one, little more than steady but heavy breathing: six. The key was in the door, which was made of thick mahogany. The lock was solid brass and until recently had been polished—the Honourable East India Company ships were built of the best of everything. He swung the door gently until it closed and then turned the key. If the men inside were serious about escaping, they could probably break the lock with a few pistol shots, but they would be unlikely to try it in pitch darkness, when the risk of being hurt by a ricocheting ball was considerable.

Ramage decided to unlock the opposite cabin and rouse one of the hostages, to warn him of what was about to happen and leave him to release and warn the others, who would know and trust his voice and could then lock themselves in the safety of their cabins. He put down his cutlass carefully to leave both hands free and made sure the knife was loose in its sheath. As he slowly turned the key he wondered how the Calypsos were going to secure those six guards without a shot being fired. A shot . . . it needed only one. The moment the guards in the other ships heard a single shot, they would massacre the hostages, twenty-four men, women and children (assuming the sixteen in this ship were safe). That was why he had emptied the priming powder from the two pistols on deck; that was the reason none of the Calypsos had firearms, even though muskets and pistols could have been wrapped in oiled silk and canvas and carried on the rafts.

He was almost startled when the door pressed against him; then he realized he had turned the key and was pulling the handle. Quickly he opened the door wider, noted in the dim light from the lantern that there was a single bed in the middle of the cabin, shut the door behind him in case it swung and banged, and crept towards the bed. He wanted all the hostages warned without raising the alarm among the guards, and the only way of ensuring that the alarm was *not* raised was by everyone acting as though the door to the guards' cabin was still open.

His outstretched hand touched the foot of the bed. Curious that they did not give passengers swinging cots, because it must be difficult to stay in a bed in anything of a sea, even though the bed must be bolted to the deck.

The cover was a smooth material he could not identify. Shantung? A John Company ship would be furnished in exotic materials from the East. Now, if he was lucky the fellow in this bed would be an Army officer—or, rather, an officer in the company's military service. If his luck was out, the man would be some pompous and panicky nabob who would need a good deal of convincing. In fact it might be easier to leave him and try the next cabin.

He ran his hand along the bed as he crept softly towards the head of the bed, listening for breathing to determine where the sleeper's mouth was. Here was the body and he ran the tips of his fingers lightly along it to get some idea of where the man's head was, in case he shouted. Then his hand was cupped over a yielding mound of bare flesh; a mound topped by a

199

firmer summit. It took him a moment to realize he was holding a woman's bare breast in his left hand but a moment later his right hand was on her face, pressing down on her mouth.

She started wriggling as he grasped a shoulder with his left hand and hissed: "Don't scream, don't struggle, I'm from the—"

At that moment she bit the heel of his palm but he risked another bite, whispering urgently: "From the British don't make a noise!"

Finally she seemed to be wide awake and her hands were pushing him away, but without the violence or urgency of a terrified woman.

"Do you understand?"

He felt her trying to nod and experimentally lifted his palm half an inch from her mouth.

"I understand, but don't suffocate me!"

The voice was calm, musical and verging on deep, but quite firm, and asking: "Who exactly *are* you?"

"That doesn't matter, but I want you to—"

"My dear man, I'm not given to the vapours, but although I can see nothing I have the impression I am in the grasp of a naked man. A naked Englishman, so he says, although what difference that makes . . ."

"Madam," Ramage whispered desperately, conscious of the minutes slipping by, "my name is Nicholas Ramage, and I command the British frigate. A couple of dozen of my men are swimming over here and will be climbing on board in a few minutes. It is absolutely vital that they overcome the guards without a shot being fired, and I want you to unlock their doors and warn the rest of the hostages—the passengers, I mean—to stay in their cabins no matter *what* happens."

"I'll warn them. You must have swum over; you feel devilish damp. I'll give you a towel in a moment."

"Listen," Ramage said urgently, "you do understand what you have to do? Each of the cabins is locked with the key still on the outside. The point is, people will recognize your voice, so—"

"I understand perfectly! What about the scoundrels in the cabin opposite?"

"They're asleep and locked in. But if they wake up they might start shooting."

200

"And the two guards on deck?"

"Unconscious and tied up."

"You *have* been busy. Very well—stand back and let me get out of bed."

"Let me help you, ma'am."

"Please stand back. It's so hot in here that I sleep—well, without the encumbrance of a nightdress, as you probably realized!"

Drunken guards, barracudas, bare breasts, a cabin full of snoring pirates... even in the urgency of the situation Ramage had most certainly registered a breast—a fine one, that much was certain—but he had been too tense to make the obvious deduction that in this hot and airless cabin the rest of the body was almost certainly naked.

"I beg your pardon, ma'am," he whispered. "Incidentally, I am not entirely naked."

"It's—well, let's say 'miss' for now. And nakedness is of little consequence in the dark."

"There's a lantern outside," Ramage said and could have bitten off his tongue.

"Thank you for the warning."

He heard the rustle of material and then she whispered: "Lead me to the door, I can't see a thing."

"Keep whispering or I'll never find you."

"Ramage... Ramage... Captain Lord Ramage... damp and smelling of seaweed..." The teasing whisper led him to her. So she had known the name. Well, for the moment he was concentrating on remembering where the door was, because it fitted so well and the lantern was so dim that no light penetrated the crack.

"I don't use my title," he said, and suddenly bumped into her. To stop falling they both held each other tight as though embracing.

"Good morning, Captain," she said, gently disengaging herself, "you are really not properly dressed for paying social calls."

Ramage took her arm and led her to the door. "I'm tempted to take you hostage."

"You'll have to make an exchange with the privateersmen. At the moment they claim me."

He opened the door but she was through it and turning left

to the other cabins before he could glimpse her face, and before he could catch up she had unlocked the first door and slipped in.

The best thing he could do was wait beside the guards' cabin until she returned. A minute or two later he saw a blur of white as she came out of the cabin and went to the next. Finally, after she left the last cabin, he walked across the corridor to wait at the door of her cabin, but she slipped into the next one and a minute or two later a middle-aged man with muttonchop whiskers came out, faintly absurd in a gown, and whispered: "Ramage—everyone has been warned. We'll wait in our cabins with the doors locked. And—thank you!"

With that the man went back into his cabin after removing the key. Ramage then saw that all along the corridor people were removing the keys, to lock the doors from the inside.

He hurried back up the companionway and went to the ship's side, listening for the sound of swimmers. There was no sound and no swirls of phosphorescence. A rolled-up rope ladder lay on top of the bulwark; he untied the lashing, let it unroll and heard the end land in the water with a splash. On the other side he found a similar ladder and unrolled that.

Then he picked up the lantern and walked over to stand at the starboard entryport. He was out of sight of all the ships but the *Calypso,* and he held the lantern so that he could be seen by the swimmers. Almost at once he felt a tug on the bottom of the ladder and heard a faint swishing of water. A minute later Rossi was jumping down from the top of the bulwark, waving an acknowledgement of Ramage's signal warning him to be silent.

"The rest of the men are close behind, sir," Rossi whispered. "We went slowly, as you said, so we are not without the breath." He looked round and said, a disappointed note in his voice: "*Mamma mia,* you have not made the capture alone, *Commandante?*"

"No, I've left the easy part for you." Ramage smiled and looked down to see two more men already climbing the ladder.

Within three minutes he was counting his boarding party and found them all present, with Martin and Paolo. He looked round for Jackson, pointed to the two men under the barrel of the guns, and whispered: "They might be coming round soon. Gag them, please."

The American waved to Rossi and Stafford, pulling his sodden shirt over his head and tearing two strips off the tail. Out of the corner of his eye Ramage saw Jackson lift the first man and bang his head on the deck, and then proceed to gag him. In the meantime another seaman was cleaning the wick of the lantern and stirring the molten wax with the tip of his finger to level it out. The lantern suddenly gave a brighter light and Ramage glanced round nervously: someone watching from the *Lynx* might well become suspicious of the shadows thrown by the group of men. "Put the lantern down on deck, under the table," he said hurriedly.

As soon as Jackson came back to report both men unconscious and gagged—not bothering to mention that one had given signs of recovering—Ramage gathered the men round and in a whisper now getting hoarse explained the position.

"If the total of eight guards is correct, then the six off watch are sleeping in a cabin below. I've locked the door on them. They'll probably be in hammocks because they prefer them and the passenger cabins are each fitted with one large bed.

"We've got to rush them and make sure they don't fire pistols. You see the two pistols on this table: the two men on watch were sitting here drinking, their guns within easy reach.

"The doorway into the cabin is the standard width. This is how we do it. You, Orsini, will carry this lantern; I'll take the one that's hanging from the deckhead outside the cabin door. Riley," he said to one of the seamen, "you will stand by the key of the door. When I signal, you'll unlock the door and pull it open—towards you: it opens outwards.

"I will go in first holding my lantern high and Orsini will follow with his. As soon as I go through the door I want you all to start shouting—anything to make a noise: I just want to confuse those men as they start waking up. Confuse their brains and dazzle their eyes.

"Martin, Stafford, Rossi, Riley—you'll have had time to see into the cabin by now—follow us. Orsini and I will take the two hammocks to the right, the rest of you take the four on the left. Aft, in other words.

"Cut the hammocks down. A good slash with a cutlass should cut the lanyards at the foot or head and tip the occupant out."

"And then, sir?" Orsini inquired.

"There are so few of them that we can take prisoners," Ramage said regretfully, "but kill a man if there's a risk he'll otherwise use a pistol. Now," he said as Orsini picked up the lantern and turned towards the companionway, "follow me. And watch your cutlasses—don't let them bang anything."

The steps of the companionway creaked, and as he crept down Ramage felt that the ship was suddenly holding her breath and listening: she had stopped her gentle pitching so that there were no groans from the hull and spars to mask the sounds they made.

The lantern below was burning steadily, the air having the faint sooty smell of untrimmed wick. Glancing down the line of doors he saw that all the keys were now missing except for the first on each side. The key was still on the outside of the cabin in which the "Miss for now" had been sleeping. He knew the shape of one bare breast; he had not the faintest idea whether she was ugly, plain or beautiful. An intriguing voice, a good sense of humour, and very self-possessed in an emergency. She was probably coming home from India after being a teacher, or some old woman's companion. But for the "Miss" he would have assumed she had been sent out to India to find a husband, succeeded and was now on her way home again...

Why the devil was he thinking about her at a time like this? He unhooked the second lantern and gave it to Orsini and waited while Riley crept to the door and reached out for the key with his right hand, holding the brass knob with his left and glancing over his shoulder to make sure he would not bump into anything as he flung open the door.

Ramage checked the men behind him: Martin, Jackson, Rossi, Stafford and then the seamen not specifically chosen for the cabin. The cutlass blades shone dully in the lanternlight; he noticed Orsini was using his dirk in his right hand but had a long, thin dagger in a sheath at his waist. Jackson had a cutlass and a knife—he had developed Paolo Orsini's liking for a *main gauche*.

He found himself staring at the grain in the mahogany door. "Miss for now." The passengers were in for a rude shock in a few moments: the bellowing of his men would echo in this confined space, although no one outside the ship would hear. How was Aitken getting on with the capture of the *Amethyst*? At least he had heard no shots...

He pointed at Riley, who turned the key with a loud click and flung back the door with a bang. Ramage plunged into the black space as the men behind him started shouting. In a moment the lantern showed hammocks slung from the deck beams at various angles, bulging like enormous bananas.

He slashed at the lanyards of the nearest one on his right, took a pace to one side to avoid the body that slid out of the canvas tube as it suddenly hung almost vertically, and reached across to cut the lanyards at one end of the next one.

Orsini, cheated out of a hammock, crouched over the body of the first man, managing to hold up his lantern while pointing his dirk at the privateersman's throat and shouting bloodcurdling threats down at the staring eyes.

Ramage's man, caught up in the folds of the canvas, began swearing and obviously thought his shipmates were playing a joke on him until the point of Ramage's cutlass prodded the fleshy part of his right thigh.

From the left hand side of the cabin he heard above the yelling an angry shout end in a liquid gurgle, as though someone's throat had been cut. The noise made Ramage's victim try to scramble up, attempting to pull something from the folds of a blanket he had been using as a pillow. Ramage gave him another jab with the cutlass. "Keep still, or you're dead!"

The man gave a grunt of pain and flopped back flat on the deck. "Wha's going on?"

The yelling was dying as the last of the hammocks was cut down, but the thud of a cutlass blade being driven into the deck was followed immediately by a scream of pain, which cut off as sharply as it began.

Ramage's lantern was too dim to show him what was going on, and all he could do was to wait for his own men to report. To encourage them he called: "Calypsos—have we secured them all?"

"I've got your man, sir," said Martin.

"I've got mine, sir," Orsini muttered. "Alive," he added, "at the moment."

"This *stronzo* here, I have to kill him," Rossi grunted. "He have a pistol in his hammock."

"Prisoner, sir," Jackson said, followed by Stafford's "'Ad to prod my fellah, sir, but 'e'll live."

205

"Prisoner, sir," Riley said and added, raising his voice in warning, "a *dead* prisoner, if 'e don't keep still."

Ramage turned to Orsini, who was nearest the door. "Get your man out into the corridor where the others can secure him."

The privateersman yelped as the midshipman prodded him to his feet. "Ow! You'll do me 'arm," the man complained.

"Yes, I just want an excuse!"

"You're just a bloody murderer!"

"You were ready to kill the hostages," Orsini said, and to judge from the short, sharp scream the man gave, he must have punctuated his remark with another and stronger prod.

Ramage watched as Orsini, lantern held up, followed his prisoner through the door, where the man was seized by eager Calypsos.

"Now you, Jackson..." The American coxswain had an armlock on his prisoner, so the man lurched out of the cabin bent double. "Rossi, you wait a minute. Stafford, are you ready?"

"Aye aye, sir. Up, you murderous bastard. No, you're not," he said in answer to a muttered complaint Ramage could not quite hear, "that was only a prick. Get movin', or I'll spit you like a suckin' pig ready for the fire!"

Riley followed with his prisoner and by then Ramage's man was scrambling to his feet, assuring Martin and Ramage that he too had surrendered, and his pistol was still in the folds of his hammock.

Outside, in what was in fact a lobby, Ramage saw several prisoners lying crumpled on the deck and before he could say a word one of the Calypsos had landed Martin's prisoner a savage punch that drove him to his knees, as though praying for mercy. A moment later a second punch sent him sprawling.

Ramage stood and watched. Eight guards captured and only one of them killed. He knew that every one of the Calypsos was filled with a fierce hatred for the privateersmen because they knew the eight men were on board the *Earl of Dodsworth* for one reason only—to murder the hostages if they thought it necessary. Men who could murder women in cold blood, Jackson had commented hours ago, should not expect too much mercy when their turn came...

A Calypso hurried down the companionway, dragging the

end of a rope. "Here, cut off what lengths you want: the rest of the coil's on deck—it'll kink if I pitch it down."

It took about five minutes to tie up the men. Ramage was just going to call to the passengers that all was well and they could leave their cabins if they wished, when they remembered the dead man.

"Rossi—take a couple of men and get your privateersman up on deck. Wrap him in a hammock so you don't spill blood everywhere."

"When we have him on deck, sir?"

"I'm not reading a burial service over a man waiting to murder women," Ramage said bluntly.

"Si, va bene; capito Commandante."

"Orsini, take three or four men and bring down those two privateersmen stowed under the guns. Jackson, drag these men back into the cabin as soon as they're secured: we'll use it as a cell for the time being. Martin, unhook the ends of those hammocks and collect up any pistols you find. I'll hold this lantern so you can see what you are doing."

The cabin was a strange sight: six hammocks, each suspended at one end but with the other hanging down on the deck, looked like sides of beef suspended from hooks in a slaughterhouse—an effect heightened by the large black stain surrounding the body lying among them, and which Rossi was beginning to turn over.

Suddenly Ramage began to shiver, his body feeling frozen although he had only just wiped perspiration from his brow and upper lip.

"It's cold, sir," Jackson commented conversationally, and Ramage realized that several of the men were also shivering. The long swim, the excitement, the relief that now it was all over? Ramage began chafing his body with his hands; it was enough that they felt cold; the devil take the reasons.

"The *Amethyst* . . ."

"Yes sir, I was wondering about her," Jackson said, and Ramage realized he had spoken his thoughts aloud. "If anything went wrong, I think we'd have heard shots by now. Nothing else for us to do tonight. Let's hope tomorrow night goes as well as this."

CHAPTER FIFTEEN

A rather embarrassed Ramage, after carefully adjusting his stock, walked nearly naked along the corridor and, knocking on each door, repeated like a litany: "This is Captain Ramage, of the *Calypso* frigate: you are all free now, but please do not go up on deck."

Several people called their thanks; he heard one man begin a prayer in a firm, clear voice. He turned after knocking at the last door and walked back towards the cabin, which was now a cell containing seven bound prisoners guarded by three Calypsos who, armed with cutlasses, were sitting on chairs just inside the door.

As he went to pass the next to last door on his right, it opened and a woman in a gown came out, her face hidden in the shadow thrown by a lace scarf over her head.

"You must be cold," she said, "and still damp. Come, I'll get you some dry clothes."

She held his arm and opened the door of her cabin.

"Can we borrow that lantern?" she pointed to the one back on its hook, now that the Calypsos in the cabin had their own. He walked over and lifted it down as she asked: "Where is everyone? It sounded as though there were scores of you!"

"Most of them are up on deck now. The privateersmen are tied up and under guard in that cabin opposite."

She led the way into her cabin: "And no one was wounded?"

"None of my men. One of the privateersmen was killed."

"Good," she said, without bitterness. "They are truly wicked men. They were going to murder us."

"Well, only if we tried to rescue you!"

"No," she said quietly. "Several days before you arrived, they decided there was no hope of getting ransom from us. Or, rather, it would take too long. So they decided to kill us on the day they took all the prizes away. When you arrived they realized they could use us as hostages to stop you capturing them."

Suddenly Ramage realized the cunning of Tomás and Hart, and he hoped that Aitken and his men would have the same difficulty as Rossi.

As though she guessed what he was thinking she asked, as she unlocked a trunk: "What about the passengers in the other ships?"

"I hope by now those in the *Amethyst* have been rescued by some of my men."

"And the rest—in the *Heliotrope* and the *Friesland*?"

"We tackle them tomorrow night. Tonight, I mean."

"Do you mean to swim across to them?" She stood up and looked at him, but the shawl still threw a shadow over her features.

"Yes. Obviously we'd be seen if we used boats."

"But surely you have done enough, saving us."

Deliberately misunderstanding her, he said: "The *Earl of Dodsworth* is merely one of four with passengers, although the other privateer—yes, there is a second one—may bring in more any day."

"No, I didn't mean that," she said. "You said one of your lieutenants was dealing with the *Amethyst*. I meant, cannot more of your lieutenants go to the other two ships? Is it usual for a frigate captain to swim around naked doing everything?"

"I am not naked," he said stiffly, "and you offered . . ."

"Of course!" she lifted the lid of the trunk. "Forgive me, I know nothing of naval ways and was curious. The colonel commanding a battalion is not expected to lead every patrol, that I *do* know."

"You have the advantage of me there," Ramage said ironically. "I know nothing of how the Army goes about its business."

"Well—" she tossed a pair of breeches across to him, and

209

followed it with a shirt and a uniform jacket which was of a very dark colour, difficult to distinguish with the lantern, probably green, with heavy frogging across the front "—you are going to look like a soldier for the rest of the day. It will all fit. Do you want shoes? They're in another trunk. Hose, a clean stock—I don't imagine you will want to continue wearing your own—and do you want to try a hat? No? It would have suited you."

He had put the lantern down on a table as he caught the garments she threw to him. That deep, vibrant voice: one did not hear it with the ears alone, and as he watched her he was thankful he could hold the bundle of clothes in front of him.

"You seem—er, knowledgeable, about men's wear, 'Miss for now'."

"Yes." She was not being unpleasant; it was a matter-of-fact agreement with what he had just said. She shut the lid of the trunk. "Now, to see if some shoes fit you. Come and sit on this trunk; the other one is here next to it."

She unlocked it and by the time he was sitting she had selected a pair of shoes which, he noticed, had heavy silver buckles already fitted. Half a dozen other pairs, which she had taken out and put down on the deck, also had the buckles fitted. The owner must be a wealthy man; most people transferred the buckles when they changed shoes.

"These fit comfortably."

"They look rather large."

"They'll be just right once I am wearing hose."

"Of course," she said, obviously irritated with herself for forgetting and moving Ramage to search through the first trunk. "Well, have we forgotten anything else?"

"No, I'm now well equipped. Will you please thank the owner for the use of part of his wardrobe?"

"That won't be possible, so you can thank me. I'll leave you this cabin as a dressing room. I shall be next door. Perhaps you would knock when you've finished."

With that she was gone, and he still had very little idea of what she looked like. A definite sense of humour—she was enjoying telling him nothing about the ownership of these clothes and she neatly evaded any hint that they belonged to a husband or a brother. A young man, he noted, glancing at the waistband of the breeches. Not her father nor an uncle. He examined the buttons on the jacket. They had a curious design carved into them—were they ebony? Anyway, not the usual number indicating one of the foot regiments, yet the sword he had seen in the second trunk was not a cavalryman's sword. Well, he had all day to find out more about her...

Breakfast brought the first crisis. Stafford lit the galley fire at the regular time noted by Southwick, sunrise, while Rossi searched everywhere for food for the passengers. Ramage and Orsini were planning to serve them with an elaborate meal to celebrate their release, and Aitken had already signalled that he had taken the *Amethyst*.

But no food. When an embarrassed Rossi reported that he could find only seamen's fare, Ramage realized that he would have to go below and ask "Miss for now". He had purposely remained under the halfdeck, out of sight from any other ships, because his Army garb was unmistakable and Southwick had never reported seeing anyone being exercised in such a uniform. He had intended meeting the passengers formally after they had breakfasted and the tables in the great cabin had been cleared.

By now daylight was penetrating below, making the lantern-light weak and yellow. The wind had not come up yet and he found the air below was still and stale, thick with the sooty smell of burning candlewicks.

He felt self-conscious in his strange uniform. The Calypsos were already dressed in their usual shirt and trousers—a bag on the raft (already hoisted on board out of sight) had been used as a travelling trunk by the seamen who, Ramage thought ruefully, had had more foresight than himself. He nodded to the men guarding the prisoners and knocked on her door, expecting to wait for a few minutes while she dressed. She would be hard put to try to hide her face now, he thought, but he had persuaded himself that the reason for the shawl over her head had been because she *knew* she was plain, and was enjoying the unexpected and brief flirtation with the captain of the frigate. She would have a long, horsy face, straight hair, a large bulbous nose that went red in cold weather, and a mouth with thin lips. She would smile readily, of course, in that eager-to-please way of an elderly woman's companion...

By now the door had opened and the face smiling at him

211

was beautiful. It was as if he was standing within inches of a Lely portrait, the doorway being the frame. It would be called *La Belle Inconnue*.

"You should not stare," the voice said.

"I'm not staring, I'm stunned," Ramage said without feeling any connection between his voice and the words. "Breakfast," he added lamely.

"Oh, you are hungry? Mrs Donaldson's turn with me this morning. It takes about half an hour to prepare."

Ramage pulled himself together and gave a brief bow. "Ma'am, you—"

"'Took me unawares'," she supplied.

"—took me unawares," Ramage repeated gratefully and grinned. "I came to ask 'Miss for now' where my men can find the food to prepare the passengers' breakfast."

"In a 'John Company' ship the passengers supply their own victuals." She obviously enjoyed using such professional words. "And dress visitors, too, when necessary," she added mischievously. "I'll collect Mrs Donaldson. I'm afraid your unexpected arrival has upset the routine we had to start when the pirates took all the crews ashore."

"*On* shore," he could not help teasing her. "People go *on* shore; only ships go 'ashore', usually accidentally."

"Captain, you must give me lessons in the nautical language; it will be invaluable when I return to the land of drawing room chatter."

And the devil of it was that he did not know if she was serious or teasing *him*. She smiled and walked past him along the corridor to tap on a door and call: "Mrs Donaldson . . . it's our turn to prepare breakfast, and we have a guest."

"Three guests," Ramage called, remembering Martin and Paolo. As she waved to acknowledge that she had heard he thought of Gianna, and suddenly she seemed even more distant in both time and space.

The great cabin of the *Earl of Dodsworth* was impressive. Athwartships, in front of the sternlights, was a long table with a smaller one at each side of the cabin running parallel to the centre-line and leaving a hollow square between for stewards using the big sideboard at the forward side of the cabin.

As Ramage walked through the door, Martin and Paolo

behind him, he saw that half a dozen people were sitting at the big table—clearly "the captain's table"—while six more sat at one side table and two couples at the other. He saw her walking across the cabin towards him, obviously acting as the hostess.

The light from the stern windows was behind her. She was wearing a light mustard-coloured morning dress, nipped in at the waist and tight across the bust, but flaring out from the hips. Her hair was not quite blonde—tawny perhaps—but the light reflecting on it showed it was brushed out loosely, not braided.

He was deliberately avoiding looking at her face: he had seen every man and woman in the cabin was watching him and the men were rising—and yes, the women were clapping gently!

She gave a little curtsy and said: "Because I am the only person who has really met you . . ." She paused for a moment and Ramage glanced up: there was no mistaking her meaning. ". . . I have been given the task of introducing you—all three of you," she corrected herself, "to everyone present."

Ramage took Paolo's arm. Now he would hear her name! "May I present Lieutenant Martin and Midshipman the Count Orsini."

Paolo took her hand and kissed it.

"Ah, we have been reading about the Count's exploits in a recent copy of the *Gazette*," she said and no one but Ramage seemed to notice that she had not offered her name.

She led the way to the top table and introduced him first to the elderly man who had come from the next cabin, and the grey-haired woman sitting next to him, a woman whose fine-boned face still had an almost haunting mature beauty.

"The Marquis of Rockley, the Marchioness: may I present Captain Ramage, Lieutenant Martin and Midshipman the Count Orsini . . ."

Rockley? Somewhere in Cambridgeshire. Friends of the Temples and of Pitt. As he went through the ritual of being introduced, Ramage tried to place the couple more exactly, but in a few moments he was being introduced to the next couple. He recognized the name as belonging to a Kentish landowner active in Parliament. The last man was an officer in the military service of the Honourable East India Company, and Ramage apologized for his borrowed uniform, admitting to be uncertain to which regiment it belonged. The man laughed a little too loudly at the idea of a naval officer in a soldier's uniform, but the woman with him looked embarrassed.

Ramage managed to glance at "Miss for now" but she was looking away, deliberately it seemed. What was unusual about this uniform?

Finally, with the last introduction completed, and before the woman had shown them to their chairs, the old Marquis stood up and tapped a glass with a knife to get everyone's attention.

"If I may have a moment . . . you all know the identity of the gallant captain who gave us a sleepless night and at dawn presented us with our freedom. I know you want me to give him our thanks, and ask him to thank his officers and men as well. We know he and his men have more work to do tonight, and our prayers will be with them."

No reply was needed and amid clapping and hearty "Hear, hears" Ramage sat at the head of the table, finding the Marquis on his right and "Miss for now" on his left. Just as he noted the white cloth and napkins and was wondering what was going to happen next, Rossi marched in carrying a huge silver tea urn, followed by Jackson and Stafford with trays of various dishes.

She was smiling at his bewilderment. "A surprise for you: we hatched it up while slaving round the galley fire!"

"I don't get such service in my *own* ship," Ramage protested mockingly. "I have one incredibly slow steward . . ."

"The terms of the peace treaty," the Marquis said. "Could you give me some idea . . . ?"

Ramage, realizing that this would be the first information from anything approaching an official source that the Marquis had heard, apologized for not having mentioned it earlier and told him all he could remember.

"A sad business," the Marquis commented. "We won the war and now we've lost the peace. Still, Bonaparte will try again. Now tell me what brings your ship to this strange island?"

Ramage described the omission in the Treaty and the British government's intention of taking advantage of it. The Marquis nodded. "I should not care to be one of the garrison," he commented.

A few moments later he asked: "Do you know India, Ramage?"

Ramage shook his head. "Their Lordships have kept me in the West Indies and the Mediterranean, I'm afraid."

"Breakfast tends to be a more social occasion out there than in England. It is not unusual to have guests arriving unexpectedly for breakfast."

"It is not unknown in the Ilha da Trinidade," "Miss for now" said, laughingly easily.

"I hope you have made our apologies for not sending out the proper invitations, Diana," the Marquis said, smiling.

"His Lordship hasn't left cards yet, father."

She was watching him and he saw that she was a woman who could smile with her eyes. And talk, too, and at this moment her eyes were saying: "There—now you know my first name, and you have met my parents, but you wonder about that uniform you are wearing."

It all passed in a moment and Ramage said in a humorous apology: "My card case is in another uniform, which I forgot to bring with me."

"Think nothing of it," the Marquis said, pushing his cup towards Rossi, who was unused to wrestling with a large urn and its two taps. "We half expected you. In fact your arrival has cost me a guinea."

Ramage raised his eyebrows questioningly and Diana said: "My father didn't think you could rescue us before the pirates cut our throats..."

"The guinea?"

"Oh, I bet him a guinea you would find a way."

"Obviously you are an optimist! If he won he could hardly collect!"

She shrugged her shoulders as though dismissing any such thoughts of losing. "After all, you *did* find a way."

Her matter-of-fact acceptance of it all irritated him; too much was being taken for granted.

"We shan't know if we've been successful until nightfall."

The Marquis was quick to spot that Ramage had not spoken out of pique. "In what way, Captain? After all, we're free and our former guards are your prisoners."

"Yes, but supposing a boat comes from the *Lynx* and they

215

find they have neither guards nor hostages now in this ship or the *Amethyst* . . ."

"What will they do?" the Marchioness asked.

"I can only guess, ma'am. Certainly raise the alarm, which will mean the hostages in the *Heliotrope* and *Friesland* will be murdered, then probably the *Lynx* will try to escape."

"Will she succeed?" Diana's voice was almost a whisper.

"I doubt it. My second lieutenant, now in command of the *Calypso*, has his orders."

"But has he enough experience?"

Her question was so harshly spoken that her father murmured: "Diana!"

Ramage suddenly found he had lost all appetite for breakfast. "All my officers have been in action many times. The two left on board the *Calypso* have been in battle more times, I imagine, than the people in this cabin have seen a full moon rise. Now, if you'll excuse—"

He put his hands on the table and began pushing back his chair. She touched his left hand with her fingertips and murmured: "I'm sorry: please stay. Don't spoil our first breakfast."

"Our only one," Ramage muttered, "And I feel none too comfortable in these absurd clothes."

She was the only one to hear him, and she went pale, withdrawing her hand. "That was unworthy of you."

The Marquis, sensing currents he did not understand, turned to talk to his wife. Ramage then realized that to leave the table now would puzzle or embarrass everyone present, quite apart from taking him away from the immediate presence of the one woman he wanted to be with at the moment. What made him behave like this? Normally he did not take offence at what were obviously intended as ordinary remarks. Why now, he asked himself. The answer was almost stunningly simple: he was behaving like a spoiled child because he had thought that, however obliquely and however mildly, Diana was criticizing him. Not even that—almost questioning his judgement. Not even that, he had to admit, repeating the phrase as though deliberately nagging himself: because she knew nothing of the way a ship of war was run, and nothing of the *Calypso*'s officers (except himself and Paolo, whose name must have lodged in her memory). She did not know, and could not know, that

216

Wagstaffe and Southwick were more used to being in battle than in a drawing room.

"Am I forgiven?" she asked quietly, and the tone of her voice showed it mattered to her.

"There's nothing to forgive, but I forgive you twice, so that you have two in reserve, like Papal dispensations."

She smiled with her eyes. "We are making progress from our first meeting!"

Quite involuntarily Ramage glanced down at her bosom: the scene of the first meeting, he thought to himself, is now modestly covered. He looked up to find her blushing slightly. Her eyes flickered down to his left hand, as though she had momentarily lost control of them, and he knew she was thinking the same, and the memory was not as displeasing as it might have been.

Stafford came round with a napkin-covered basket of hot rolls. "Bit 'ard, sir and madam," he apologized, "but they're yesterday's bake, 'otted up. No time to make fresh this morning."

"Thank you, Stafford," she said with a smile that made Ramage feel unreasonably jealous of the Cockney, who went on to the other tables.

"You know Stafford?"

"Oh yes—remember, we were all slaving away in the galley: Jackson, Rossi and Stafford. They're very proud of themselves, too."

"Oh? In what way?"

"They were boasting that they had served with you longer than any of the others in the *Calypso*. They were telling Mrs Donaldson and me how they helped you rescue Midshipman Orsini's—is she his aunt, the Marchesa di Volterra?"

"Yes, aunt," he said, his voice as neutral as he could manage.

"I had the impression she was much younger. And very beautiful."

"She is young. Only a few years older than Paolo."

"And he is her heir?"

"At present, yes."

"You mean, if she doesn't marry and have a son of her own."

"Yes," he said. "A son or a daughter. If she dies childless."

217

"Is that likely?"

"She left England recently to return to Volterra, so I don't know what she's doing."

"Travelling through France? Isn't that dangerous? I wouldn't have thought Bonaparte . . ."

"We tried to warn her."

"But *noblesse oblige*." It was a comment, an acknowledgement rather than a judgement.

"*Noblesse* hardly obliges you to put your head in a noose," he said sourly.

"Perhaps the Marchesa knows her own people best."

"No, she has yet to learn *Non ogni giorno e festa*."

"My Italian is sketchy but from Latin, 'Not every day is a *festa*'?"

"Yes, now try, *Non ogni fiore fa buon odore'*."

"Hmm . . . 'Not every flower makes a good odour'?"

"'Not every flower smells sweet'—yes, it's impossible to make direct translations, but she trusts Bonaparte's treaty."

"Your Italian sounds fluent."

Was she changing the subject from Gianna? "It should be: I was brought up there as a child."

"And you love the country."

"Yes, that helps, too. But my French and Spanish are good enough, although at the moment they are not my favourite peoples."

A sudden smell of hot food made him turn, and he saw his three seamen placing covered dishes on the sideboard. Jackson came over and whispered to Ramage, who spoke to Diana. She nodded. "We always do help ourselves. It all smells delicious."

Rossi came up the companionway to the halfdeck holding several shirts in one hand. He saluted Ramage and said: "For the 'guards', sir. I took the brightest the prisoners were wearing, so they'll be seen from the *Lynx*."

Ramage gestured to the five Calypsos who would be pretending to be guards while exercising the hostages. "I hope they're watching from the *Lynx*, so that your acting won't be wasted. And by the way: you are supposed to be *privateersmen*. Don't hit any of the 'hostages' but don't behave in a friendly fashion either. Keep two or three yards away from them."

He tried to remember the wording of Bowen's report on the days he had spent watching the *Earl of Dodsworth*. Eight women walking the deck for half an hour, followed by eight men for half an hour. They used the after companionway. The guards had cutlasses and Bowen presumed pistols, though they were too far away from him to see.

The sun was high over the island now and beginning to heat up the deck. Ramage could see half a dozen tropic birds soaring over the northern headland and the shadows were shortening on the western side of the hills. The *Earl of Dodsworth*'s decks had not been scrubbed for many days, and her captain would be shocked if he could see the stains where the guards had been swilling rum and spitting tobacco juice. He went down the companionway and called for the women to go on deck.

He could see that to an onlooker everything was normal in the *Calypso:* the two boats used by the surveyors were anchored off the beach and he had watched the men, tiny ants in the distance, start their long climb into the hills. The boat making the soundings was slowly crossing the bay, stopping every few yards for a man to heave the lead. The bosun would be commanding Martin and Paolo's boat today, dressed up in officer's breeches, coat and hat. Some time this morning the boat would, apparently by chance, pass close to the *Earl of Dodsworth,* in case there were messages to be passed.

Diana was as good as her word, calling instructions to the Calypsos. "One of you should spit over the side—well, not exactly spit . . . they delighted in trying to embarrass us."

"Spurgeon," Ramage called. "Relieve yourself at the larboard entryport."

"Well, sir . . . I . . . er, well, I don't think I can, sir, I just went a'fore the ladies . . ."

"Pretend," Ramage growled.

After a few minutes, Diana walked past where Ramage was waiting in the lee of the halfdeck. "As soon as we spread out, the guards would get excited and make us bunch up together."

Riley had heard her words and began shouting: "Come on, you women! Keep together; this ain't a parade to church, yer know!"

"Perfect," Diana said. "That's just the sort of thing they used to say."

Jackson suddenly called urgently: "There's a boat leaving the *Lynx!*"

It had to happen, Ramage thought bitterly, pulling off his

uniform jacket. A man in a white shirt could be a guard because the bulwarks hid his breeches. He stared at the *Lynx* through the gunports, using a telescope he had found in the binnacle drawer. Four men at the oars, a couple of men sitting in the sternsheets. Not Tomás or Hart. Nor was the boat in any rush: whatever she was doing and wherever she was going, it was something routine. If she came to the *Earl of Dodsworth* . . .

With the exception of the Marchioness, who was sitting in a chair right aft, the women were in a bunch, Diana being closest to him. She had very quickly worked out a way of talking to him.

"Er, Captain . . ."

He turned, lowering the telescope.

"Yes, 'Miss for now'?"

"*Lady* Diana, actually, Captain . . ." Ramage recognized the querulous voice of Mrs Donaldson, a big-boned woman who was the wife of the owner of jute factories in Madras. "Her father *is* a marquis, you know."

"Forgive me, Lady Diana," Ramage said, and from the impatient shake of the head knew he had not added to his knowledge of her. As Lady Diana she could be the unmarried daughter of the Marquis, but if she had married someone without a title, she would still be Lady Diana. Only if she had married someone with a title of their own could she have become "Lady Blank". But . . . the devil take it, he could not even remember the Rockleys' family name!

"Is the boat coming here?" demanded Mrs Donaldson.

"To us or the *Commerce*. I can't tell yet because the *Commerce* is almost between us and the privateer."

"The hostages in the *Commerce*—your men have not rescued them yet?"

"The *Commerce* has no passengers, as far as we can make out."

"What happens if the boat comes here?"

"If the men come on board, then we have lost the game."

"Why? How ridiculous! There can only be a dozen men in that boat!"

"Half a dozen," he could not resist correcting her, particularly since the number had no relevance.

"Well, you have *two* dozen! You can easily capture them,"

220

Mrs Donaldson declared. "Why, we women could deal with them!"

"I'm sure you could," Ramage said gently. "And having killed or secured them, then what happens?"

As Mrs Donaldson gave her views Ramage saw that Diana had at last realized the problem: she bit her lower lip between her teeth, but Mrs Donaldson, in a patronizing voice, announced: "Why, we add them to our prisoners and tell that horrible privateer man that now *we* have hostages, and if he doesn't go away we'll hang them all! Won't we, ladies!" She looked round her for agreement. A couple said "Yes, of course," with the eagerness of nitwits, while the others were watching Diana, perhaps unsure of what was making her doubtful but, after having her as a neighbour for so long, aware of Mrs Donaldson's intellectual shortcomings."

"I assure you, madam, that the privateer captain would not jib at the sight of a dozen of his men dangling by their necks from nooses: privateers are desperate men, and if only a few survive the action, it means their share of the spoils is bigger."

"Don't you believe it, Mr Ramage—"

"*Lord* Ramage," Diana corrected, ignoring Ramage's request in her exasperation.

"Oh, indeed? One of the Blazeys, then? How interesting. St. Kew, in Cornwall, isn't it? You must be the Earl of Blazey's son—"

"If that boat does not return safely to the *Lynx*, madam," Ramage interrupted her, "the privateer captain will give a signal which will result in all the passengers in the *Friesland* and *Heliotrope* being killed by the guards. Four men and four women in the Dutch ship, two men, two women and two children in the French."

"Oh dear me, what will happen? You must *do* something, young man; do something at once!"

"He is trying to decide now, and he doesn't need *your* help," one of the women said. "Come on, leave the captain to his business." With that the woman walked aft, followed by several of the others. Mrs Donaldson, however, stood where she was, twirling her parasol and tapping a foot.

"Young man, I *demand* to know what you intend doing!"

Ramage nodded to Rossi, who politely but firmly took Mrs

221

Donaldson's arm. "*Signora,* is down to your cabin now, the sun is too strong."

"But I don't wish—"

"This way," Rossi said, "is dangerous, too much sun." He took Mrs Donaldson's parasol and held it so low she could hardly see and, with her protesting that she *liked* the sun, the Italian had her almost trotting along the deck.

"I'm sorry," Diana murmured, "I continually underestimate you."

"Not now you don't; I've no idea what we do if that boat comes here. Kill or capture them to save ourselves, and kill the passengers in both the remaining ships—or surrender ourselves and save the others."

"How many passengers in the *Heliotrope* and *Friesland?*"

"Fourteen."

"Compared with sixteen here and how many in the *Amethyst?*"

"You have to balance twenty-six free with fourteen still held hostage."

"So you've already considered it from that point of view," she said. "Like a butcher weighing up meat."

He sighed and lifted the telescope. "I happened to know the figures; I've been living with them for the last few days. You were the first hostages to be released only because you were the nearest to the *Calypso,*" he added brutally, "and the *Amethyst* was the next nearest."

"I should have thought you would have considered it your duty to rescue the largest British ship first anyway," she said, a cold flatness in her voice.

"I'm not rescuing any particular ship. My men and I are saving lives of innocent people—or trying to."

"Don't say that to my father—he was the Governor General of Bengal."

"I know—I remembered that at breakfast."

"So that had no bearing on your rescuing us first?" Obviously she found it hard to believe.

He snapped the telescope shut with a vicious movement. "You are at liberty to question my officers when you have the chance. We knew nothing of the identity of any of the hostages."

"You mean the privateersmen said nothing to you?"

"Do they know?"

"Well, I'm sure they do. Someone must have told them!"

"I doubt it. I believe that they don't know for the simple reason that they could get almost a king's ransom for your father. A governor general's ransom, anyway. How much would the British government pay to free him? Or the directors of the East India Company? They'd pay whatever was demanded."

"Well, you've saved them the expense," she said. "It has cost you what must be a very irritating encounter with me. And if that boat comes here, I suppose everything is wasted anyway."

"The boat isn't coming here."

"How do you know?"

Ramage stared at her and then gave her the telescope. "Give it to Mrs Donaldson when you've finished. The rectangular boxes they are lifting from the water are lobster pots." He bowed and went down the companionway, knowing that his hands were shaking with anger but both surprised and pleased with himself for not showing it. Mrs Donaldson—thank goodness Rossi had understood that unspoken order. But Diana—there was no way of lowering a parasol over her. He wondered what she looked like, lying naked on a bed. Well, he would never know, but one thing was certain: she could be damned annoying fully dressed on the upper deck.

He could just make out the first stars in Orion's Belt as they rose over the hills, and he glanced across at the black shape which was the *Heliotrope*. It was going to be a long swim tonight: the *Heliotrope* was much farther from the *Earl of Dodsworth* than the East Indiaman was from the *Calypso*, and his own job was going to be a lot more difficult because he would be warning French passengers. Still, he spoke good enough French to deal with that. Much worse was the problem facing Aitken, who had to board the *Friesland* and warn a number of Dutch men and women.

It was so peaceful—and so improbable that Captain Ramage, commanding the *Calypso* frigate, should be sitting here on number four gun, starboard side, in a John Company ship anchored off an Atlantic island so small few had heard of it.

And thinking so many random thoughts his head seemed to be a mill stream in flood.

His fingers traced the "GR II" cast into the gun between the tompions. Not a new gun, by any means, but not used enough times to make a gun from the previous reign less useful. Well cared for, of course; he could feel the smoothness revealing many coats of gun lacquer, and in daylight he had seen that the ropes of the breeching, side and train tackles were in good condition: one could tell that without twisting the rope to see if the heart was still a golden brown, even though the outside had weathered grey.

It was a still night. The current kept the ships heading west of north as though they were half a dozen compass needles, but each one's heading was slightly different, so it was easy to see how the current came round the northern headland and curved into the bay with a scouring movement before meeting the southern headland and running out again.

That faint scent, crushed nettles and yet containing the muskiness he associated with the East he had never seen, and then the rustle of silk and the voice he knew he would never forget. "You sit there with head bent like Atlas carrying the weight of the world on his shoulders," she murmured.

He reached out and took her hand in a movement which seemed quite natural. "The weight of *my* world, and that's quite enough!"

"We haven't made it any lighter—people like Mrs Donaldson and me. 'You must do something at once.'" She mimicked Mrs Donaldson. "I shudder every time I think about this morning." She gave a curious start, like a suppressed hiccough.

"You've been crying, too. Not about that, surely?"

He felt her fingers let go of his hand but he held on. "Answer me, 'Miss-for-now'."

"Yes, I've been weeping like a silly young woman, but not over that."

Ramage suddenly remembered the military uniform he was wearing. Had the sight of someone about the same size as its owner provoked sad memories? Of a distant husband, a dead lover—or what? Was she a widow mourning her husband or had she gone to India with her parents to marry a fiancé who had died of one of the East's many diseases?

He twisted round on the breech of the gun so that he could

look at the dark shadow which was Diana, and he held her hand in both of his. In a few hours he would say goodbye and probably never see her again, but he needed to know.

"Over what then? It's not vulgar curiosity that makes me ask."

She gave a muted, unhappy laugh. "Captain Ramage," she said, with almost mocking formality, "I met you only eighteen hours ago. We have not even been formally introduced. My mother would have a fit if she knew I was up here alone with you..."

"Would your father?"

"I...well, I doubt it. He has a wider understanding of...problems."

"We have known each other eighteen hours; in three more we shall say goodbye—if you stay up that long. So you can answer my question without worrying about blushing when you meet me at breakfast tomorrow, because for us there is no tomorrow."

She lowered her head and gave another dry sob which she tried to disguise with a laugh. "It was a silly reason and of no possible interest to you."

"You could say possibly no concern of mine, but certainly I am interested, or I wouldn't have asked."

"Please, Captain Ramage, forget it."

"My name is Nicholas."

"I've been thinking of you as Nicholas; I suppose because you finally called me Diana."

"Finally...it took long enough. We wasted so many of those eighteen hours, 'Miss-for-now'. But tell me the reason." He could not prevent himself from returning to the question but she shook her head.

He let her hand go and said, without trying to hide the sudden bitterness he felt: "It must be important if you wish to keep it secret. Anyway, I can guess it, I think."

She looked up suddenly and he thought he had shocked her.

"What have you guessed?"

"This uniform you lent me—it belongs to someone of whom you are fond and it brought back memories."

"It brought back memories," she said, "but the trunks are in my cabin only because the purser was afraid that if they were stowed below the rats might damage the clothing."

He thought for a moment. *Had* she answered his question? He shook his head, as much to try to make his brain work more clearly as a sign of disbelief, but she said in a small voice: "The uniform has no significance; I would never have given it to you if it had."

"We met under unusual circumstances..."

"Yes, I was naked and we were not formally introduced," she said unexpectedly. "And for that matter you were almost naked, too."

"I've thought about it many times since."

"You are trying to embarrass me."

"It was dark. I didn't see your face for hours. Anyway, why were you crying?"

"Oh, don't keep harping on that. I was unhappy. Now I am going to say goodbye and leave you here thinking of the beautiful Marchesa. My father has already thanked you again for having saved us. I can only repeat his words. Thank you, Nicholas."

With that she was gone: she was barefooted, he realized, and in a moment she was hidden in the shadows cast by the masts and rigging.

So she thought he was sitting here alone in the dark "thinking of the beautiful Marchesa". He began to feel guilty when it came to him that in the last hour he had not thought of Gianna at all. He cursed the boastings of Jackson, Rossi and Stafford. They had told a romantic story of a young naval officer rescuing the beautiful Marchesa from under the feet of Bonaparte's cavalry, but they had not mentioned—because they did not realize, or never knew—the other side of it. A man and a woman could fall in love—no one could stop that. But there was much that could prevent them from even thinking of living happily ever after.

At some point in the voyage to Trinidade, Ramage now saw as he sat on the gun, hoping that Diana would return as quickly and silently as she had vanished, he had finally made up his mind about Gianna and the future. Without thinking about it openly, he had made the decision that mattered: he was not prepared to do something which made the twelfth Earl of Blazey, his son, as yet unborn, into a Roman Catholic, and forcing all the subsequent earls into a dual loyalty, to the British monarch and the Vatican.

His own father, the tenth Earl, had never mentioned the question of religion to him, even though he knew that at one time there was a question of marriage. The old Earl was very fond of Gianna: for the past few years, while Gianna was living with his parents, they had considered her more as a daughter than a refugee.

Unknown to himself, he had reached his decision. In her own way, Gianna had made a definite choice in deciding to return to Volterra. Did those two facts combined mean that the courtship, if that was the word, was over? In returning to Volterra, Gianna had obeyed the dictate of *noblesse oblige*. In turn, that meant that for reasons of state she would marry an Italian, a Tuscan whose family would be powerful enough to be a strong reinforcement for her own.

What about Paolo? For months Ramage had had the feeling that, perhaps without realizing it, Paolo was building his life round England and the Royal Navy. Yet he was Gianna's heir, and Ramage forced himself to think about it: if she was murdered by Bonaparte's agents, or even traitors among her own people, he would be the new ruler of Volterra. Paolo might be the ruler already, he told himself with a shiver.

Traitors and treason . . . there would be enough of both round the court in Volterra: the pro-French group would hardly welcome Gianna back. But had *he* been disloyal to her? Somewhere on the way from Chatham to Trinidade he had fallen out of love with her. His feelings in recent weeks, he realized, when he had worried about her safety, pictured her in a French jail, imagined her threatened by a Tuscan assassin, had been the anxiety a man would have for a much-loved sister; it was not the freezing fear for the safety of a future wife.

Had Gianna undergone this same change? It was not so much a change of heart as a change of direction. Had she begun to change while she was England, so that this made it easier for her to return to Volterra? The more he thought about it the more it seemed he was using it as an excuse for himself. Gianna had returned because it was—as she saw it—her duty. He had tried to persuade her not to because—as he saw it—the war was not over, despite the Treaty, and it was her duty to remain in England until she could return to rule her people in safety, knowing that her work for them could yield results.

All very convincing, he told himself, and now you can think

of very little else but a woman you have only known for eighteen hours and will never see again.

He slid down from the gun and, clasping his hands behind his back, walked towards the fo'c'sle. Well, in at least one way Diana had done him a good turn: she had, quite unwittingly, forced him to think clearly about Gianna, and the thinking about her had brought the knowledge that his feelings for her had changed. Not died, but changed. He now accepted, too, that since the walls of religion and their inheritances would keep them apart, there was no question of him going to his grave a bachelor because his love was forever out of reach. St Kew needed a landlord and his parents deserved a grandson.

Noblesse oblige again, of course! He had not thought of the phrase for years, but now Diana had mentioned it in another context, did he want to be the eleventh and *last* Earl of Blazey, after his father died? It was one of the oldest earldoms in the kingdom. He was an only child and by not marrying and not having a son, did he want to see the end of it?

He turned and made his way aft. It would soon be time for him to start off alone for the *Heliotrope*, the rest of the men following later. They had prepared the raft, and Ramage pulled his stock from his pocket. It was dry now. Jackson was waiting with the cutlass and knife. The wind dropping had left a warm night, and as the excitement of the second stage of the operation began to seep through him, the uniform felt particularly hot and oppressive. He felt an irrational hatred for it—irrational because she had made it clear it had not belonged to anyone she loved. He stopped for a moment. Loved now, but could it have been someone she *had* loved?

The devil take it; he would never see her again. Jackson stepped forward and helped him out of the jacket, and then he sat on the breech of a gun to pull off the rest of his clothes.

Over in the *Amethyst*, Aitken would be preparing. The second stage . . . and if it was successful the third stage would be the last one. It was, he reflected, an odd way to survey an island.

CHAPTER SIXTEEN

He came out of the blackness as though swimming up from a great depth and heard Jackson and Rossi talking in a jumble of words before sinking back again. The next time he surfaced, quietly and smoothly like a dolphin, he knew that he was cold and wet, and he could hear Diana's voice. The third time, when he managed to stay with them longer, he realized that he was lying on the deck of a ship, soaking wet and with a dull, pounding pain in his left arm, close to where the scar was still white from the musket ball which hit him at Curaçao.

"Nicholas," she was saying, her voice urgent. "Can you hear me? Nicholas . . . Nicholas!"

He thought he was answering but everything seemed so far away. He shouted and his voice came out as a whisper, and he wished the pain in his arm would stop. "Yes . . . yes." That seemed about all he wanted to say. Quite why he was lying flat on his back, this awful pain in his arm, feeling that he was going to vomit any moment, and with something soft against his face, soft and warm, and moving slightly all the time, he did not know. Now someone was approaching with a lantern . . .

The light showed that he was lying by the mainmast of the *Earl of Dodsworth* and his head was cradled in a woman's arms. But he had swum away from the East Indiaman hours ago and boarded the *Heliotrope* alone.

What was happening in the *Heliotrope?* All those passengers, two of them children. He had explained what they were to do in French, and then the *Calypso*'s boarding party had arrived. Yes, now he remembered that a privateersman had woken and roused the rest and there had been a desperate fight in that small cabin...

"Jackson! Jackson!" he shouted, and she heard him whispering, his teeth chattering with the violence of the shivering.

"He wants you," she said to the American, the wetness of his hair soaking through her frock and chilling her breasts. While the American and the Italian continued tying the bandage round his arm, his face was as white as a sheet in the lantern-light: the cheekbones stuck out like elbows, the skin of his face stretched taut as though all the blood and much of the flesh had drained away in the sea while the men towed the raft with him lashed to it.

He was dying, of that she was sure, and her last words to him had been unpleasant; she had turned her back on him and walked away when all she wanted to do was kiss him and have him hold her. Now they had brought him back to die in her arms.

"Sir, it's Jackson," the American crouched over him, his ears close to Nicholas's mouth. Diana listened intently. Some last message for the Marchesa? No, he would give that to the young count. But she must not have these bitter thoughts now; if he died, two women would have loved him.

"Wha' happened?"

Jackson knew what his captain wanted to know. "We saved the hostages, sir. The guards in the cabin were roused. One caught you with a cutlass as you spitted a man going for Spurgeon with a knife."

"Di' we lose anyone?"

"Spurgeon, sir. The privateersman stabbed him the same moment the other one slashed you with his cutlass."

"Wha'm I doing here?"

"Now, sir," Jackson said soothingly, "you rest now. The *Lynx* heard nothing. Mr Martin's in command in the *Heliotrope* and Mr Aitken's taken the *Friesland*."

The American straightened himself and shouted aft: "Look alive with those blankets! Sorry, ma'am," he said to Diana, "but the captain's mortal cold."

It was no good explaining to this seaman that the passengers were so bewildered as to be almost helpless; that being seized by privateersmen in the first place had been a great shock;

being suddenly rescued in the middle of the night was a second one; and now, having the man they regarded as their saviour dragged bleeding and unconscious up the side of the ship must seem like the end of the world to them.

God, he was shivering so violently. Now he was whispering again, every word taking so much effort. She reached out and tugged Jackson's shirt as he bent down to help Rossi with the bandage, which was a strip torn from a sheet.

"*Calypso* . . . I must get to the *Calypso* . . ."

"Yes, sir, as soon as we can. Three of the men have swum over to fetch Mr Bowen and a boat."

"Jackson, why bring me here?"

She realized that the American knew it was pointless to give soothing answers. "You'd have bled to death a long time a'fore we reached her, sir. We started off for her but we couldn't swim fast enough towing the raft, and when you kept on bleeding in spite of the bandages and tourniquet, we reckoned we needed somewhere quick with dry bandages and a lantern."

"Nicholas," she said, "they're trying to make you a hot drink, but they're frightened the glow of the galley stove might be seen from the *Lynx*. Will you sip this brandy?"

"Come on, sir," Jackson said and uncapped a flat silver flask. Finally he said: "It's no good, ma'am. I know what he's like from other times. He hates spirits."

"Other times?" she whispered.

"We really thought we'd lost him the last time, didn't we, Rossi?"

"*Mamma mia*, when we blew up that Dutch frigate, I thought we were *all* loosed."

"Lost," Jackson corrected from habit, and said to Diana, "He'll be all right soon, ma'am; you wait until Mr Bowen arrives."

"Who is he?"

"Our surgeon. Ah, about time!" he growled as two men arrived with blankets. "We only needed two or three! Here, take that end and we'll slide one under him and use it to lift him."

"Where are you going to take him?" she asked anxiously.

"Nowhere, ma'am. If you'll fold those other blankets into a mattress. Keep out a couple to go over him. Then we can lift him on to it."

Reluctantly, like a woman having a suckling child taken away from her, she lowered his head and helped Rossi cradle the wounded arm.

"He's so cold," she said to no one in particular.

"Ma'am," Jackson said, "if you'd just walk away for a minute or two . . ."

"Why?" Her voice was harsh.

"Oh . . . I just want to—well, remove his wet clothes!"

She leaned over, saw the pin shining in the lanternlight among the folds of silk, and pulled it out, and then unwrapped the stock. The triangle of curly black hair glistened and the men gently lifted the blanket. She held the stock for a moment. There was not a hint of warmth in the silk; it was as though it had been a corpse's loincloth.

Once he was lowered on to the makeshift mattress she took one and then the other blanket and covered him, leaving the left arm outside so they could keep an eye on it. Already blood was seeping through the bandage, a spreading black stain in the candlelight. His eyes were closed, his breathing shallow. She had earlier watched the rise and fall of his ribs and any moment expected it to stop, as if the effort was too much.

The loss of blood and the shadows thrown by the lantern emphasized his features. His nose was thin and slightly curved, like a beak, and the bone made a white ridge. The cheekbones frightened her; it was almost as if parchment covered a skull. Above his right eye there were two scars on the brow, thin, white bars on the skin, which itself seemed almost grey. The eyes, closed now, were sunk even deeper under heavy brows. His hair, wet and tangled, looked like a clump of seaweed tossed carelessly on a beach by a wave.

His right hand was plucking at the blanket and trying to reach across to his left arm. Before she could move, Rossi had leaned over and with surprising gentleness put the hand back under the blanket. The lips moved and Rossi bent down and listened.

"I think he wants you, ma'am, if you're 'Diana'."

She felt a surge of pleasure, then realized that this Italian seaman had probably misheard a murmured "Gianna" as "Diana". He was thinking of the Marchesa.

"Nicholas . . ."

232

"Diana," he whispered, and there was no mistaking it, "they shouldn't have brought me here."

Misunderstanding him, she said: "Don't worry, Mr Bowen will be here at any minute. It's not a bad wound; it is just that you've lost a lot of blood."

"No . . . I meant—" he seemed to lose consciousness for a moment, then she realized he had shut his eyes to fight off a wave of pain "—I'm sorry to have frightened you . . . but the *Lynx* is next, and then home."

Not knowing quite what he meant, she smoothed the hair from his brow and said: "Don't worry about the *Lynx* now, all the hostages are safe."

"Yardarm . . . both of them," he murmured and seemed to lose consciousness.

"Yardarm?" she asked Jackson.

"Yes, ma'am," the American said briskly, touching the side of his captain's throat to check the pulse, "those privateersmen will hang from a ship's yardarm. Maybe not all of them, but the leaders. Not the *Calypso*'s," he explained. "We'll probably take 'em back to England for trial."

"You have to capture them first."

"Oh, I'm sure the captain has a plan for that."

She wanted to shake the American. Did the fool not realize his captain was dying? That he was slipping away from them even now, like smoke in the wind? And they could do nothing to prevent it: the great gash in his arm, now bound up and with a tourniquet above it, was not the problem. He was dying because as his men had swum with desperate haste to the *Earl of Dodsworth* with him lashed to the raft, his blood had been draining from his body with every pump of his heart. The men who had tied the first tourniquet could not see—did not think to look—that it had come undone.

As she began to weep, she understood that, such was their faith in him that a mention of the *Lynx* brought the confident comment that the captain would have a plan . . . In her imagination she saw him dead, and remembered the funeral service, and the dreadful business of the body sewn up in a hammock and tipped over the side from a plank. One of the seamen had died of a fever off Capetown.

Jackson's body went taut for a moment, then he hurried to

the entryport. He came back a few moments later and said: "It's the boat with Mr Bowen."

Obviously they had faith in this man Bowen. It was a pity that the *Earl of Dodsworth*'s regular surgeon was a prisoner along with the rest of the ship's officers and men in the camp on shore.

Suddenly a man appeared out of the darkness behind her and knelt beside Nicholas. A hand went down to his face and a finger pushed back an eyelid. "You still with us, sir?" The voice had a bantering note which infuriated her. Was *this* Bowen?

"I didn't cover one of their pawns," Nicholas murmured. It was an extraordinary thing to say, but Bowen laughed and turned to the plump, elderly man now standing beside him, a man with flowing white hair and carrying a box with a rope handle.

"Put it down there, Southwick. We ought to have brought the chessboard. Now, Jackson, what happened?"

She wanted to tell him first to do something about the terrible pallor of his skin, to make him drink some brandy to stop this awful shivering.

"Cutlass slash across the upper arm, sir. We put a tourniquet on, just as you showed us years ago, and a bandage, and lowered him on the raft to tow him back to the *Calypso*. We hadn't gone above a hundred yards when Rossi reckons he'd never cover that distance alive, so we made for this ship, sir."

"Why the devil didn't you go back to the *Heliotrope?*"

"She's French, sir. All that gabbling and panic with the passengers. They wouldn't keep out of the way once they saw Mr Ramage had been wounded—he'd spoken to all of them, o' course, when he first got on board. Oh yes, and Spurgeon was killed. It was trying to save him that led to Mr Ramage getting cut."

Cut, indeed, she thought, not knowing that Jackson was using a slang word regularly spoken in the West Indies to describe a sword wound. It originated among the Negroes, when they slashed each other with machetes, but she had never heard the phrase.

Bowen had knelt while Jackson talked and was unwinding the bandage Rossi had just put on.

She said: "It's a clean wound, I can tell you that."

"Thank you, ma'am," Bowen said courteously, and continued to unwind the strip of sheet.

"You might start it bleeding again."

"It is still bleeding," Bowen commented. "But don't you worry. Perhaps you'd like to return to your cabin, ma'am? The sight of blood..."

Jackson coughed and said: "The lady helped us hoist Mr Ramage on board and she found the tourniquet had come adrift. Then she cleaned the wound—the basin of water is still over there."

"My apologies, ma'am," Bowen said, and detecting more in Jackson's words than the bare meaning, added: "Perhaps you would care to help me. A woman's touch is gentler than that of my clumsy but well-meaning shipmates. Now, Southwick—" he paused as he began to lift the bandage clear "—open the medicine chest for me and stand by with the pad of cloth you'll find in the top left-hand corner. Rossi, let's have that lantern closer..."

He now had the wound uncovered and seemed to be talking to himself. "Ah yes, chipped the humerus bone slightly but no fracture because the blow was directed at a sharp angle downwards... missed the main artery... veins bleeding—that seems to be the main problem... Muscle torn but probably still functional..."

He bent over Ramage's head. "Still with us, sir? Ah, good. Would you try to move your left hand slightly? Ah—yes, it hurts. Now just wriggle the fingers. That starts more bleeding but tells us that no ligaments have been cut. You'll be able to carve a roast in three or four weeks. Southwick, stand by with that pad... the lady did a very good job of cleaning the wound; nothing for me to do there. Now, I'm going to release the tourniquet for a minute or two, and then retie it. Except for the lady, you all know why, but as it looks rather alarming, should I explain, ma'am?"

She nodded, finding that she now had complete faith in the man: he seemed far removed from her idea of a naval surgeon, which in turn was based on the rather tough individual presiding over the *Earl of Dodsworth*'s medicine chest.

"Well, if we leave a limb cut off from its blood for too long, the flesh can die and gangrene starts, so we release a

235

tourniquet for a minute or two every twenty minutes, and then tie it again."

He loosened it, waited and retied it with skilled fingers. "Pad, Southwick—perhaps you would hold it in place, ma'am, while I apply the bandage. No, there's no need to press, and it's not hurting him. He's in pain, but that's from the whole wound."

As he prepared to roll on the bandage he leaned over and sniffed and commented: "He's refused the brandy again, eh?"

"'Fraid so, sir," Jackson said. "Even when the lady tried."

Bowen looked up at her for the first time: up to this moment he had rarely taken his eyes off Ramage's wound or his face.

"You notice, ma'am, that we all seem to be rather familiar with the, er, routine of patching up our captain. The fact is he does get himself knocked about. I remember the last time, at Curaçao, was just like this except that—"

"Jackson told me," she said hurriedly. The strange thing was she had not felt faint when she had to retie the tourniquet, wash the wound and staunch the bleeding; when she believed he was dying and thought that if he was to be saved she would have to do whatever was necessary. But now, with Nicholas obviously not dying—not even in any danger, according to this surgeon, who was clearly an extremely competent man— she could feel the strength going from her knees, and the lantern was beginning to blur.

"The brandy, Jackson," Bowen snapped. "The lady."

Southwick bent down and caught her as she slid sideways. "There, m'dear, just have a sup of this . . . gently, it'll make you cough . . . now swallow."

"Put her down on her back," Bowen said, "and get her head on a level with her heart. Now, ma'am, breathe deeply, and when you feel better, I'd be glad of your help."

Quickly she sat up, the faintness vanishing. "Yes, what can I do?"

"Just hold his forearm up high enough for me to pass the bandage round . . . You see, you don't feel faint while there's something for you to do: when you thought he was dying, you took control. Now you've no responsibility, you get the vapours, like some silly young woman in a London drawing room!"

Bowen was right, of course, and she smiled at him. "I don't like brandy, though!"

"Just as well," Bowen said cheerfully. "I nearly killed myself with it, years ago. You'd never believe I once had a flourishing practice in Wimpole Street...took to brandy..." He continued winding the bandage, pausing now and again to straighten an edge. "Lost all my patients—they shunned a drunkard. So I became a naval surgeon...My first ship was commanded by Mr Ramage, who decided no drunkard was going to tend his sick...So he and Southwick here, this man with a head of hair like a dandelion run to seed, decided to cure me...Succeeded, although it was a grim business for both of them—"

"Not too pleasant for you either," Southwick said.

"No, it wasn't. Anyway, I've had not a drop of alcohol since. A new man, a new life, thanks to these two. I'm not telling you that story, ma'am, to frighten you off brandy, which you obviously dislike, but to show you that old Southwick and I do our best to keep an eye on him."

Had this man Bowen guessed? Was she being too obvious? That seaman Jackson was watching her, smiling. And the white-haired man, too. She bent her head and concentrated on holding Nicholas's arm.

Finally Bowen said: "That's it. Perhaps you'd close the medicine chest again, Southwick. It's no good offering him any Tincture of Opium, to make sure he sleeps, because he'll insist he has to stay awake. Now, how do we get him down into the boat?"

"Oh, no!" She said it before she could control herself, and continued hurriedly: "I mean, he must stay here. We have plenty of cabins with comfortable beds—enough for all of you. And fresh meat and eggs—just what he'll need while he convalesces."

She saw Nicholas's right hand signal to Bowen, who leaned over as he whispered something.

"We'll see about that!" the surgeon said disapprovingly. "Aitken and Southwick can deal with them!"

Again the hand signalled and Bowen listened. "Sir, with respect, I'm beginning to think it would be best if you stayed in this ship."

"Southwick..."

Bowen moved back to let the white-haired man move nearer.

"Get a stay-tackle rigged . . . Lash me in a chair . . ."

"Aye aye, sir," the old man said reluctantly.

They were taking him away. It had something to do with the *Lynx*. If only they would go away for a few minutes . . .

She watched as Southwick and the seaman went to the ropes and began pulling on some and loosening others.

"Ma'am," Southwick called, "could you ask a couple of men passengers to bring up a chair with arms?"

She ran below, hurriedly gave instructions, and came back to find Bowen sitting crosslegged on the deck beside Nicholas. She called to Southwick that the chair was being brought up and, kicking her skirt sideways, sat opposite Bowen, with Nicholas lying between them, apparently asleep, his bandaged left arm lying across his stomach.

Bowen looked across at her and said quietly: "The cutlass slash will soon heal—you cleaned it perfectly. The weakness, which looks so distressing to you, as though he's dying, his face so pale, his voice weak, is simply the result of losing so much blood. But the human body is very resilient. It'll have made up that quantity of blood in a matter of hours. By breakfast time he'll be grumbling. By dinner time he'll be impossible!"

"Thank you, Mr Bowen. I . . . well, I thought he was dying when they brought him on board."

"So did Jackson and Rossi, and the other men, until you got to work. They say you spotted the tourniquet was loose, and stopped them panicking."

"That's not true, but it is nice of them to say it."

"Ah, well, here comes the chair. I'll go and see what Southwick and the men are going to rig up."

As soon as the surgeon had left she turned the lantern so the light was not in his eyes. In fact, he was almost in shadow.

"Are you awake?" she whispered.

"Yes . . . where has everyone gone?"

"They are arranging a chair, so they can lower you into the boat. Are you warm enough?"

"The shivering . . . it's reaction, not cold . . . Thank you for helping me; I heard what Bowen said."

She shook her head, her eyes swimming with tears. "You will rest now, promise me. The *Lynx*, whatever you plan, can be done by your officers. This man Southwick, he's obviously a very competent man."

"You didn't—" he winced, and then continued "—think so yesterday."

"Your chair is nearly ready," she whispered.

She leaned down and her hair tumbled over them. He was still shivering and as she held his face in her hands the skin was cold.

She kissed him and said: "I'm going now—I'd rather you didn't see me cry like a baby." She stood then and ran aft to the companionway but had to wipe away the tears that blurred her vision before she dared to walk down the steps.

CHAPTER SEVENTEEN

It was a few minutes past nine in the morning when the surgeon's mate sitting beside Ramage's cot saw that his eyes were open and called to the Marine sentry: "Pass the word for Mr Bowen an' tell him the captain's awake."

Bowen arrived almost immediately, and grinned when he saw Ramage watching him.

"How's the patient feeling?"

"My arm hurts like hell, I feel dizzy, and I can still taste that dam' soup you made me drink. It was too hot and it burned my tongue."

"Your recovery has obviously started, sir," Bowen announced, feeling under Ramage's armpit. "Ha, no swelling there. No more than the pain you'd expect in the arm. No throbbing?"

"No, it just aches," Ramage said grudgingly. "The pain of those stitches has gone."

"An excellent piece of embroidery, if I may be allowed to boast. Two weeks and I'll be taking them out and you'll be admiring a handsome scar which will impress the ladies."

"Yes, I shall parade through the drawing rooms in a ruffled shirt with the sleeve rolled up. Now, call Silkin: I'm going to wash, he can shave me and help me dress, and then you can rig up a sling."

Bowen shook his head. "You must stay in your cot for at least three days. You've lost a lot of blood, which the body must make up. Exsanguinated, that's what you are, sir, and it means—"

"I can work it out, and I hate your medical terms. Pass the word for Silkin, please and—"

"Sir, I must insist that you—"

Ramage's eyes narrowed and Bowen stopped talking; one did not insist when the captain was in this mood.

"Bowen," he said, "I appreciate your concern, but let us keep a sense of proportion. I have a minor flesh wound and have lost some blood and feel a trifling dizziness. Spurgeon is dead. That's the very small price we have paid so far to rescue forty men, women and children hostages. We have two dozen privateersmen under guard in the four prizes we have captured. There is a fifth prize but she has no passengers— only two or three privateersmen on board as shipkeepers."

Ramage struggled and sat up in the cot, making it swing with the effort, and holding his bandaged left arm with his right hand.

"However, all we've done up to now is grab the animal's tail. The head, with a mouthful of sharp teeth, is still there at anchor. The *Lynx* still has enough men and boats to recapture the prizes the moment she realizes we've taken them."

Bowen nodded. "I understand that, sir. We have to deal with the *Lynx.*"

"Exactly. And this morning. Any moment now they might discover what we've done."

"I appreciate that, sir, but surely Wagstaffe and Southwick—"

"Bowen! Can you picture me lying here while all that's going on?"

"Well, sir . . . I'm only advising . . ."

"For my own good. Yes, thank you. Very well, now, pass the word for Silkin!"

It took half an hour to get Ramage washed, shaved and dressed, and Bowen then spent fifteen minutes with squares of nankeen cut off from the roll kept by the purser, making a sling for the wounded arm. While an impatient and cursing Ramage tried to hurry the surgeon, Silkin bobbed between them, trying to make his captain drink hot tea and eat a soft-boiled egg which had been spread on a piece of ship's biscuit.

Finally Ramage sat at his desk, his arm resting on the flat surface and his face pale and wet with perspiration, his hand shaky and his knees only doubtfully reliable.

"So the survey boats and the one doing the soundings went off as usual?" he asked Wagstaffe.

"Yes, sir. One of the young seamen wore a hat and jacket of Martin's, and that painter fellow Wilkins wore one of my coats and hats today and went on shore with the surveyors."

"Wilkins? What on earth for?"

"He mentioned something about the *Lynx* being so close to the beach. He took notebooks and sticks of charcoal with him."

"Does he want to sketch the *Lynx* then?"

Wagstaffe looked away and said noncommittally: "I think he had in mind that—well, he wants to do a painting of the *Calypso* capturing the *Lynx*, and he'd get the best view from the beach: the *Lynx* is barely a hundred yards out."

Ramage thought for a moment and then realized that almost the last place for an artist to be would be on board the *Calypso*.

"How many men are we short?"

"Twenty-two are away in the prizes (Orsini, Jackson and Rossi came back with you last night, sir: Bowen needed help to hold the chair upright across the thwarts). Twenty-four in the survey and sounding boats: forty-six men, and Aitken, Kenton and Martin. I didn't send Orsini off in the soundings boat this morning."

"Why?"

"He was rather concerned about you, sir, and until you woke . . ."

"Orsini is simply another member of the ship's company. Remember that, Mr Wagstaffe."

"Aye aye, sir," the second lieutenant said, thankful that it had passed off so easily. The boy was sure the captain was going to die, and that combined with the knowledge that both men were very worried about the Marchesa had made him agree that Orsini could stay on board. But the way things were going, the *Calypso* was not going to be the best place to spend the day...

"Now listen carefully," Ramage said. "First things first. The captain must be comfortable. I want that armchair from the *Earl of Dodsworth* put down on the larboard side of the binnacle box, where I can sight the compass."

Both Southwick and Wagstaffe laughed with him, and the lieutenant said: "I knew that chair would come in useful! The bosun was proposing to heave it overboard!"

"Now," Ramage continued, his voice becoming serious. "Guns on both sides loaded with grape but not run out, of course. Decks wetted and sanded, but make sure no one from the *Lynx* can guess what's going on by seeing water pouring out of the scuppers or spot the washdeck pump rigged...I want the lashing on the bitter end of the anchor cable untied down in the cabletier, so that we can let it all run out: I don't want to lose time and make a noise cutting the cable with an axe—"

"Can I buoy it, sir?" asked Southwick. "Seems a pity to lose an anchor and a new cable."

"Yes, by all means. Men to have arms listed for them in the Watch, Station and Quarters bill, but again, make sure no one is seen from the *Lynx* marching round wearing a cutlass. Leave the grindstone down below! But make sure the topmen have sharp knives—I want those gaskets cut: don't waste time untying them. The sails must be let fall and sheeted home and the yards braced in moments, not minutes."

He paused as a wave of dizziness made the cabin tilt, and for a few moments he could not understand why both Wagstaffe and Southwick were sitting horizontally, but after a few deep breaths it passed.

Southwick then took a deep breath, as though he was going to dive over the side. "That chair, sir. Supposing we put it right aft, on the larboard side against the taffrail, then you'd—"

"—be out of the way of the quartermaster and not such a target for sharpshooters in the *Lynx*," Ramage said.

242

"Well, sir, that's quite true; a sitting target, if there ever was one," the master said, making no attempt to hide the fact that he was offended.

"What time do we start, sir?" Wagstaffe asked tactfully.

"We can start as though we intend airing sails. Send four or five topmen aloft to let fall the foretopsail, untying the gaskets; but make sure the maintopsail and mizentopsail gaskets are cut. That'll save us a few minutes."

"The Marines, sir?"

"Is Renwick on board?"

"Yes, sir: I stopped him going on shore with the surveyors. All the Marines are on board."

"Very well, they will be sharpshooters, but must dress as seamen. That man Hart will suspect something if he sees groups of Marines in uniform."

"And the prisoners we take, sir: there may be several British. I suppose they'd be different from prisoners of war?"

"There's no war," Ramage said deliberately. "All the Lynxes are pirates. The British—well, that'll be for the Crown lawyers to decide, but they're probably traitors as well. The matter won't arise unless we have prisoners, of course."

"No, sir," Wagstaffe answered, and then stared at Ramage as he realized the real significance of what his captain had just said. The lieutenant leaned forward as Ramage said quietly: "Those brave fellows were prepared to murder women and children, and I'm afraid that if we take them to England some clever man of law may charm a judge . . ."

"Aye, charm, bribe, call it what you will," Southwick said. "No matter what happens, no one in England is going to believe what we've seen and heard out here. Pity we can't try 'em on board."

"Well, we'll see," Ramage said judicially. "Let's see how many prisoners we take."

Diana stood on the afterdeck of the *Earl of Dodsworth* with the other women, six Calypsos still pretending to guard them. Since the rescue, Mrs Donaldson seemed rarely to be more than a yard way, prattling, questioning or grumbling.

"This Lord Ramage," she said. "Why doesn't he take his ship and *sink* these wretched pirates? After all, his ship is bigger."

"He was far from well last night," Diana said mildly.

"Oh, a mere cut on the arm, so my husband said, and he saw him when he carried a chair up. What they wanted a chair for, I don't know. With arms, too!"

Diana could see that the *Calypso* was built for speed and for fighting: she had never before compared a frigate with a merchant ship, but the *Heliotrope*, for example, was a positive box while the *Calypso* was lean, seeming to contain power, like a coiled spring. Like Nicholas, she thought, like Nicholas when he was not wounded.

"You saw that Lord Ramage last night," Mrs Donaldson said. "*Was* he badly wounded? They fetched the surgeon from that frigate, so my husband said."

"No, a mere cut on the arm, just as your husband said."

"Then why all the fuss? Why isn't he *doing* something? After all, his father's an admiral and a peer of the realm, so you'd think the young fellow would have—well, some sort of tradition."

"It isn't tradition he needs," Diana said quietly. "It's blood."

"Blood? My dear, do you mean he lacks breeding? Isn't he really the Earl's son? So the Countess was faithless, eh? Well, one can never be sure, my husband always says."

"Blood," Diana said, even more quietly, "that flows through the body. He lost most of it in the sea between here and the *Heliotrope*. He might have died and then," she added, hating the woman's vulgar and crude mind, "the pirates would have come back and probably taken you to the *Lynx*."

"Oh, la!" Mrs Donaldson squealed, and fainted like a tent collapsing, and Diana walked away to the taffrail, angry that she had let herself be provoked by the woman.

She looked across at the *Calypso* again. Which was Nicholas's cabin? She could picture Bowen with his medicine chest, and Southwick, too: they would have seen him already this morning; might even be with him now. He could have had her cabin, then she could have sat with him, and helped Bowen.

Obviously nothing was being done about the *Lynx* today, which was hardly surprising, except to a woman like Mrs Donaldson. The important thing was that all the hostages had been freed, the privateersmen guarding them locked up, and their place taken by British seamen. This pretence that they were all still hostages had to be kept up until Nicholas was ready to deal with the *Lynx*, but today all the Calypsos deserved a rest, and as soon as he was strong enough Nicholas would be giving orders to his officers. In the meantime the *Calypso*'s boats were going about their usual business, two taking the surveyors to the shore, and one finding out the depths in the bay by dropping a lead weight on a rope into the water. Nicholas had been droll when describing that, but she could not now remember which was correct, "swinging the lead" or "heaving the lead". One meant malingering, and she thought it was "swinging", but she noticed that the sailor on the boat swung it before he let it go. Yet that was "heaving" too. It was very puzzling.

He commanded more than two hundred men in the *Calypso:* the sailor who told her that said there were four lieutenants and the master—that was the white-haired old man she had seen last night. It was a good thing the sailor had explained, because the man who commanded the *Earl of Dodsworth* was called "the master" although referred to as "the captain". It was very different in the Royal Navy, apparently, where the man commanding the ship was a lieutenant or a captain, depending on the size, but, like the *Earl of Dodsworth*'s master, was referred to as "the captain". And a master in the Royal Navy by no means commanded the ship (unless he was something called "master and commander" but she did not understand that and it applied only to small ships). Indeed, "the master" was not even a commission officer like the lieutenants; he was only a warrant officer, like a sergeant major in the army.

The waiting and the not knowing . . . On the one hand she was relieved that he was not attacking the *Lynx* today; on the other it meant another day and night—of worrying without being able to say a word to anyone, without confiding: just having this secret which she could share with no one. Hardly a secret, even; more the type of thing—so she imagined—that a young Catholic girl might confess to her priest. Yet it was all so hopeless (and so innocent, really) that it was doubtful if a young girl would find it worth mentioning, and certainly a priest would not be interested.

So hopeless and so innocent—yet it was tearing her apart: she could not sleep because of it; she wondered how she was going to get through a day—let alone every day from now on—without screaming or having hysterics. She went down the companionway to her cabin: tears were very close, and if that Donaldson woman continued prattling after her friends had helped her over this latest attack of the vapours, Diana knew she would scream at her.

Love you could not admit to, love that was not returned, love for a person already in love with someone else—was there any worse instrument of torture? The rack? The ducking stool? The garotte? Childish toys, mere irritants. She shut her cabin door and sat on the bed. Nicholas Ramage. He had returned her kiss when she said goodbye. But was that because he knew that once the *Lynx* was captured all the ships would sail from Trinidade, a farewell as the ball came to an end, or... she forced herself to think of it, although she squeezed her eyes tight shut, as though at the same time trying to keep it out. Or did he know, or have a presentiment, that he would be killed while capturing the *Lynx?*

The more she thought about it the more certain she became: he knew he was going to die. He loved another woman, so this farewell kiss was in the nature of a thank you to "Miss for now" for cleaning his wound. If he knew he would survive the attack on the *Lynx,* why the farewell kiss? If he lived he would meet her again before the ships sailed; he must know, too, that now Papa had retired as Governor General of Bengal and was returning to England, they were bound to meet again in London society. It was curious how angry he had become over wearing the military uniform.

"Miss... miss!" Someone was banging on her door. "Miss, quick, on deck, the *Calypso*'s getting under way!"

"I'm coming—thank you..." She wanted to stay in her cabin and pretend nothing was happening, but instead she would have to go on deck and watch the *Calypso* carrying Nicholas to his death, and listen to people like Mrs Donaldson cheering, and repeating some banal remark of her husband's.

The sunlight sparkling off the sea was dazzling; the sky was an unbelievable blue and cloudless, the island seemed utterly peaceful, holding the bay in its arms. Even the *Lynx* seemed small and innocent. Then she turned to look at the *Calypso.*

She knew she would never forget the sight: the wind was making the sails curve, pressing out the creases in the canvas, and the *Calypso* moved through the water slowly but with infinite grace, a swan borne across a lake by a breeze.

Suddenly she saw the smooth black sides, with the white stripe (was that what they called a strake?) seem to move and grow red rectangles, and she realized that the port lids were being raised. A moment later she saw the guns themselves protruding like black fingers. But why was she stopping now, the sails flat and flapping?

Southwick did not often disagree with what the captain did, but he considered now was such a time. To be honest, it was what he *thought* the captain was going to do, since Mr Ramage had not said anything. It looked as if he was going to take the *Calypso* up to the *Lynx*, lay the frigate alongside the privateer and board. And the trouble with privateers was that they always had enormous crews. They did not need many men to handle the ship—the *Lynx* with her schooner rig could make do with fifteen men—but they needed plenty of seamen to send away in the prizes she took. Now was a good example: one privateer had five prizes, and would eventually need five prize crews, although admittedly in the case of the East Indiaman they would probably force some of the original ship's company to work at gunpoint. And the privateersmen would be desperate: they would realize that unless they escaped the *Calypso* they would end up on the gallows, and to them the sword would be preferable to the noose.

The old master looked ahead. The *Calypso* was at last gathering way, picking up a breeze after running into an unexpected almost windless patch in the lee of some hills. A windless patch like that, had it continued, could have wrecked everything.

After successfully letting the anchor cable run, bracing the foretopsail hard up after leaving it for half an hour "to air" and letting fall the remaining topsails, sheeting them home and bracing them hard up, the *Calypso* had moved off to windward like an old warhorse hearing gunfire in the distance. Then the wind had died.

Looking at Mr Ramage sitting in his armchair, the white cloth of the sling making it seem he was wearing some strange new uniform, one had to admire his calm: he glanced at the sails and at the windvanes and simply told the quartermaster to bear up a point. Sure enough the *Calypso* had enough way on to keep moving through the windless area, and when the wind picked up again it had backed a point, to north by west.

The course to the *Lynx* meant the *Calypso* would pass close to the stern of the *Amethyst*, with the *Friesland* also on the starboard side farther over towards the southern headland, and then even closer to the *Heliotrope*, while the *Earl of Dodsworth* was already on the larboard beam with the *Commerce* ahead of her.

The wind was settling down to north by west although the bows of all the ships headed more to the east, particularly the *Lynx* and *Commerce*, closer inshore. With a lighter wind they were more affected by the current sweeping round the headland and up into the bay, so they were partly wind rode and partly current rode.

Steering for the *Lynx* and slapping the *Calypso* alongside, though, seemed unnecessarily risky to Southwick for another reason: getting alongside with the privateer to windward or leeward and hooking on to her with grappling irons risked the *Lynx* cutting her cable so that both ships drifted as they fought, probably fouling the *Heliotrope* and ending up on shore.

Admittedly the captain must be worried about the chance of the *Lynx* escaping him: she might be able to cut her cable and set enough canvas to slip round between the *Calypso* and the shore—that was the main reason why the *Calypso* suddenly let fall her sails and cut her cable, to give the *Lynx* as little time as possible. But the privateer's fore and aft rig gave her an enormous advantage. The *Calypso* was like a bull trying to trap a calf in a corner of a field: not so much from the point of view of relative strength, but from size and clumsiness.

Still, the hinges of the *Calypso*'s port lids squeaked as they swung up and Southwick felt more confident as he saw the men haul on the tackles that sent the guns rumbling out. The powder monkeys were already lined up along the centreline, each behind a pair of guns, and squatting on the wooden cylinder in which he carried the next flannel cartridge, the one needed for the second round.

The decks glistened wet in the sunshine; the sand sprinkled unevenly on the planking and soaking up the water made light patches and dark, and already the heat of the sun was drying it. Southwick felt the hilt of his sword. The captain always referred to it as his "meat cleaver", and he hoped he would get a chance to use it in the next few minutes: they were fast approaching the *Lynx*.

Ramage found the sunshine dazzling. Normally it did not bother him, but he was still dizzy from losing all that blood, and he had a headache. That was not surprising, but it did not help him concentrate.

The first few hundred yards had gone satisfactorily, anyway. The foretopsail let fall "to air" had not aroused any interest in the *Lynx:* they would have seen the two survey boats landing at the beach as usual, and even now the boat doing the soundings was being rowed across the bay, seamen heaving their leads and the depths and course being written down.

He had been watching the *Lynx* as he gave the order to let the cable run and let fall the main and mizentopsails, sheet home all three sails and brace the yards hard up. The sails were filling and the *Calypso* was already sliding through the water before he saw any response from the few figures moving about the *Lynx*'s deck. Although in the glass they were only tiny, he could imagine the shouts, followed by Hart and Tomás hurrying up on deck and sizing up the situation. That was the moment the *Calypso* ran into the windless patch. He had seen it before they set any sails—a smooth area of water surrounded by tiny ripples—and knew the *Calypso* would carry her way through it.

Now she had picked up the wind again. It was infuriating having to sit here in an armchair, but he knew he had not the strength to stand. Wagstaffe was standing at the rail on the forward side of the quarterdeck, Southwick stood behind him, and Orsini was a couple of feet to one side of the chair, ready to run messages.

Glancing from one side to the other he saw that the *Calypso* was midway between the *Amethyst* to starboard and the *Earl of Dodsworth* to larboard. Was she watching? What was the significance of those two trunks full of uniforms and men's clothing? A man's clothing, he corrected himself: a man about his own build with slightly larger feet. Did she love him? Was he even alive?

Trinidade, a speck in the South Atlantic that few men knew about and even fewer visited, but here he had found a ship carrying out her own private war against everyone, and a woman he did not yet love in the deepest sense of the word (because he hardly knew her in the usual way) but who filled his thoughts to the exclusion of almost everything else.

The *Lynx* was dead ahead and he could see the men rushing around on deck. He could imagine the pandemonium—the magazine was locked and where the devil was the key? Perhaps Tomás and Hart were arguing with each other: should they cut and run or stay and fight—or did they have the choice anyway? The privateersmen would be shouting in various languages—English, French, Spanish and Dutch for sure, and there would be others.

That night in the *Earl of Dodsworth* before he swam to the *Heliotrope:* sitting on the breech of the gun in the darkness before she came up to him, he had seen himself—his life, rather—with an almost frightening clarity: he had felt guilty that Gianna was fading in his memory, that he did not think of her nearly as frequently or in the same sort of way as before. Then he had realized that without either of them understanding it at the time, each had discovered that there was no choice. Each was drawn by a force that love could not overcome—or perhaps love showed them there was no happiness waiting for them even if the force was overcome. He saw how they had never had a choice, even had Gianna not decided to go back to Volterra at that time. It had an inevitability about it; the same inevitability that was taking the *Calypso* up to the *Lynx*.

He turned his head. "Mr Southwick..." As soon as the master was standing beside him he gave him his instructions and the old man grinned. A relieved grin? It seemed so to Ramage, as though Southwick had expected him to do something else. Anyway, the master took the speaking trumpet from its rack on the forward side of the binnacle box and walked over to Wagstaffe, telling him to report to the captain.

The second lieutenant looked cheerful: his hat was at a rakish angle, his silk stockings were obviously new (and worn because Bowen had told Ramage, who made it a standing order, that silk, not woollen stockings should be worn in action: wool dragged into a wound made the surgeon's work ten times more difficult).

Ramage told him the orders just given to Southwick. "Now, we'll be firing our starboard first, unle: something unforeseen happens, so get the extra men over on that side. After that, a certain amount depends on what the *Lynx* does, but seconds are going to matter. This is what I *want* to do."

The lieutenant listened, nodding a couple of times. "Aye aye, sir," he said, and walked back to his position at the foreward side of the quarterdeck. He borrowed the speaking trumpet from Southwick and shouted orders to the guns' crews.

No ship in the Royal Navy ever had enough men to "fight both sides". Usually there were enough to load and fire all the guns on one side, with only one or two men for each gun on the other side. If both broadsides had to be fired, then one was fired first and several men from each gun ran across to the corresponding gun on the other side to fire that while the men left behind began to sponge and reload.

The *Heliotrope* was now on the starboard beam (no wonder that had seemed a long swim from the *Earl of Dodsworth*) and the *Commerce* to larboard. Ahead, only her transom visible and her two masts in line, the *Lynx*. Once again he raised the telescope. Her gunports were still closed and beyond her, on the beach, he could see the Calypsos and the two surveying parties running towards their boats. The artist Wilkins would have to be left behind if he wanted to sketch the action from the shore.

He eased the sling slightly: his arm was beginning to throb, but at last he was coming to life; the chill which had seemed reluctant to go since they dragged him from the sea on board the East Indiaman was now being replaced by a warm glow; the sky was deep blue again, the hills of Trinidade fresh green, the sand of the small beach almost white, and the sea in the bay a patchwork of dark blue, pale green and brownish-green, warning of the depths.

The dark, mangrove green of the *Lynx*'s hull, the buff of her masts and white of her topmasts, the black of her rigging— they showed up in the telescope as though she was fifty yards away instead of five hundred.

He hated sitting down: usually at this point before battle he would be free to pace along the deck beside the quarterdeck rail, but now he had to be in an armchair like some ancient dribbling admiral, hard of hearing and even harder of comprehension, bald of pate and watery of eye. He laughed at the picture and noticed Wagstaffe glance round and grin. Paolo began laughing and Ramage glanced up at him questioningly.

251

"You look very *commodo*, sir."

"I'm comfortable enough, although I'd sooner be walking, my lad, but at least I'm not missing anything!"

He gave Paolo the telescope to replace in the binnacle box drawer: there was no need for it now. Four hundred yards—and he could see five or six men looking over the *Lynx*'s taffrail. "Can you see any men on her fo'c'sle?"

"No sir, but it's partly hidden from here by the masts."

The chances were that they had not begun cutting their cable. No men were casting off the gaskets of her sails. Had they all panicked? Frozen with fear as they saw the frigate beating up to them, guns run out on both sides? He pictured Tomás and Hart and knew they were not men likely to panic. Then he glanced at his watch. He tried to guess how long had passed since those two or three privateersmen had pointed and raised the alarm. Two or three minutes, he saw; not enough time for Tomás and Hart to do anything—yet.

Three hundred yards and the privateer was dead ahead: they must be wondering which side the *Calypso* was going to grapple. The colours of the *Lynx* were bright now and he could distinguish a thin man from a fat one. Judging distance was the hardest job of all.

"Wagstaffe, warn your men to be ready as the target bears. Southwick—" he paused. Two hundred yards. His eyes followed an imaginary curve round to larboard which would be the *Calypso*'s course as she tacked. It had to be done slowly to give the gunners a good chance, but not so slowly that she got into irons and drifted helplessly. One hundred yards. That popping was from the muskets of a few privateersmen at the taffrail. In the moment before he shouted the order to Southwick he realized that the privateersmen were still trying to guess which side to defend against the *Calypso!*

"—put her about, Mr Southwick, slowly now!"

The master bellowed a few words at the quartermaster, Jackson, who snapped at the men on each side of the wheel. Slowly, it seemed so slowly that for a few moments he thought he had left it too late, the *Calypso* began to turn. For a long time it looked as though her bowsprit and jibboom would ride up over the *Lynx*'s stern as she rammed the schooner, then the speed of her turn increased as the rudder started to get grip on the water. Southwick held the foretopsail backed just as the frigate swung north, with the *Lynx*'s stern appearing to move slowly along her starboard side.

Ramage heard a thud from forward and saw a puff of smoke beginning to drift down the *Calypso*'s side. Then another as the second gun fired in the frigate's raking broadside. More popping—loud from the muskets of Renwick's Marines, soft from the privateersmen; then the thumping of the frigate's remaining guns formed a deep background to the descant of flapping sails, squealing ropes and Southwick's shouted orders as slowly the *Calypso* went about on the other tack, swinging past northeast and heading west-north-west before she picked up enough way for the rudder to act.

The wind was so light that the smoke of the *Calypso*'s guns did not disperse and in a few moments the quarterdeck was covered in a thin, acrid fog which set Ramage coughing and clutching his wounded arm as the spasm shot pain through his whole body. In a moment Paolo was bent over him, holding a handkerchief over his nose and mouth to filter out the smoke, but almost as suddenly as it appeared the smoke vanished and the sun was glaring down again on the quarterdeck.

Still coughing, Ramage twisted round in the chair. The *Lynx* was on the starboard quarter, dust hanging over her stern, and beginning to slide under the *Calypso*'s taffrail as the frigate continued her turn.

It was working! "Mr Wagstaffe—are your men ready at the larboard side guns?"

The second lieutenant waved, a confident gesture to reassure the captain.

Still the *Calypso* continued turning: having fired all her starboard guns into the *Lynx* while tacking northwards across her stern she was turning to pass southward across the *Lynx*'s stern again and fire all her larboard guns, loaded with grapeshot, into the unprotected stern, yet another raking broadside which every ship feared.

"*Mamma mia!*" Paolo exclaimed. "We've smashed half her transom with the first broadside!"

"Only half? All those 12-pounders loaded with grapeshot should have done more than that!"

Grapeshot: they sounded innocent enough to a landman, but even for a 12-pounder they were formidable. Nine small iron balls, each weighing a pound (and the size of a duck's egg) comprised a single round. Each of the *Calypso*'s guns on the starboard side had blasted nine one-pound shot into the *Lynx;* one after another, like a funeral bell tolling, until eighteen rounds had been fired—a total of 162 grapeshot.

Now the frigate was almost round again, bracing the yards and trimming the sails as the eye of the wind passed across her stern. Now she was steering southeast on the larboard tack to cross the *Lynx*'s stern again.

"They're opening her ports, sir! I can see a gun run out!"

"They have only half ports," Ramage shouted above the thumping of the sails and squeaking of rope rendering through blocks. "Only *one* gun?"

"She's rolling, sir. I can see a second gun on this side. But—well, both have been run in. Now they're running them out again!"

Ramage realized what was happening. "The grapeshot have cut the breechings. The guns are running in and out as she rolls. But why the rolling? Has she cut her cable?"

Paolo snatched the telescope from the binnacle drawer and adjusted the focus. "Yes, sir! She's drifting! Some men are cutting the gaskets on her mainsail!"

Southwick was standing beside the chair. "I took us too close that time, sir," he said apologetically. "The gun captains complain we passed the *Lynx* too fast. They want us about fifty yards off."

"You'll have to bear away: they've cut their cable and are drifting."

Southwick peered ahead and gave a helm order to Jackson and at almost the same moment Ramage heard the groan of the tiller ropes rendering round the barrel of the wheel as the helmsmen pulled at the spokes.

"She's not drifting fast," the master commented. "Half a knot; perhaps a little more."

The trouble was, every yard of drift to leeward took the privateer towards the cliffs which ran in a curve round to the headland to the southwest. That section of the bay had not been surveyed yet. The *Calypso* could very easily slam into a reef, or even a single rock, that the *Lynx* with her much shallower draft could pass over without noticing it.

"You'd better have a man ready with the lead," Ramage said to Southwick, who sniffed.

254

"He's standing by, sir, but the muzzle blast from the guns could bowl him over."

Ramage bit off a sarcastic retort: the *Lynx* was turning slightly to starboard as she drifted. In a few moments she would be in the sights of the first gun on the larboard side.

"Orsini! Tell Mr Wagstaffe to load the guns on the starboard side with roundshot. Use roundshot in all guns after the larboard guns have fired."

Southwick looked round, having heard the instruction. "Aye, sir, the grapeshot is just pecking at her!"

But the master was wrong. "Don't judge it by what you see on the transom! Just imagine all that grape sweeping through the ship from stern to bow. Cutting the beggars down in swathes!"

The second and third guns fired almost simultaneously, followed by the fourth, fifth and sixth. The longer range—fifty yards, perhaps a little more—gave the gun captains more time to adjust the elevation. The training would stay the same, about at right-angles to the *Calypso*'s centre-line, and each gun captain would tug on his trigger line, attached to the flintlock, as the *Lynx* slid from forward aft across his field of view.

Now the smoke was pouring aft and rising over the quarterdeck. He held his breath, then tried to breathe shallowly, but in a few moments he was gasping and then coughing and once again it felt as though his left arm would burst under the jabs of a sharp knife.

A heavy double thud almost beside him warned that the last two guns had fired and Southwick, yelling "That's it; round we go again!", began shouting into the speaking trumpet to wear the frigate. Ramage saw a pall of dust lying over the privateer, the surest sign that the shot were tearing into the wood and slowly ripping the ship apart.

Again sails slatted; the yards creaked and rope rattled the sheaves of the blocks as the *Calypso* seemed to spin and sail back almost in her original wake, only this time with her starboard guns slowly coming to bear. The first half dozen had fired when suddenly Ramage saw a huge blast of flame and felt, rather than heard, a roaring blast, and everything went black.

CHAPTER EIGHTEEN

Southwick was sitting in the chair by his cot. Ramage's arm felt as though the point of a cutlass blade was still embedded in it. But his right leg—the lower part felt heavy. And painful—especially when he tried to move his foot.

"Good evening, sir," Southwick said and sniffed. A relieved sniff, Ramage noticed through a haze made up of dizziness, pain—and, he was surprised to discover, hunger.

"Keep absolutely still, sir, while I pass the word for Bowen. He's been very busy."

Busy—the word chilled Ramage. "Wait—" the word came out as a croak: his throat was sore. "Have we lost a lot of men? What happened? All that flame—"

"Easy sir," Southwick said reassuringly, pushing Ramage back in the cot. "Only two men dead, but twenty or more wounded."

"Oh God." So he had failed. It had looked so simple. It *was* so simple. Get the *Calypso* under way and tack and wear across the *Lynx*'s stern firing raking broadsides until she surrendered. They were firing the third when there was that dreadful flash.

"Let me pass the word for Bowen, sir." The master went to the door and spoke to the Marine sentry, and when he came back he said, almost accusingly: "You've lost a lot more blood again. No one realized the quarterdeck had caught it."

"Why?" Ramage hardly recognized the noise that came out when he spoke.

"Well, young Orsini and I were over the side in the sea,

256

Jackson was unconscious and the two men at the wheel were dead."

"What were you doing . . . in the sea?"

His head was spinning; he was spiralling down and down as though caught in a whirlpool, and night had fallen before he came round again, to find Southwick dozing in an armchair, the sleeping cabin lit by a lantern.

His brain was muddled. He had dreamed that Southwick had been swimming in the sea with Orsini. Curiously enough the master's hair was plastered down on his head, as though still damp and sticky from salt water.

Southwick saw that Ramage's eyes were open and jumped up at once to kneel beside the cot.

"Before you pass out again, sir, Bowen wants to know if you're warm enough, thirsty or hungry."

"Thirsty," Ramage said, and then repeated it, trying out his voice and finding it was still hoarse but nearer normal. "Hot soup."

Then he remembered something. Not only had he dreamed Southwick and Orsini were swimming together, but there was talk of him losing a lot of men. And what was he doing here in his cot anyway?

"What happened?"

Southwick sniffed—had he not just done that? "You get a warm drink inside you and some food, and I'll tell you what I know. Mr Wagstaffe's in no state to talk at the moment, no more is Jackson, and the other officers weren't on board: they only saw it from the shore . . ."

"But that terrible flash . . ."

"Yes, yes, sir," Southwick said soothingly, "all in good time. Bowen is most anxious you don't get excited."

"Excited!" Ramage grumbled wearily. "How can I help it when you won't tell me anything?"

Southwick finally caught the despair in his captain's voice and as he walked to the door to talk to the sentry said over his shoulder: "Don't worry, sir. There's nothing to worry about."

When the master came back, having ordered hot soup, he found Ramage propped up on his right elbow, a wild look in his eye, his hair matted and filled with dust. "The *Earl of Dodsworth,*" he muttered, "something happened to her!"

Southwick looked puzzled. "She's all right, sir. The hostages were a bit startled, I expect, but that's all."

"And the rest of the hostages?"

"They're quite safe, sir. There's nothing to worry about. Once you've a pint of hot soup inside you, I'll tell you all I know. And Bowen will be here in a few minutes for a chat about that leg of yours."

Leg, for God's sake. An arm and a leg. Anything, it seemed, to prevent him from getting over to the *Earl of Dodsworth*. Not that he had any excuse to go over, he told himself. She would have seen the attack and whatever happened next. At the moment she probably knew more than he did.

The sentry's hail told him that Bowen was coming, and even by the dim light of the lantern Ramage could see that the surgeon was exhausted.

"What happened?" Ramage asked. "Southwick won't tell me a damn thing. Why did we have so many casualties? We oughtn't to have lost a man. Was it because I was knocked out? Did—"

He was running the words together, almost as though he was drunk, and Bowen knelt beside the cot and without answering motioned to Southwick to bring the lantern. Then he pushed up one of Ramage's eyelids, inspected the eyeball for a few moments and then felt the pulse in his right wrist.

"How do you feel, sir?"

Ramage seemed to stir himself at the question. "I'm all right. The arm is better but why is my right leg so stiff? It doesn't hurt much but I can't use it!"

"Don't try to for a few days: it's bandaged up. I don't think you've broken a bone, but several muscles were wrenched and there's considerable swelling."

"But what happened?" Ramage, his voice getting stronger, had clearly recovered enough to become angry. Recovered enough, Bowen guessed, to try to scramble out of his cot— and probably fall over as it swung slightly. The cot, being a rectangular box slung low in what was little more than a large hammock, was easily capsized by someone trying to get out to one side without distributing his weight evenly.

A knock on the door and Silkin's voice heralded the arrival of the soup, which Ramage drank from a large mug with ill grace as Southwick supported him. He swallowed it all, refused more, and said to Bowen: "Well, now tell me."

"Southwick will tell you the earlier part in a moment. I am treating twenty-three men, apart from yourself, for various kinds of wounds, from widespread contusions to broken limbs. Jackson was hit across the head but should be fully recovered in the next twenty-four hours. Two men are dead—the men at the wheel. An enormous splinter seems to have spun across the deck and cut them down."

"None of the twenty-three men are in any danger, then?"

"No, sir: I've got them all cleaned up and bandaged, and where necessary, splints have been applied."

"What happened to Southwick and Orsini, then?"

Bowen gestured towards the master, and Southwick said: "Well, sir, you probably want to hear the whole story. I can tell you most of it; it's just the last part that someone like Stafford will have to tell.

"You remember we were just crossing the *Lynx*'s stern for the third time? I'd said the gunners wanted us to pass farther off, to give them more time to see the target. Then we started firing that third broadside. The first six guns had just fired after I'd said something about 'Now round we go again!' and that the grapeshot didn't seem to be doing more harm than a wood-pecker—"

"Yes, yes, *go on!*" Ramage said impatiently.

"Well, that's very nearly the end of the story. There was an enormous flash and bang, and there was just a big ball of smoke where the *Lynx* had been. What was left of her—lengths of planking, chunks of masts and yards, even bits of bodies—were hurled for hundreds of yards. Scores of big pieces of timber hit us, sir, some coming in almost horizontally like round shot, some falling on us a few moments later like sleet. But the force of the explosion, sir! It blew me and Orsini off the quarterdeck clear over the bulwarks into the sea. A dozen others were blown over from the maindeck, and we were all swimming round in circles while the *Calypso* sailed on with no one in command and no one at the wheel."

It was too much to comprehend, Ramage decided, listening to this story lying in his cot and watching Southwick's sun-tanned face in the light of a guttering lantern... "Well, then what happened?"

"Stafford can best tell you about the ship, because he led a group of men and hove her to. Those of us in the water swam round in the wreckage wondering what would happen next, then we saw the ship heaving-to and suddenly we were being hauled into the survey boats, which you remember we saw getting away from the beach. As soon as we were all on board they rowed like madmen towards the *Calypso*, and I saw then that Mr Martin had reached the ship from the *Earl of Dodsworth* and I guessed he was staying hove-to until our two boats reached him. Mr Aitken was rowing over from the *Friesland*. I'd guessed Mr Wagstaffe was out of action. To be honest, sir, I thought he'd been killed, along with you: I couldn't see how anyone could live through that explosion unless he was lucky enough to be blown clear over the side."

"What did happen to Wagstaffe?"

Bowen coughed and took over the story. "He knows nothing more than you and Jackson about the explosion, sir. You were all knocked out together. But (and this I saw as I ran up on deck; because the action was over, it was easier to start treating men there than carry them below) Stafford was getting some men together. They were stunned from the explosion but very quickly he had them backing the foretopsail.

"Just about that time someone saw a dozen or so men swimming in our wake and reported to me, but there was nothing we could do for the time being—I didn't know how badly hurt were the men lying round on the deck. Two dozen looks like four dozen, with all that mess. Oh, then there was the fire, sir, which—"

"Fire!" Ramage exclaimed, lifting himself on his right arm. "Fire on board this ship?"

"It was soon put out, sir, so rest easy while I tell you about it. Some of the burning debris from the *Lynx* landed on our sails. The maincourse took fire, but it was furled so some men soon beat out the flames. Fires broke out on the maindeck but all the men knew what to do; every cartridge was tossed over the side, all the larboard broadside was fired off because the guns were loaded, and the deckwash pumps and buckets soon had everything under control without getting up the fire engine."

"Under control? What else burned?"

"Well, sir, some riggings, gratings, one side of the quarterdeck ladder—that sort of thing. It wasn't a conflagration, so the men could leave it while they did more urgent things. Heave-to the ship, tend to the wounded, look for you, that sort of thing. They were getting worried about you: there was only Jackson, knocked out, and two dead men by the binnacle (which was not even scratched). Then they found you still in your chair—which was just matchwood—lying under the muzzle of the aftermost gun on the larboard side. Apparently your leg was jammed in the wreck of the chair and it was only the back and one leg of the chair that stopped you from falling out through the gunport."

"So you and Stafford took control?"

"Not me, sir, because I was busy with the wounded. Stafford was splendid. Then the moment the ship was hove-to, Martin and then Mr Aitken managed to get on board—they had been trying to intercept us, but until we hove-to, we were making five or six knots. Anyway, they came on board and Mr Aitken at once took complete command.

"He sent off Martin with the soundings and survey boats to collect the privateersmen prisoners in the five ships—I gather Martin made the prisoners row, threatening to shoot the first man that flagged."

"So Aitken is in command? Where are we?"

"Mr Aitken is in command, yes, sir, and making a good job of it. We are back where we slipped our anchor—Mr Aitken picked up the dan buoy under sail."

Southwick grunted his approval. "Made a very good job of it. I thought he'd have used the boats—we have five towing astern by now—but he got the cable on board and sailed the ship up on it while the men heaved in the slack. Couldn't have done it better myself."

Ramage eased back into the cot again and stared up at the deckhead, the beams appearing to move when the lantern, which Southwick had returned to its hook, swung slightly as the ship gently pitched.

"The *Lynx*," he said. "Did you find any survivors?"

"We sent a boat to look," Southwick said. "They found no complete bodies. The water is so clear they rowed around looking for a long time. They could see some of the privateers' guns lying on the bottom a hundred yards apart. We were lucky some of them didn't land on us."

261

"I think those privateersmen were lucky," Ramage said, although he was talking to himself. "We'd have taken them to England, where they'd have all been hanged. They might have escaped with jail if they hadn't used the passengers as hostages. Tomás and Hart were quite prepared to murder them."

Southwick reminded Ramage of the privateersmen being held on board as prisoners.

"I'd forgotten those. They probably stand less chance in court than the others actually in the *Lynx*, because if Tomás or Hart had actually given the word, they would have been the murderers. What happened to Renwick, by the way?"

Bowen shook his head. "I'm sorry, sir, I forgot to mention him. He's all right now, but he was knocked out by one of the *Lynx*'s half beams; it flew on board, hit the mainmast and then fell on him. He's a trifle sensitive about it, sir; reckons it's an undignified way for a Marine officer to be put out of action!"

"Undignified! His captain nearly went over the side in an armchair!" Ramage burst out laughing at the thought of it, but a moment later was gasping with pain as the spasms of laughter wrenched at his arm and leg.

Once he had his breath back again, he said: "Well, I suppose that's it. You've no other surprises for me, I presume."

The two men looked at each other, and seemed reluctant to speak.

"What's the matter?" Ramage was alarmed. Was it about Paolo? He suddenly remembered Southwick had only mentioned him swimming.

"Well, nothing the *matter*, sir," Southwick said. "It's just rather irregular, and I don't know how to tell you."

Ramage grinned. "Oh, come *on*, let's get this report over with!"

"It's not a report exactly, sir. Aitken discussed it all with Bowen and I, and as I knew more about it than the others, I took the responsibility. Well, that's to say I—er, I agreed that—"

"Southwick!" Ramage snapped. "You sound as though you plan to jilt a blushing maiden."

"Ah, yes, sir: you remember that lady in the *Earl of Dods-worth* who cleaned up the wound on your arm?"

Ramage nodded warily. He had asked Southwick earlier if everyone in the East Indiaman was safe and had been assured they were. Now here was Southwick backing and filling, and Bowen looked damned uncomfortable.

"Well, sir, she and her mother have been waiting to see you since soon after we anchored."

"Waiting? What, you mean you signalled the *Earl of Dodsworth* when I'd recovered enough to receive visitors?"

"No, sir," Bowen said firmly. "They insisted that one of the East Indiaman's boats be lowered, collected every scrap of clean cotton and linen in the ship, and had themselves rowed over to help tend our wounded.

"They spent several hours helping me clean up and bandage the men, then took over the galley and made them soup. They— well, the daughter, because the mother was busy with Wagstaffe—helped me sort out your leg and splint it, sir, and did your arm again. They wore themselves out."

"Have they gone back to the *Earl of Dodsworth* now?"

"Not exactly, sir, because they know they'll be able to help me again when it comes to changing dressings and checking that each man is comfortable."

"Where are they, then?"

"We made up a bed for the mother on your settee, sir, and the lady's resting in the armchair. They're both waiting in your day cabin. Can I show them in now, sir?"

CHAPTER NINETEEN

Walking his own quarterdeck using a cane had its funny side, at least as far as Diana was concerned. The click of the ferrule on the planking, she said, sounded like a wooden-legged, black-eye-patched pirate captain walking up and down, a parrot on his shoulder, and shouting foul oaths because no ship came over the horizon to provide him with a victim.

It was two weeks since the *Lynx* had blown up and the bay looked strangely empty. Strangely because he had first seen it with the privateer and her five prizes anchored there. As soon as all the ships' companies were freed from their prison camp (with the privateersmen prisoners on board the *Calypso*, closely guarded by Renwick's Marines), there had been a round of official calls on Ramage, by then transferred to his settee each day.

The first visitors (apart from Diana and her mother) had been the captain of the *Earl of Dodsworth*. As befitted the captain of a John Company ship, he came in considerable state, but he was a pleasant and plump man, pink-faced and perspiring under a wig that did its best to hide his complete baldness. He made no secret that, during the long days as a prisoner, he never expected to see his ship again. The arrival of the *Calypso*, he said, had not given them any hope because the pirate guards—he resolutely refused to refer to them as privateersmen and was, of course, perfectly correct—had warned them that all the passengers, still held in the ships, and everyone in the prison camp, would be killed if any rescue was attempted.

On a later visit to the frigate, the *Earl of Dodsworth*'s captain, John Hungerford, also made no secret of the fact that after the rescue, and with the *Lynx* destroyed by the *Calypso*, the passengers had met in the saloon and then called him to hear what they had been discussing: they did not want to sail on to England alone.

He had explained to them that there was now a treaty of peace signed with Bonaparte, but they had pointed out that the *Lynx* had been a British ship, and two of her victims had been French. What they were afraid of, he said, was yet another *Lynx* like the one that had recently hove in sight.

Ramage was not sure whether Hungerford was being tactful or he had not expected the *Calypso* to catch the *Lynx*'s sister ship, but it was unlikely that their Lordships at the Admiralty would view the episode with much favour.

Dusk was warning of night when the second privateer came into the bay. Aitken had realized immediately who she was. The *Calypso* had slipped her anchor and sailed at once in chase, the men loading and running out the guns by the time the frigate passed the headland, but the privateer, making the best use of her fore and aft rig to work up to windward to round the eastern side of the island, then turned northeast, sailing into the darker half of the horizon. By the time the *Calypso* had settled down to chase it was completely dark, and dawn brought an empty horizon, except for the grey smudge of Trinidade in the distance.

Ramage, still confined to his cot by the leg wound, had been puzzled by one thing: where were the second ship's prizes? Tomás and Hart had hinted that their fellow privateer was due with more victims, so had she failed to find any? Bad weather in the English Channel could delay sailings for a month, and that could be enough to account for a lack of outward-bound ships. Or she could have her victims anchored somewhere else. If so, where?

For once he was not bedevilled with choices: looking for prizes was ruled out by the fact that there were no known islands that the privateer could be using: Ascension, Fernando de Norenha, St Paul Rocks—all were too frequently visited. Finally he concluded that the privateer was simply intending to rejoin the *Lynx* and help take the prizes to wherever they were to be sold off. Indeed, she could have been away arranging the sale at some port on the South American coast.

Hungerford had brought many invitations for the *Calypso*'s officers to visit the *Earl of Dodsworth* for dinner, but more thoughtful was the request that one of the *Calypso*'s boats go alongside the East Indiaman to collect some cases of spiced foods for the *Calypso*'s men: things with sharp tastes that would tempt the men after weeks of salt tack.

The *Amethyst*'s captain had been the next visitor, and he confirmed that the ship was indeed one of Mr Sidney Yorke's fleet, and Mr Yorke himself had told him about the voyage he had once made across the Atlantic with Mr Ramage and Mr Southwick, discovering how Post Office packets were being captured by the enemy.

The French captain of the *Heliotrope* and the Dutch master of the *Friesland* came together and, to begin with, were chilly and formal, protesting to Ramage that the *Lynx* had been British, and implying that Ramage must have known of and approved her activities even though a peace had been signed.

This had been such an outrageous suggestion that Ramage had immediately told Aitken, who had escorted them below, to see them to their boats. Taken aback by this treatment, both men had stood there grumbling in a truculent duet until Ramage, from his cot, had held up his hand for silence. Gesturing to the Dutch captain of the *Friesland*, who spoke good English, he had then pointed to Aitken.

"This officer swam alone in the night to board *your* ship secretly and warn your passengers and, when his men followed him, they captured the privateersmen and freed your passengers, eight of them. If I'd helped the *Lynx* people capture your ship, I'm damned if I see why I'd risk my own men freeing her." He pointed at the Frenchmen, "I swam to *your* ship and my men followed. This—" he raised his bandaged arm "—is my souvenir of that. All your passengers were freed.

"A day after that my ship destroyed the privateers' vessel and you were all rescued from the comparative safety of the prison camp. So your passengers are safe, your ships undamaged, and now the pair of you have the gross impertinence to imply that I, or the Royal Navy, or my government, were in league with the *Lynx*.

"Pray tell me," he said quietly, "are *you* responsible for the

266

French and Dutchmen we've found among the *Lynx*'s guards? One of my officers has drawn up a rough muster list for the *Lynx* by questioning the survivors—the guards we captured— and it seems she had one hundred and ten men altogether. Nineteen of them were British, forty-one French and twenty-seven Dutch. The rest were Spanish or from various other countries. So I bid you good day, gentlemen."

Both captains were immediately apologetic, pretending they did not notice Aitken waiting to escort them up on deck. Would Captain Ramage favour the passengers of the *Heliotrope* by taking dinner with them? Not to be outdone by his French companion, the Dutch captain of the *Friesland* gave his invitation. Ramage thanked them gravely and Aitken led them out. By contrast the French master of the *Commerce* hurried over with a case of his best wine, alarmed to hear of Ramage's wounds and swearing that the wine he brought, from his own part of France, was famous for restoring the blood.

The *Heliotrope* was the first of the ships to resume her voyage—she was bound for Honfleur—and she was followed next day by the *Commerce*, for Nantes. The *Friesland*'s captain visited Ramage again, still apologetic and asking for a copy of the terms of the peace treaty, and after discussing it with Ramage and displaying a remarkable realism as well as frankness, sailed for the Channel, cursing that the delay caused by the privateers meant that he would arrive in winter.

The *Amethyst* was bound for Calcutta, and her master decided to fill extra water casks, to make up for the amount used while at anchor. He was pleased to find two boats from the *Calypso* sent to help him.

While the merchant ships, except for the *Earl of Dodsworth*, prepared to resume their voyages and sailed, the surveyors continued their task of scaling down Trinidade's length, breadth and height to a large sheet of parchment. The masons and Renwick and his men had blasted and dug out the sites for the batteries and then built the floors, walls, magazines, kitchens and other outbuildings with the bricks the *Calypso* had brought out as extra ballast.

The botanist, Edward Garret, took parties of seamen to three flat areas he had inspected and set them to work with spades, forks and hoes, finally reporting to Ramage that all the Irish and sweet potatoes were planted.

Ramage had been disappointed to find that Wilkins did not visit him. Lying in his cot or on the settee in his day cabin, he would have enjoyed chatting with the artist. However, one day he discovered that Wilkins was being taken over to the *Earl of Dodsworth* by one of the survey boats on its way to the shore, and collected in the late afternoon when it returned. Neither Aitken nor Southwick seemed to want to discuss it.

Why should an artist want to spend his days on another ship? Presumably to visit someone. Who? Presumably a woman—he was a presentable, handsome and lively young man. But the only unattached woman—Ramage still did not know whether she was married or unmarried—was Diana. Was Wilkins seeing Diana?

The first time he thought about it he felt sick with jealousy: his throat seemed to knot, his arm hurt and he clenched his fists. Various of Wilkin's remarks took on different meanings; the devil had wheedled Aitken into providing him with transport. And—he finally admitted to himself—perhaps Wilkins was seeing her quite openly: he would have no inkling of Ramage's feelings for her, so he could not be accused of being deceitful. Well, perhaps not deceitful, but he was hardly being open about it.

Then, going hot with embarrassment, he recalled that Diana and her mother visited the *Calypso* daily, sometimes in the morning and sometimes in the afternoon, and always during these visits, which often lasted a couple of hours, Wilkins was over on board the East Indiaman.

Well, what *was* the fellow doing? Certainly he had done some good paintings of Trinidade and its flora and fauna. The fact was that the island lacked much interest, and Wilkins had concentrated on the shore and the sea lapping it. He had done a series of remarkable oils showing in detail the main seashells, introducing Ramage to a new world of colour and beauty he had never dreamed of. In fact one of the main reasons he was impatient to be able to walk properly was that he wanted to join Wilkins, who had been swimming and diving on the reefs and among the rocks at the bottom of the cliffs, collecting even more shells. The after part of the ship reeked with the smell of turpentine because so many of his canvases were propped up drying. Anyone visiting the frigate, Southwick had commented, would think her rigging was being treated with turpentine, not Stockholm tar.

Bowen had long since agreed that Ramage's leg was not broken: the swelling was caused by the bruising of the muscle. Finally he agreed to remove the bandages and look at the limb again. Bowen was a firm believer in covering a wound and leaving it alone for as long as possible. Uncovering it and exposing it to the noxious vapours in the air, he maintained, was the root cause of gangrene.

Diana and her mother arrived an hour after Bowen had inspected the leg and pronounced it sufficiently recovered to be without bandages, providing Ramage kept it covered with a silk stocking and was careful not to bang it. The cutlass wound on the arm, inspected at the same time, was healing well—entirely due, in Bowen's opinion, to the prompt cleansing by Lady Diana the moment Ramage had emerged from the sea.

The Marchioness enjoyed her daily visits to the *Calypso;* it was, she told Southwick, a most pleasant way of chaperoning her daughter. She and Southwick and Bowen formed a little coterie at the after end of the quarterdeck, under the awning. Ramage's one armchair was always brought up for the Marchioness, and the master and surgeon would, as soon as she raised her eyebrows and regretted there were no seats for them, produce canvas-backed chairs, and sit round her.

Diana and Ramage, in the meantime, would stroll back and forth across the quarterdeck, and occasionally along the maindeck and on to the fo'c'sle, while talking of a dozen subjects. All too often, Ramage found himself making comparisons with Gianna. It was quite unintended, and he remembered vividly the first time. Somehow the subject of music had come up and they began discussing composers. Diana mentioned her favourites and they were Ramage's, and he was relieved because although Gianna did not dislike music she was oblivious to it. Now here was a woman with whom he could—for a brief while, anyway—discuss this symphony and that, each of them humming sections and then arguing, or playing the game of naming a piece, with the all-too-frequent answer from Ramage with his acknowledged bad memory: "I know it well enough but can't remember the name."

After music there were books and authors, and the game

of completing quotations. Diana or Ramage would give the first few words and the other had to complete it and name the source. Shakespeare was the favourite; they agreed that Lear was the least favourite of his plays. She knew far more poetry than he, but was anxious to teach him.

The walking about the deck soon restored the muscle in his right leg, and he was able to stop using the cane. Then David Williams and Walter White, the two surveyors, asked to see him and reported they had finished all the field work for their survey and the draughtsmen had now completed their first draught. The final drawings, White said, would be done in London, "because it is impossible to do a good job in the Tropics."

"Why not?" inquired a puzzled Ramage. "We're not rolling or anything."

"No, sir, it's the heat and the ink: it dries so quickly on the pen that they can't draw a line more than six inches long. It means the line starts off black but turns grey after a couple of inches . . . Makes the drawing look very patchy, sir."

Martin and Orsini completed their soundings of the possible anchorages and Ramage took the *Calypso* out for three days to run a few lines of soundings round the island, up to two miles offshore. The frigate had only just anchored again, an hour before noon, when a boat came over from the *Earl of Dodsworth* with a letter. It was from the master, Hungerford, and was a formal invitation. The master of the *Earl of Dodsworth* and his guests requested the pleasure of the company of Captain Ramage and his officers to dinner tomorrow at half past one o'clock.

When Diana and her mother paid a visit later, they were vague about it: there was nothing special about the occasion, as far as they knew; simply that Hungerford understood that Captain Ramage was now recovered enough to be able to visit the *Earl of Dodsworth*, and was now looking forward to entertaining the officers of the *Calypso*. Starting, Diana had suggested, what would presumably become a regular social exchange between the two ships during the long voyage back to England.

Ramage was thankful that his arm had healed enough for him to leave off the sling: he had become thoroughly exasperated with having Silkin cut up his food, and then having to eat everything one-handed. Even breaking a piece of bread was a major effort using only one hand. He still needed the sling by the time evening came, when tiring muscles made the arm throb like a bad headache.

Wagstaffe insisted on remaining on board as the officer of the deck while the rest of them went off to the *Earl of Dodsworth*, and Ramage was thankful to accept his offer. The second lieutenant pointed out that he had not taken part in any of the captures, and obviously the passengers on board the East Indiaman were going to be expressing their thanks.

It was another beautiful day: the sun hot and bright, sea and sky the usual startling blue, and Ramage and his officers were rowed over to the *Earl of Dodsworth* in the *Calypso*'s launch to find the John Company ship's deck splendidly cool. More awnings had been stretched so that no sun touched the deck between the mainmast and the taffrail, and more canvas had been laid on the quarterdeck like a huge carpet. Many chairs were scattered about and two large tables bore decanters, jugs and glasses.

Ramage was met at the gangway by Hungerford, who turned to greet Aitken while the Marquis of Rockley stepped forward.

"Ah, Ramage, it's good to see you well again. I've been receiving daily reports from my wife and daughter, but nothing beats seeing you with my own eyes."

"I've been a trouble to a number of people," Ramage said apologetically. "The leg business was particularly annoying. Getting slashed across the arm by a cutlass is one thing, but being blown across one's own quarterdeck in an armchair seems almost like carelessness!"

The Marquis laughed and, taking Ramage's arm, led him towards the other passengers waiting on the quarterdeck. "To tell you the truth," he murmured, "the two women have loved every minute of your convalescence. They've never had their very own wounded hero to fuss and worry over!"

Those Army uniforms: their owner had never been wounded, nor did he rate the description of a hero! Who the devil was he?

Ramage kissed the Marchioness's hand and answered her inquiries about his health. He turned to Diana and, knowing every passenger was watching, kissed her hand with the expected politeness, and then turned to accompany the Marquis

271

and walk round, talking to the other passengers, all of whom he had met the day before he'd swum to the *Heliotrope,* and all of whom now wanted to hear from his own lips every detail of everything that had happened since.

Was his Lordship *sure* that the wicked leaders of the pirates had been killed when the *Lynx* exploded? Was he certain that none could have escaped and swum ashore? Was there the *slightest* chance of them meeting another pirate ship on the voyage home? Would the privateersmen imprisoned in the *Calypso* be hanged when they reached England?

One woman, and Ramage recalled she was a Mrs Donaldson, proclaimed loudly that the pirates held in the *Calypso* should be tried before the ship sailed from Trinidade, and hanged from gibbets erected along the small beach, their bodies left hanging in chains as a warning to any more pirates who might visit the island after the *Calypso* had gone.

Several of the passengers—Mrs Donaldson among them, Ramage noticed—were happily drinking and keeping the stewards busy fetching fresh glasses. Soon Aitken, Kenton, Martin, Southwick and Paolo were mingling with the passengers, and quite naturally Ramage and the Rockley family became separated as the new faces attracted attention among a group of people who had been together for many weeks, from the time the *Earl of Dodsworth* had left Calcutta, making her way down the muddy Hoogly river to the sea.

The Marquis was anxious to hear more details from Ramage about the recent treaty with Bonaparte, and again expressed his doubts. The French, he declared, were determined to have India, and Bonaparte was prepared to play a waiting game. However, once he heard that his own views were shared by Ramage and that many powerful figures in London, including the Earl of Blazey and most other admirals in the Navy List except St Vincent, felt the same, he let the subject drop.

The Marchioness said, out of the blue: "I've been telling Diana that she must make more use of her parasol: her face is getting quite brown; quite unbecoming, in my view."

Diana smiled impishly at Ramage. "Well, let us hear *your* view, Captain."

Ramage felt his own face turning red beneath the suntan because he had been encouraging Diana to lose the cream colour on her cheeks, and let the skin turn golden in the sun. Indeed, most nights he had gone to sleep imagining her whole body a golden brown, and he suspected that Diana had guessed.

He looked up to find the Marquis chuckling. "You poor fellow, you *are* in a fix! Do you upset the mother or the daughter—the problem most young men face sooner or later! Well, I'll add my pennorth by saying I think she looks beautiful whether peaches and cream or golden, and I see that Captain Hungerford wants us to lead the way down to the saloon!"

He was thankful for the Marquis's intervention, and then saw that the Marchioness was smiling and as she passed close she whispered: "Don't think you'll always escape as easily: I am a golden dragon, the highest rank of the species!" Ramage was surprised and pleased to see Wilkins among the guests. He was very well dressed and obviously quite at home among the passengers.

Hungerford led the way down the companionway and directed the Calypsos to their seats. The master of the *Earl of Dodsworth* sat in the centre of his table, his back to the sternlights, with the Marquis on his right and the Marchioness to his left. Aitken was on the Marquis's right. Southwick at the Marchioness's left, with a woman passenger separating Martin from Aitken and Orsini from Southwick. Strictly speaking, Southwick as a warrant officer was junior to Martin, but Southwick clearly was one of the Marchioness's favourites.

Ramage found himself seated exactly opposite Captain Hungerford, with Diana on his right and Bowen beyond her. On his left was another woman passenger who, had Diana and her mother remained in India, would have been the most beautiful woman on board the *Earl of Dodsworth*, and she seemed to accept her secondary role with good grace, seating herself as Ramage slid her chair with an ease that most women would envy and a softly breathed warning to Ramage not to hurt his arm.

As soon as everyone was seated, Hungerford rose and took a deep breath. "My lords, ladies and gentlemen: I have three tasks before we begin this dinner. First, for the benefit of our guests, our bill of fare. Pease soup, as you who have voyaged with us so far know very well, is a speciality of this ship and I dare claim it as unique. We have legs of mutton, and can only apologize that it isn't lamb, but our ewes proved barren. There are fowls for those who like white meat, hogs' puddings, hams, duck, pork and mutton pies—" he paused to consult a list "—corned round of beef, mutton chops and potatoes, removed by plum pudding. And port wine, sherry, gin, rum and of course porter and spruce beer."

Ramage glanced at his officers. Martin and Orsini were glassy-eyed with the prospect and Aitken was obviously hearing John Knox inveighing against gluttony and preparing to ignore him. Southwick had that comfortable smile one associated with Friar Tuck, and was surreptitiously undoing a button of his coat.

Captain Hungerford continued: "So much for what is to be placed before us. I now welcome our guests, only three of whom are known to the majority of you." With the skill of a man who for years had known that one of the most important tasks of a John Company master was to make the passengers feel comfortable, he then introduced the Calypsos, starting with Ramage and ending with a confident Orsini.

"These are the men to whom we owe first our lives and second our freedom. I believe Captain Ramage (incidentally he does not use his title, so I am being neither familiar nor disrespectful), first boarded this ship in a rather unusual way, and the second time was very very unorthodox—" he paused while the passengers laughed and then cheered and clapped "—so it is my pleasure on behalf of all who voyage in the *Earl of Dodsworth*, to give you our thanks."

Ramage was aware of some scraping and scuffling behind him, particularly puzzling because some of the passengers were deliberately not looking in that direction while four or five others' curiosity was winning. Aitken, Southwick and his other officers facing into the saloon were openly staring.

He felt Diana's hand clasp his beneath the tablecloth and press it (reassuringly? sympathetically? affectionately? It was impossible to tell, and a moment later it was withdrawn). Then Captain Hungerford, unable to restrain a grin, said: "If those seated at the other side of this table will turn and face in the direction I am looking..."

Stewards appeared from nowhere to turn the chairs, and as soon as a puzzled Ramage sat down again, facing the length of the saloon with a table to the left and another to the right, he saw in the space between them Wilkins's easel, the one the carpenter had made for him. A green baize cloth covered whatever canvas was on it.

Hungerford said: "Lady Diana . . ." and she stood up, as though to perform a role for which she had been prepared, and walked to the easel, standing to one side. "It gives us all great pleasure," Hungerford continued, "to ask you, Captain Ramage, if you will accept this as a small token of our gratitude. It will show you something which, I am told, you did not actually see for yourself. If you will go up to the easel . . ."

She was waiting by the easel and watching him, and the look in her eyes seemed to be giving him some secret message he dare not believe. When he was within three or four paces of the easel she leaned across and removed the cloth with the grace of a provocative dancer, and he found himself on the *Calypso*'s quarterdeck watching the *Lynx* exploding in a great ball of fire. The painting was so real that in the instant of surprise he nearly flung his arms over his face to protect his eyes from the bulging flame. He looked away and caught her eyes and knew he had not been mistaken those few moments earlier, but there was so much confusion: the *Calypso*'s guns spewing smoke and flame, the *Lynx* exploding, Diana's face so close, and—

Quickly he stepped back, bewildered, and almost at once he saw Wilkins and realized that the artist had given him a few moments in which he could pull himself together. Two steps and he was grasping Wilkins's hand, congratulating him, and there was a sudden uproar of cheering, clapping and the clinking of knives tapping glasses. Then they were all shouting "Speech, speech, speech!" and he turned back to explain to her that for a moment the ball of fire had blotted out everything, and her eyes said yes, she knew, but *noblesse oblige*, and if it helped she loved him, and one day he would know all about that military uniform . . .

He turned back towards Hungerford. "I don't know what to say." He stopped and everyone in the cabin realized that he was simply speaking his thoughts aloud. "The beginning was just like that, then it all went black . . ."

Suddenly, he swallowed, stood straight because the deckhead in the saloon was high, and with what seemed to many of the passengers as easy nonchalance, bowed and said: "On behalf of myself and every man in the *Calypso*, I thank you for commissioning, and Alexander Wilkins for recording on canvas, this instant in our lives. I shall always treasure it, and it will hang in my family's house in London so that when in future any of my Calypsos want to come and look at it again, or any of you good people, you have only to knock on the door. I cannot guarantee that I shall always be there because, as you know, I am in the King's sea service, and I fear the present peace will be brief..."

CHAPTER TWENTY

The two surveyors came to his cabin next morning with the draft of the new chart of Trinidade and its waters. With Southwick's help they had determined the exact latitude, and the longitude as close as the *Calypso*'s chronometer would allow. Their task, though, was simple enough. White unrolled the parchment and pointed to the numbers representing heights on land and depths in the water.

"We have to name the hills, bays and headlands... We'd like you to choose the first ones, sir! At least, one or two bays have been named already, but..."

Ramage glanced up. "Who named them?"

"Well, sir, the Marquis and his family—and, well, sir, the passengers in the *Earl of Dodsworth!*"

Ramage pulled the chart round and stared at the writing. The bay in which they were anchored had, pencilled in, "Ramage Bay", while the headland forming the southern corner had been called Ramage Head. The next bay to the west, where the only accessible stream for fresh water ran into the sea, had been called "Calypso Bay". The beach which the survey teams had used was now "Potence Beach"—a grisly mixture of French and English, since *potence* was French for a gallows.

"What will Lord St Vincent think of me if he sees my name written all over the chart?" he demanded.

"The Marquis, sir," White said hurriedly, "we mentioned that to him, and it seems he knows the First Lord very well, and had already drafted a letter to him about what you did. Now he's going to say that he insists..."

Ramage sighed. "Well, Mr Dalrymple at the Hydrographic Office can always change them later. Now, let's name the rest. This next bay to the west, we'll call that Rockley Bay, in honour of the Marquis. This first bay on the north side could well be named after the First Lord. Write them in, White: Rockley and St Vincent. We'll leave the next two—some of the Lords Commissioners may have ideas. But this little bay here, at the southern end; I want that named 'Aitken Bay'. He saved the *Amethyst* and *Friesland*."

He looked at the chart carefully. Renwick had worked hard at building the batteries and was in the attack on the *Lynx*. The biggest battery, which covered the watering place in what was now to be Calypso Bay, was at the top of a hill which was 1,430 feet high.

"That will be Renwick Battery," he said, tapping the place with his finger. "Here, where you have the maize and potato fields marked, just call it 'Garret's.' The old West Indies hands will think it is the name of a sugar plantation!

"Now we have three batteries left. This one covering the landing beach—Potence Beach, rather—we'll name for Wagstaffe; that one for Bowen; and this one here, covering the northeastern side of the island, for Southwick."

He paused a minute or two and White coughed. "Orsini, sir: might we suggest the reef just on our larboard side? It is the nearest to where he helped you..."

"Excellent: pencil it in. He'll be so proud." Probably more proud of that, Ramage thought, than of all of Volterra, if he inherits it. "And this big shoal in Calypso Bay—that's Martin's. Poor Kenton has been left out a good deal, so we'll give him this big shoal of rocks in Rockley Bay."

White swallowed hard. "I seem to be interfering a lot, but

everyone in the gunroom was most anxious that I should ask you if—well . . ." He stopped, overcome by nervousness.

"Who are they suggesting?"

"Mr Wilkins, sir. He's such a good shipmate, and that painting . . ."

"I agree entirely," Ramage said. "Have you any suggestions, or should we change some of these round?"

"No, sir, we know which is his favourite hill: it's this one overlooking the bay; you've seen several of the paintings he's done from that."

"Wilkins Peak, eh? Good, write it in."

Aitken followed the surveyors and reported that the last of the casks of fresh water were being hoisted on board. "We've located thirty-five tons, sir, and Kenton tells me that if he'd had the boats and casks, he could have loaded five times as fast."

"So a large squadron could water here in a matter of hours?"

Aitken made an expansive gesture. "A small fleet in a couple of days. And digging potatoes and harvesting maize at the same time!"

"Very well, then you can start hoisting the boats in. The *Earl of Dodsworth* is weighing tomorrow at nine o'clock. We can start to weigh about ten o'clock. We'll be spending the next six weeks or so in her company, so we can afford to let her get ahead for an hour or two!"

"It'll mean a slow passage for us," Aitken commented.

"Only if there are light winds. She's a lot bigger than us and can carry more canvas in a blow."

"Can, sir, but will she?"

"She'll have to if she wants to keep us with us! Don't forget she wants to sail in company with us. We are not under orders to escort her—after all, we are at peace, despite a privateer or two. We're doing Captain Hungerford and John Company a favour . . ."

"So we could lose her in the night after a week or two," Aitken murmured.

"We could, but we won't," Ramage said, and knew that if he was honest he would admit that if he had his way he would bring the Rockleys on board the *Calypso*, just for their peace of mind, and leave the *Earl of Dodsworth* to follow.

Aitken was just leaving the cabin when he turned round. "By the way, sir, Orsini wanted to see you. May I send him down?"

Ramage nodded, puzzled by the formality; normally if Orsini had anything to say he approached on the quarterdeck with a smart salute.

A few minutes later Paolo came into the cabin and stood to attention. The boy was growing quickly, Ramage realized; he had to stand with his head bent to avoid bumping the beams.

"Sit down," Ramage said, gesturing to the armchair, but Paolo shook his head nervously. He was holding a small canvas wallet, a flat bag suitable for carrying documents. "I'd prefer to stand, sir: this will only take a minute or two."

Ramage looked up from the chair at his desk. "You sound very serious, Paolo!"

He rarely called the boy by his first name, and then only when they were alone. But at this moment something was obviously troubling him.

"It's the date, sir."

Ramage frowned and glanced down at his journal, which he had been filling in when Aitken arrived. There seemed nothing unusual about the date: it was not the King's birthday, the anniversary of the Restoration of Charles II, the King's accession or the Queen's birthday, or any of the other dozen or so days when the King's ships fired salutes. Paolo's birthday was some time in August.

"What about the date?"

"It is six months to the day since we sailed from Chatham, sir."

"Allora!" Ramage exclaimed, surprised that it was so long, but still puzzled that it had any significance. *"E poi . . . ?"*

Paolo began to undo the two brass buttons holding the wallet closed. "I have a letter for you, sir."

"A *letter?*"

Obviously Paolo was not going to be rushed. He now had the flap of the wallet open, and he looked up as though this was only another stage in whatever duty he was performing.

"I had to deliver it to you exactly six months after we sailed from England, sir. And that's today, if you would be pleased to refer back in your journal."

"I'll accept your word for it. Is it so important?"

279

"I gave my word, sir."

"Very well," Ramage said hurriedly, determined not to show any impatience or offend Paolo's prickly sense of honour.

"May I have the letter, then?"

"Yes, sir," Paolo said, making no move to hand it over. "I have to explain . . . My aunt gave it to me when I visited her in London at your father's house. She made me promise to give it to you on the exact day."

"Which you are now doing," Ramage said encouragingly. Whatever it was, Gianna had clearly threatened Paolo with the *mal occhio* if he failed, and no matter how intelligent, God-fearing and sophisticated an Italian, he was always wary of the evil eye.

"Which I now do, sir," Paolo said, pulling the letter from the wallet and taking three steps to place it in Ramage's out-stretched hand.

"If you will examine the seals and make sure they are intact, sir?"

Ramage looked up at the youth. "Paolo!"

Orsini flushed and almost stuttered as he explained: "Sir, my aunt said I was to say that as soon as I delivered the letter."

Ramage turned over the letter, recognized the seals of Volterra and saw they were intact, and said solemnly: "I have received the letter safely on the due day and the seals are unbroken."

He looked up and saw tears forming in Paolo's eyes. In a few moments the poor boy would *fa un brutta figura.*

"You may go!" Ramage said quickly and the boy almost ran from the cabin. He had held back the tears long enough to avoid "making a bad figure", but too late not to reveal that he knew something of the contents of the letter, and what he knew had upset him.

Deliver six months after the ship sailed . . . which was also six months after she left England for Paris on her way to Volterra. Ramage turned the letter over and over, strangely unwilling to prise open the seals and unfold the page. The paper was thick and he recognized it as her own, not the note-paper used in Palace Street. Was it a letter telling him . . .

Suddenly he slid his fingers under the seals, opened the four folds and smoothed back the flaps. He read it through hurriedly to get the general sense and by the time his eye reached her signature he was angry, relieved and confused, all in the same instant, and his hands were trembling. He then began to read it again, slowly and carefully.

My dearest,

I am writing this while you prepare to leave England in the *Calypso* and I pack to leave with the Herveys for Paris and then Volterra, but there will be one great difference: you will return to England, but I never shall.

Paolo will give you this letter in six months' time. By then I hope I shall be blurred in your memory, just as I pray you will be blurred in mine.

The reason is one we have talked over so frequently. My love and duty lies with my little kingdom. Your love and duty lies in England, the Navy, and the Blazey estate.

You must accept that we can never marry, because our religions are different and the people of Volterra would never accept a *straniero* after the years of French occupation. They will need reassuring by a ruler they know and trust—a role I hope to fill. They will expect heirs to be born—and you and I can never give them any because we cannot marry.

But please, Nico, look into your heart. You have known all this for years, but you have fought the knowledge, denied it, and tried to devise ways round it. You have failed because there *is* no way, and slowly this has affected us: slowly you have fallen out of love with me. Small things I say and do irritate you; the prospect of me going to Volterra makes you angry, but I think that without you realizing it the reason is that, inside you, you know this is the only answer; that we can never really be together. I mean as lovers.

For myself, yes, I have loved you deeply and perhaps I always shall (who can promise the future?), but now I go to Volterra in the certain knowledge that I shall marry another man and bear his children, and the succession will be secure for the future in my little kingdom.

I am weeping now, of course, and my memory goes back to a young woman in a cloak pointing a pistol at you in the Torre di Buranaccio at Capalbio. It was a strange meeting and since then we have loved each other, but for both of us that page in the story of our lives must turn.

By the time you receive this I shall either be in Volterra and perhaps already married to another man, or Bonaparte will have had his agents dispose of me. Either way, I have left your life and, my dearest Nico, I hope you will find a woman you love and who will love you as deeply as I did, and whom you can marry.

Think of me occasionally, as I shall think of you occasionally, if Bonaparte spares me, but only occasionally. If Paolo can serve with you, I shall be happy, but I suppose he will become a lieutenant and go to another ship. He worships you and you have become the father—uncle, anyway—that he never knew. He has never forgiven me because he thinks I should have broken our relationship long ago, since we could never marry. At his age, solutions are so simple.

> So farewell, my Nico,
> Your Gianna.

His eyes blurred with tears. So she had known all along what he had for so long refused to admit to himself, that the hopelessness of it all had killed his love for her. Killed? No, not killed; changed its character. He had loved her as a woman, and as a mistress, to the exclusion of all other women. Then it had cooled until in the last year or two he had loved her as he would a favourite sister. And she was right about the irritations and the anger he had felt about her going to Volterra. Anger, yes; but much of it was guilt, too.

A guilt, he realized as he folded the letter carefully, that he need no longer feel. He stared at the polished top of his desk, his eyes following the sweep and curve and twists of the mahogany grain. So by now she could be married, and knowing Italian marriages and the demands of politics, perhaps already carrying another man's child.

He put the letter in a drawer and locked it. He could believe her wish that he would meet a woman he would love. The damnable irony, he reflected sourly, was that he never fell in love with women who were free to love him. Gianna held in the chains of religion and the heavy inheritance of a kingdom; Diana held by—what? Something represented by a trunkful—two trunkfuls—of military uniform. Where was her heart? Probably buried in some grave in the plains and hills of Bengal.

If the peace held, he would send in his papers, find some good plain woman of respectable family, marry her and spend the rest of his days in St Kew. There was more pain attached to love than joy, and months at sea gave too much time for black thoughts; of unfaithfulness, of handsome Army officers dancing quadrilles, of—he stood up, grabbed his hat and went up to the quarterdeck, where the sun was bright.

It was particularly bright because the men were taking down the large harbour awning which almost completely shaded the quarterdeck. Soon it would be rolled up and stowed below and the smaller one, heavily roped, rigged in its place.

He looked at the island half encircling the bay. It was so peaceful that the events of the past weeks were impossible to believe—except that his left arm still pained him and his right leg ached, and he could see four or five Marines with cutlasses and pistols exercising some of the privateersmen who clanked across the deck in irons.

Wilkins Peak, Rockley Bay, Garret's, Aitkens Bay, Wagstaffe Battery... They had all come to the Ilha da Trinidade and had (on paper) changed it. But Trinidade had changed all of them permanently: no one, privateersmen now in irons going to face trial or English aristocrat travelling home in a John Company ship, surveyor employed by the Admiralty Board or artist with a plentiful supply of paints, would ever be the same again. The memories would have changed them in some way.

After taking his noon sights five days later and working them out, Southwick walked over to Ramage, who had been pacing moodily up and down the weather side of the quarterdeck for an hour, and now stood at the rail staring forward at the horizon. Staring, Southwick knew, but not seeing.

"First five hundred miles, sir," the master said. "Only another four thousand or so to go and we'll be in the Chops of the Channel. Our latitude is fourteen degrees thirty-nine minutes South and the longitude is twenty-three degrees forty-seven minutes West."

"That's an average of four knots," Ramage said sourly. "At

this rate it'll take us more than forty days. Six weeks. That's if we don't spend a couple of weeks slamming about in the Doldrums—"

"Deck there, foremast here . . . the East Indiaman's making a signal."

Kenton, the officer of the deck, looked with his telescope and took the sheet listing the flag signals agreed between the *Calypso* and the *Earl of Dodsworth*: single flags which represented complete sentences.

"For you, sir," he told Ramage. *"The captain of our ship invites the other captain to dinner."*

Ramage tried to appear casual. The sea was reasonably smooth, the trade wind clouds marched in orderly procession, the *Calypso* was up to windward on the *Earl of Dodsworth*'s larboard quarter. He looked at his watch—he would be expected on board about one o'clock for dinner at two. Usually he was not fond of large dinners: taking up a couple of hours and involving too much food and too much wine (and too much talking about extremely boring subjects), they left him with a headache and an uncomfortable feeling in his stomach.

All of which did not matter a damn now because here was his first chance of seeing Diana since the day before both ships had left Trinidad. Five days, did Southwick say? It could have been five months.

"Acknowledge the signal and accept the invitation," he told Kenton. "Then in half an hour I want the ship hove-to a mile ahead of the *Earl of Dodsworth* while you hoist out a boat to take me across. I'll keep the boat and make a signal when I'm ready to return. You'll see the *Earl of Dodsworth* heave-to."

"Aye aye, sir," Kenton said and saluted. Heaving-to and hoisting out a boat made a welcome break in the boredom of keeping station on a John Company ship day after day . . .

Half an hour later Ramage, in his second-best uniform and wearing the obligatory sword, climbed down into the jolly boat, settled himself in the sternsheets as Jackson draped a light tarpaulin to keep the spray from spattering his uniform and watched the *Calypso* with interest as she drew away, seeming huge and almost clumsy from what was little more than the height of the wavetops.

The East Indiaman was sailing down on to them and in a few minutes would luff up and back the foretopsail. It would make a diversion for the jaded passengers who, even now, would be exclaiming over the tiny boat...

Two hours, probably three, before he would return to the *Calypso*. Would he manage to speak to her privately—or, at least, with no one able to hear what was said—during that time? What a stupid position to be in. He wanted to ask the question because he wanted to know the answer. Yet the answer could bring such black misery that the rest of the voyage would be like being transported to a penal settlement in Australia. Some people preferred not to know the worst, but he was too impatient to be able to bear the suspense. Someone had once said to him: "Why be unhappy today when you can put it off until tomorrow?" That made sense if the unhappiness came unexpectedly, but waiting until tomorrow to be certain of something you half expected—no!

"Sir," Jackson was saying and Ramage glanced up, startled to find the bowman about to hook on to the *Earl of Dodsworth*, whose sides reached up beside the jolly boat like a black cliff.

Two ropes covered in green baize hung down almost to the water, one each side of the battens, and held out clear of the hull by buoys. He flung off the tarpaulin, jammed his hat hard on his head, swung his sword behind him and stood up, grasping a rope in each hand as the jolly boat lifted on a swell wave. A moment later he was climbing up the ship's side, conscious that the muscles in his right leg and left arm were still not completely knitted.

Hungerford and the Marquis were at the entryport to greet him. The master was soon apologizing for their slow progress; the Marquis regretting that Ramage had been unable to accept the two previous invitations to dinner.

"Paperwork, sir; I'm trying to get my reports written while things are fresh in my mind," Ramage lied. It would hardly do to tell him that he had been so miserable he did not want to speak to anyone, least of all Diana's parents.

A few minutes later he was among the East Indiaman's passengers, smiling, kissing the Marchioness's hand and then Diana's; making small talk with the woman who had sat on his left at dinner when they presented the painting, reassuring Mrs Donaldson (already a little tipsy) that indeed, the *Calypso*'s men were keeping a sharp lookout for pirates...

Then, as if by chance—but he realized the two of them had

285

been circling like fighting cocks to arrange it—he found himself with Diana, and no one else within a couple of yards.

She wore a pale turquoise dress which had a fine lace overskirt. Her tawny hair caught by the wind and free of pins and clips had strands bleached blonde by the sun; her skin was gold and her eyes, green flecked with gold, were watching him, as though she knew he had something to say to her.

"Your leg and arm?" she asked quickly, as though to dispose of them at once, although to her they were important questions she was afraid he would brush aside.

"Still giving me twinges, but otherwise fine: you saw me climbing up the side."

"Yes, and your leg gave way twice."

"I didn't notice it. Diana—"

Suddenly everything was quiet but for the drumming in his ears; drumming from the pumping of his heart. She moved slightly, so that she was standing with her back to the rest of the passengers and obscuring his face. She said nothing, her eyebrows slightly raised.

When he hesitated she said quietly: "You look as if you're seeking the answer to the riddle of the universe."

"I am, to *my* universe." This was not the way he had wanted the conversation to go: he wanted to ask the question casually, instead of making it a single issue of vast importance.

"Captain Ramage's universe must be enormous." She was smiling, but he knew she was trying to lessen the tension which had suddenly sprung up between them.

"Nicholas's is very small," he said, and ploughed on. "That uniform—whose is it?"

She blinked and then her eyes were wide open with surprise. "What uniform?"

"The military uniform you lent me the day . . ."

"Oh yes! The day you were using a stock as a loincloth! Most dashing you looked, but you needed something, well, more substantial, before you met people like Mrs Donaldson!"

"You haven't answered my question," he reminded her.

"But Nicholas, it's such a silly question! What on earth does it matter?"

"It matters to me," he said stubbornly.

As soon as she realized he was serious she said quietly: "Does it *really* matter to you all that much? It was just a uniform which fitted you."

"Yes, it matters. I must know."

Suddenly she began to go pale and instinctively she touched his arm. "You think it is my husband's?"

"Yes. What else can I think?"

She shook her head slowly, as though trying to make herself understand something.

"You are jealous of him?"

"Of course." The *Calypso* looked a fine sight over on the starboard quarter but seemed remote from him.

"Why? Why should you be jealous of him?"

He sighed and was just about to turn away and return to the other people: it was the husband's uniform, she loved the man, and she had not the faintest idea that she was loved by the captain of the *Calypso* frigate.

"It is of no consequence now, ma'am," he said stiffly, and then forced a smile. "We must rejoin the others."

"No, wait. It *is* of consequence why you should be jealous of him."

"Flattering for you, ma'am, but hardly of consequence to a married woman."

"Answer me!" Her voice was low and her fingers grasped his arm.

There was nothing to lose: a few minutes' embarrassment and he could leave the ship and return to the *Calypso* after taking a bowl of soup, claming his arm was paining him.

"I have fallen in love with you. So naturally I am jealous of your husband."

She held his eyes. "Listen carefully, Nicholas," she said softly. "My father went out to India three years ago as the Governor General of Bengal, and he took his family with him. He found he disagreed with much the Honourable East India Company is doing, so he resigned, and we are returning to England. All but one of us."

Now it was his turn to be puzzled. "All but one? Your husband?" Yes, of course, he had died out there.

"All but the owner of the uniforms. He has resigned his commission with the Company—he was my father's ADC—because he wants to remain out there for another year or two. His uniforms are in the trunks, although for the life of me I don't know why they were not burned before we sailed."

"Let's join the others," Ramage said miserably.

"But you still don't know who owns the uniforms!"

"I can guess, though why you didn't stay with him, I don't know."

"My brother is a pompous bore," she said.

"Let's join the—your *brother?*"

She was laughing as she nodded. "Why are you in such a rush to join the others?" she asked innocently. "Does my company bore *you?*"